by the same author

THE EMPEROR OF LIES

STEVE SEM-SANDBERG

The Chosen Ones

Translated by Anna Paterson

FABER & FABER

First published in 2016
by Faber & Faber Ltd
Bloomsbury House
74–77 Great Russell Street
London WC1B 3DA
This paperback edition published in 2017

Typeset by Faber & Faber Ltd
Printed in the UK by CPI Group (UK) Ltd, Croydon, CR0 4YY

A CIP record for this book
is available from the British Library

ISBN 978-0-571-28847-2

2 4 6 8 10 9 7 5 3 1

For See

decursus [*Latin.*]: flow, stream; [*med.*] course of treatment;

Although every kind of cripple is offered an opportunity to work and every effort is made to suit that task to each one of them, we must not forget that the survival of the fittest is not based on compassion and charitable attitudes but rather a struggle in which the stronger and more competent must and will be victorious, if only for the benefit of sustaining the species . . . We must be prepared to grasp that, as a consequence of the war, many of the incompetent, or, in other words, 'negative variants', are likely to reproduce and so heighten the risk that the proliferation of such negative variants will, to an extent greater than at present, generate a need for support and hence a burden for the next generation. Thus, while it may sound cruel, it must be stated that the continuously increasing demands for support for such negative variants is ill-advised in terms of management of human assets, as well as wrong in terms of racial hygiene . . . Improvements in quality must begin with the child. If it is the case that we are unable to manage reproduction according to qualitative goals, then we should at least make every effort to promote high-quality breeding practices. Child-care provision, regulated in accordance with biological and social principles, is part of this.

Julius Tandler: *Krieg und Bevölkerung*
(*War and Population*, 1916)

The care institution 'Am Spiegelgrund' is charged with the duty of subjecting all mentally deviant children and young people, from infanthood until they come of age, to the most precise and attentive examination leading to a full assessment of their mental and physical skills and abilities, before directing them to the appropriate care home or institution. In addition, these experiences will be collected with a view to later scientific study.

Currently, we manage 15 groups of boarders consisting of 30 children per group and two double groups – that is, each with 60 boarders. We maintain our own unit for infants and young children with an average bed occupancy of 50, and also units for two groups, each containing 30 school pupils with psychopathological conditions. [. . .]

We require, already at the time of admission [. . .] that the referring authority, whether it is – as has so far been the case – a young people's social service or a healthcare department, should provide us with a complete report of the grounds for the transfer of the child and a thorough family history, in which information concerning all heritable handicaps and environmental factors with damaging effects is especially valuable. Furthermore, a careful account of school performance is also required to allow assessment of any matters of concern raised by deficiencies in the upbringing of the child or other noteworthy defects. [. . .]

At the time of admission, it is the immediate duty of the institution's medical officer to establish the child's status somaticus *and to suggest appropriate treatment to mitigate any physical health deficits; should a condition already be under treatment, a complete medical history is required. The examination will take cognisance especially of internal medical and neurological issues. [. . .] Also, the institution's medical officer will obtain, during visits by the child's parents or close relatives, or after summoning such persons, a detailed case history with regard to hereditary biology as well as to psychiatric and somatic conditions. All boarders will immediately have their height and weight measured and photographs taken for anthropological purposes after a brief evaluation of anthropological status. Until such time as we have in place the necessary equipment and the required scientifically trained support staff, the child's status will be brought up to date through exact anthropological and phrenological measurements and completed by dactyloscopic records of skin patterns on hands and feet.*

Once settled into our institution, the boarder will undergo a psychological assessment that in part also serves as an intelligence test as per currently accepted methodology, but which is somewhat expanded and readjusted to aim not so much at establishing an intelligence quotient (although for practical reasons we will still keep this aspect) as to enable us to arrive at an overview of the child's personality and to assess that he or she has the mental and physical abilities critical for upbringing and training. In the context of the written appraisals of meticulously selected themes which in particular ways are suited to offer insight into the inner mental processes of the child or young person, and also not infrequently provide important data on the development of his or her character, we will furthermore acquire quite spontaneously written text samples that very often complete our insight into the boarder's character in the most remarkable manner. These psychological tests will be administered by trained and experienced psychologists who have been specially selected for this task and are under the supervision of academic psychologists with pedagogic experience. In joint meetings and through constant scrutiny of our results, we will attempt to arrive at a methodology appropriate for our particular purpose.

Hans Krenek: *Beitrag zur Methode der Erfassung von psychisch auffäligen Kindern und Jugendlichen* (*A contribution to methods for assessment of children and young people with psychological abnormalities*, 1942), Archiv für Kinderheilkunde (Archive of Child Medicine)

It is certainly legitimate to write a history of punishment against the background of moral ideas or legal structures. But can one write such a history against the background of a history of bodies, when such systems of punishment claim to have only the secret souls of criminals as their objective?

Michel Foucault: *Surveiller et punir* (*Discipline and Punish*, 1975)

I

Fostered Children

The Institution They brought him to Spiegelgrund for the first time in January 1941, on a cold, clear winter's morning when the pale light closest to the ground shimmered with frost. Near the top of the mountain that rose behind the pavilions, Adrian Ziegler remembers seeing the institution's church, its dome green with verdigris against a blue sky, an unreal blue like that of postcards or colour-printed posters. The car stopped just inside the hospital gate, in front of the buildings that housed the directorate and the administration. A nurse came to escort them, first to meet the elderly director, a grave, pale gentleman in a dark suit, who signed the documents, and then to a pavilion to the left of the main entrance, where a doctor was waiting to examine him. Another nurse was there as well and she shouted at him to undress at once and step onto the scales. Adrian would claim that he had no idea who the doctor was until much later. It was only then, when he finally saw the medical report and recognised the signature of Doctor Heinrich Gross, that he identified the Spiegelgrund doctor as the man who pursued him for the rest of his life, even long after he had been set free. But on this first day, the doctor is simply a frightening stranger in a white coat who forces his jaws apart as far as they will go, and then probes and squeezes the bones in his skull and spine with strong fingers. The examination lasts for an hour and the doctor uses instruments that Adrian has never seen before. The top of his head is measured using a kind of circular tool with a sharp point at the tip. He is told to sit on a tall seat made up of a loose board with flaps on either side and then Doctor Gross lowers another measuring thing to determine the distance between his eyes, and between each eye and his chin. Next, the doctor pulls on a pair of gloves, prods Adrian's testicles and pushes a finger up his anus. When the examination is done, the escort nurse comes to collect him. It is still early. They walk along a corridor where the white winter daylight bounces off the monotonous pattern of rhomboid floor tiles and it will often come back to him afterwards how the floors and walls in corridors and dormitories glowed with an unearthly luminosity as if alive in their own right, independent of the children who stayed there and somehow more substantial than they were. But, of course, the nurse has no patience with him. *Stop staring and come along, we haven't got all day!* They go outside through a door at the back of the building. Now, he has his first glimpse of the extent of the place that will be his home for several years, of its many pavilions lined up side by side, pale and shut-off in the long, frost-white shadow below the mountain. All the pavilions look the same, with barred windows and plain brick frontages broken by bays. The narrow tracks of a tramline apparently link the pavilions. From a little higher up, a small train comes along, three freight wagons pulled by a red and white locomotive. It looks like a toy train. He is to be housed in pavilion 9, in the third row to the left of the central path. The nurse pulls out a huge bunch of keys from her apron pocket and flicks through them with practised fingers until she has located the right one. The dormitory doors must be locked even though it is mid-morning. If there are any children behind the doors, they aren't making the slightest noise. The nurse leads the way to a store cupboard next to the washroom and hands him a towel and a piece of grey institutional soap. He has a bath and afterwards she inspects his fingernails and ears, then lets him have his clothes back. She gives him a pair of felt slippers to wear indoors and a short, grey woollen jacket, but he isn't allowed to put the jacket on even though the corridor is as cold as sin. She leads him to a tall white door with *IV* painted on it. At first, he thought the children behind that door were just sitting very still and holding their breath. Later, he thought maybe they were already dead but pretended to be alive for his sake. So he wouldn't lose heart straightaway.

The River Adrian would sum up his early childhood as hardly the happiest years of his life, but at least a time he could look back on without feeling ashamed. He used to spend his summers with his favourite uncle, one of his mother's younger brothers who lived out in Kaisermühlen. His real name was Ferenc Dobrosch, though his sister called him Franz. At the time, Adrian and his siblings had the surname Dobrosch, because their mother wasn't married to their father. Ferenc said that that Dobrosch was a Hungarian surname even though it didn't sound the slightest bit Hungarian, and explained that the entire family came from a couple of small villages in a part of Hungary that now belonged to Slovakia. Adrian's mother insisted that the family name was Slovakian and in no way Hungarian, not that it mattered since it was just as good as any Austrian name because all names are fine in Austria, or had been in the old days. Uncle Ferenc had no education to speak of but was a hard-working and enterprising man who earned a living from occasional jobs that he seemed to pick up easily, or at least he did back then. During the summer, he minded the animals down on the allotments at Hubertusdamm, where many of the plot-holders used to keep cows or goats on the old floodplain between the high-water dam and the river. Adrian and his little brother Helmut helped to feed the animals and were rewarded with a churn full of fresh milk to take home. The animals were calm and warm. If it rained, they would stand close to each other, as if asleep. Ferenc and Adrian lay on their backs on the ground. It was covered in animal dung and rubbish like old tyres and nails from the workshops along the road, so if you were running around barefoot you had to look out or you might get hurt. The air was moist after the rain, the summer sky high and bright. Dense insect swarms rose like pillars above the puddles in the river mud. Ferenc wore an old suit jacket and a beret, but had nothing on under the jacket. His hairy, sun-scorched chest was dotted with red insect bites and he would squeeze the worst ones with his hard nails, then suck the blood from his fingers. It didn't hurt one bit, he said. Sometimes, he taught them things. How to cheat hunger by chewing grass, for instance. Lying there, looking out over the river, Ferenc said that the river was a curse on the land. Once, Kaisermühlen had been one of the numbered city districts – it was the 2nd Bezirk – and the local farmers had come here to have their grain ground to flour in the water-powered mills. Then the emperor ordered dams to be built across the old branching creeks of the river to direct the flow through a new main channel dug along a line that changed the relationship of the land to the river. For instance, what had been the *left* bank of the Donau ended up on the *right*, cut off from everywhere else by the river. From then on, Kaisermühlen was changed by word of mouth into Hunger Island. People would come looking for work but never managed to cross the river. The same thing happened when they dug the Panama Canal, Ferenc said. And then, as now, many of the labourers had drowned. Adrian asked if he knew anyone who had been a navvy on the river channel but no, Ferenc had been too young at the time, though he had heard that relatives on his father's side had worked there. They mostly took on foreign labour, though, because the work was so dangerous. The men had died from typhus or were carried off by the river and surfaced months or even years later, so you never knew who they were or where they came from. Adrian liked the river, especially on clear days after rain, with open sightlines in every direction that meant you could see faraway places like Kahlenberg and the Reichsbrücke and the tower of the Kaiser Jubiläumskirche in Leopoldstadt. He also liked to watch the river, the controlled but irresistible power of the flowing water, and the way it and the sky exchanged light, so that the river looked different from one hour to the next. At dawn, the wind would raise ripples across the mass of water which later, at dusk, could be so still and translucent it seemed you might walk on its glassy surface. This was when they would set out for the walk back home, Ferenc in front carrying the milk churn, followed first by Adrian and then his little brother. Helmut was only three and it was hard for him to keep up. He was a slight, blue-eyed boy with a shock of blond hair. Seeing him, no one thought that this little boy could be Eugen Ziegler's child, not even Ziegler himself, who accused the mother of having produced this Dobrosch offspring with another man. All the same, Adrian, who shared his life with his younger brother, thought Helmut's ingratiating smile and the unconcerned look in his eyes made him a dead ringer for their father. The boys walked barefoot because their mother thought it was silly to wear shoes when it wasn't necessary.

Simmeringer Hauptstrasse Adrian grew up in Simmering. But not just grew up, as he would say later in life. Apart from the time I was kept at Spiegelgrund, I've spent my whole life in Simmering. They had me adopted but even then, where would I end up but in Simmering? Why, I was jailed in Simmering. In Kaiserebersdorf prison. He laughed when he said that but the listener understood that, to Adrian, it had been something like a curse. There are places you never seem able to leave behind. When Eugen Ziegler moved to Simmering, the Social Democrats had only just set in motion the gigantic building projects which they were determined would once and for all *wipe poverty off the map*, as their election posters claimed. Simmeringer Hauptstrasse was still its old self, as it had been for several centuries: a heavily trafficked through-route that linked a network of workshops, shops and pubs. The family lived in a nineteenth-century building which, like most of the larger ones in the neighbourhood turned a 'respectable' front towards the street while the tenements around the inner courtyard were crawling with dubious, lower-class life forms. The house was only two storeys high, but wide, with two separate stairwells on either side of a broad gateway for wagons that wasn't broad *enough*, Adrian said, because the oak uprights on either side were deeply scored where loads had scraped past, on trucks as well as horse-drawn wagons. There was a pub in the building next door and the landlord preferred to unload the heavy beer barrels in the yard. Mr Streidl, who owned the shop at the front of the building, brought his stock in the same way. The flats were reached by narrow galleries along the inner frontage, one for each storey. The Dobrosch-Ziegler family lived on the first floor, at the far end of the gallery on the right. Tucked well away in a corner of the yard, where the latrines were clustered under a tall horse-chestnut tree, there was a wash house that served the entire building. Every day, regardless of weather or time of year, the women would be doing the laundry and some would bring hordes of noisy children. One of Adrian's earliest memories is of coming home on an overcast day in the winter, when a billowing cloud of sour-smelling steam fills the big room, washing hangs on the line in the gallery and over the cooker, and Emilia and Magda, their faces glistening with sweat, lift the big pans of boiling water and shout at him in loud, shrill voices to keep out of the way or he'll get scalded. Emilia and Magda (Magdalena) were his mother's younger sisters and, because neither of them had yet got herself a husband, Adrian's father had condescended to let them live with his family. The flat actually consisted of this kitchen and another, slightly larger room where one wall was covered in mould. That so many people could share this place was really beyond all comprehension. Adrian's uncle Florian, his mother's older brother, occupied a kitchen alcove. Florian had always been what was known as 'peculiar' and never got round to getting a job, despite his sister's endless nagging and despite Eugen, Adrian's father, who whenever he came home would have a go at Florian; although, Adrian said, you wouldn't catch him saying that he had *come home*, that was below his dignity at the time, only that he had *dropped by*, often bringing booze with him and being generous at first, when he would offer everyone a drink, until suddenly he lost interest and broke into a violent rage that almost always targeted Adrian's mother and her brothers and sisters, whom he abused, called parasites and vermin, and claimed that they stayed in the flat without his permission and that he had to pay for them all, though there was of course no truth in that, Adrian said, because Florian was only one of the Dobrosch brothers who lived with them, and Uncle Ferenc paid for him, always adding a little extra when he could since Ziegler himself never contributed a cent even though he kept telling them about the big business deals he had on the go. Eugen Ziegler treated Uncle Florian especially badly. Adrian clearly remembers one particular row, when his father grabbed a handful of his uncle's long, black fringe and slammed Florian's head against the wall, as if it was a wrecking ball. And did it over and over again. The regular, dull thuds sounded like the back of a wedge axe hitting the chopping block. Florian didn't try to resist or defend himself; the whites of his eyes swivelled further and further up and back into his eye sockets. This was one of the few times that Leonie, Adrian's mother, dared to speak up against Eugen. She shouted that he was to leave her Florian alone and, if he didn't, she would leave him and never come back. She might well say that, but if she walked out, what would happen to *the others*? They were all her dependents: her brother and her sisters and her growing number of children. Instead, she wiped the blood off the floor, hid the empties under the sink and set Uncle Florian to glue the kitchen table leg that Eugen had broken (he was good at simple, practical things, was uncle Florian; all his sense of the here and now seemed concentrated in his hands). And so Leonie pulled on her beret, buttoned up the brown cotton coat she wore in all weathers, and went to catch the 71 tram to Schwarzenbergplatz and then go on to Wieden or Josefstadt, where she spent all day cleaning for one wealthy family after another, scrubbing their floors and beating the dust from their carpets, though some of her employers might live really far away, as when she had to walk all the way to Salmannsdorf in Döbling because she didn't even have the money for the ticket. What Leonie Dobrosch earned from her skivvying was barely enough to pay the rent so she would try to bring back scraps of food, leftovers from the tables of the well-to-do that she had begged them to give her, things like day-old bread or potatoes or *Knödel* that could be fried up, but before cooking the family meal she had to start cleaning and tidying all over again the moment she arrived, because everything went to pieces at home when she wasn't there. She had only one day a week that she could call her own: Sunday. Once a week, she threw them all out and allowed no one back in – you'd be told off if you so much as showed your face in the door – got down on all fours next to a bucket of water, scrubbed the floors and covered them in newspaper afterwards. When the floors were done, Leonie sat down at the kitchen table, on her own or with Florian for company (he alone was allowed to stay), and just stayed sitting there, doing nothing, saying nothing. Because the children had nowhere else to be and because wherever they happened to end up they'd sooner or later be chased away, they ganged up, regardless of age, and drifted from place to place, sometimes begging for things to eat or to trade. They stole, too; mostly easy pickings like fruit and vegetables from the open boxes grocers displayed outside their shopfronts. Adrian, whose aunties rarely had time for him, had belonged to the local gang since the age of just three or four. The children ran about down by the old hospital barracks in Hasenleiten, or by the Donau canal where the banks in the summer were miracles of cool stillness under the canopies of the trees, or they might go to the field with the huge gasometers, monumental brown-brick structures which loomed over his earliest childhood. When they lived on Simmeringer Hauptstrasse, he was often the youngest of the child drifters and would quite often get lost. One story that was repeated about him in the family (his sister Laura kept telling it) was about how Adrian once, when he was four, apparently fainted outside the Sankt Laurenz church. It was in the middle of winter and it took time before anyone spotted the tiny snow-covered bundle at the bottom of the church steps. The verger found him in the end. Since no one knew anything about him and there was no one to ask, the parish priest's housekeeper took pity on the child and brought him home with her, gave him a bath, a meal, and a bed to sleep in. This was the first time he had a bed to himself instead of sleeping at the bottom of his aunties' bed or sharing with Helmut or Laura. He spent three days with the kind lady and then his mother, brimming with shame and worry, came to collect him. Not that she was ashamed because he had been looked after by someone else. The other children had of course said where they had been that day, and she'd had a shrewd idea where her little boy was all along but hadn't wanted to get mixed up with the police (like most people in her position, Leonie Dobrosch dreaded anything to do with the authorities) and, besides, what had happened had happened and the boy might as well stay and sit down to a few decent meals. This was also how Adrian Ziegler himself saw it many years later: his mother had in a way already handed him over to strangers. And it had seemed easy to do because she felt that, when all was said and done, staying with the priest's housekeeper was *for his own good,* perhaps even a lucky break. Later on, in Spiegelgrund, he would have nightmares about that housekeeper with her hard, thin-lipped mouth and her unkind eyes with bright blue irises that seemed to suck in everything they saw but never offer anything in return. One day, she had fixed him with those blue eyes of hers and asked him if he knew who He was who was throned in Heaven and what His Son was called and then, when he had no answers, she had smiled haughtily, turned away and refused to explain. At home, they talked of neither Heaven nor Earth. They hardly ever mentioned anything that wasn't right there in front of you. Only Ferenc was given to hold forth about whatever came into his head and his siblings would often rebuke him for it. When the psychologists at Spiegelgrund asked Adrian where his mother and father came from, because they naturally had to find out what kind of blood flowed through his veins, he couldn't answer that question either. The past was the *one thing* no one spoke about at home because it was guaranteed to cause trouble. That his mother had been a sewing machine operator in a Vorarlberg factory for many years before she moved to Wien and got pregnant by that man Ziegler, was something he learnt while at Spiegelgrund, and then only by chance, when one of the staff decided to punish him by reading aloud from his notes; and as for who, or perhaps rather what Eugen Ziegler really was, that is, what he was in terms of *biological heredity*, Adrian would grasp only when, after being fostered for four years, his foster parents rejected him and sent him off to reform school in Mödling, where the staff informed him that he'd never be any good, what with his father being of Gypsy stock. But then, something happened. Perhaps it was simply that the war began. One morning, in October 1939, he was told to go to the director's office. There was a surprise for him, the director said and he opened a door that Adrian had thought just led to a cupboard and none other than his Gypsy King father popped out, like a rabbit out of a hat, beaming at his son as he declared that it was time they let bygones be bygones and started afresh. By then he was ten years old but hadn't seen his father since he was six and even before then, only a few isolated occasions many months apart. The director told Adrian that he was to go *home* with his father. And seemed to expect him to be happy. Actually, he had never been more scared in his life.

Portrait of a Father Eugen Ziegler took a great deal of pride in his appearance. Before going to bed, he smeared nut oil into his strong, dark hair and kept it in place by pulling a ladies' stocking over his head. Whenever he might be coming to stay the night, Leonie always put a towel on the pillow to protect it from the oil. To Adrian, a towel on the pillow at bedtime meant that his father was on his way home. Though the towel on his father's pillow was often untouched, he remembers how hopeful he would feel every time and then how overwhelmingly disappointed, because his father was a great one for making generous promises about the special things he would bring next time he came home. A toy car, perhaps, or a steely marble or a collection of colourful bottle labels that he had showed Adrian once, promising that, next time, he'd have got hold of another collection just like it for his boy. Then next time, and the next and next again. At times, if and when his father did come home, it could be grim. He often arrived so late at night that Adrian was asleep and never heard the noise of the door slamming. In the morning, his mother was lying half on top Eugen's body as if she had tried to wrestle him down during the night or as if something inside her had broken and left her unable to move away on her own. Eugen Ziegler kept very quiet about himself and his relatives, which was strange for someone usually so cocksure and boastful. He had told Adrian that the name *Ziegler* had to do with his descent from one of the thousands of Czech labourers who had travelled to Wien to labour in the brick works – the Ziegelbrenners – without whom no houses could have been built in this city. Or so he said. Ziegler became his name because he was a Czech, and moulding and firing bricks was what the Czechs did. It didn't take Adrian long to realise that this was no more than a tale. Sometimes, his father would speak of his work as a handyman in a railway station somewhere in eastern Slovakia, and how he had just happened to get on a train to Donetsk in Ukraine where he got himself a job at a steel mill and stayed for years. The revolution had just ended and thousands volunteered to go to Russia because they were fired up by Lenin. I've always been a communist at heart, Eugen Ziegler would say, beating his breast. This was sheer bombast. Ziegler had no heart but reckoned he could get away with pretending that he did or, at least, that being so handsome would make up for the defect. As Auntie Magda kept saying, Eugen's looks made women turn their heads. Well, *a certain kind* of woman, Auntie Emilia would add. When Adrian asked her if his mother was one of these women, Auntie Emilia told him that Eugen had been different in those days. But if Adrian went on to ask more about what he had been like, in *those days*, the answers became vague and muddled because one wasn't to speak about what had been. Still, it was fact that Eugen Ziegler spoke Russian, so there might have been a grain of truth in the story about running off to Donetsk. Once, he and Adrian almost paid with their lives for his language skills. It happened in the autumn of 1939, just weeks after Eugen had collected Adrian from Mödling and they were planning to start a new life. They lived in the 3rd Bezirk, on Erdbergstrasse, which is only a few blocks away from Rochusmarkt. Every day, Eugen would go to the pub to negotiate business deals and, every night, his oldest son Adrian was told to go and walk him home. On the slow, unsteady way back to Erdbergstrasse, Eugen, who was usually dead-drunk, would go on about how Wien was no longer the city it once was, the streets were crawling with *Piefkes*, he said, traitors and Nazi swine, and, once, when he saw two of them in Wehrmacht uniforms on the square at Rochusmarkt, he swayingly pulled up in front of them and, before Adrian had time to react, let out a stream of Russian abuse, all presumably meaningless to the soldiers. What they did grasp was that this man spoke Russian. *Spitzel*, a fucking spy, Adrian heard one of them snarl as he whipped the rifle off his back. Adrian grabbed his father's arm and managed to drag him behind one of the remaining market stalls where they crouched, squeezed tightly together, and heard the two soldiers run past, rifles rattling against the buckles of their Sam Browns, the heels of their boots thumping on the cobbles, and then Eugen pulled his fingers through his hair and turned his face, stinking of alcoholic fumes, to Adrian and hissed:

If you ever get matey with one of these Nazi swine I'll kill you, you hear me?

It would take six long years before the Nazis were run out of Wien but when it finally happened, a new life also opened up for Eugen Ziegler, incredible as it may sound. Earlier, his business deals had to be managed hand to mouth. 'Business' had always been hugely important for him. No day would pass without his doing deals and Adrian couldn't remember him speaking about anything else. Much later, Adrian would recognise more than a little of this in himself. My father, he said, was incapable of living with what was closed or already decided or concluded in some way. He existed in the present and for the promise of something to come. When the business was done and he was left facing the results, so many tons of brown coal or cubic metres of logs, he had no idea how to handle the goods he had acquired, or even how to transport the stuff. When he turned up at home, it was never to see me or Helmut or even our mother, whatever he might claim at the time, but to persuade Uncle Ferenc to fund the delivery of his brown coal on time or the down-payment on something he was after, Adrian said, and the rows with my mother broke out every time because he kept trying it on with Florian or Ferenc, and Leonie refused to allow either of her brothers to do business with Eugen. You don't know what you're doing, she would say. Leonie, who always stepped into the breach, was the one who got hit. When Eugen Ziegler beat up his woman, he went about it in a properly systematic way. First, everyone else was ordered to leave the flat. They gathered in the yard to wait while the screaming Leonie was hauled from wall to wall. The punishment could last from about twenty minutes to more than an hour, with increasingly long breaks in between bouts. Then the beating seemed to be over, until they heard a terrible scream and it started all over again. If in the end Eugen was too drunk to storm out in a rage, he collapsed exhausted in a corner while Leonie limped around, picking things up and tidying as always. Adrian remembered the time when his father had ordered a schnitzel and a beer to be brought from the restaurant across the street. Abusing Leonie must have made him hungry. Without a word, the table was laid with a white tablecloth and they all stood around watching the head of the household eat his supper. He ate as methodically as he beat his woman, but something about the way he brought fork and glass to his lips showed that he was out of his head with drink. Before going away, he emptied the coffee tin of the money Leonie and Ferenc had saved up for the rent. He left afterwards, without a word to anyone.

I know it's no fault of yours, Mrs Dobrosch, the landlord, Mr Schubach, used to say when Leonie went to see him the next morning and, with an ingratiating smile on her lips, asked him to be allowed to wait with the rent. It's that man Ziegler, a bastard who doesn't know how to behave decently. But, you know, this can't go on.

Foster Home And they were evicted in the end, on a day in May 1935. Adrian remembers that it poured with rain. Ferenc and Florian had carried the sticks of furniture the family still owned down to the yard: Leonie's bed, the bed all the children had slept on in turn, and the much-hammered kitchen table, always glued together again by Florian; the chairs, and the wardrobe for Leonie's dresses. She had packed Laura's, Adrian's and Helmut's clothes into a large suitcase. They had nothing to cover their things with and it rained so hard that the drops bounced many centimetres up in the air when they hit the wooden surfaces. Adrian still remembers this. Their neighbours had come out to watch from the galleries outside the flats. And the boys with whom he and Helmut used to drift around the streets. Now, they stood still and silent, just staring. Next to them, their fathers in their vests, leaning uncaringly against the railings with thin fags squeezed flat between their fingers. Everyone was waiting for Eugen to drive into the yard in the lorry he claimed to have got the use of, but he didn't come, with or without a lorry, and finally Leonie had had enough of being stared at, told her children to come along and walked away. Laura went to stay with Auntie Emilia, who in the nick of time had managed to rent a room in a flat on Taborstrasse. Adrian and Helmut were led by their mother to the children's home called the Zentralkinderheim on Lustkandlgasse. She told them afterwards that she nearly fainted on the way there and simply had to sit down on the pavement outside the entrance to a railway station, the Franz Josefs Bahnhof. A man had come along to ask if the lady was feeling unwell and then he fetched a glass of water for her from a nearby café. Which was the only ounce of kindness anyone showed me during that entire time, his mother said. He can't remember any of it and has little memory of what it was like in the Lustkandlgasse institution, despite he and Helmut spending almost all of the summer there. He stayed close to his little brother all the time, in the playground and when the food was served. Everybody liked little Helmut, who was blond and merry. *Ein hübsches Kind*. The nursery staff was keen for them to wash properly and, one day, they were helped to dress neatly and comb their hair before being brought into a large room with walls covered in white and black tiles. There were tall benches along the walls and, on these benches, children stood lined up. He and Helmut were to climb up onto a bench and Adrian was told to hold his little brother's hand tightly and wait obediently for *his turn*. Suddenly, the room filled with strangers. He was so scared his legs felt like jelly and his one thought was that he mustn't pee himself now that all these high-ups were around. The strangers walked slowly along the benches and examined the children carefully. One of the ladies who stopped in front of Adrian and Helmut wore a red dress with a white lace collar. She scrutinised Helmut from top to toe and turned to the nurse:

and the red lady said, *I'll have him, he looks nice*
and the nurse said, *in that case you must take the big one as well*
the red lady, *oh no, I don't want him, he's too ugly*
the nurse, *I'm sorry but we don't separate siblings*
the red lady, *well, too bad, if I have to I'll take the ugly one as well.*

That was that. He and Helmut went with the red lady for a ride on the 71 tram. It was August and he was enjoying the warm wind that blew in through the half-open windows when, after a while, he became baffled by the oddly familiar street outside. Then it dawned on him: the tram was going along Simmeringer Hauptstrasse. This was literally home from home. He even caught a quick glimpse of the greengrocer, Mr Gabel, keeping an eye on the fruit boxes he put out on the pavement every morning. Mrs Haidinger, the lady in the red dress, was sitting opposite him and, as soon as she saw him turn to look out, she reached across the centre aisle and twisted his head to make him look straight ahead. Afterwards, she didn't take her eyes off him for a second, as if she was worried that he would run away at the next stop or maybe do something worse, like jump at her throat. At close quarters, Mrs Haidinger looked rather less impressive than she had done in the tiled room. Below the hem of her red dress her legs were big and knobbly, and when she smiled, her closely packed, short white teeth reminded Adrian of a crocodile. She acted differently with Helmut, touching him all the time, patting his blond curls, and when they stepped off at Zentralfriedhof to change trams, she went into a shop near the cemetery gates to buy her new little boy a bar of Bensdorp chocolate that cost ten *groschen*. Obviously, Adrian got nothing because he was so ugly. They got off at the Kaiserebersdorf stop and took a shortcut across the fields and deserted building sites. That way, it was only a ten-minute walk to the Haidingers' house. Over on the far side of the fields, you could see the jagged outline of the chimneys of Schwechat and when the wind came from that direction it carried the rich scent of malt from the breweries. Mrs Haidinger lived in a large bungalow built to house two families. Mr and Mrs Haidinger, together with her parents, stayed in the rooms on the left, and on the right were her brother Rudolf Pawlitschek and his family. The two lines of the clan were feuding and Mrs Haidinger's notion of bringing back a couple of foster children did nothing to improve the atmosphere. Mr Pawlitschek was a cripple. Just below his shoulder, where his left arm should have begun, was nothing but a small flap of skin. It might be because he wasn't *serviceable*, as Mrs Haidinger put it, that he was such an angry, bitter man. He called the children *mongrels* and did everything he could to make them feel worthless and rejected. Adrian was set to work from his first day in the Haidinger household. The large back garden included a barn with pens for cows and goats, and a hen house and rabbit hutches. Adrian had to collect greens for the rabbits, clean dung from the coops and hutches, then scrub them with soda. The goats had to be tethered and moved on when they had stripped the patch of land within reach. If Mr Haidinger needed to water his lettuces, onions, strawberries and tomatoes, Adrian was to haul buckets of water from the well and barrow them to the right plot. He was never paid any wages for his labour. Even though he shared a bedroom with his little brother, they didn't see much of each other. While Adrian worked, Helmut accompanied Mrs Haidinger on her visits to relatives and friends and brought back gifts, new toys or chocolates from the Konsum. Much later, Adrian realised that the city council in Wien made large payments to foster parents who gave the children the *right kind of home*. The benefits not only covered Mrs Haidinger's outlays for board and lodging of both children but also left her quite enough to spend on new clothes for Helmut, *who grew so awfully quickly*, and probably on quite a few outfits for herself. Years later, the thought of this still upset Adrian very much. If all that money was there for the asking, he said to his mother, why not give some of it to you so we could have grown up at home? But his mother only shrugged helplessly in the rather childish way she had adopted of late and replied that she really couldn't say. But perhaps the authorities had decided to give you just one chance in life to bring up your children the right way, and perhaps she had squandered hers when they had been forced to carry their belongings down into the yard and Mr Schubach had had thrown them out and left them all in the rain while their neighbours lined the galleries, smoking and watching the spectacle.

March 1938 The wireless was always on in the Haidinger household. It was silent only if the battery had run down and then Adrian had to take it to an electrician in Schwechat to be charged. The batteries were heavy and there was always at least one to carry each way, the discharged one that he brought to Schwechat and the fully recharged one that was needed back home. The Haidinger and Pawlitschek families called a ceasefire when it was time to gather around the radio. Together, they listened to speeches by Mr Schuschnigg, the Federal Chancellor, and to the debates about the betrayal of Austria, and were excited to hear the news from Steiermark about the Heimwehrverbande, the local Territorial Army unit that refused to take sides against their German brothers. The day Hitler came marching in, a group of them went off to Heldenplatz: Mr Haidinger, Mr Christian, who was a neighbour and a member of the Patriotic Front, and *old* Mr Pawlitschek, the father of the man with the missing arm. Pawlitschek senior was a large man with a stiff, bristly moustache. He was a *convinced* Nazi, Mrs Haidinger said, as if, even among the NSDP members, some were less than *wholly* convinced. Adrian was allowed to come along on the outing because they needed someone to carry the provisions. They took the tram to Schwarzenbergplatz and walked up Ringstrasse, past the Imperial Hotel where old Mr Pawlitschek insisted that Hitler and his entourage were quartered. When they passed the Opera House, he also pointed out that jumped-up Jews were the only ones parading around in there. The pavements of the wide avenue were crowded with people waving banners and handkerchiefs, shouting *Heil Heil Heil!* all the time. By the time the group got close to Heldenplatz, the crowd was too dense and they had to cross to the museum side and finally, after re-crossing the tram rails, they once more ended up so far back that all they could see of Hitler was a small, grey blob on the distant balcony. But I did see him, Adrian would say afterwards. Well, sort of. He had been overwhelmed by hearing the Führer's voice booming through the loudspeakers high above everyone's heads, even though the words of the great man's speech were almost impossible to make out because the sound bounced all over the place and was anyway drowned in the wild noise made by the tens of thousands of voices shouting and screaming while people waved their swastika-emblazoned banners and stretched their arms straight up in the air to return his salute; but, Adrian said, all he could think of was how to place his feet so that he could quickly bend down and then get out from under if he risked being trampled on. A few weeks later, his form teacher in the school at Münnichplatz was replaced. The new one, a Mr Bergen, had the title 'Magister' and was probably a *convinced* Nazi, perhaps even a party member. He started to pick on Adrian straightaway.

There was a poem by Ottokar Kernstock that should be read with a special kind of solemn emphasis at the end of each sentence and Mr Bergen would read it aloud, standing by the teacher's desk, and then all the pupils had to repeat after him:

Das Hakenkreuz im weissen Feld
Auf feuerrotem Grunde
Gibt frei und offen aller Welt
Die frohgemute Kunde
Wer sich um dieses Zeichen schart
Ist deutsch mit Seele, Sinn und Art
und nicht bloss mit dem Munde.[1]

Over and over again, Adrian was told to stand in front of the class and recite the poem by heart and, every time, he lost track. Besides, the way he pronounced some of the lines made his reading unintentionally come across as a comic turn, perhaps especially when he got to '*um dieses Zeichen schart*'. By then, everyone was in fits of laughter and Mr Bergen's face had flushed as red as the Nazi banner. It didn't take long for the form teacher to make a personal call to Mr and Mrs Haidinger. He told them that innate stupidity clearly made the bastard boy they had adopted unteachable. Mr Bergen added that they had actually been wrong to take him on. The teacher seemed to know how it had happened and had presumably heard it from someone else. The foster parents weren't likely to go unpunished for their bad judgement. Mr Haidinger took it out on Adrian afterwards. He went for the most straightforward approach, ordered the boy to strip

1 The hooked cross in a white field / On a fiery red background / Offers freely and openly to the whole world / The joyful message / That everyone who treasures this emblem / Is truly German in soul, mind and origin / And not only a camp-follower.

to the waist and come along to the tool shed where the spare rabbit hutches were kept and where, just as he would when flaying a dead rabbit, he hung Adrian on a hook on the wall using the rope tying his wrists, then took his belt off and whipped the half-naked child until not only Adrian, but Haidinger too, was screaming insanely. Light seeped into the shed and Adrian saw Helmut watching them, eating one of Mrs Haidinger's titbits and smiling in exactly the same nervously submissive way as their father when he was scared.

Mr Pawlitschek's Money Rudolf Pawlitschek had this habit of boasting about his prowess as a huntsman, never mind that he had only one arm. Once, Mr Pawlitschek invited Adrian into his room next to the hallway and told him that he would be allowed to watch how one went about greasing a hunting rifle. The rifle hung on a hook above Mr Pawlitschek's bed. While he outlined some of his sporting feats, he took it down, laid it across his parted thighs and extracted a tin of gun grease and a cloth from the drawer in his bed-side table. The cleaning started with Mr Pawlitschek ramming the muzzle into his left armpit and then rotating the gun by alternately tightening and relaxing his grip with what was left of the stump on his shoulder as he wiped it down using strong, even strokes with the cloth. It looked funny. His armpit kept releasing and catching the gun while his right hand rubbed and rubbed on the same spot. The effort made Mr Pawlitschek sweat copiously and, all the while, the sweat seemed to soften his sour, twisted face until a grimace almost like a smile was spreading across it. When Mr Pawlitschek had finished and put the cloth and the tin of grease back in the drawer, Adrian caught sight of a bundle of bank notes squashed in at the back. It became instantly fixed in his mind. Every morning, as he dragged himself to the school on Münnichplatz, his thoughts circled around the money and the image stayed with him all the hours he spent sitting on the seat Mr Bergen had exiled him to, right at the back of the classroom, where he was left to his own devices because Bergen persistently, patiently ignored Adrian and directed his questions to the other children. Adrian thought that he would count the money one day when Mr Pawlitschek wasn't at home. He wouldn't do anything else, only count the notes to find out how much the stash was worth. The right moment arrived sooner than he had dared to hope. When he came home from school one afternoon, the Haidingers and the Pawlitscheks (senior and junior) were out and the rifle had gone from its hook on the wall, so Adrian opened the drawer, removed the tin of gun grease and the cloth, then the notes, pulled off the rubber band and started counting with trembling fingers. Sixty Reichsmarks. In that moment a decision was made, but not by Adrian; as he explained later, instead his mind had been made up *for* him. Actually, it was more like an incontrovertible fact rather than any kind of choice because what to do next *must* be done for the simple reason that the money was in that drawer and this was the day when no one was in, except the cows and the rabbits. It took him only minutes to put the notes in his pocket, pack some clothes in his satchel and catch the tram towards Schwarzenbergplatz. Far fewer people were out strolling along the Inner Ring than on the afternoon when Adolf Hitler's cavalcade ploughed through the huge crowds, and soon Adrian was stopped by a policeman on his beat. In the thirties, school-age children were not usually drifting about on their own in central Wien. Besides, guardian or no guardian, this boy with his dark tinker's face and grass-stained pants, the only trousers Mrs Haidinger let him wear when he was at home and made to clean the rabbit hutches, didn't come across as a believable schoolchild. The officer, pretty certain that he had caught an experienced pick-pocket whose school satchel was nothing but camouflage, felt vindicated when he found the bundle of bank notes. Adrian was taken to the police station, the money was properly counted and he had to confess all. He was Adrian Dobrosch (not yet Ziegler!) and, yes, he had taken Mr Pawlitschek's savings, intending to keep half for himself to pay for food and somewhere to live, and give the rest to his mother for the rent. Tell me, who's your mother? the policeman asked with a cunning smirk, as if he reckoned he was about to catch an entire gang of thieves, but Adrian fell silent at that point.

The Tinker's Lad But they already knew all they needed to know. Mrs Haidinger wouldn't have him in the house and, once he had got his money back, Mr Pawlitschek requested that he should be allowed not to bring a charge. The thing was, who would be responsible? On paper, which was what mattered, the Haidingers were Adrian's parents. The boy was dispatched to the institution for abandoned children on Lustkandlgasse in Alsergrund, the Kinderübernahmestelle or 'KüST' as it was known for short. This time there was no chance that he would be stood on a bench like some circus animal and ogled and, with any luck, chosen by a lady in a red dress who bought you chocolates in Konsum afterwards. He was there for two weeks, presumably the time it took for the documentation about him to be shuffled by officials from one department to another until his adoption papers were cancelled, and then he was transferred to the old orphanage in Mödling. It was known as the Hyrtl'sche Waisenhaus and looked like a medieval fortress, a large brick building with high flat-fronted towers and a chapel in an inner courtyard. Very soon after the Nazis had taken over the government, the Waisenhaus was turned into a reform school for undisciplined children. Adrian was to be sent to Mödling twice. The worst tour was the second one, in early spring 1943. He does not remember much from his stay in the autumn of 1939, just large, draughty rooms and apparently endless corridors and stairwells, where they were never to be seen alone but always in a troop, singly or in pairs, in *Einzel-* or *Zweierreihen*, always on their way to somewhere, to the dining hall or the gym, with one of the older boys in the lead shouting out orders over the sound of angrily tramping feet that echoed down the deep shafts of the stairwells. During the first weeks, he was tormented by guilt. He had not deserved the care offered to him by the Haidingers, or by anybody else for that matter. He had no idea what Mrs Haidinger would decide to do with Helmut. Keep him or make him suffer an even worse fate, which would be Adrian's fault? He didn't know anything and the uncertainty pained him more than being pestered by the other boys, who remarked on his looks, his dark skin and oddly shaped ears. They used to ask what kind of glue he used to stick his ears so close to his head. One day, his group leader told him that he had to go to the office. The director, Mr Heckermann, seemed short where he sat ensconced behind his big desk. His moustache was kept narrow, probably not to outdo his lips, which were even narrower, and together the twin lines of lips and moustache made a shape like a small beak. Heckermann's slightly frail, bird-like body could look threatening, as it did now, when he raised his shoulders and asked Adrian to state his surname. Scared, Adrian shrugged in instinctive mimicry as he replied in the firm, military style that everyone in the school was to use:

Dobrosch!

That ugly, insubordinate name had never sounded more repulsive. Like when one opens an old tin can and some rotting, stinking sludge pours out. For a moment Mr Heckermann looked disgusted, but then his moustache-beak opened again:

You're wrong there!

What are you supposed to do when a person in authority asks your name and then says you're wrong? Adrian closed his eyes, convinced that this was it, he was finished. *You're wrong because from now on, your name is Ziegler!*

When he said that, Adrian dared to open his eyes again, saw Mr Heckermann standing behind his desk, and in the next moment, as already mentioned, the grinning Eugen Ziegler emerged from a cupboard and stepped forward to hug his prodigal son.

Uncle Florian's Warm Hands It was a little like a baptism. At least, that's how Adrian saw it. He had stepped out of his mother's ineffective shadow into the radiance of his father's name. Eugen Ziegler had abused Leonie Dobrosch constantly for ten long years; he had abandoned her and their children countless times, just as no one could have kept track of all the times he had come back home, drunk or broke and, hence, repentant. But when father and son left Mödling together, Eugen put his arm around his son's shoulders and explained to him that nobody could separate them because, by now, his father and mother were *married for real*. This was his happy message and he had wanted to tell Adrian face to face, he said, but the paternal arm around the boy's shoulders, meant to seem strong and protective, was actually no more than one long plea for support. Naturally, it was all because of the war. What else? Unless Eugen Ziegler could prove that he had responsibility for the upkeep of a family, he risked being picked up in the street and driven to the front line, or maybe even some worse place. As it was, the authorities had found him a job on the assembly line in the Floridsdorf locomotive factory. They worked round the clock out there, building locos for the Deutsche Reichsbahn. The job had strings attached, though:

Ziegler had had to promise to take his wage packet home to his wife, hand over all the money and then she had to sign for it. Also, the factory foreman had apparently said that once is enough, Ziegler, if I hear you're coming to work pissed or not taking all the money home you'll be out on your ear. And even though his sobriety might have slipped some evenings and weekends, officialdom had the whip-hand and, throughout the war years, Eugen Ziegler dragged himself along to Floridsdorf every day and did his bit on the production line that was to build more than 1,000 engines of the type DRB Class 52. They lived in the 3rd Bezirk at the time, in a modern flat with a bath-tub and a toilet, and had the authorities to thank for that as well. Ferenc still stayed in Kaisermühlen even though he had got a job in St Pölten, driving coal trucks for a haulage company delivering to businesses that weren't too pernickety about paperwork like orders and receipts. The job was dangerous because they had to drive at night with the headlamps off and might at any moment get caught by the police. Adrian's mother was beside herself with worry, but she worried even more about Uncle Florian. He had never been a problem for as long as he was with them. True, he could be confused at times and it could be confusing to talk to him because his speech was so slurred and rambling that it was hard to understand him. But he was a kind man, and if only he had some way to use his hands he was as precise and diligent as you could wish (but you always had to *place* whatever it was in his hands). For instance, it happened that Mr Gabel, the greengrocer, allowed him to come along on trips to the wholesaler out in Kagran. When they returned, Adrian remembers, Florian would be wearing tough gloves and an apron that made him look like a real stevedore. In the spring, he would help Ferenc with cleaning and waxing the boats in the marina at Alte Donau. Seated on a small stool, he would sit in the white sunlight holding the brush as delicately as if he were painting on a costly linen canvas. His sister, Adrian's mother, always used to say that Uncle Florian had such warm and sensitive hands. But after the eviction, all this came to an end. No work could be found for Florian. He stayed for a while in a hostel for single men in Brigittenau but could never settle down among strangers, and then his mindset and behaviour changed, he became restless and wandered in the streets, *playing the fool*, as his sister said. By the autumn of 1937, she had managed to find him a bed in the mental asylum in Gugging. The relief lasted only a few months, until the Anschluss. The old hospital board was replaced only weeks later and Florian was transferred to Steinhof, where he shared a ward with forty deranged men who sat or lay on their beds, sometimes tied down and screaming because there was no one who came to look after them. Leonie would visit her brother at least once a month, always on a Sunday. Adrian has a clear memory of how she would get dressed before the visit, standing in front of the mirror, something she normally did not do. She'd put on a grey, woollen cardigan and a beret. Her face always looked blurred with crying when she came back from Steinhof. She complained that the staff treated Florian worse than they would a dog and that her brother was *fading away* in front of her eyes, more and more at every visit. (The abyss that separated how they lived then, during that last, unreal year of freedom, from the insanity that was to take over, was so deep that it would take many years before Adrian managed to join up the two periods of time: the one that came *before* he was sent to Spiegelgrund and the other that began *after* he had become a registered inmate. He realised only then that the gravelled paths between the pavilions that he had to take to the school building every morning were the very same that his mother had taken on her Sunday visits to uncle Florian just a few years earlier. It was not only that it was the same place, but also that the Spiegelgrund staff *recognised* her when she delivered him, because almost all of them had been working at Steinhof as asylum nurses. In their eyes, his mother was one of those *crazy women* who would turn up at every which time and make nuisances of themselves by asking about husbands or brothers or children, even after it should have been clear to them that there were no more Steinhof patients left to ask about. It must have been how they looked at her when she came to visit him, Adrian, the only time she did. For one thing, she was dressed exactly as when she visited Uncle Florian, the same skirt and woolly, grey cardigan and worn coat and beret, so she had presumably stood in front of the mirror and prepared herself in the same old way, her eyes anxiously fixed on her reflection while she applied shiny red lipstick to her thin, pale lips.) In October or November 1940, Uncle Florian and forty-or-so other males had been herded onto buses run by the charity GeKraT (Gemeinnützige Krankentransport) and driven to Hartheim. Leonie Ziegler had not been informed of this. The official letter arrived several weeks later and announced that Mr Florian *Dobrocz* – some ill-educated clerk had either misheard or simply couldn't spell – had suddenly succumbed to pneumonia and, despite every effort by the staff, his life could not be saved. Adrian remembers when the letter arrived. The family was seated at the table. So far, one Sunday night after another, his father had sat down, calm and sober, at the carefully laid supper table and, every week, put up in silence with his wife's tearful face and endless wailing about dear Florian with the warm hands who was simply fading and receding away from her, but this Sunday he could take no more. Enraged, he stood up with such force that the table rocked and sent plates and glasses flying, then crashing onto the floor. He had had it with all the miserable moaning and groaning, he shouted, then he left and slammed the door after him. At first

Leonie sat very still, then she hid her face in her hands and wept so wildly her shoulders shook. But it might be that none of this had happened by then. In March 1938, Helga was already born and, just over a year later, Leonie had become pregnant again with Hannelore, who arrived in February 1940. Adrian was a pupil in the school on Erdbergstrasse. Just as in the Münnichplatz school, it was understood that he was an *imbecile* and, as such, placed at the back of the classroom. By then, the other children in the class wore uniforms with a Hitlerjugend pin on the jacket lapel and, once a week, went off to a *Heimabend* at someone's home after school. When his classmates asked him why he and his sister never came to someone's house for these evening get-togethers, which after all were compulsory, he didn't know what to say. When Eugen Ziegler had received a document stating that he was *wehrunwürdig*, he probably felt a certain sense of relief, but for his children the fact that Ziegler was classed as unfit for military service meant exclusion from the Deutsches Jungvolk and presumably all other organisations with a link to NSDAP. Adrian was dead keen to wear the same uniform as the others. It wasn't because he was crazy about uniforms or the stupid Home Evening singalongs but because the uniform was the one thing that could stop his father from beating him up. All children in an HJ uniform were under the personal protection of the Führer, and no one could punish them except, of course, the Führer himself. At Spiegelgrund it grew quite boring, the way they kept insisting that the Führer was the greatest friend and protector of children. Adrian Ziegler had realised that long ago, and nothing that was to happen later would make him doubt that it was true.

A Christmas Celebration (and its consequences) In December 1940, the Ziegler family celebrated their first Christmas together.

Helmut joined them once the reluctant Haidingers had been persuaded to 'hand him back for the duration'. They'd had family Christmases before in the Simmeringer flat, with a tree and all the trimmings, but it always ended with everyone, uncles and aunties included, waiting around at the table where the place laid for the head of the household stood empty. With any luck, he would turn up near midnight, drunk, alone, or with mates he had fancied bringing along. If he was on his own, he'd be furious because there was nothing but *sweet rubbish* on the table and would take it out on Leonie, hit and kick her, shouting that she was a useless slut not worth wiping the floor with. This time, though, they would have a proper Christmas. With one week to go until Christmas Eve, Adrian and his father walked to Rochusmarkt and picked a real fir tree to take home. At school, one of the teachers, who clearly wasn't a totally convinced Nazi, allowed them to write essays on the theme *My Best Christmas* and even let them build their own nativity cribs. Adrian's sister Laura became so excited at the thought of all the fun they'd have over the festive days that she spent an entire afternoon dashing in and out of the shops on Mariahilfer Strasse. She made one of her friends from school distract the shop assistants while she picked all the lovely, shiny things she could find room for under her sweater, like many-coloured glass balls and glittering strands of tinsel. They were sitting on the steps leading up to the Westbahnhof platforms, tarted up like little princesses with tinsel threaded through their hair, when the police caught up with them. It wasn't the first time that Laura had been caught shoplifting. Most of it was small-scale, like pencils and erasers and other things she needed for school, or chocolate and fruit from the stalls in the market. But times had changed. Before, staff from the departments of social services and health had at least tried to be sympathetic and helpful, but now everyone was relentlessly strict. Vagrancy and larceny were crimes, and correct punishments had to be meted out. Laura's behaviour was especially vexing, as she obviously 'tempted others to follow her'. When the social workers came for a home visit two days into the new year, they took note of the fact that Adrian, Helmut and Laura not only shared the same bed but also played 'Mummy-Daddy-Children' underneath a rigged-up tablecloth and, furthermore, that Adrian and Helmut were both naked, all of which was interpreted as *an indication of incestuous relationships* in the family. *The children are dirty and malnourished, and their manners have been allowed to degenerate. They are rebellious and foul-mouthed.* The report included a long passage about Adrian Ziegler, who is described as *an insolent and degenerate boy who, when adults are talking, incessantly interrupts with obscene expressions and invectives.* I can't remember any of us being insolent, Adrian commented when he saw the report much later. On the other hand, I do remember how they interrogated us one at a time, he said, and tried to make us say things about our parents that were not true. For instance, they wanted me to tell them about my mother, how she was slovenly and had failed to look after the family, and then I burst into tears. I knew that my mother had worked, unselfishly and unaided, for more than twelve years, doing her best to keep her children clean and in decent clothes, seven of us in the end, and have food put in front of us every day. They could never make me say that she had failed to look after us. The family was split up again. They decided that Mrs Leonie Ziegler (née Dobrosch) had enough on her hands with her two youngest. The authorities looked for a new foster family for the eldest, Laura, who was almost fifteen and needed to prepare for her *Pflichtjahr*, when she had to go away and learn how to do practical tasks in the house and on the land. A place in a children's home on Bastiengasse in Währing was found for Helmut.

Adrian was sent to Spiegelgrund, which had just been designated a specialist clinic for children with severe psychiatric or neurological conditions, but which also served as a reform school for boys and girls with disciplinary problems. Spiegelgrund was the place of last resort, the end of the road for those thought effectively irredeemable. He didn't know all that at time, of course. When he was registered on that January day in 1941, the form recorded all measurable facts about him in neat typescript:

Height: *135 cm*
Body weight: *34 kg*
Skull type: *Flattened; somewhat deformed; 'Gypsy type'*
Ears: *Semitic curvature but shapely; close to skull*
Hair colour: *Dark*
Overall pigmentation: *Dark*

Doctor Gross had made just a few entries under 'Other characteristics': *R. shoulder blade protruding slightly; feet smell badly; L. shin, an approx. 30cm long scratch.* The form has three photographs attached, two from sideways on and one from in front. The photos show an eleven-year-old boy who looks perfectly healthy. His shoulders are raised a little and his half-open mouth and scared eyes complete the picture of a child who surely could harm no one.

II

A Healer of Souls Needs No Eyes

My name is Anna Katschenka. I have worked as a nurse for twenty-two years. My service at Spiegelgrund began in 1941. Doctor Jekelius was the institution's acting medical director at the time. I believe Doctor Türk had taken up her post there by then. Later, Doctor Illing took over the directorship. If I remember correctly, this change took place in July 1942. Between 1923 and 1934, I was a member of the Social Democratic Party and, subsequently, of the Austrian Patriotic Front. Since the post-war regime changes, I have not taken any further interest in politics. I have never belonged to the National Socialist German Workers' Party (NSDAP) or any of its organisations. In June 1929, I married the medical student Siegfried Hauslich. Our marriage was dissolved on grounds of incompatible differences of personality and interpersonal antipathy. My ex-husband was a Jew. I met Doctor Jekelius for the first time after my dismissal from service in Lainz, when I was referred to him for treatment of my recurring depressed moods. His treatment was successful and I came to trust the doctor wholeheartedly, which is why I applied for a nursing post in his clinic. A few days after starting work on the wards, Doctor Jekelius called me into his clinical office. He reminded me of my professional oath and promise of confidentiality, and emphasised that I must not, under any circumstances, disclose any details of individual cases treated in the hospital, nor was I to ask unnecessary questions. He put it to me that I had by then seen with my own eyes the miserable state of the children when they arrived at the clinic and observed that some of them were incurable. He then went on to explain to me how the clinic managed the children afflicted by such conditions. I remained very attached to Doctor Jekelius after his recruitment to the Wehrmacht in January 1942. I wrote to him when he was on active service and visited him several times. There was no romantic relationship between us at any time. Doctor Jekelius was a National Socialist and I never was. Personally, I have never cared for politics.

Doctor Jekelius He inspired confidence from the start. At first, she thought it was just a matter of the way he observed her and addressed her, but later she realised that his entire being contributed to the impression he gave. The way he moved was so remarkably graceful and relaxed. Like an animal, on his guard but never self-conscious. Several years later, when he was hounded and became the target of a hate campaign, and even some of his especially loyal colleagues began to distance themselves from him, whether out of cowardliness or an acute sense of fear, he was accused of being a fraud. Still, she felt certain that someone who inhabited his body with such confidence and was so trustful of all its senses couldn't possibly defraud anyone. It is easy to lie in thought or speech, but the body doesn't lie. Later, when the preliminary investigations started up, she felt not the slightest need to try to cover anything up, and spoke quite openly about how she came to look for a post in his clinic. Back in 1939, she had spent a long, anxious year on the nursing staff at the home for the elderly in Lainz. Doctor Herz, the Minister of State in charge of the home, committed suicide immediately after the Nazi takeover. Professor Müller, head of the medical department where she worked, was forced to leave. The staff kept changing, one wave after another. Anna Katschenka, who had never before doubted her own competence, began to feel inadequate, and her sense of insecurity made her subject to recurring fits of depression and an unending series of headaches and stomach upsets. She worried that her new superiors were in some indefinable way displeased with her and thought her poor at her job. To her, loyalty and trustworthiness were central ideals. It mattered very much to her that the authorities should regard her as *worthy*. Her medical problems, she would confess to Jekelius, were rooted in the fact that she lived in fear. Of course, she feared that she would be sacked for political reasons. More than that, she dreaded what the consequences would be of no longer belonging, of not being seen to exist in her own right, of not being needed. It was relevant that both her father and her brother had been forced out of posts at various points in time after the Patriotic Front came to power in 1934, and that the survival of her family now depended on her alone. When her physical symptoms became unbearable, she turned to her superiors, and Doctor Dipold, a consultant who had taken over from Professor Müller as medical director, had recommended her to get in touch with Doctor Jekelius. Jekelius himself had changed his place of work and taken on the post of senior consultant at the Steinhof alcohol and drug rehabilitation clinic. However, he had kept his former practice going and still saw patients for a few hours in the afternoon at his Martinstrasse surgery in Währing. The patients had to ring the bell at the garden gate and cross a paved terrace edged on both sides by great trees whose crowns had come to join, forming a shadowing arch. Almost like a pergola. Because it was a warm summer's day, the surgery window was open and they had their first long talk against the background noise of sparrows flying in and out of the leafy canopies outside. She had been quite worried about that first encounter. Maybe he would be contemptuous, even displeased when he realised that his patient was a registered nurse. He might have taken note of this but she couldn't tell. Instead, he enquired meticulously about her previous jobs and muttered approvingly if a familiar name of a professor or consultant turned up. He smiled when she finished her account, and went on to say that she must surely regard him as the oddest of all the doctors she had met. This claim put her on the back foot. Why so? she asked. Because of my accent, he said. It's from Siebenbürgen, my whole family is from there. (True, his precise High German had a slight Saxony intonation, but she had taken no special notice and, insofar as she thought anything about the way he spoke, it was how well his melodic voice went with his smoothly co-ordinated body). She suspected his remark to be more of a diversionary tactic, a way to make her relax a little. Then, he told her a story.

In Hermannstadt, where he grew up, he had cared a lot for one of his aunts who throughout his youth suffered from recurring depressions. For that reason, his parents had forbidden him to go and see her. He usually played by a small stream near their house. They called it Stinkystream because it carried so much smelly rubbish. When he was playing on its bank, he hoped all the time to find something that might cure his aunt. One day, he came across a small, white packet and brought it to her at once. The moment I took the wrapper off, my aunt burst out laughing, Jekelius said and looked straight at her. Can Nurse Anna guess what was in the packet? he asked.

She shook her head.

Lausex.

What's Lausex?

A delousing insecticide. Given the right dosage, the contents of that packet could have killed some seven thousand people. There, I see that you're laughing, Mrs Katschenka! And so did my aunt. She laughed so hard she could not stay upright, neither sitting nor standing. The next day, our family doctor called to tell my parents that my aunt felt much better, thanks to their son's timely intervention. He told me, *you must study medicine, Erwin!* Do you know what I replied? I said, *then I think I'd rather become the emperor of Germany!*

They laughed. And then sat together in silence. From outside came a noise as if someone quietly, discreetly, was scrunching up crisp sheets of paper. It was the sparrows dashing in and out of that dense mass of leaves. She had forgotten about them for a while.

Why do you tell me this? she finally asked.

Perhaps, he replied, because what you need is just someone to snap their fingers in front of your face – *like this!* – and, suddenly, the world looks different. Put it this way: to cure disease, truly to heal, doesn't exclusively mean doing something to, or even *for*, the patient. The person who is ill is part of a *context*, and that is what must be changed: the very way we understand illness. I would be happy to discuss this further at your next appointment.

A Healer of Souls Needs No Eyes

You ask if I had a relationship with Doctor Jekelius and it makes me proud to be able to say: yes, I did, although not in the coarse sense that you might have had in mind. I had never before in my life trusted anyone as I trusted him. When I first sought him out, it felt as if I was anaesthetised, body and soul. I felt nothing if I raised my hand or touched something, as if unaware that I had a hand, and then he came along and placed his hand on mine and my sensibility came back, and the mobility of my fingers. A healer of souls needs no eyes, was what I once wrote to him after he had been wounded on the battlefield and could neither move nor see. By now, they have robbed him of everything: his body, sight, hearing, and his honour, too. But there is one thing no one can take away from him, and that is what he did for me. He gave me my life back. Does it follow that I must also be close to him in other ways, such as politically? This is what you imply but, of course, it is not so. I knew all the time that Doctor Jekelius was a National Socialist. However, politics never meant anything to me.

The Vocation Anna Katschenka had known that she wanted to be a nurse ever since she was ten. That was her age when her sister died from an inherited thickening of the heart muscle. Everyone had known about her heart trouble and that it might be fatal at any moment. Anna's sister had found it hard to keep up with the other children, and soon became breathless and had to sit down to rest. She was perfectly fine when they played what their mother called 'quiet games', and could even be a little protective of Anna. The day before she died, Anna's sister had been swinging her legs to and fro as she perched on the edge of her bed and they had pretended that her legs were little wild creatures that Anna had to catch, but once the wiggling feet had been caught and shoed and the laces were tied, Anna's sister stood up but was breathing oddly and sweating, and her face was flushed. The following day, her bed was empty, the bedspread stretched flat and tightly tucked in. They had removed all the pictures, and the books from the shelves, and even the 'secret box' where Anna's sister had kept her pretty things, her rings and necklaces, together with saved-up letters and a diary. It seemed they felt nothing of hers could remain, now that she was dead.

Whosoever doth not bear his own cross, and come after me, cannot be my disciple. So therefore whosoever he be of you that forsaketh not all that he hath, he cannot be my disciple.

She had told Doctor Jekelius of a memory of the funeral. Anna and her mother, who had been deeply affected by her daughter's death, were leaving the church together, walking arm in arm. Above them the mighty church bells had swung and hammered and banged incessantly with their massive brass clappers. She used to say that the bells had called her into service, but at heart she knew that nothing so uplifting had taken place. It had been a dreadful moment. For perhaps a second, all went black as the overwhelming, choking din of the bells took her over. It was as if the Lord had hurled back down to Earth each one of the dead child's frail heartbeats, transformed into a crushing weight of iron that boomed and trembled, boomed and trembled, until the sky seemed like a gigantic heart about to break. Her mother had clapped her hands over her ears and moved closer to the wall as if looking for shelter. But the wall, too, broke, and the pavement cracked and sagged under their feet. Anna's hand, from now on to be a *helping hand*, could not reach her. No hands could help. From that day, Anna Katschenka's mother never went outside. She said that she dreaded the looks in people's eyes. Perhaps more than their eyes, she dreaded those whispering voices that, even as she sat beneath the stone arches of the church, had begun to creep into her mind, every one of them murmuring that she had failed to save her daughter's life. From then on, her child's heart failure took shape and became a dominant presence during all her waking hours, just as being blind or paralysed can dominate someone's life. It meant that every objection, every attempt to inject some uncertainty into the absolute truth of what the mother said about her dead child only served to make the illness stronger still, because it brought back memories of shame and guilt. Anna, from now on, was the one charged with preventing the chaos and disintegration in the outside world from getting through to her mother, and seeing to it that her mother heard only what was cheerful or encouraging, and nothing that maimed or tore apart. Day after day, Anna did her bit to create a provisional world order that was sound and harmonious, even though her mother had long since stopped believing in anything of the sort. One of her sayings used to be: *the healthy don't shun the light*. This was one of her mother's many incantatory phrases that Anna now made her own. To prove just how healthy and tough they all were, her father would sometimes spend an evening displaying his photos from the time when he was a sportsman. He had been a long- and medium-distance runner, and could be picked out in the group pictures from championships in strange cities as a tall, gangly young man standing among his teammates, all with their arms loosely draped across each other's shoulders. The young sportsmen belonged to the Wiener Arbeiter Turn- und Sportverein and the banner above their heads read *WAT Ottakring*. As an older man, Anna's father had been asked to take on the honorary post as the society's treasurer. He used to sit at the kitchen table most evenings after supper and run his index finger down the columns of paid and unpaid membership fees, or else he went to the sports ground and settled down alone on the empty coach's bench with a stopwatch in one hand and a notebook in the other, checking his son's lap times on the track below as Otto trained for the hundred-metre hurdles in the club championships. Into the light, then out of it.

Blood Anna loses blood. Warm, sticky, dark blood. When she pushes her hand between her legs, it fills her cupped palm. It is menstrual blood, as she knows perfectly well. What she can't understand is why such a lot of it pours out of her. Headaches and nausea follow in its wake and she, usually such a good pupil at school, who hangs on the teachers' every word and is diligence personified, has to ask leave to go to the lavatory too often during lessons and must walk out while everyone in the class giggles and looks the other way. To tell her mother about this affliction is unthinkable. To her father, she says it is just nerves. But, in the end, it is the ageing printer, a shy and inhibited man with little idea of women's health problems, who takes his young daughter to see the doctor. They learn that Anna is anaemic and needs to take the prescribed tablets. At school, she gets called Woodlouse because of her greyish, unnaturally pale skin, set off by greasy hair and teenage pimples. How she *hates* this physical self that grows and swells and wants nothing more than to wallow, languid and bland. She hides behind a wall of chilly self-control. She has few friends at school but stays top of the class. The healthy body that she never before felt ashamed to see in full sunlight has changed irrevocably into an alien continent. That is how she sees it. Like the school's wall maps of Africa or South America. Her skin is like a coastline, long and thin. Beyond it, there are endless forests through which the blood flows, in narrow winding streams or in huge glossy rivers, only to end in internal lakes in cavities enclosed on all sides by the vault of a sky that has no inner or outer surface but exists only as the boundary of the truly boundless inner world. This childlike idea of the body stays with her even much later, when she has learnt so much more about human anatomy. When the migraines come, the headaches establish a hold over this alien continent, and when she sleeps, her dreams are inner seas and skies in which she travels. Unlike the world out there, it is pleasingly easy to move from one internal place to the next. Her feelings, which she is quite capable of concealing from everyone, can in moments transport her mind from the black bog of despond and self-contempt onto the high plateau of willingness to forgive herself. Pain, she soon learns, is another way of travelling.

The Healthy Don't Shun the Light To be a nurse is no longer her vocation. Training has become a compulsion: the only way to make the alien continent her own while at the same time keep it at bay. Control it. She follows her father's advice and takes a three-year course in domestic science and then gets a poorly paid job as nursery nurse at the children's hospital in Leopoldstadt. If your background is ordinary, it is hard to land a good traineeship. It was only in May 1924 that she found an opening. Wien had been a federated state in its own right for a couple of years and the city council was under Social Democratic control. Now, the hospital in Lainz offers a three-year course leading to registered nurse status. Anna Katschenka sails through the preliminary exam. The training also includes voluntary work, and the following year Anna's class is recruited to run the first aid station at the large sports championships held by the Austrian labour organisations at Trabrennbahn – the trotting course – in the Prater. Her period is due just then and, in the morning, dizziness overwhelms her as usual despite her attempt to deal with it by lying in bed with her feet higher than her head to force the blood to run back into her head. (But there's nothing else for it. This is her baptism of fire. And she wouldn't miss it for anything in the world.) Here they are! Twenty-odd dutiful nursing students, *Pflegeschülerinnen* in freshly starched uniforms. In front of them, out on the race track, thousands of young male and female athletes are marching in perfect formations behind their colourful club standards, while above them the span of the sky is as high and deep and blue as it can be on a summer's day, and a light breeze toys with the pennants on the packed terraces. Afterwards, she remembers the conductor in his absurd tailcoat, leading the orchestra from his podium with amusingly snappy baton movements while the music emerged from the laughter of the audience and the noise of marching feet: the crisp bleating of the brass section, the twittering of the flutes and the heavy, rhythmic, but somehow distracted *thump-thump-thump* of the percussion. Once the athletes' walk-past was completed, the procession swung round and, led by the standard bearers, marched towards the exit and she craned her neck to spot her brother among them when, in an instant, nausea hit her again. Her next memory is of lying flat on her back in the grass with some of the other trainee nurses bending over her, so many of them that their faces screened the sun, and black night seemed to envelop her. It was in this shame-filled darkness that she heard the voice of her husband-to-be for the first time:

Let me through. I'm a doctor.

She later said to Doctor Jekelius that, from that day on, she took to heart that a vocation like hers was not a call coming out of the blue, not a gift from a merciful God, but something you must struggle for all your life.

He introduced himself as Hauslich, Siegfried Hauslich, she went on to explain. All that about being a medical man was just something he said to make an impression. He told her, much later and with not a trace of shame, that he had been watching her at a distance for months and waiting for the right moment to make himself known to her. They had gone walking together after that first encounter, up and down the Prater Hauptallee to 'let her get some air' and, during that short time, he had not only harangued her with fussy medical advice but also made her tell him what her parents' names were and where they lived. Only a few days later, a letter addressed to her father arrived in which Mr Hauslich introduced himself as the holder of pre-clinical degree, claimed to have grand ambitions and also to enjoy the patronage of Julius Tandler, presumably because Anna had let slip, against her better judgement, that her father was a great admirer of Professor Tandler, who as a leading city councillor had done so much to improve the health and social services for the working classes of Wien. Hauslich explained to Anna's father that Professor Tandler had helped out with bursaries from his personal funds and that he would surely also support Anna's studies. One believes what one would like to be true. Is that not so? Afterwards, her father happily overlooked the fact that everything Hauslich said was empty chatter and meaningless boasts, and yes, even that he was a Jew . . .

And Doctor Jekelius, *are you telling me that Hauslich was a Jew . . . ?*

She said, *yes, what did you think?*

Doctor Jekelius, *if he was a Jew, why did you agree to marry him?*

She looked straight into his large face with its receding hairline, powerful hawk nose and the clear, sincere eyes below dark, dense eyebrows (he seemed relaxed and deep in thought but his eyes were alert) and knew that she had confided too much to back out now. Doctor Jekelius had already learnt all there was to know about her dead sister and how her family had attempted to recover from the defeat of their inability to keep her alive. And now, about *the shadow*, the shaming black mark in her past that was the man she had had the misfortune to marry and who was a curse she still had to live with. It was my father who insisted that we should marry, she told him. My father was very serious about not making distinctions between people. It's the *character* that matters, not someone's faith or blood, he used to say without realising that in this case it was precisely Hauslich's character that was the problem. By then, it should have been blindingly obvious that he would never do the right thing by anyone, let alone complete his medical training. He was a charlatan. Who could tell how many people he had already deceived with his pretty talk? Before the wedding, she had already started in her first post as a nurse in the maternity unit at the Brigitta-Spital on

Stromstrasse. So it was *she* who supported *him* while he lived in a rented room in the neighbourhood but expected any time soon to move into the large flat that his wealthy uncle was renovating for them both. The flat, falsehood like all his promises, never materialised. One evening she decided to confront him, went to his shabby room and told him that if he did not qualify as a doctor, start paying off his debts and find a decent home for them both, she would divorce him. The pathetic man had burst into tears, kneeled before her and begged her to stay with him, insisting that ever since that day in the Prater he had loved her madly, blindly. She stuck to her guns. Her father, who rarely allowed anything to upset him, was furious with her. But he was no longer her guardian, she had made up her mind and nothing could stop her. There were jobs going at the unit for infectious diseases at Karolinenspital and she applied happily, even though she knew how demanding the work would be. Her years at the Karolinenspital under Professor Knöpfelmacher would provide her experience of nursing children. Her first two years at the unit coincided with one of Wien's worst-ever epidemics of diphtheria. She was the charge nurse in a ward with beds for forty-five children and, within one month, thirty of them had died. Can you imagine what it was like, Doctor? What it was like to hold a four- or five-year-old child in your arms and watch, powerless, as the small life slipped between your fingers? The one factor that made the years in the unit bearable was Professor Knöpfelmacher's personality, his courage and strength of character. But 1934 brought changes that turned absolutely everything upside down. Professor Knöpfelmacher was forced to leave, as were many of the doctors. I worried, too, through nights of desperation. The Patriotic Front was in power and one of the things they did was send my father to prison because of a rumour going around that he had embezzled money belonging to WAT. They suspected that the money had been spent on arming the Socialists. My father was freed in the end and I had meantime managed to arrange for a transfer to Lainz, so all could have turned out well in the end if the Nazis hadn't come to power. And this time, they had of course found out about everything.

Doctor Jekelius, *sorry? Who? What had they found out?*

She said, *they said that of course they couldn't have an employee who had previously married a Jew.*

Doctor Jekelius, *aha, that man Hauslich, yet again . . . !*

There was something about the indifferent, uncaring way he pronounced the hated name that made exasperation suddenly explode inside her:

Can you have the slightest sense of how I felt, Doctor Jekelius? What it was like to have fought all my life to stay sane and well and so escape from the suffocating influence of this man and then, when I had succeeded after years of faithful service, to be told that my work had been in vain?

Jekelius's face remained unmoved:

Nothing you have done is in vain, Mrs Katschenka.

And, much later, when the war had ended, when Spiegelgrund stood shut and empty after the discovery of what happened to the interned children, she would be able to recall, almost word for word, what they had said to each other that day, which was to be the last time she came to him for treatment. How she had tearfully confessed to him that it was work that kept her well, nothing but the good, self-sacrificing work, and he found a handkerchief for her in his jacket pocket, unfolding it in his calm, measured way. *I understand your predicament very well,* he said. And then, *you are in the front line.* And, *you have nothing whatsoever to be ashamed of.* A few months later, she learnt that Jekelius had been appointed medical director at the clinic for children and adolescents that had opened in the old Steinhof asylum. The Wien city council's new department of health was advertising for staff at the recently established Wiener Städtische Jugendfürsorgeanstalt, 'Am Spiegelgrund'. After hesitating for a while, she took her courage in both hands and phoned them. Later, this would be held against her because, by then, she had surely realised whose interests Jekelius served and what they were up to at Spiegelgrund, though this was something she would consistently deny. Again and again, she would repeat what she had told Doctor Jekelius the first time they met: that all she wished for was to be allowed to work with children again. And this time, her application was not returned as it usually was, with a covering letter to the effect that her qualifications were 'insufficient' or even 'unsuitable', but instead she was called to a face-to-face interview in the personnel department and found to her great surprise that the long conversation never touched on subjects such as her previous marriage or her father and brother's illegal political activities. When she, just one week later, received written confirmation that the post was hers, she wept with happiness. She felt certain that in the future, too, Doctor Jekelius would hold out his hand to support her.

III

Spiegelgrund

Steinhof The asylum had existed as a concept long before she saw it with her own eyes. In the Steinhof, one would say. This or that individual was in the Steinhof. And this would always be said quietly, almost in a whisper, with a distant look in one's eyes. Her grandfather had been a Steinhof patient for many years and when she was nine or ten and, as they thought, old enough, she was taken along to visit him. She remembers narrow lobbies full of men in the institutional uniform; how the staring, oddly bright eyes in their coarse, unshaven faces would fix on her and follow every step she took. She remembers the screaming, high-pitched and repulsive, as if from animals taken to slaughter, that would rise suddenly from behind the open doors of the wards and which often triggered frenetic activity, sending staff along the corridors at a run, with the long, effective strides of trained athletes. But just as often, the screams would be completely ignored. A mat of sound was ever present beneath these frightening outbursts, woven from thousands of mumbling voices, incessantly muttering and whispering. Somewhere far inside this huge cathedral of sound, her granddad lay quietly in bed. Dad, don't you recognise me? her father would ask every time, on a sliding scale of anxiety. Her grandfather didn't recognise anyone, it seemed, but now and then he would reach out and touch Anna's head the way you tentatively touch an object you would like but don't dare to hold. Her mother, who never came with them, opined that her father-in-law was paying the price of a life of drunkenness and she missed no opportunity to tell them about all the sacrifices her husband had been forced to make for his alcoholic father. However, for the son, these visits were no sacrifice. Afterwards, father and daughter would walk for a while in the hospital park and maybe climb the hill to Otto Wagner's lovely church with its copper dome, green with verdigris, and its great gate guarded by four angels with raised, golden wings. Anna remembers the hospital site as always thronged with people of all ages. Some of the strolling groups would include a patient in his pyjama-style daywear but there would also be people dressed for a picnic, or entire families, the boys in knee-length shorts and the little girls with bows like small propellers in their hair. The trams taking you away from Steinhof would always be crowded. It felt as if the whole city had enacted a communal pilgrimage and happily went home in unison. A few years later, Anna's granddad was moved to the Ybbs hospital and no more visits were made, at least not by her. The family would sum up what happened as: the old man was lucky to die in good time. What that was supposed to mean, no one cared to explain.

Has Sister Anna Worked with Idiots Before? When she starts work, she discovers that Steinhof has changed and no longer has anything but the walls and the façade ornamentation in common with the hospital site she once visited with her father. It is January 1941. The day is overcast and still. Near the imperial clock by the main entrance, the Nazi flag droops, as if glued to the flagpole. Set among the bare trees in the park, the pavilions look like bunkers with their high, solid walls and window grilles. Anna Katschenka presents herself to the administrative office in pavilion 1 and is given instructions about where to go next, but she is soon met by the matron, Klara Bertha, who comes walking briskly down the wide drive. Bertha is a strongly built, middle-aged woman with, in some people's eyes, striking good looks. Arguably she would have been respected, whatever profession she had taken up. In conversation (with patients or colleagues) she comes across as slightly reserved, someone waiting patiently if a little irritably for what the others have to say before finally delivering her response, distinctly and explicitly. On the way towards *their* pavilion, she points and describes with pedagogic clarity which of the pavilions still belong to the 'old' Steinhof establishment and which to the new institution for children and adolescents. She explains that the odd numbers, as in 3, 5, 7, 9, 11 and 13, are 'theirs'. We have tried to avoid mixing former inmates with, for instance, the children from Lustkandlgasse who have been placed in pavilions 3, 5 and 9, and those from Juchgasse in number 7. Pavilions 15 and 17 hold only psychopaths of both sexes and also younger children who are very ill or malformed, which means that they don't just need specialised care but also constant supervision. And that is where Sister Anna will be nursing. Anna Katschenka points out her previous experience of dealing with severely ill children and takes the opportunity to mention her many years in Professor Knöpfelmacher's unit. Matron smiles patiently, almost sadly, as she waits for Sister Katschenka to finish and then says: I'm afraid that there's very little hope for these young lives. By then, they have reached the right place and the door is opened by a young nurse who introduces herself as Nurse Hedwig. Behind her, several other members of staff emerge from doors along a narrow corridor. Bertha introduces some of them by name and qualifications: Emilie Kragulj, Hildegard Mayer and Cläre Kleinschmittger. Kragulj and Mayer had worked before as psychiatric nurses at Steinhof but had been seconded to the children's wards and had to relearn on the job. Same difference, Mayer says. Her tongue is as quick as her body is heavy. Nurse Kleinschmittger, Bertha continues, is the charge nurse for one of the wards for very young children. There are three types of patient in pavilion 15: infants, children aged less than three, and slightly older children, up to the age of six or seven. We employ tutors who are meant to instruct the third age group but, regrettably, most of the children lack the ability to learn even the simplest things. When Bertha has completed the sentence, Kleinschmittger turns to Katschenka and smiles. Her smile is meant to please but is tinged with nervousness. One might even read jealousy in it, a keenness to guard some spoken-for territory. Or else it is simply that she has no idea what she is supposed to say or doesn't dare to speak at all. Meanwhile, Doctor Gross has descended the stairs, apologising loudly for having been delayed by a telephone call, and quickly takes the lead in what turns out to be an improvised tour of the premises. Like most of the pavilions on the site, number 15 is constructed around a central flight of stairs, which makes for an easy subdivision of each floor into two wards. Two doctors, Gross and Marianne Türk, who used to work at Steinhof, share the medical responsibility. Anna Katschenka is due to meet Doctor Türk later. She is a short, slim, middle-aged woman with something tense and withdrawn about her that marks her out as one of those doctors who set about their daily work with the kind of goal-oriented persistence that leaves no room for anything else – neither errors of judgement nor moments of compassion. Quite unlike Doctor Gross, who speaks with many vague but big gestures and who has already acquired the apparent distractedness often displayed by men conscious of their own importance, a manner that entails constantly changing subject and register and seems ultimately intended to make everyone they talk to feel insecure. *Has Sister Anna worked with idiots before?* he suddenly asks without stopping to listen to her answer. He moves on, as if the question had been quite beside the point, and instead opens wide the door to one of the wards and steps inside, immediately followed by Bertha, Kleinschmittger and

Mayer, who seem to be swept along in his wake. The wards are not that large. Each long wall has room for five to ten beds, and the changing tables and basins. The bedsteads with their high end-rails are made of white-painted metal. Along the short walls, some beds enclosed in metal netting stand a little apart, presumably to make it easier to keep an eye on them. In one of the netted beds, a nearly grown-up girl is crouching, leaning a little forward. Oblivious of the staff, her jaws are grinding like millstones while her gaze makes helpless attempts to hang on to objects within her field of vision: a blanket, a pillow, the inside of the bed rails, which her fingertips explore intently as if investigating an enigmatic script. All the children, not only the infants, are in their beds. Gross walks from bed to bed, pointing this way and that. He could be demonstrating objects in a museum. She only catches fragments of what he says: *idiocy . . . spastic diplegia . . . we have cages for epileptics as you can see here!* He indicates the girl in the netted bed. For Anna Katschenka, the children are still nameless and suffer from nameless diseases. She sees bodies: bodies just lying there, the already exhausted attachments to gigantic skulls that sometimes look absurdly beautiful, the distended cranial bones covered with blond baby hair and fragile networks of pale-blue blood vessels. Some bodies have been preyed on by tumours until so emaciated that the skeleton is about to pierce the skin, the ribcage protruding through the loose skin-folds over chest and abdomen, the sharp edges of forehead, cheek and jaw bones stretching the weakened sphincter muscles around eyes and mouth. The bodies emit shrieks and odd noises which are everywhere, the alien sounds ranging from hoarse shouting to gurgling and cooing. A little boy with cleft palate groans like a rutting animal when they are about to pass him, and Doctor Gross stops and points: *Cheilognathopalatoschisis. Alcoholic mother who abandoned the infant when she saw what it looked like. One can't entirely blame her!* With an exaggeratedly caring gesture, the doctor helps the malformed child to stand by supporting his right arm. The split in the boy's palate is wide enough for them to see straight into the moist membranes of his gullet. When Gross touches him, the boy's coarse, wild groans change into helpless gurgles and she finds herself looking into a pair of shiny blue eyes that express a lucid awareness more alarming than any scream. But most of the children are silent as they sit or lie on the beds, their fingers spread out or stuck between wet lips, their gazes dull or absently following the white-clad procession, and it seems as if the incessant sobs and moans that fill the large room from floor to ceiling don't come from anyone in it but from somewhere far away, like a vast, distant wave of discordant noise that has taken tens of thousands of years to reach this place but is finally breaking through the dams and is about to swallow everyone and everything on the ward, the children in their beds and the professionals bending over them. But a slightly older child, whose skin has a doll-like pallor, lies on her back deep below the uproar, her face turned indifferently towards the murky surface high above her where space and voices blend. Her face has grown and suggests five or six years of age, a much too large head in relation to her short torso and thin but shapely limbs. Looking more closely, her every feature seems chiselled with extraordinary precision. Her hands, which rest on the coverlet, have slender fingers and pink, half-moon-shaped nails, and her doll's face with its porcelain skin and pointed chin is given distinction by her small, lovely mouth that has a slight, almost ironic twist. Her eyes are a deep blue beneath their heavy, aristocratic lids, the sweep of her high forehead ends where a mane of thin blonde hair with a reddish shimmer grows from what Anna Katschenka's mother would describe as 'a perfect hairline'. And it is perfect. The thin, exactly delineated roots run like a neatly stitched seam across the forehead, along a line that is reminiscent of a Cupid's bow. (Anna Katschenka has had to learn these finer points, as her own hairline is less than perfect.) This child is Sophie Althofer, Nurse Kleinschmittger explains as she stops by the girl's bed and draws attention to her presence next to Katschenka by pretending to tidy the coverlet. Her mother comes in almost daily, she adds, at which Doctor Gross, who patently disapproves of nurses chattering while he is prepared to hold forth, clears his throat and loudly announces the diagnosis: *Achondroplasia, combined with imbecility of the worst order.* Not even the mother has managed to get a single, sensible word from this girl, he says as he turns to Anna Katschenka with a smile, as if to advise her against even trying. And then the performance is over. Matron instantly picks up the change of tone and addresses the group of nurses: *Sister Cläre, will you show Sister Anna the practical side of things.* Anna Katschenka follows Cläre Kleinschmittger into the corridor and then into the lavatories and shower rooms. Sister Cläre also demonstrates the sluice room and the correct places for washbasins and bedpans, then shows her where the first aid cupboard and the linen stores are, and goes through the order of towels and bed-linen items on the shelves. Anna stays in the sluice room afterwards and watches as Hedwig Blei, the young woman who opened the door when she arrived, busies herself with rinsing out bedpans. Nurse Hedwig is young and vital. Her arms are broad and strong, and there is a band of freckles across her nose. She seems unfazed as she upsets the hierarchical order, speaking to a superior without being spoken to first. Pointing to a jar of hand cream that she has put next to the sink, she says that *people from the countryside know how to look after themselves* and then explains that it is the same cream she learnt to use when she was younger and was asked to treat the inflamed sores on cows' udders. Then, in reply to Anna's question, she says, *yes, well, I'm from Grünbach in Mühlviertel. You know, this cream is good for chapped skin on the hands as well.* For a moment, the two pairs of hands are placed side by side on the workbench and young Miss Blei can't refrain from asking, *I can't help seeing that Sister Anna perhaps isn't married?* And carries on, now energetically rinsing off bottles and glasses, so she doesn't notice how Anna stiffens. Instead, Nurse Blei adds that *a job like this is simply impossible to combine with having a husband and children, that's what I've always thought. Much wiser to wait!* On their way out, they pass little Sophie with her pretty doll's-house face that looks too mature, too clever for a child. Anna feels that the girl's gaze follows her but Sophie's pupils shelter below her elegantly curved eyelids. Her exquisite lips curl disdainfully.

Conditions of Service She did not know what exactly she had hoped for as she took up her new post because her expectations had been more linked to the person of Doctor Jekelius than to the work, but nothing had prepared her for having to nurse such badly afflicted children. It was not that she was unused to caring for ill children or, of course, for physically and mentally debilitated old people. The patients they were responsible for here were, however, so severely disturbed by neurological and other malformations that they fell outside the normal range. Her training had taught her to deal with injuries and common illnesses, but little or nothing about how to nurse children who had no control whatsoever over their limbs, who any second might attack her with wildly flailing arms, hissing and spitting and biting, or children whose inner torment was so terrible that they screamed all the time, unending ululations without any apparent relationship to the cause of their pain, let alone how they could be made better or even soothed in any way other than the morphine-based medication that was routinely prescribed in quantities that frightened her. She also felt that she was being constantly watched, which didn't help at all. Every hesitation was recorded, every hint of her being ill at ease or put off by something interpreted as being unable to cope. Nurse Mayer especially seemed to see it as her duty to keep an eye on the new recruit. Even though she was formally Katschenka's inferior, she had ways of showing that she disliked *how* she had been told to do something, or simply disliked being told anything at all, and indicated her displeasure by perhaps a raised eyebrow or a faint smile, before going about her tasks with studied slowness. Mayer was an old hand, as she put it, and like many of the other ex-psychiatric nurses, she handled the children in her charge as if they were insensate, pulling the screaming little bundles out of bed and carrying them under her arm like parcels, or perhaps more like small animals on their way to slaughter. Meanwhile, Cläre Kleinschmittger would hover in some doorway, her eyes flickering anxiously while her gaze stayed fixed on Anna's every move. Their eyes never met and they never exchanged more than a few words, but Kleinschmittger seemed always to be surrounded by one or several colleagues such as Nurse Sikora, Erna Storch and Emilie Kragulj, and Katschenka saw them together more than once in a corridor or the corner of a ward, standing in tight little clusters, whispering together only to fall silent the moment she came past. Finally, her concern had become an incessant, deep-seated ache and, one afternoon, she knocked on the matron's door and asked leave to take half an hour off work in order to speak with Doctor Jekelius. Doctor Jekelius is away on business, Matron Bertha replied curtly, and her tone suggested that it was an unheard-of impertinence even to mention his name. Sister Anna can of course talk to me if the matter is a practical one, or refer it to the personnel department. Anna Katschenka had by then realised that Doctor Jekelius's role was not only that of medical director of the Spiegelgrund institution but that he also acted as the right hand of Councillor Max Gundel, who was in charge of the new department of public health. It had been Gundel who drove the decision to merge the city's many children's homes and reform schools into one institution: Spiegelgrund was his creation. Jekelius had been charged with overseeing that all children 'who required special treatment' were taken to Spiegelgrund, a responsibility that led to much arduous travelling. When Jekelius was not on site, the administrative side of his work was handled by Doctor Margarethe Hübsch. Doctor Hübsch was a robustly built, middle-aged woman with severe features. She wore her blonde hair pulled back into a strict bun, dressed for work in two-piece suits with the NS-Frauenschaft pin ostentatiously placed on the lapel, and greeted people with the German *Heil*, as was the rule by then but which Anna Katschenka found awkward. Anna was of course used to working within a framework of discipline that meant employees knew what was expected of them and what the limitations of their rights were. She had always been content with the clarity of this. However, she had now joined an institution run on militaristic lines, as if the hospital had turned into barracks, and it made her feel ill at ease. She was unused to the way her superiors addressed the staff. Doctor Knöpfelmacher had been firm and decisive but often ready with a kind, encouraging smile. Doctor Hübsch, on the other hand, was either formal, bordering on brusque, or else given to ice-cold sarcasm. Katschenka felt insecure and, always, there was Nurse Kleinschmittger, lingering in a doorway, as if looking forward to when Katschenka would make some mistake or annoy one of the doctors. Anna lay awake night after night, arguing with herself. She couldn't afford the risks entailed in resigning. For instance, returning to Lainz would be out of the question. There was just one way out, as far as she could see. She told her mother one evening that she would be going out after supper to meet a friend, and set out to catch the 8 tram. That was the line she travelled on to work every morning but, this time, she stayed on board until the Alser Strasse stop and then walked briskly up the hill to Michelbeuern. It was only when she stood in front of the wide iron gate on Martinstrasse that it dawned on her quite the enormity of what she was about to do. It wasn't just that she was being *pushy* (which was completely out of character, of course) but also that she clung to the belief that he would be able to put a stop to, or at least mitigate the effects of, the choice he had himself suggested that she should make when she had consulted him. The healer of souls needed no eyes. Would he be able to see that this particular post did not suit her? But she doesn't get round to ringing the bell. Standing on the pavement opposite the gate, she is as incapable of stepping forward as of walking away. A few cars pass by. When the noise of the last one dies away she hears footsteps on the cobbled pavement. She turns. It is he. She recognises his light, vigorous gait immediately, despite the darkness. Suddenly terrified that he might catch sight of her, she slips into a gateway, the sound of footsteps grows fainter and when she dares to look he is gone. He must have turned the corner already. She runs the same way, well aware of what a pathetic figure she makes. The street in front of her is deserted. Did the ground open up and swallow him? And then she hears a car engine start. Just some fifty metres away, two powerful headlamps light up. The car glides out of the garage and, as it reaches the street, the light falls on a woman waiting on the pavement. The car stops near her, the window comes down and she bends forward to say something. It is Jekelius in the driver's seat, Anna is certain of that. She has no idea who the woman is. Anyway, with a laugh, a small affected giggle, the woman gets into the car. They drive past

Anna but neither one pays any attention to her. As she walks back to the Alser Strasse tram stop, she doesn't feel disappointed, only empty. Her mother doesn't ask where she has been. She knows that her daughter doesn't have any friends and especially not anyone whom she might like to visit at this time of night.

Mother and Daughter Only a few days later, she meets Mrs Althofer in the office in pavilion 1. Sophie's mother wants to speak to Doctor Jekelius and, when she learns that he is away, asks to see Doctor Hübsch. Mrs Althofer is in many ways the spitting image of her dwarf child. The same reddish-blonde hair springing from the same perfect hairline. Their curving eyelids are similar, too, but the mother's eyes look so heavy that she can't lift them enough to see Anna Katschenka's face. *A meeting was arranged for today at nine o'clock but it would appear that Doctor Hübsch has preferred to be unavailable*, she says as her gaze slides past Katschenka to follow the stair rail. Sister Katschenka says that this is not a matter she can deal with and suggests that the office staff could set up a new appointment. But Mrs Althofer insists that the agreed meeting should take place and eventually becomes very loud on her daughter's behalf. Apparently Doctor Hübsch had personally assured her that her daughter would get well and now, what's happened to that promise? *You're keeping my little girl locked up day and night! You don't give her anything to eat or drink! You treat her worse than a base animal!* Next, Anna Katschenka is baffled to find herself holding Mrs Althofer's small, clenched fists in her hands. For a brief moment, the surprise they both feel at the prevented exchange of blows dampens the underlying fury and the two of them, the ward sister and the mother, stand on the stairs with their faces close together. Then a door slams a little further upstairs and a white-coated Doctor Gross bends over the railing to speak to them:

Doctor Hübsch is off sick today,

but if you wish, Mrs Althofer, you can speak with me . . . !

Later that day, Doctor Gross will enlighten Katschenka and her new colleagues about exactly what type of woman they are dealing with in Mrs Althofer and, particularly, what kind of *mother*. One of those who can't make up her mind: will she or won't she let go of her child? And because she is incapable of squaring her conscience, she continues to haunt the periphery of the institution where her child is being cared for, all the while complaining loudly about how appallingly the little girl is looked after and how unpleasant the staff are to her mother. Nothing but a charade, from beginning to end, Doctor Gross emphasises, because in her rational moments, Mrs Althofer knows that she can have her child back any time she so decides. Against medical advice, that goes without saying, but no matter. That right belongs to her in this situation, as it would to *all* mothers. The problem is that, in her heart of hearts, Mrs Althofer doesn't *want* to. She is aware that if she ever were to hug Sophie's shrunken, malformed body to her breast again, she would be at an utter loss as to how to handle this new burden. It is a fact that she doesn't have the time to look after her child. She has to work. Food is hard to come by. Who would look after little Sophie while her mother carries out her office duties? As Mrs Althofer has repeatedly pointed out herself, she has a responsible post as the trusted secretary of a large legal firm. And Mrs Althofer's own mother, who selflessly used to care for her granddaughter while her daughter was at work; well, the old lady has spent the last few weeks in hospital with an attack of gallstones. And Mr Althofer has been called up. So typical of how families live nowadays. There's a war on, after all. Each and every one of us must be prepared to make sacrifices. We can only conclude that Mrs Althofer's stubborn meanderings amount to nothing more than her way of quieting a constantly nagging, very uneasy conscience. Because, by coming here and badgering members of staff and complaining, Mrs Althofer at least gives the *pretence* of doing something even though she knows deep down, as does everyone else, exactly what a repulsive and miserable condition this child is in, how depressingly feeble and *unworthy* it has become. Yes, Mrs Althofer knows full well but cannot bring herself to state it in so many words, Doctor Gross says. She would really be so endlessly grateful if we could only lift this burden off her shoulders but is unable to put *that* into words, as well; like all these mothers who keep accusing us of stealing their children.

Decursus Morbi In the evening, Sophie runs a high temperature. Anna Katschenka is not on duty at the time but one of the day nurses had made an entry in the case notes: before the onset of the fever, the girl had been very restless for several hours, first noted early that afternoon. *The child twists and turns, also emits short, almost inaudible shrieks.* The following morning, the perfect hairline is edged with a ribbon of small, shiny drops of sweat. *The child is febrile. Temp. 38.5.* During the months and years that follow, Anna Katschenka, as the ward sister, will be responsible for keeping case notes up to date. Back then, another hand is making entries in Sophie Althofer's notes. The writing is stronger than Katschenka's, with neat rows of sloping letters. The notes include something of the patient's earlier history. She was *a much longed-for girl*, born to two apparently perfectly normal parents. Their only child. At birth, it was noted that the baby had shorter than normal limbs, with hands and feet especially reduced in size, and a protruding breastbone – one of the so-called pectus anomalies, the 'pigeon chest' or *pectus carinatum.* The misshapen thorax is associated with narrowing of the ribcage and sharp-edged ribs that threaten to compress the internal organs. Various treatments were used at an early stage, beginning with a cradle designed to straighten the limbs. On the family doctor's advice, Mrs Althofer gave the infant a nightly bath in rock-salt brine. All available nutritional supplements were purchased, including Vigantol oil, Bio Malt and cod liver oil. At the age of three and a half, the child suffered from severe headaches in connection with a cold, and later fell ill with a high fever and strong muscular pains. The tentative diagnosis was polio. The child's mental development, which had been normal, became affected and she stopped speaking or in any other way communicating with others.

21/01/1941
[. . .] the child was admitted to Spiegelgrund as her mother stated 'I cannot cope any more'.

22/01
[*notes in Doctor Gross's writing*]
[. . .] The child is well nourished, overall status good. Deep tendon reflexes elicited bilaterally and at normal power. Babinski reflex and Rossolimo's sign negative.
The child tends to lie on its back, hardly ever moves its pathetic stumps of arms and legs. Cannot sit upright without support, the head falls backwards due to an apparent lack of muscle power. Pupils fix on stationary objects but she does not reach or grasp. No real eye contact possible.

On examination, the child gives an impression of *a marked degree of idiocy*.

02/02
[*notes alternately in Doctor Gross's and Doctor Türk's writing, with added entries made by the day duty nurse*]
[...] Sophie appears not to suffer from any physical pain but will emit an incessant low, wailing sound (especially on days when her mother has visited).
Sophie is calm and biddable but will not eat unless spoon-fed & seems not to feel hunger in the ordinary sense.
Weight reduction: 800g. [...]

08/02
Strong epileptiform convulsions. The girl is tied down to prevent self-inflicted injuries. She still refuses nourishment. Luminal prescr.

09/02
Continued muscular spasms, less extensive.
As the restlessness is not reduced by the evening, administration of Luminal.

11/02
Condition not improved. Visible decline in the child's overall status.
Further weight loss recorded: 800g.
Generally weakened. Apathetic.

At this point, Mrs Althofer writes a letter to the board of the institution and demands that they should let her have her child back. Her stated reason is that she felt unable to establish contact with her daughter on her latest visit, an experience she describes as 'something completely new'. Even though Sophie has chosen not to communicate 'as people normally do', Mrs Althofer insists that mother and daughter had developed 'their own language' and that they could speak fluently with each other. The girl had been happy and often laughed. *When I held her by her waist and lifted her high in the air she would choke with laughter and whisper in her tiny voice, 'Thank you, Mummy!' It is with deep distress that I have been forced to realise that my girl is no longer herself. You have written* [Mrs Althofer refers to a letter from Doctor Jekelius] *that no amount of wishful thinking can make my daughter well again and that at Spiegelgrund she will receive all the care and attention a child needs. Are you telling me to be grateful that my daughter seems no longer able to recognise her own mother?*

> *16/02*
> [. . .] Fever 39.0°. Suspected viral bronchitis. Decongestant prescr.

When Katschenka checks on her that evening, Sophie seems to be sleeping peacefully for the first time in weeks. Her smooth features show no sign of the earlier distortion. Anna would like to stop and place a hand on her face. But there are so many children. Soon afterwards, she is called to pavilion 17, where a boy is banging his head against the wall. He has to be restrained. In the other ward, a boy has come down with scarlet fever and must be isolated at once. Hildegard Mayer is bullying a girl, she shouts and hits the child. Nurse Mayer really has an awful temper. By the time Katschenka returns to pavilion 15, Sophie has been moved to the gallery wing. Her temperature has gone up again and she is breathing irregularly. Each breath seems to be ejected separately, one by one, from her misshapen chest.

The pallor of her face has turned grey, and her skin is unnaturally glossy, like a sheet of shiny, thick paper. There might well have been glimpses of awareness in her eyes before but now they are empty beneath their heavy lids. Anna thinks that her face shuts you out, like a blank wall. Later that day, a so-called *Schlechtmeldung*, a bad news announcement, is put in the mail.

Wien, 16 February 1941

For the attention of Mrs Althofer
I regret to have to inform you that your daughter's health has undergone a severe decline. Her condition must now be regarded as worrying.

Professor, Dr E Jekelius
Medical Director

The following morning, two of them wash Sophie Althofer's body. Katschenka props the corpse upright while one of the nursing assistants pulls the mattress and sheets off the bed. The child's body is lighter than Anna had imagined and easy to hold: the strongly arched pigeon chest fits into the bend of her left arm. They suddenly hear a shrill, piercing scream from the corridor, and Anna briefly fears that Mrs Althofer has arrived and that she is to be the one who hands the dead girl over to her mother. But it is a child who screams. The note about Sophie's declining health had been put in the post after a deliberate delay to make it too late for Mrs Althofer in case she decided to come along. But she might not come at all, just as Doctor Gross had explained earlier: the mothers may well be tremendously loud and pushy while their children are here, but once the little ones have died, they'll write and ask us to 'look after the practical issues' and that they'll pay us for our expenses, thank you kindly.

The Procedure A few days after the death of Sophie Althofer, the office finally informs Anna Katschenka that Doctor Jekelius wishes to see her. Does a child have to die before she is offered the reward of an audience with him? The Jekelius she meets in his study isn't the humorous, pleasantly jovial doctor she remembers, or believes that she remembers. He doesn't get up to greet her, and carries on leafing through documents while taking occasional notes. She is left to stand there. When he finally turns to her, he moves in the old, relaxed, carefully controlled way but his face is like a stone wall. There is no way to get through. He slowly places one hand on top of the other and asks if she is becoming familiar with the routines and pace of the ward work. She says yes, since that is obviously what he expects. This unchanging face of his frightens her. He goes on to say that he assumes she has by now observed the miserable condition of most of the children, taken on board the fact that many of them are incurable and also understood how the institution deals with this type of case. She thinks of Sophie, and the far too high dose of phenobarbital she was given, and of how strangely light, almost weightless the child's body had felt in her arms. Tears fill her eyes. There is nothing she can do to stop them. She feels in her uniform pockets for a handkerchief, can't find one and tries to turn her head away. Weeping is so undignified but Jekelius doesn't seem to have noticed that her feelings have got the better of her. His face is still rigid as he leans forward over the desk. I shall now have to remind Sister Anna about the professional oath that binds you and the pledge of confidentiality that you will have made at the same time. As you know, you are, under no circumstances, to communicate any details whatsoever with respect to any individual case to anyone outside the institution. And you are not to ask any unnecessary questions. Has Sister Anna grasped these implications? She nods. The corners of her eyes have almost dried and now she thinks that maybe Doctor Jekelius's stiffness is related to the message he is trying to convey to her. He sits back in his chair to unlock one of the drawers in his desk, finds a thin sheet of typescript and hands it to her. It is some kind of certificate with a signature at the bottom and the Nazi emblem in the upper left-hand corner. She is far too tense to get a grip on what the lines of typescript actually say. As Sister Anna can see, this circular carries the Führer's own personal signature, Doctor Jekelius points out. It means that legally, this document has the same status as an already enacted piece of legislation. He pauses to give her time to take in the overwhelming significance of this but, somehow, she is struck mute and also feels unable to grasp what he is trying to tell her and what the circular has to do with any new laws and regulations. She stares at the piece of paper in her hands. So, that's what Hitler's signature looks like? Doctor Jekelius continues to speak but in a gentler voice, as if he has sensed her confusion. What we do in certain circumstances, he says, is confined to *extreme cases only*. And our interventions aren't crimes, neither morally nor legally, as you can see now. On the contrary, the measures we take should be seen as acts of mercy in the spirit that has always guided medical science, that is to ameliorate or remove sources of pain and suffering. Then he explains the practical aspects of the procedure, how for each patient certain forms are to be completed and sent to the Ministry for Internal Affairs in Berlin, where a dedicated medical committee scrutinises the submissions with great care and sees to it that every individual case is tested before their decision is made and which it is our duty to carry out. But, by now, she has ceased taking in what he says. She gets up, politely excuses herself, but she really must leave. They are waiting for her down in the pavilion. Presumably, he believes that she is upset because of the information he has just entrusted her with and his gloss on the words in that document. She is upset but that isn't why. Often that day, as well as during many of the days and nights that follow, she returned to the thought of how differently she would have reacted if he had taken her into his confidence rather than laying on that performance. How she would then have understood not only the words he used but, with a will, embraced the meaning of it all. However repellent the new legislation he had spoken of appeared to her, she would nonetheless have been completely loyal to it. Now, it seemed as cold and abstract and impersonal as Jekelius himself. And what of those monstrous children, was there nothing for them except the law? No mercy, no love, no life? She lay awake all night in her old girlhood bedroom in her parents' flat on Fendigasse. Although their area was usually calm and quiet at night, she seemed to hear a chorus of voices rising from the street: loud, high-pitched voices speaking across each other and then yet cut through by other ones, as sharp and shrill as officers' commands. The ultimate decisions are not made by us, but by them, in Berlin. All we can do is knuckle under and do as we're told. None of us can be regarded as personally responsible. We are obliged to obey current legislation. We have no reason to feel guilty.

Two Lives From that time, she seems to lead two lives. With her parents, she chats contentedly about her new, secure post at Steinhof and the remarkable Doctor Jekelius who looks after his staff so well. Sometimes, she also tells them about the children she cares for at the institution, the *poor little things* – that's how Hilde Mayer describes them – with their comical notions, and about the games the nurses think up to amuse and distract the few who have enough sense to be distracted. She never says a word about the circumstances that have led to the children's institutionalisation or gives the slightest hint of any of the repulsive defects and health problems they suffer from, but instead manages to suggest that these are quite normal children, though maybe a little slow to develop. Doctor Jekelius had assured her that euthanasia would be considered only in extreme cases. He expanded on this theme: only when we are one hundred per cent certain that being cared for in this institution will never lead to anything better than conditioned responses that please the staff; only when the child is so retarded or afflicted by such grave defects of hereditary or racial biological origin that the only predictable outcome is endlessly drawn-up pain and degradation; only then will we choose to abandon attempts to extend artificially the tormented existence of such children and instead end its life, something we will do, as instructed, in the most humane way possible. However, Anna Katschenka had no doubt at all that the committee in Berlin had been notified of just about all of the children in pavilion 15 and that new patients were routinely referred on admission. Nor had it taken long for her to understand that most of the children on the ward had already been prescribed the 'treatment' but some were still there only because it was due start later. She never grasped the logic of the timing. On her daily rounds, all she knew was that some of the children were 'sentenced' but not whether they had weeks or months to live. However strange and distressing she found it, nothing stopped her from carrying out the necessary day-to-day work. Children rated as unfit to live still had to be washed and changed regularly, and fed with solid or liquid food as required. Those who couldn't swallow must somehow be *made to* in the end, and those who were immobile had to be turned to prevent bedsores developing. And all ought to be talked to and cared for, perhaps even sung to, as Anna found herself doing to a little girl whom no one and nothing could comfort. She sang the same songs she had once sung to the children in Professor Knöpfelmacher's infection wards. They were childish verses and riddles, like the one about the fox who stole all the hens in the coop. Then the knotted, hard muscles in the little girl's face relaxed slowly and the large, infantile mouth began sucking on its own tongue, then two fingers went into her mouth and she fell asleep. A few hours later that same girl woke and convulsed badly. They had to tie her hands to bars at the head end of the bed to stop her from scratching her face. While Nurse Sikora tried to bottle-feed her, Anna Katschenka phoned for Doctor Türk who came at once, as tight-lipped and focused as ever, inspected the girl's throat and prescribed scopolamine injections since the child clearly could no longer chew and swallow on her own. A week later, the girl had to be moved to the gallery wing where the most severely ill children were cared for or, more to the point, where they kept the children whose 'treatment' had advanced to the last stage and who had only a few hours left to live. Along the wall, opposite the row of tall windows with the ventilator panels always open to let the persistent stench of Lysol and faeces escape, the febrile children were bedded down under thick white duvets. It looked like a line-up of little mummies. Some might cough, making rough, painful sounds as if a spoon was scraping the inside of their frail chests. Most of them lay quite still, their lids half closed over cloudy eyes. The hardly audible breathing of one child after another would cease and all that was left of them was the mess on the sheets. The alkaloid agent that was pumped into their bodies to dull their restlessness and convulsions seemed, at least in these huge quantities, to affect the mucous lining of the intestines and cause the faeces to become semi-liquid and stained with blood. The bitter stench of shit mixed with medication was so overpowering that nothing you washed the floors with could remove it, and however often you cleaned and aired the place, it was still there. The smell would never go away. Outside, the corpse-porters were waiting with their covered carts to take the bodies to the mortuary, where they were washed and made ready for the post-mortem examination. The soiled bed linen was bundled up and the packages taken on the little train to the laundry. And that was it. A casual visitor might have been surprised at how quiet and orderly the procedure was. No one struggled to save lives here. No *dashing about*, as Nurse Mayer might have put it. The two ward medics, doctors Türk and Gross, came and went at their own serene pace. If some especially interesting case had been admitted, the doctors might all turn up and cluster around the bed. Their discussions could become lively but rarely loud. Doctor Jekelius never joined these case conferences. Often, it was Doctor Gross who took the lead with his usual pompous authority. And it was also Doctor Gross who usually decided about whether to carry out encephalographic examinations on the children, or any other investigations. The young patients who had been subjected to lumbar puncture, and especially those who had to have several punctures, which of course took much longer, were often in terrible shape when they were returned to the ward. It took just a few hours for some of them to fall ill with nausea, vomiting and severe spasticity. And then it was time for scopolamine injections again. Instinctively, Katschenka knew that it was wrong to up the dosage of pain-reducing and tranquillising agents to this extent, especially for very sick children. But what right did she have to express medical opinions? She assumed anyway that the cases that were selected for cranial X-rays were already so ill that the child's relatives would have given their consent, and she also hoped that these investigations were carried out in order to reach the high scientific goals that Doctor Jekelius always invoked. Besides, it was a comfort to see that in the end the children became calm and somnolent after all their pain, although it was impossible to make them take any nourishment afterwards. What was truly hard to deal with was the way all these interventions were undertaken without a word being exchanged about them, and in an atmosphere of gloom and mutual distrust. She would sometimes catch Nurse Kleinschmittger watching her as she stood in front of the drug cupboard with her list of prescribed medications, as if weighing up what Katschenka might know of all that was unsaid and simply taken as read when it came to the running of the ward. Would she reach a stage at which what was left unsaid would become unbearable? But, no, of course there was no such stage. Rather, it was a relief when one of the members of staff turned what they all knew into a joke; someone like Nurse Mayer, whose uncaring, coarse manner could feel liberating. *Isn't it soon time for little Fritzl to have his next shot?* she might say, all mock innocence. Or Emilie Kragulj, who was simply thoughtless, would lift one of the most malnourished children and say *the doctor will come soon*, unintentionally making Nurse Kleinschmittger smile even as her restless eyes nervously flickered across the room to check on Katschenka. All this meant that they formed a collective after all, without trying to and without any real understanding between then. What they were not allowed to talk about or even mention in front of the others made them bond more tightly than anything else they might have in common. The shadow of all that was unsaid would never disappear. It was no ordinary shadow because somehow those on whom it fell were induced to lean further into it. Katschenka has that darkness inside her. She can't explain her awareness of the shadow in any other way. When she went home in the evenings, she sat in the tram and all around her people would crowd in, with the workaday briefcases squashed under the arm or between their knees. They were all pure, spotless, and it showed. She paid attention to how she dressed but avoided anything startling, and carried out her duties flawlessly; the shadow grew as flawlessly. She realised that it would soon invade her so thoroughly that none of it would show anymore, inside or outside her. Then, not even the fact that it existed would seem remarkable.

Existence and Will One May morning, she is again told that Doctor Jekelius wishes to see her. This will be the first time he has spoken to her since he showed her that circular but, to her relief, he seems to be in a gentler mood, even expressing regret that he has so little time to spend at Spiegelgrund, since when he is not with Councillor Gundel to discuss urgent matters, he often has to attend medical conferences. And then there's the problem with all the provincial hospitals under Wien City Council's control, where local clinics look after children who should be transferred to Spiegelgrund and which he is duty bound to visit. These last few weeks, he has carried out numerous inspection-tours of such clinics. And herein lies the reason why he has asked her to come to his office today. A journey to the Bruckhof hospital in Totzenbach has been scheduled and the plan was that Doctor Hübsch would accompany him, but now she has informed him that she is ill and cannot travel, so he wonders if Sister Anna might be prepared to assist him instead? Of course it is to be seen as an in-service duty. He adds that he will drive an official car and that expenses will be paid.

Sister Anna could perhaps see it as a change from her routine?

They set out early in the morning, on a Monday in July. It must have rained the night before because afterwards she clearly remembers the sloshing sound made by the tyres as the car sped through the quiet streets. The air had a fresh saltiness about it, as always after rain. Doctor Jekelius had offered to collect her at her door but she had declined. She had no wish to be observed from inside the house. In that case, she would have to go to the trouble of coming to his home; she knew the Martinstrasse address, of course, he added with a little smile. She recognised at once the car she had seen that night when a strange woman had been waiting for him. In daylight, the glossy new Opel Kapitän convertible is if anything even more impressive. Jekelius looks suitably sporting in his plus fours, matched by a checked tweed jacket and a cap of the same material. The cap makes his face look more angular than usual, which both attracts and alarms her. She feels a twinge of fear because he suddenly seems a stranger, as if she were landed with an unknown companion. They drive with the top down along Hernalser Gürtel, where the rumbling traffic is already building up to the morning rush, then past Westbahnhof towards Linzer Strasse. He is at ease behind the steering wheel and chats about how pressed he is for time, what with all these inspections and, of course, all the administrative work. She finds it more and more difficult to keep her mind on what he is saying. The sun, still low above the horizon, is dazzling. As they speed along, the wind makes her eyes fill with tears (he clearly has no intention to raise the hood). She congratulates herself that she put her hair up properly and used a scarf to keep it in place. Her mother always went on about how only prostitutes let their hair hang loose. And would add that such girls of course want to hide their faces. (She wonders, why suddenly think about all that?) Jekelius carries on talking but has moved on to the necessity of advancement in medical research and how the profession, despite all the progress during the last few decades, still persists in holding positively medieval views on what constitutes illness. So, what *is* illness? he asks her. It is probably a rhetorical question, because he only glances fleetingly at her where she sits picking at the ends of her scarf. Illness, he says, is something that afflicts people *blindly*. Or so it is believed. A punishment sent by

God whose hand reaches out from heaven and singles someone out for no rhyme or reason. But, on the contrary, nothing to do with the body happens at random. The biology of heredity has demonstrated with unassailable clarity that there is no disease of the organism; no, not even ordinary infections, which cannot be explained in terms of inherited factors. *The causes of damage are already lodged within the body, long before we see the first symptoms of disease.* It follows that medical science must adopt a different perspective of time. Taking a patient's history should not only entail asking if Mr A has had symptoms of this or that illness before. A useful, goal-oriented examination must include the patient's entire medical history as well as his social and racial background. Sister Anna surely understands that we should learn to see time as a space, but above all learn how to make the art of healing more fit for purpose. How many dimensions would you say there are, Mrs Katschenka? (The question is so abruptly asked that at first she doesn't take on board that she is supposed to say something. But when she turns towards him, his eyes still look straight ahead and both his hands grip the steering wheel.) Most people would reply that there are three, he goes on without pausing. Three dimensions that define space and then, perhaps, time as well. However, personally, I would answer that there are only two. The first dimension is existence. Most people live in it. And in existence, only the most base and trivial needs are recognised. When someone who simply exists falls ill, he experiences a base, animalistic need to be cured. He doesn't for a moment consider why he fell ill, why the illness afflicted just him or what would be the use or sense of curing him. The other dimension is the will, which is outside the reach of most. Your will enables you to prove that you, in yourself, feel free to rule over the material and physical contingencies of your own life and the lives of others. Duty and law both derive from the will. Likewise, the freedom to sacrifice yourself for a higher cause. Likewise, the ability to think in categories such as lifetimes rather than just lives, or in terms such as peoples or races rather than individuals who are either well or ill. For as long as medical science operates only at the level of human existence it will never truly heal, only remove or mitigate the symptoms and, even so, only temporarily. Medicine acts, as it were, blindfolded. It remains unaware of precisely *whose* symptoms are removed or, worse still, if such a removal has any significance or is useful in a wider context. The enlightened form of medical science that encompasses both dimensions always intervenes with some defined intention. This is when it becomes possible to treat also in order to *cure*. That is, you remove not only the external symptoms of the disease but also clarify its fundamental causation, and can hope to eliminate the factors that have allowed it to emerge and take hold. This might sound strange, coming from the mouth of a medical man, but it is my whole-hearted, firm belief that even the most severe conditions can be cured by the action of the will alone. Our Führer is the sovereign incarnation of the will, of course, he adds quickly. It is actually said unemphatically, as a dutiful afterthought. He is driving very fast by now. It occurs to her (and it might well be the effect he wanted) that they are leaving mere existence behind and are travelling exclusively in the dimension of the will. She quite enjoyed the speed at first but she is beginning to feel sick. It scares her that she has no sense of *where* she is, whether the countryside is spreading wide and open around them or, on the contrary, if they are hurtling so fast through a narrow tunnel that its walls can't be made out, and suddenly the *old* nausea overwhelms her, taking her over as brutally as it did that time in the sports ground on the day she met Hauslich.

Please, I have to ask you to stop for just a moment, Doctor Jekelius . . .

She didn't mean to, but she has touched his arm. He turns to her and his eyes look dismissive and stern. In the shade of the brim of his tweed cap, his jawline looks hard, even threatening. But he does slow down and then stops outside a rustic building that seems to be some kind of inn. He stares at it for a while before, in a sudden rush, he says that he must make a phone call, leaves her and slams the car door shut. After a while, the engine sounds in her head die down and, with them, the dizziness and nausea. All is quiet around her now. The sun shines in a cloudless sky. It is baking hot. She sticks her arm out and touches the car door. The sensation of hot metal against her skin is pleasurable with just a hint of pain. The realisation of how quickly feeling sick can give way to feeling so wonderfully well makes her a little ashamed. She closes her eyes. In the silence, she hears the chirping of grasshoppers and smells the rough odour of decaying grass from the roadside ditch. When she opens her eyes again, she sees larks swirling high above the ripening cornfields. She turns to look for Jekelius and catches sight of cardboard boxes on the rear seat. The boxes are packed full of tins and jars of preserves. She can't resist taking a closer look. Cured ham, asparagus, *champignons*; desirable luxury goods in these deprived times. Who are they meant for? They are travelling on duty, after all, so all this can hardly be intended for the staff or the patients at the hospital they are going to inspect. She quickly straightens up when she sees him walking towards the car. The sun is behind him and his slim body seems to dissolve and reform in the heat haze that rises from the tarmac. She waits, ashamed again, with lowered head and thumping heart. They're waiting for us at Bruckhof now, is all he says before starting the engine.

The Boy Pelikan and the Fourteen Holy Helpers The Bruckhof hospital is not in Totzenbach as she had assumed but stands surrounded by fields and meadows about a kilometre outside the village. Apart from the main building and a chapel, there is also a long, wooden building on the hospital site: a barn, perhaps, or stables, or a tool shed. The hospital building is three storeys tall, with a splendid Baroque gable and a high, sharply sloping roof topped with an onion-domed turret. Jekelius parks in the narrow shade in front of it, removes his cap, takes a white coat from his doctor's bag and pulls it on over his jacket. The institution's director, a red-cheeked, elderly man, is already waiting on the steps to receive them. Accompanied by two nurses in neatly ironed, white uniforms, he leads the way in a nervous, slightly affected manner. The doors to the wards open into long corridors and the whole scene reminds her of Steinhof as it looked in the 1920s, when her grandfather was a patient there. It smells the same, as stale as if the place hadn't been properly aired for decades. There is something almost sculptural about the bright sunlight that enters through the windows high above the heads of the few patients who have dared to step outside the wards. They are ushered into a smallish room with bare stone walls and a single tall window looking out over the garden. Someone has put a vase full of fresh wild flowers in the window alcove, a gesture that seems somehow touching. The staff has already picked the children to be examined. She can hear their voices on the other side of the door, excited and angry as children always are when jostling for a place in a queue. The director invites them to sit down at a desk in the middle of the room. On it, patient records and case-note folders are tidily arranged and opened for the inspector and his assistant. The two nurses stand by the door, ready to assist as required. Looking indifferent, Doctor Jekelius leafs through the list of patients and then agrees with the director that the children will not be called in alphabetical order (the records are not consistently sorted that way) but according to the ward and room where the child's bed is. The voices outside suddenly fall silent, and one by one (as their names are called) the boys and girls come in to stand in front of them, like little actors at an audition, looking confident or scared or trying their luck with frankly ingratiating smiles. Some are obviously imbecile, with protruding lips, wet with saliva. Most of them seem to find it difficult to stand still in the same spot, or to speak coherently enough to string together more than a few sentences at one time, or to speak at all without constantly becoming distracted. They are not intimidated, though, and look curious and intently interested in what is going on. One of the boys tries to grab hold of the spatula used to examine the inside of his mouth and then becomes intrigued by the doctor's little reflex hammer. Jekelius works calmly, with that thoughtful concentration she has come to think is typical of him. His expression fascinates her, withdrawn and distant but very alert at the same time. He is sparing with comment, but now and then uses a Latin term or some short description, for instance of the appearance of the limbs, or of skin rashes and scars. She makes a note in the margin of the patient's record of the remarks she has understood. Finally, the room is empty, no one waits in the corridor and the hospital director, visibly relieved, comes over to them. She looks through the list of children again. All names have been ticked apart from one.

Someone called Pelikan is missing, she says. *Karl Pelikan.*

Jekelius looks hard at her for a long moment. The director is pressing the palms of his hands together in front of his chest, almost as if praying.

Why haven't you had Pelikan called? Jekelius asks. The director closes his eyes and Jekelius turns to one of the nurses: *this Pelikan, is he not here any longer?*

The nurse, *oh, yes, Doctor . . . Doctor —*

Doctor Jekelius, *Please, would you bring the child to us immediately.*

Pelikan is brought. He is a thin, gangly boy of about thirteen or fourteen. Two men support his shoulders but he can walk on his own, though in an odd, jerky, foot-dragging way. Instead of stepping straight into the room, he drags his body along the whole of the short wall next to the door and the two men follow him obediently. She thinks: like royalty. His long, narrow face seems as strangely twisted as his body. His eyes are screwed up below sternly pulled-together eyebrows, as if observing Jekelius with profound distrust, possibly even contempt. Briefly, confused embarrassment fills the room. The two men who support Pelikan are unsure whether to keep propping him up or to set him down, and Doctor Jekelius offers them no instructions. He just stands there, intently scrutinising the boy's face until the hospital director clears his throat and says, clearly still troubled:

Master Pelikan here works for us in the office, he's . . .

Doctor Jekelius waves impatiently at him to shut up:

Sister Anna will read to us from his hospital record instead.

> ***Pelikan, Karl*** (***Karel***). Born 1927. The youngest child of four.
> Father: Forest ranger. Mother: Schoolteacher.
> K initially developed normally; learnt reading and arithmetic early. Joined in children's play but worried because he was unable to run as fast as the others. At the age of eight, complained that he found it hard to raise his arms or to carry heavy objects.

She looks up and sees Pelikan staring at her, from his throne of supportive arms. His gaze is so penetrating that she gets lost in the text she is reading. The room is very silent. Then, a new conversation starts up between Doctor Jekelius and the institution's director, in a different, more factual tone:

DIRECTOR: Pelikan walked normally until he was ten.

DOCTOR JEKELIUS: This looks like a severe case of muscular dystrophy. It usually starts distally in the limbs. Can he raise his hands?

DIRECTOR: He can read and write, he's . . .

DOCTOR JEKELIUS: What about his speech?

DIRECTOR: His speech is perfectly normal. Like you or me.

DOCTOR JEKELIUS: [*to Pelikan*] Say something . . . !

KARL PELIKAN: [*stutters*] J-j-j . . .

DOCTOR JEKELIUS: And what is the nature of the work he carries out?

DIRECTOR: He works in the office. He stamps letters, Doctor Jekelius.

DOCTOR JEKELIUS: Stamps letters?

DIRECTOR: He is a great help to us in the office, where he undertakes many other practical tasks in addition to stamping letters.

DOCTOR JEKELIUS: But all this is of course completely beside the point. It's clear for everyone to see that this boy is subject to progressive atrophy and, as you will understand yourself, this is not the right place for keeping cripples. Young Pelikan ought to be transferred to the kind of institution where he will receive appropriate care. His future capacity for work is something you, Doctor, and I should discuss in private, if there is an opportunity?

The two medical men leave the room together. Young Pelikan, too, leaves in his mobile throne, followed by the two nurses who both turn in the doorway and curtsey to Anna, as if to some superior. Because she doesn't know what to do next, she returns to the car. Soon afterwards, Jekelius comes along and insists that they must drive into Totzenbach. Someone lives there whom he must visit. But first, he has a couple of phone calls to make in the hospital. Sister Anna can go ahead into the village to pass the time, he says. It sounds like an order and she obeys. There is a cemetery on the village side of the hospital. It is surrounded by tall poplar trees that cast a basketwork of swiftly changing shadows over the gravestones. Some of those buried here must have been patients who died in the hospital, but most of the graves are for staff, all female. The tall headstones have the same year chiselled into them: 1918. The year of the Spanish flu. She recalls Jekelius's long lecture on the way here: were these nurses themselves the cause of the infection that killed them? A narrow path runs from the wooded burial ground between broad fields towards the village. For a while, she follows a slow stream with wooded banks until houses and farms close in around her and she is in Totzenbach. She has arrived at a ruined castle with a moat that looks more like an overgrown ditch. The castle seems to have been recruited as an army base: parked military trucks and troop-transport vehicles are parked everywhere along the moat. It is midday. The heat encloses her like a bell jar. She feels dizzy again and recognises the spasms at her temples that announce a headache. When ten minutes have passed without any sign of Jekelius, she walks slowly towards the church at the far end of the village main street. There are hardly any men around, only women and children. Yet another sign of the war's silent presence. A flock of boys and girls come running from the school building and set off, shouting and laughing, down a road lined by flowering pear trees with large flower clusters far out along their branches. She is looking for cool places where she can settle down to rest, and when she sees the door to the church transept standing open she walks inside, then stops in front of a low stone relief on the wall of the porch. It is a triptych and the central panel is crowded with allegorical figures. She stares vacantly at the scene for a long time before she suddenly recognises two of the Fourteen Holy Helpers in Need: Saint Christopher holding the infant Jesus in his arms and Saint Catherine with the wheel. And then she realises that they are all there: Saint Barbara with the tower, Saint Blaise with the crossed candles, Saint Margaret with the dragon. When she was little, she had to learn about them in school, the fourteen names and attributes of each saint. Irrespective of where you were or what affliction you suffered from, there was always a Holy Helper to pray to and the hope of a pair of protective or supportive hands, like those escorting young Pelikan from his hiding place. There should have been a helper for her mother, too, someone to save her from the insane time warp that made everything seem to slip out of her hands. Perhaps Saint Florian would serve, he who blessed and secured the sanctity of the home when fire and warfare lay waste the land? She notices next that the two worshippers kneeling on either side of the frieze's central panel, a man and a woman in prayer, have had their heads knocked off. But the vandals have spared the saintly helpers. Only time has worn their bodies smooth. There is the sound of a car engine in the distance, and from inside the gloomy transept she sees Jekelius's large Opel Kapitän slowly approach along the tree-lined street. Some of the children have climbed up into the pear tree closest to the church but one little boy is too small to follow them on his own. He stands around on the ground below while excited voices call from inside the canopy and then go silent when Jekelius gets out of the car and stops near the tree. He first looks up, then at the boy, who tries his luck by expectantly stretching both arms into the air.

Jekelius grabs hold of him and lifts him up into the anxiously waiting tree. Then, he walks to the passenger side of the car and silently holds the door open for her. She climbs in. He stays silent all the way back to the city. Even though he has not commented on the day's events, she feels that he all the time wanted her to be there, not exactly as an assistant but more as a witness. He intended her to watch his assured, decisive examination and evaluation of the children of Bruckhof, and liked her to see the affectionate firmness with which he lifted the little boy up into the tree. And then she recalls the scene in Martinstrasse, when that woman was impatiently waiting while Jekelius manoeuvred the car out into the street. It has struck her that she is now taking the woman's place. She briefly wonders if he, too, is aware of that, only to push the thought right out of her mind. It is too absurd and irrelevant to follow up. Instead, she leans back, allows herself to be dazzled by the setting sun and thinks of nothing else until they drive into suburban Wien.

IV

The Boys and the Mountain

The Quiet Hour There were around fifteen, maybe twenty boys in their dormitory and their section probably held sixty or so, I can't quite remember, Adrian Ziegler says. Generally, remembering is hard for him. The others agree. It is as if their memories are somehow smudged, or as if much of what was once stored has been corroded. When Ziegler is shown photographs of the boys, he recognises most of them but can't for the life of him work out where or when he has met them. He remembers their nicknames even when their proper names are lost. Apparently, one of them was called Cape (for Cape of Good Hope); there was a Miseryguts, and an Escape-artist whose real name was Pawel Zavlacky. He instructed Adrian, with all the precision of an experienced locksmith, about the locks in their section that could be hooked or picked, what kind of tools there were and how they functioned. Easy locks, like those in the doors between the day room and the corridor, or the dormitory doors, could be picked with any kind of object that was pointy enough, like a filed-down nail or a knitting needle. Or a piece of a tin lid. Tin lids could be hammered into a point as sharp as an awl. In the toilets and the shower rooms, the window latches were fastened to the wall and secured with bolts, so to break these you needed stronger kit. Another snag was that the windows were barred on the outside, so just breaking the locks didn't do the trick. To get out, you had to be slim and agile like a *real* escape artist. Zavlacky boasted that he had lost count of all the times he had got out of the place. Adrian had only seen him escape once and thought he had died in the process. Just over a year later, Zavlacky was caught and incarcerated again, and by then it had been like meeting an entirely different person. Spiegelgrund did this to people's bodies and minds: deformed them almost to death. The children who didn't manage to escape or disappear some other way ended up in pavilions 15 or 17. The idiots were kept in 15. You could hear them screaming and moaning in the summer when it was warm enough for all the narrow ventilation panes at the top of the row of windows to be left open. Their noises would hang in the moist, still air between the pavilions and became somehow tangible, almost fleshy, and you could hear the slow, heaving intakes of breath that preceded the long screams, and the whimpering from those who couldn't breathe in enough air. Adrian slept in the second bed, counting from the main dormitory door. The younger children were usually placed in the middle and the older ones, like Zavlacky and Miseryguts, and later Pototschnik, closer to the door. The bed on Adrian's left was Julius Becker's and the one on Becker's left was Jockerl's. Jockerl was a bed-wetter. Hannes Neubauer slept closest to the window. Neubauer was one or maybe two years younger than Adrian, a small, solid boy whose spotty, scarred head was as round as a cannonball and, apart from scattered pale tufts, almost bald. His expressionless face gave nothing away, his eyes were a pale, almost transparent blue and his mouth was tight but with slightly upturned corners, as if smiling at something only Hannes could see. He sometimes wandered about for days without looking at anything much or saying anything in particular, seemingly only to carry his round, blond head from place to place rather than to be with others, a habit that might have made people take him for a hopeless idiot had it not been for him actually talking to them from time to time. He had to name everything he saw and might say: *a chair*. Or: *a plate*. The words could also come tumbling out of him in long, incomprehensible sentences in which only the swear words could be picked out clearly because they were recognisable, although he sometimes used really strange ones, like *schiache Hustblumen* or *g'fäulte Marillen* or *leck mich du Amerikanische Tuttelaffe*. What normal person would ever say anything like that? But the words would keep pouring out of Hannes until he suddenly stopped talking and then he looked blank and seemed to wipe them away with the back of his hand as one does when wiping snot or saliva from one's face. His father was an officer in the Wehrmacht and fought at the front. That's why Hannes was in Spiegelgrund. Not because he had said or done anything stupid, or misbehaved, but because there wasn't anyone at home to look after him. At least, that's what he said. In a manner of speaking, Julius Becker's parents were war victims too, but that was different and, unlike Hannes, he never spoke about them. Becker normally didn't speak at all unless there was someone he could harangue. Miseryguts said it was because Becker was an *intellectual* and it was a fact that he looked like one: tall, with narrow shoulders, thick hair as curly as a Negro's, and small round glasses with chrome rims that he treasured and always tried to hide in some safe place. The other boys worshipped Julius but hated him as well. They thought he was god-like because he wasn't at all like them. And probably detested him for the same reason. He would tell them about another, much larger and better world that existed *outside*, or that was what he claimed anyway, when he bothered to say anything at all. He was sure there were *good powers* working for his release. His time inside was limited, come what may. Or so he said. All the time, according to Adrian, it was as if Becker had something to long for, some hope for himself, and that made the rest of us feel sick because we too had of course something to long for, only we had been told it was just crap, and no one was waiting for us to come outside, let alone anyone who could be said to have *good powers*, and so we knew that life inside was not about keeping yourself to yourself and digging in for the duration, as Julius saw it, but precisely the opposite; that is, you had to become as invisible as possible to avoid becoming the target of the fury of the nurses, to never resist and instead try and eliminate your real self to make it possible to play along and pretend to do what they wanted, given that what they did want wasn't what they said, which was to make us better people, Adrian explained, but to get rid of us, wipe us off the surface of the earth once and for all, which of course meant that the only remaining way out of there was willingly to agree not to be. The fact was, Julius was always afraid. Fear was the price he had to pay for his belief in something outside worth having faith in or longing for. When he sat on his bed, he always perched on the edge, with his legs together and his thin shoulders raised. His posture was the same when he ate. And he was always on the lookout for a confidant. Julius confided certain things to Adrian that he only understood much later. For instance, Julius's father, who had been a top legal advisor to the Schuschnigg government, had resisted the demand to let the Nazi insurgents out of prison and had himself been imprisoned just after the Anschluss. The Nazis had gone after Julius's mother as well and made her work in the armaments industry. He didn't know where she worked or at what, but he said that someone he called his 'at-home uncle' knew and the 'at-home uncle' would visit sometimes, bringing short letters or secret notes from Mrs Becker. The uncle also sent Julius parcels that contained food and warm clothes and added useful items like shoe polish, plasters and antiseptic cream. These last three things in particular infuriated Nurse Mutsch (*. . . who does he reckon we are? Doesn't he think we're minding the children's every need . . . ?*). One day, she made up her mind that she had to stop this special gifts business.

She acted during what was called 'the quiet hour'. Every afternoon, once they were back in pavilion 9 after their lessons, and before they went off to queue for their supper, the children were made to sit down for the quiet hour. This meant that they went to the day room, where they sat, straight-backed and with their hands visible on the tabletop. They were allowed to read books or do their homework but not to say anything or ask any questions and, while they sat there, Nurse Mutsch or bony Nurse Demeter would keep an eye on them so, naturally, the nurses' beady eyes would register *all* there was to see, every failing and every mistake their charges had been guilty of that day, every sign of indiscipline or disobedience which then, as the compact silence gathered in the room, would surface, urged on by bad conscience as heat drives sweat from the pores of the skin. Such is the wickedness of children (so they were told) that it is as impossible to choke it off at birth as it is to stop it being found out. Which was why Mutsch chose to produce the new parcel from Julius's would-be uncle during the quiet hour and put it down in the middle of the table, in front of fifteen pairs of frightened eyes:

. . . *now, let's see what we'll see*, she says and holds up a pair of scissors.

. . . *scissors,* Hannes says.

She begins to cut. Fifteen pairs of childish eyes follow Nurse Mutsch's brisk movements as she plunges the scissors into the parcel, cuts the coarse string, pulls the folded ends of the wrapping paper back and puts her hand inside. The parcel is so big that her massive forearm disappears. Then it re-emerges and she begins to line up her finds. There are little jars with preserved apricots and pears, and she twists the lid off one of them, makes pincers of her right thumb and index finger and extracts one of the halved, syrup-soaked pears, golden-grey and soft, and pops the entire piece in her mouth, then licks her fingers, not to miss a drop of the wonderful syrup. Her hand goes back into the parcel and out comes a box of original Manner Kex, the Neapolitan wafers layered with chocolate cream. Looking thoughtful, she opens the box and starts eating, slowly and systematically, crunching on one wafer after another. By now, all eyes have swivelled to fix on Julius. In the beginning, he just sat there, looking as scared as everyone else and unable to believe what was happening. But when Nurse Mutsch has munched her way through all the fruit in syrup and all the biscuits, and gone on to examine the warm socks the uncle had packed, and the handkerchiefs and the spare leather bootlaces, he gradually begins to shake. It is a strange fit of the shakes that starts at the top of his body, around his head and shoulders, but he manages to control it so that he sits still, or almost still, back straight and hands on the table as per orders, but the lower part of his body is less controllable, his hips rock on the seat, his thighs tremble and his feet rattle against the floor like drumsticks. Nurse Mutsch stares at him:

What's up, do you want the toilet?

Julius opens his mouth as if to answer.

Big or small?

Julius opens his mouth again but Mutsch is too impatient to wait for a reply. She looks for something to wipe her hands on. There is nothing obvious nearby so she grabs one of the carefully folded socks from the parcel, uses it to wipe her mouth and nose, finds her bunch of keys and picks up a couple of the precisely measured strips of toilet paper that she keeps in readiness next to her place at the table and walks with firm strides to the door, unlocks it and holds it open for Julius who slowly, as if reluctantly, gets up from the bench and walks towards her,

come on, what are you waiting for do you think we've got all day . . .

and then the door slams behind them and from the corridor the others can hear Mutsch's voice, muffled but still perfectly audible, then the keys turn in the toilet door lock. Shortly afterwards, the door to the day room opens again and Nurse Mutsch returns. Without a glance at anyone, she sits down and carries on exploring the parcel. When she can't find anything more, she makes a bundle of the wrapping paper and takes the rubbish to the nurses' cubicle. There's a discreet knock on the door. Mutsch admits Julius, and as he walks to the table it is obvious that he has managed neither the small nor the big stuff but that everything is as it was before – except there is no parcel now, only Nurse Mutsch, who carries on staring at Julius and, next, slowly but surely, he starts shaking again and now Mutsch is ready for him.

Do you want the toilet again?

Julius shakes his head but by now there's no telling if this means no, or if the disturbance of his body has reached his head, and Nurse Mutsch gets up and walks over to him to issue an order, *get a grip on yourself,* and next (when Julius still hasn't managed to subdue his shakes) slaps the side of his head with the flat of her hand, his glasses go flying and *no one allowed you to stand*, she says when he makes a reflex attempt to pick the glasses up, and then *sit down*, she says as she bends to pick up the glasses before returning to her seat at the head of the table. She holds the glasses in her fist, her fingers wrapped around them so firmly that everyone can see how tightening the grip just a little would squeeze the thin frames to breaking point and the glass would be crushed. Please, Julius pleads quietly, and Nurse Mutsch goes, *you just stay where you are, nice and proper, and you'll get them back at the end of the quiet hour*. Julius sits where he sits, trembling as hard as ever. One can almost hear the skeleton rattle inside him. He doesn't put his hand up to be allowed to go to the toilet and Nurse Mutsch doesn't anticipate any request by asking him if he wants to go. No need for that. A little later, the silence is broken by a liquid, rustling sound and soon afterwards they see a puddle spreading under the table, over which Julius droops, wet and still shaking like a rattle. Nurse Mutsch watches him with something akin to satisfaction. *It's when one doesn't think before one acts that everyone can see what kind of a weakling one really is*, she says with distaste, and even though she is looking in another direction no one fails to realise that she is talking about Julius.

Wake-up Call All days begin exactly the same way. At 5.30 a.m. punctually, their tutor or *Erzieherin,* Mrs Rohrbach, unlocks the dormitory door and steps inside followed by the day staff. Mrs Rohrbach blows on a whistle she has hanging from a strap around her neck and uses a short, rubber-coated metal stick they called 'the clapper' to bang underneath the metal bars at the ends of the beds.

Aufstehen, heraus aus den Betten!
Bettnässer vortreten!
(Get up, out of your beds!
Bed-wetters, step forward!)

This was worst for the newcomers, who had not yet realised what shame can mean, and very bad also for those who were still naïve enough to imagine that resistance might not be entirely futile and in vain flapped about trying to grab what little there was to hold on to: bed-ends, door frames, basin edges. Your grip was of course removed sooner or later, one way or another. The day nurses used to work in the lunatic asylum and were as strong as bears. In the wash-room, apart from the ordinary shower cubicles, there was also an old-fashioned, high-sided tub of cast-iron. A shower head at one end sprayed ice-cold water into the tub that was already full of wet linen towels. One of the nurses would drag the troublesome bed-wetter to the tub and the other one would stand guard at the head end. As soon as the child had been thrown in and tried to crawl out of the mass of wet towels, one of them would grab an arm or a leg, raising the limb for long enough to force the culprit's head and shoulders under the freezing water again, and possibly get him entangled in the towels, which would soon block both his mouth and his nose. The term for this practice was 'dunking'. As soon as a boy had been dunked, he was hauled up again and made to stand on the cold tiled floor, shivering, barely able to stay upright, as moist and shiny as an eel and with a face as blue as a plum. Jockerl was one of the boys who got dunked quite often. Jockerl's bed was close enough for Adrian to pick up the sweetish, ammoniacal pong of urine, often before he had woken up properly, as if that smell could penetrate his sleep and reach into the place in his mind where fear had rooted itself. Soon he would hear Mrs Rohrbach hitting the bed with her clapper and next the screaming as Jockerl was pulled off his peed-on sheet and dragged into the washroom, and the slapping of the shower water against the side of the tub followed, and the boy's desperate calls for help that ended in helpless gurgling as the water rushed in and choked him. But Jockerl was tough. Despite the beatings and clips round the ears that threw his little body like a wet rag from one tiled wall to another, he always managed to get through and find a place at the long row of wash-hand basins where the other boys were already getting on with brushing their teeth. Jockerl was a head shorter than the rest of them but always carried himself as straight as a spear and was often first back in the dormitory for the next stage, which was bed-making. At this point, Mrs Rohrbach positioned herself at the far end of the room with her back to the window and started clapping her hands to match her counting aloud . . . *one two three four five six* . . . and for Jockerl it was important to keep ahead of her every command. When Mrs Rohrbach called out *twenty* he had already stretched the sheet over the edge of the mattress, when she reached *forty* he had folded the blanket over the sheet and at *sixty* he had put his toothbrush in the glass exactly where it should be, the glass lined up edge to edge with the right corner of the bedside table, and folded his towel, placed it on the middle of the three shelves, and put his indoor and outdoor shoes, laces untied, on the floor below. Julius Becker was useless when it came to practical things like these and Mrs Rohrbach had noticed that soon enough. Time after time, she would do rounds to check Julius's bed. She wouldn't say anything, only start, almost thoughtfully, to count again, just for Julius . . . *one two three four five* . . . and then she went on counting more loudly . . . *six seven eight nine* . . . and at *ten* she gave up and tore blanket and sheets from Julius's hands and shouted:

that's not the right way

don't you know how to do it

and he still couldn't do anything right with his listless hands, even less keep his eyes and lips under control,

you're to begin again and get it right this time

and Mrs Rohrbach started counting again . . . *one two three four* . . . but now she had the clapper ready and Julius knew what to expect. He faced up to his failure and before he had even lifted the sheet, fell crying to the floor in front of Mrs Rohrbach's feet. So, with one firm grip under his chin, their tutor in good manners would pull him upright, then hit him with the clapper, one blow for each correct bed-making action he had failed to complete:

. . . *one two three four* . . .

And so it went on. Day after day after day. Always the same ritual, Adrian said.

Those who had got away without punishments *that day* were made to stand and wait until everyone else had been dealt with and one of their guards came along to order them to line up for the march to the school pavilion. Sometimes Julius would join the rest of us, sometimes not, Adrian explained. If not, it was because they had made him scrub the dormitory floor or clean the toilets or sentenced him to four or six hours standing punishment. There was no loyalty among the boys. Each one of us had his own confusions to deal with. We kept getting punished for being careless but were actually as guarded and distrustful as old men. Alliances were formed though, some of them baffling. Like the one between Hannes and Jockerl. On their way to the school pavilion the boys passed the institution's kitchen and, next to it, the central-heating boiler that spewed out disgustingly thick, black smoke from its chimney. One day, Jockerl asked what they might be burning in there and Hannes turned to him and said:

They burn bed-wetters like you, didn't you know?

Even though he was in their section, Jockerl behaved in many ways like a small child. When he was told something, his face softened, melted somehow, and his eyes had an inward look, as if trying to visualise in his head what he had just heard. Miseryguts gave him a shove and said, *hang on, it's not your turn yet*, and suddenly everyone laughed and formed a cluster around the little one, the most gullible of them all, and Jockerl blanched and became as pale as when they hauled him out of the bath in the mornings or when they gave him a *Wickelkur*, a wrap-up cure, and watching that is something I'll never forget, Adrian said: they wrapped him in wet towels and made him stand in the bitterly cold corridor until all the towels had dried. It took fourteen hours. To cure him of his bed-wetting once and for all, they told everyone. That's what they wanted us to believe. That what they persecuted us for was something that was already part of us.

The Führer's Signature on a Piece of White Card A framed portrait of the Führer hung on the corridor wall. In those days, identical portraits were hung on the walls of all official places; the Führer, who gazed into the distance but had a steadfast look on his face, was seen a little from the side. His facsimile signature was placed below the image. Every single corridor in Spiegelgrund was graced by a portrait just like that, or at at least a similar one. If you were given a 'standing-still' punishment for six or fourteen or however many hours, you had to stand in front of the Führer picture and if you failed for just one second to stay straight as a post with your eyes fixed on the great leader, you were ordered to keep standing for double the number of hours. This was how the Führer came to form part of the jumble of stories that Hannes Neubauer wandered around and mumbled about to himself. The stories were all about heroes and their brave deeds. It could be about von Humboldt, who discovered the source of the River Amazon and fought battles with the Indians, or about wartime heroics, the kind of stories you read about in the copies of *Der Stürmer* that were lying around everywhere. The tabloid was packed with pictures of steel-helmeted soldiers who were always portrayed sideways on, like the Führer, but unlike him were toting automatic pistols. In Hannes's versions, the hero was his father, who (or so Hannes would claim) kept being dispatched on secret missions to different places. What about your mum then? Adrian couldn't resist asking (he had after all a special bond with his mother) and Hannes said that soon after he was born, his father had *shown that shameless slut the door*. You can't trust women, Hannes Neubauer told them, all women are false and treacherous and greedy and only out for your money. So said the boy with the round head without as much as a flicker of his blue eyes, although this shocked even hardened types like Zavlacky and Miseryguts. Big words from such a little lad. Hey, is that true of Mrs Rohrbach, too? Zavlacky hazarded with an ironic smile. Satan's handmaidens, the lot of them, Hannes replied promptly and added that they mustn't worry. His father, an army officer of the highest rank, had already sent a message with a devoted courier to reassure his son he was on his way and Hannes must prepare to decamp. As time passed and his father failed to turn up, the preparations to leave changed more and more into priming everyone for a collective rescue action. His father would come not only for Hannes himself but also for his friends, whom he had trusted and confided in, and his father had therefore secretly selected to be set free as well. Meanwhile, they must all be ready to obey Neubauer's commands. The order to make a break for it might come at any time and then they would move into a *safe place* which had been set up for them inside the mountain. What mountain is that? Zavlacky asked dubiously. What kind of warrior are you? Hannes replied, sounding just as dubious, and his little smile, playing in the ever-upturned corners of his mouth, hinted at the ongoing planning for the top-secret rescue action but also that it was all kept inside the ball of Hannes's head, which was sealed like a bank vault, and that he would give nothing away unless he had decided in good time that the person he told was worthy. Though not even the normally self-contained Neubauer could always manage to keep himself under control. One day, when their teacher, Mr Hackl, had spoken with his usual engagement about all the sacrifices that their proud soldiery made while on the front, Hannes gathered some of his most trusted companions around him in the furthest corner of the area fenced in with steel netting that passed for their 'schoolyard', and showed them his scars. Most of them had already noticed the marks on his body and wondered. From a distance, they looked a little like rough skin or spots of dirt. But now they were allowed to observe him close up and realised that the blemishes were clearly the kind of scars that only a real fighter would sustain. Hannes showed off a deep gash left in one of his armpits once the doctors had cut out what he described as a *lump*. What such a *lump* could be no one quite knew, but Miseryguts actually probed the hollow with his finger and could confirm that there would have been room for an egg inside it. And everywhere on Hannes's body, on his shins, under one elbow and across both his thighs, long scars ran like narrow winding ribbons or blood vessels. On his back and the back of his head, the healed patches looked more like the pits after chickenpox but Hannes insisted that these were burns from the time he had almost fallen backwards into a cauldron full of boiling tar. The top of his head was marked by scars from long slashes and there was a skin ridge down the side of his neck which he told them was due to a sliver of glass that his father had surgically removed using a kitchen knife and a cloth soaked in alcohol as the only anaesthetic, a necessary operation because if the piece of glass had been left it might have started to move around inside his body, maybe get all the way to the heart;

and Hannes . . . *so that one just had to be cut out! . . . you see, if the black blood seeps through, you go septic and that's the end . . .*

and if Adrian had leaned forward just then, he too could have let his fingers slide along the strangely twisting skin ridges or pushed a finger inside the temptingly smooth, shiny hollow in Hannes's armpit, but at that point Hannes turned and started to button up again . . . *though some people have black blood already so there's no point.*

. . . *but I'm not a Jew*, was all Adrian could think of saying.

. . . *you're a tinker, and that's the same thing*, Hannes replied.

Adrian had been called *tinker* before and now it had happened again, with the same unquestionable authority and correctness as when Zavlacky was named the Escape-artist or Jockerl the Punch-bag, and then Hannes walked away, old wounds and all, his back as straight and his manner as untroubled as always, looking ahead with his usual innocent blue eyes that seemed to see nothing other than the convictions that filled his head, although on the outside so peaceful and childlike and blond that even Nurse Mutsch, who would not otherwise open her hands for anyone, now and then couldn't resist stroking it with her fingertips. The fact was that Neubauer the Warrior's heartless contempt for the opposite sex was in no way returned by the despised females. Or at least not by Mutsch, who liked having a little helper:

There's a supper portion missing. Neubauer,
you run along to the kitchen and fetch it.

And soon Hannes Neubauer became the only one of the boys in his section to be trusted with keys. It might well have been why Miseryguts started paying court to Hannes, who had obviously become liked by the staff. They were as tight as thieves for a while, Adrian recalled: the large Walter Schiebeler (that was Miseryguts's real name) with his big clumsy feet, whose body twitched involuntarily, and the always restrained, introverted Neubauer with his weird ideas and bursts of almost incomprehensible talking. At one point, Neubauer informed Schiebeler that at night, when they were all asleep, the Führer in the corridor picture would transform into a fighter pilot. His perfectly combed hair turned into an aviator's helmet and his eyes were protected with special goggles that allowed him to see in the dark and fog and enabled him to complete his raids at all times of day and night and – *just now!* – he was piloting his plane in a death-defying dive straight down towards the hospital site and . . .

ra-tat-tat-tatt-tatt-ta!

. . . sounds of explosions followed his flight path and, one after another, they would all burn in the flames, all the idiots and children and doctors and nurses and tutors, and the horrible female guards they called *Aufseherinnen*, and the psychologists too – every single one would be blown up, even the hateful Mrs Rohrbach who would be incinerated in an especially intense, sparking ball of fire.

However, Miseryguts was less intrigued by the fighter pilot angle and more by the facsimile signature below the portrait and the way it could be seen as composed of two parts. First, the name *Adolf* with its *A* sticking up skywards while the *f* pushed off downwards like a slanting flash of lighting. And then, for some reason several centimetres further along the line, the surname started off with a complex spiral twirl that could, on a good day, be taken to be an *H*-curl but which then whirled off downwards into an ever denser (and ever more undecipherable) cyclone. If only one could have a signature like that! Miseryguts muttered wistfully to himself. Unlike most of the Spiegelgrund boys, Miseryguts didn't come from an ordinary children's home but from the Juchgasse reform school where they placed many of the children who had at first been held in police cells. In other words, Miseryguts was a real thief. Perhaps all this had something to do with how critical he always was about everything, not only his signature but the Spiegelgrund food (what was served up at Juchgasse had been much better) and Mr Hackl's ideas about what to teach them, and every time he expressed his displeasure with something, he grimaced and rolled his shoulders as if shaking off some hugely uncomfortable sensation; *can't you sit still?*

Nurse Mutsch kept saying to him but it was a fact that he couldn't. He moaned about Mutsch as well, called her a pig and, true enough, there was something pig-like about her broad face and large, blank, nearly transparent eyes that looked like the glass eyes on stuffed animals; unblinking eyes that seemed to grow larger the longer they were fixed on you and were always full of grudges and a wish to hurt. Anyway, Miseryguts convinced Hannes that the two of them should try to imitate the Führer's signature. He reasoned that in the mail deliveries to the institution, many letters arrived daily that required children for various purposes and Miseryguts was pretty sure that, while some of the letters would be typed and some written by hand, all would be finished off with large, flamboyant signatures like the Führer's. If only they could put together a letter like that, of course best of all a letter signed by *A. Hitler* himself, Miseryguts fancied they would be allowed to leave immediately or, at least, to reunite with their parents. Walter Schiebeler was stupid, stuttered and shrugged for no reason, and couldn't write a single syllable if you tied the pen to his hand. Hannes knew all this and, besides, he wasn't even sure if Schiebeler truly believed in these insane notions of his or if the handwriting exercise was only an attempt to get a grip on the enormous restlessness that plagued him. Even so, Hannes and Miseryguts, an unlikely pair, joined forces in a two-man forgery gang. Mr Hackl handed out pens and paper but because paper was scarce they were told to write on both sides and the sheets were soon used up. Mutsch and Demeter would also dole out paper during the quiet hour if the boys were meant to write or draw something but the results were collected afterwards and, according to Miseryguts, went to the psychologists who studied the children's work for hours on end to try to figure out where their souls were located (. . . *where is the soul really?* Jockerl asked because he had listened and wanted to join the discussion but *pinheads like you have got no souls. . . !* Miseryguts told Jockerl and slapped the back of his neck). Anyway, Miseryguts had somehow managed to get hold of a few pieces of torn card and they shared these and settled down to work. During the quiet hour, they obediently busied themselves with what looked like their homework, but everyone noticed that they quickly swapped papers with each other the moment Nurse Mutsch turned her back. Julius Becker saw it (he couldn't help noticing because he sat between them) and let out an unmistakable, quite loud whimper. Nurse Mutsch turned round. As usual, her wide-open, always disgruntled, glass-ball eyes swivelled Becker's way:

Willst du noch einmal aufs Klo? (Do you need the loo again?)

'Needing to go to the toilet' had by now grown into something like a joke between them. Every time Mutsch asked Julius that question, a sarcastic grin spread over her lips and Julius did not dare to say no. Every time, he obediently got up and Mutsch, sighing heavily, would tear off two bits of toilet paper, no more than about ten centimetres each, from the roll under the table and they disappeared out into the corridor (one could still hear their voices), giving the pair of prospective forgers a chance to carry on handing bits of paper to each other, if possible with even greater intensity. But then it happened that Nurse Mutsch came back to the day room sooner than expected and, because Hannes couldn't stop himself from saying the first thing that came into his head, he uttered the two words *Julius Becker*,

and Mutsch (who stopped in the doorway), *what's it with Becker?*

Again, Hannes looked blank so it was up to Miseryguts to think of something:

. . . he's spying in the nurses' room!

Mutsch said nothing, turned at once and shot back out into the corridor:

BEE-EEECKER! They heard her powerful shout outside, her rapid footsteps and then what sounded like a massive thump followed by a scream, and in a little while she reappeared, dragging Julius and intoning *I knew it I knew it I knew it . . . !*

She didn't tell them exactly what she knew, but from then on Julius was not allowed to go to the toilet. They were sitting opposite each other for hours and Nurse Mutsch didn't take her eyes off him for a second. Julius looked nowhere, not down at his work, not around; he seemed to have no gaze of his own at all. Everyone knew that this was the end for Julius. Adrian knew it, and Hannes and Miseryguts knew. Even Jockerl knew it thanks to the strangely intuitive sense that made him aware of everything that went on in the section and, because he was kind, Jockerl did his best at least to ease Julius's fall from grace. In the mornings, when Julius as usual would stand helplessly holding his blanket and sheet, Jockerl would run up to him and say *come on, I'll help you make the bed* and since he had already finished his own bed-making, his fingers would dance over Julius's things, tucking the coverlet under the mattress just so, and turning the blanket back with the fold precisely where it should be. The part of the blanket that was folded back over the coverlet and in under the mattress was to be exactly fifty centimetres wide in order that the name on the blanket – *SPIEGELGRUND* – should be easily visible from the passage between the beds where Mrs Rohrbach paraded up and down during her daily inspection. Naturally, Mrs Rohrbach was never taken in by Jockerl's smart handiwork. She pretended not to notice for a couple of days, possibly to get a better insight into what was going on behind her back, and so the beat of her rhythmic counting *seemingly* continued unchanged . . . *one two three four* . . . and Jockerl's hands also continued to flit skilfully over the bedclothes while

Julius found himself just standing by, ever more at a loss; until, one day, Mrs Rohrbach struck:

It would appear Becker thinks he'll be allowed to keep servants!

She had already grabbed Julius's ear. Next, with her free hand, she pulled the sheets and blankets out of Jockerl's arms and not only from Jockerl's bed but all the beds on that side, including the ones she had already passed by, no matter if they had been properly made or not. Ruthlessly, sheets, blankets and mattresses were pulled apart until the air suddenly filled with a blizzard of small and large pieces of paper, whirling like confetti. I had never before seen Mrs Rohrbach so taken aback, Adrian Ziegler said a long time later. But that morning, with all those small pieces of card and cardboard adrift and floating down onto her alarmed face, for once she had no idea of what to say or do. Instead, Nurse Mutsch was the one to step in and, with her hand against the small of her back, which was always sore, she bent to pick up the bits one by one. Soon, all became clear. Not only did she recognise the wrapping that had contained Julius's treats from home, all the paper and cardboard that, after guzzling the contents of the boy's parcel, she had stored in the nurses' room in the certain expectation that, sooner or later, such tough, good-quality items would come in handy one day; she also recognised, of course, the signature that had been multiplied every which way on each piece of paper: *Adolf Hitler* with the front leg of the *A* slung like a spear towards the upper edge of the paper, followed by the flashing descent of the *f* with its hissing hook, followed in turn by the whirlwind of the surname that began like a huge lasso at the top only to drill down into a darkening jumble of pen-strokes. And once these elements had become clear, the rest was easy to work out. Julius's obvious nervousness during quiet hour, his incessant requests to go to the toilet and then Walter Schiebeler's unprovoked admission that Becker had used his toilet trips to snoop in her private room. Nurse Mutsch cupped her hands to hold the scattered fragments, then held out her makeshift bowl to show them to Mrs Rohrbach at the same time as she straightened to whisper something. Mrs Rohrbach looked up from the papers to Julius Becker. She already held one of his prominent ears in a firm grip. Her face paled slightly but she didn't lose her composure. She steered the crying Julius out between the beds with determined movements and, as the two of them came past Jockerl's, she reached out and grabbed him as well, in the passing, or so it seemed. The other boys were left standing guard helplessly by their untidy beds. When the dormitory door slammed shut behind Nurse Mutsch, they heard her ask if she was to call the office. What Rohrbach replied, they couldn't hear. But the group must have stopped in front of the portrait of the Führer, because they suddenly heard Mrs Rohrbach say in an almost tearful voice:

Now you shall have to confess to the director what you've gone and done!

Afterwards, there were blows and slaps, Jockerl's screams, the sound of keys that rattled and a key that turned in a lock and a door that opened on screeching hinges and shut again with a bang. Then something else: a hard, hollow thumping noise that at first seemed never to stop and, when it finally did, was replaced by nothing but silence.

Decursus Everything within is a world, growing blindly and without hope. The grass that grows inside your chest already reaches the sky. It must not stay like that. Growths must be removed. All that is left must be suitable for writing down on a sheet of paper, a single sheet or perhaps a half, a febrile membrane, nothing. Then the nurse wipes your forehead with the same movement as when one clears a windowpane of condensation in order to see out. But you cannot see out into that darkness and, if you did, you would disappear into it yourself. It is that kind of darkness.

The Boy and the Mountain Hannes Neubauer would explain later how all that about the scissors came about. But he spoke about the Mountain first. The Mountain is something inside your head but it also exists outside of you. When you're in the Mountain, they can do anything they like with you. They might beat you up, kick you, try to strangle you. You won't notice because you're inside the Mountain. There's no time inside the Mountain, Hannes said. That's why there's no pain either. Even so, the Mountain is a dangerous place to stay because, without time or pain, you don't notice that you're there. Everyone who enters the Mountain must be prepared to die in there. That's why you've got to try to be inside and outside it at the same time. Or perhaps you should sit very close to the entrance, Hannes said, and then he sat down in his special way, on top of his bed, like an Indian, with his legs crossed under him and his eyes looking straight ahead. What Hannes didn't say, not then and not later either, was that he had owned a doll when he was about four or five years old. A girl in the house next door had lent it to him but he had come to regard it as his. So, when he was told to hand it back, he gouged its eyes out with scissors, cut off the dolly's curly black hair and stuck it onto his own head with some glue he had found. Then he went off to ask his father: do I look like Mum now? It had made his father furious. He ripped the bits of hair off his son's head, glue and all, put the gluey curls in a large ashtray, set fire to it and then turned the ashtray upside down on top of Hannes's head. Like a potty. A burning potty. Seems I'd better teach you a thing or two, he had said and laughed. Ever since, Hannes's head bore the scars of his scalp being on fire. Only tufts of hair ever grew back on his round head. Shortly after the scalp-burning episode, Hannes had to move. The war had begun and the Führer had given his father, the high-up Wehrmacht officer, a secret task so grand and so dangerous that no one must know about it or even mention anything about it. Hannes had to go and stay with a strange woman who said she was his father's sister although that didn't make any sense. She was dark-haired and ugly and didn't look anything like a proper Aryan, not at all like Hannes's father. Besides, she spoke very odd German that kept getting snarled up. Are you a brave warrior? she would ask in her weird, lumpy voice, and Hannes would say that he was. In that case, she mumbled, you will find there is a great big mountain where all the brave warriors are gathered, waiting for the day when they will be called, one by one, to defend the nation by fire and sword until the last man has fallen. And Hannes had asked: how will I know when it's time for me to come outside? When your father comes and gives you the secret password, that's when you will walk out of the mountain, his aunt had replied. But, until then, you must be more patient than most. But though he was supposed to be patient, his aunt was not. All the time while he was staying with her, she was on the phone, speaking away in her own strange language and, in the end, she said that she didn't dare to keep him any longer, he had to go for his own sake, and then they came for him in a car and brought him to Spiegelgrund. But the Mountain she had told him about remained with him. He made himself believe that because it existed inside his head, he could take it along wherever he went. And so Hannes sat at the entrance to his Mountain and waited for his father, wondering what that password might be. All the while, the Mountain inside his head grew larger and larger and, inside it, the darkness closed in ever more densely. The rhymes he muttered under his breath were the only spells he knew that could disperse the darkness. A boy went into the Mountain, and what did he bring inside? He brought a pair of scissors. The boy went into the Mountain, and what else did he bring? He brought his mother's lovely dark hair with him inside. A boy sat at the entrance to the great Mountain and outside his father waited, saying *I'll teach I'll teach you I'll teach you.*

Institutional Life Adrian Ziegler lived, on and off, at Spiegelgrund from January 1941 until May 1944. It amounted to a total of three and a half years, if you include the three to four months in the autumn and winter of 1941 when the entire institution was shifted to Ybbs. For someone as young as he was, three and half years almost adds up to a lifetime. During that period of time, the world outside was torn apart by war, and was devastated and rebuilt many times over. Spiegelgrund was the only place I could call home, Adrian used to say a little solemnly. Spiegelgrund had been set up as a place of transit but become a home for life for many of the inmates. Though unintended, such things happened. The institution was structured to be a place of selective elimination, where the weak were continuously separated from the even weaker. In that sense, Spiegelgrund was in a way a reflection of the world. You could see it in the staff they recruited. Take Nurse Mutsch: Adrian had come across her before he arrived at Spiegelgrund when she had been *Mrs* Mutsch, and had worked as a cook in the Mödling reform school. When he joined the long dinner queue of boys in institutional kit he would see her at the front, spooning out *Rindsgulasch* and *Knödel* from steaming pans. When he came to Spiegelgrund, he had recognised her at once. She had spotted him, too, but neither cared to say anything about it, and he had not told anyone about her sudden elevation from a mere cook to Nurse, or even Tutor. But perhaps she treated him better than she otherwise would have because she knew that he knew something she wanted to hide from the others. True, she did call him her *nasty little cheat*, but never *tinker*. What was Nurse Mutsch like? Not very tall, but broad and solid. Her high-cheekboned face looked shiny, as if rubbed with cream every morning. Her thin mouth, always tight-lipped, had a determined set. Round eyes, wide open and with a look in them as if everyone in the whole world conspired to humiliate and affront her in particular. Once, Adrian said, when she had turned her back, I looked at her and it was like seeing someone else altogether. She had let her hair down and it was rich and black and smoothly glossy, like the fur on a large, agile animal. She turned towards me quite suddenly but didn't seem to mind me having seen her like that. Mostly, she distrusted the children in her charge and didn't think them capable of understanding what they saw. This was why it was better not to let them see anything at all. When she ate everything in Julius's parcel, her eyes had stared emptily and indifferently ahead, while below them her jaws went on chewing and swallowing. Consuming the contents of the children's parcels was clearly something she automatically regarded as her right. I heard her say to Nurse Demeter that the big problem with the war was that there were no men around, and some women *suffered* because of it. While Julius was incarcerated in the punishment cell on the other side of the corridor, she went to him at least five or six times. Once, she left in tears, with blood on her face. She said that the degenerate child had struck her. Nurse Demeter had to give her a hug and tried to comfort her. Nurse Mutsch went on sick leave for a few days. When she returned, she still had the staring look in her eyes but her expression was somehow different. You could see that she hated the children for what they forced her to do to them.

The Chosen Ones Julius Becker was locked up in the punishment cell for five whole days. His punishment was solitary confinement or, as the term was, *einzeln geben,* and while he was held there he served as the institution's bad conscience even though nobody dared to say anything. On the sixth day, in the morning just after Julius had been released, Doctor Jekelius, the medical director, came on a visitation. Adrian had seen the medical rounds come and go before but this was the biggest one so far and, when they got up that morning, Mrs Rohrbach used the clapper to make very clear that there was *no time to lose – straightaway, off to the washrooms! Then go stand in line!* The children who hadn't had time to finish making their beds were pulled along and out into the corridor with Rohrbach shoving them from behind. Line-up meant that they had to stand in two rows, the youngest in front and the older ones behind. Jockerl stood in the middle of the front row. In the back row, Becker stood next to Miseryguts and Hannes Neubauer, who as usual didn't move a muscle in his face. They had to wait for more than an hour and were not permitted to move their feet or even straighten their necks. Their nervous minders kept rushing to the windows to see if *they* weren't coming and then, *at last,* they were on their way. Adrian, who had waited for the inspection rounds many times, still remembers in detail the sounds the medical staff made as they approached. It must have been like when the chords on a huge Baroque organ are being added together until a mighty, complex body of music emerges, music as inherently mysterious and abstract as it is terrifyingly able to fill and penetrate every space, every soul and thought. The approach of the round begins plainly: you hear doors opening and closing in the stairwell, then the harmless scraping of feet as people walk on the stairs, soon to mingle with the monotonous rumble of a group talking. The talk later splits into single voices, women and men can be heard speaking across each other, some mumbling, others sounding more insistent. The mass of sounds grows stronger and louder until, suddenly, it is as if a dam has given way, the ward doors open and the white-coated horde pours into the corridor, a dense crowd of junior and more senior doctors making up the bulk of the procession, followed by a tail of nurses and nursing assistants whispering together, but in an order related to their rank or status, and always an 'appropriate' distance of one or a couple of steps behinds the medics. This time, Doctor Gross led the procession. His head was inclined politely to listen to Matron Klara Bertha, who was apparently informing him of something of the greatest import. Doctor Hans Krenek was at their heels. Krenek was responsible for the childcare institution's educational role (in practice, he was the headmaster) and Edeltraud Baar, the psychologist, was walking at his side. Baar was an older woman who used to come along to the day room after the quiet hour and gather up their completed writing and drawing exercises. Recently she had been observed in the corridor several times, talking with Mrs Rohrbach after visiting Becker in his cell. Eventually, Adrian also caught sight of Doctor Erwin Jekelius somewhere in the middle of the cluster of doctors. He looked surprisingly young and might have been taken for an accompanying junior medic if it hadn't been for the observant look in his eyes and his restrained way of walking, as if any minute he might have to take control over where he was going and what he had to do next. He took a folder full of documents that Sister Bertha handed him but turned to the boys at once, without looking in the folder, and briefly cleared his throat. Immediately, everyone fell silent. Even at the edge of the group, where Doctor Gross had been continuing his conversation with Matron, the talk died down as if someone had turned a switch.

Children, Doctor Jekelius began,

I shall begin by reminding you why you are here.

(He spoke in the same way as he moved, in a low voice, sounding slightly tense but at the same time almost too gentle.)

I am not sure that you understand that you are the chosen ones. One day will be the everlasting day when the Great German Reich will arrive and you will be granted the delight of growing up in the light instead of enduring the shame and darkness that has been the fate of your fathers and mothers. However, you children must also be aware of the sacrifices that stepping up into this light of day has demanded. Not only have our brave soldiers who fight in the trenches been forced to risk their lives for your sakes, but you who are the chosen ones must know that obligations come with such a privilege.

Terrible offences have been committed here, in your section. The name of our Führer has been denigrated. The boys who were guilty of this have been punished but I will now make it clear to you, once and for all, that misdemeanours of this kind will not be tolerated. They must be rooted out and shall be rooted out even if they have to be burnt out of your bodies. To carry our German flag high, and to honour our Führer everywhere and at all times, are not only our obligations and highest responsibilities. These are also ways in which we prove that we are chosen. A true Aryan, proud of his race and his people, will regard the regulations of this institution as his guide and apply them rigorously. In doing so, he will become an ideal for others to follow. Even though he is not yet strong or grown up enough to bear arms in defence of the Reich and the Führer, he is still willing to make every sacrifice asked of him, as he knows that this is how he can show his true origin and his deepest loyalty. And, as for the rest of you – children! – you who believe it possible to get away with guile and laziness – for you I have the message that not one of you who have not been proven worthy will be saved. Not one. Heil Hitler!

HEIL HITLER! The reply rose from the tightly constricted throats of thirty children who all raised their arms in the correct German greeting. Doctor Jekelius had turned away as if the sight of all these suddenly far too eager boys made him weary. Next, the selection process would follow and the selected chosen ones separated from the less worthy. Accompanied by Mrs Rohrbach, a smiling Doctor Gross walked slowly past the boys in the front row. Then he turned and started to walk back, meanwhile scrutinising the boys in the back row while Mrs Rohrbach read to him from a list of names. Now and then, Gross would stop, take hold of an arm or a chin, sometimes simply using his thumb to part lips that fear had kept tightly closed or to force screwed-up eyelids apart. Now and then, he said something incomprehensible for Sister Bertha to note in the big folder. And then they reached Julius Becker. They stayed there for what must have been just a short moment but which felt like an eternity to everyone. Nobody said anything. Doctor Gross smiled. And went on to say: *We can only hope that you have improved somewhat, Becker, now that you've had time to think through the consequences of what you did.* Still, he didn't sound angry or anything, just amused. He also kept smiling (he had smiled like that at Sister Bertha, in a partly knowing, partly supercilious way) and even winked, barely noticeably, with one eye as if to send a message to say that what would happen next was a matter between him and Julius, and nobody else. How Julius reacted is not on record, because the boys could not turn their heads to have a look, but they could all see how Doctor Gross searched in the pockets of his white coat and found a small, round sweet, peeled the wrapper off with seductively slow finger movements. He then held the sweet up between thumb and index finger, delicately, as if it were a precious object, before popping it into Julius Becker's mouth, and he kept looking at him (his smile, if possible, even more comradely and encouraging) until Julius had started to suck at the caramel, at which point he nodded gently, contentedly. All the while, he kept a keen eye on the folder in which Sister Bertha now was writing very quickly as if there wasn't enough time to make a note of all essentials. And then it was all over, the procession reformed, more quietly now, though some of them were still chatting, and they set out along the corridor where Mrs Rohrbach stood, ready to open the door for them like a hostess about to say goodbye to her guests. And that was that (once more, but now it was final) and for those left behind, still standing with straight backs, and eyes locked onto the row of windows opposite, it was impossible to work out what was worst: the realisation that whatever had happened was irrevocable, that what had been decided at the inspection was a sentence that would be carried out, or the certainty that this was how things were and would be forever after, and that whatever plans they might dream up, they would never escape this kind of scrutiny and, yes, more than that, that the entire purpose of their existence here was the inspection with its crowning event when the reward for having been chosen, as promised, was the sweet that Doctor Gross with such punctiliousness inserted into the cavity of your mouth and watched to see being sucked so there was no way to remove the dank taste, mingling with the sticky sweet caramel flavour, of that alien finger inserted into your mouth and touching your tongue or the inside of your cheek. Eventually Adrian, too, would come to belong to the happy group of selected boys who were given one of Doctor Gross's sweets. For as long as the inspection continued, no one was safe.

Interrogation of a Traitor of the Fatherland From that day, Julius Becker seemed transformed. Before, he had been drifting about, scowling and withdrawn. Back then, the only time he brightened up at least a little was when his titular uncle delivered one of his rare parcels. After the inspection, Becker smiled continuously but it was a flat, dumb, joyless smile. When he opened his mouth, his gums were the colour of cement and his eyes, always directed at you but apparently not seeing you, looked as dull. Everyone knew that his end was nearing. Every day that passed with him still among them was painful. When they lined up to march off to school, Miseryguts was twisting with discomfort. He asked Hannes if they wouldn't come soon for the traitor to the Fatherland and take him away. Away, where? Hannes asked. And Miseryguts knew: to pavilion 15, of course. Julius stood just behind them but looked unmoved. His smile and his unseeing eyes did not flicker. Mr Hackl knew, too. Why else would he torment Becker with lots of questions when he hadn't as much as glanced at him before? All the schooling took place in pavilion 13, to the right of pavilion 15 and opposite the kitchen, which was on the other side of the site's central axis path that ran from the main entrance all the way to the church with the angels. Structurally, pavilion 13 was very like their own building but with the difference that the two floors had been changed to schoolrooms for four classes, all furnished with rows of coat hooks and linoleum on the floors to conserve heat. Mr Hackl taught older and younger children, and both boys and girls, but in separate classes. It was obvious that he preferred to be with the older boys, which conferred more of a sense of power and status even though, when all was said and done, each and every one of them was (as he incessantly told them) of the same ilk, all unteachable thieves and ruffians. Mr Hackl wore a monocle, though he could have been little more than thirty years old, and boasted that he was related to the great explorer Julius Payer who, in 1873, had discovered the group of islands in the Arctic called Franz Josef's Land. Or, *Emperor* Franz Josef's Land, as Mr Hackl would have it. The islands made up the world's northernmost archipelago, an uninhabitable place although nonetheless conquered by the Austrians, of course, characterised as they are by the resilience, self-discipline and willpower so typical of the Germanic race. Most of Mr Hackl's lessons, not just those in the natural sciences and geography, often ended up as long lectures on the character of mankind, how human moral strength and stature were reflected in physical activities and also, he argued, the other way round. Each lecture left him utterly exhausted, as if he had trudged across the same icy plains as Payer and his companions, so he had to support himself against the teacher's desk and wipe his forehead with a hanky. With an almost resigned gesture, he let the class take over the exploration of the topic by asking them a series of quick questions, like this one for Julius Becker:

Can Becker tell us what an evil person is?

The question was so surprising that most of them had no time to turn round to look but if Becker himself was surprised, he didn't show it. Unhesitatingly, he opened his mouth, inside which one could already see the grey bones of his cranium and said calmly, quietly, but with certainty:

An evil person is an extortionist and profiteer whose deceits and betrayals shame and dishonour the entire German race.

Mr Hackl didn't seem surprised either. He even looked pleased, as if he had recovered a little from his fatigue:

And what do we call such evil people, Julius?

We call them Jews and Bolsheviks, Mr Hackl.

And what about yourself, Becker, what kind are you? A Jew or a Bolshevik?

This time, Julius didn't have his answer ready quite so promptly. But Mr Hackl didn't care because he had got what he wanted and turned to the class:

I can inform the rest of you that Becker isn't a Jew because then he wouldn't be here. How we treat Bolsheviks is a matter I'll tell you about tomorrow.

That was the end of the lesson. Nobody said anything else. After the midday-meal break, Mr Hackl switches to teaching arithmetic. They get their 'homework' problems to solve during the quiet hour. As usual, they sit straight-backed, with their hands on the table, and stare at their notebooks. This time it is Nurse Demeter's turn to supervise them. She scans her subdued flock, eyes sharp inside her long, scoured, red-nosed face. After half an hour, Julius puts his hand up. *Do you want the toilet?* Demeter asks. Like Nurse Mutsch, she knows the routine. *Small or large?* Julius says large and Mrs Demeter sighs, goes to pick up the keys and brings two pieces of toilet paper. Julius gets up and follows her outside.

Scissors, says Hannes Neubauer.

No one has a clue what he means, as usual.

Then darkness falls and a boy walks inside the Mountain.

Guardian Angels The children in Spiegelgrund have guardian angels watching them from the summit of Gallitzinberg. Like the world's children, the angels are innumerable. They stand with their arms draped across each other's shoulders, like football players, so close that no one can get up to or past them. In case the Mongols attack, the guardian angels will protect us, Nurse Mutsch explains. To give the children an idea of the Mongols, she puts two fingers slant-wise over her eyes, bends forward and bares her teeth in a dreadful grin. Mongols and Bolsheviks are the same, really, she says. They eat children. That's why a lamp that casts a pale blue light must always be on in the dormitory when the children are asleep. If the Mongols were to attack, the nurses must have time to lead the children to the shelters and lock all the doors so the Mongols can't get in. Julius Becker doesn't believe the bit about the angels on the mountain and, on quite reasonable grounds, he doesn't believe in the Mongol story either. But he does believe in that strange, bluish angel-light that every night lifts the white-painted bedsteads and bedside tables from the floor and makes them float free in darkened space. This night, too, all the children are adrift. They are hanging helplessly inside their dreams, as if enclosed in large white cocoons. Inside one of these cocoons, Julius Becker slowly closes his hand around the handle of the pair of scissors he stole from the nurses' room. Afterwards, there will be much talk about the scissors and how Julius could have got hold of them. All tools and equipment that might hurt a child must be kept locked up in the appropriately designated cupboards or similar spaces and only Mrs Rohrbach or members of staff trusted by her have access to the keys, which means that if any such key goes missing or is suspected of having ended up in the wrong hands, the loss must instantly be reported. No report had been submitted. Nobody has seen any keys in the wrong place. Also, nobody has noticed that a pair of scissors has gone missing. However, it has of course been known for a long time that Julius Becker was in the habit of sneaking about without permission to investigate cupboards and drawers. Several of the children have already admitted as much. One morning, he was caught trying to hide writing exercises under his bed, actually quite comical efforts but nonetheless done without permission. In other words, cunning and deceit are not at all unfamiliar aspects of this child's behaviour. Why should he not also have managed to steal a pair of scissors without anyone noticing? But Julius sees the scissors quite differently: a long, thin object with properly sharp blades that feels warm to hold. At least, his fingers go warmer as he closes his hand around it. He might be thinking: I've got it now. Perhaps also: now Nurse Mutsch can't open my parcels. Or maybe he took the scissors simply to have a weapon to defend himself with. Against the other children, or against Nurse Mutsch, who came to him in the isolation cell, bent over him and spat in his face before demanding to be told what made him believe he deserved extra rations when no one else could have them, and then went for his pathetic little body, shoved his elbows and his drawn-up legs apart and hit him where it hurts most, on his midriff and genitals, on the small of his back and his neck, hit his Adam's apple until he couldn't draw air into his lungs and couldn't get a scream out either so it stuck, as if inside a gigantic, brightly lit space full of pain. Now, he has a pair of scissors in his hand but the pain is still inside him. Nurse Mutsch is still there, too. She bends over him and spits and rubs her saliva into his lips and closed eyelids. *You swine*, she says. *You have no right to live. We'll either send you to the idiots or else the doctor will inject you here and now*. And the scissors are no longer scissors. The object rises into the blue light, floating as the other objects do, he must get it back down before Mrs Rohrbach comes in and discovers it and, the moment he thinks this, Mrs Rohrbach is there. She slams the clapper against his bed, only his bed and nobody else's. *Bang bang bang bang!* it goes and all around him, the children climb out of bed and come to stand around him shouting *BANG BANG BANG BANG!* and Julius has to silence them and grabs the scissors with both hands, lifts them high up in the air and plunges the blades straight into himself, right into his middle. And then silence falls. For an instant, it seems as if even the blue angel-light dies down. But then the light comes back on and with it comes a pain too enormous to grasp and he clenches his teeth and contracts his nose and mouth to shut in the terrible scream that is raging inside him. Now he knows he can't get away with it. Not after taking the scissors. Not after what he has done with them. This time he must stab himself deeply, at best so deeply that the blades can't be pulled out and the thought of how he must do this grows so big there is hardly room for it in his head, it becomes even bigger than the pain and the glisteningly cold wave of nausea that flows through his body but, in that moment, he can't feel any hands holding the scissors. What can he do without hands? He loses his grip, manages to grab the edge of the mattress and haul his whole body around so that he lands on top of the scissors and, this time, the blades pierce the membrane lining of his abdomen, then his intestines, go all the way inside him where everything explodes, and the pain, too, and all bursts out, washes out; as if drowning, he reaches for the blanket, bites into it to hang on and save himself from the rising sea of blood that is pouring out of him and to save his scream, too, before it erupts from him. And no scream comes. Or perhaps he has already screamed, only so loudly he didn't hear it. Now all he hears is the sound of blood running over the edge of the bed onto the floor. He listens to it running, then dripping – drops falling in a rhythm that slows steadily – until, finally, the drips stop and only the bluish-violet angel glow is left, although it is also fading as the faint dawn light comes through the curtains and starts to make the white-painted beds blanch and their shapes solidify, as do the floor and the walls and the sleeping children. Daylight also brings the dry clatter of the day nurses' cork-soled sandals hurrying along the corridor outside; then, the sound of keys rattling, of double doors opening and Mrs Rohrbach entering, there's a shrill screech of her whistle, she claps her hands . . . *one two three four* . . . and everyone wakes apart from Julius who stays curled up in his bed, half on his back, half on his belly and, between his two partly clenched hands just below the diaphragm, the handles of the scissors protrude like a big white shout and there is blood everywhere: on the sheets, down the side of the bed, on the floor, even around Julius's eyes and mouth. His lips are twisted into a rigid grimace. But for the fear in his eyes, even after death, one might have thought he was lying there, laughing Mrs Rohrbach straight in the face.

V

Black Keys, and White Ones

She Who Waits I didn't know her, Hedwig Blei says (speaking about Anna Katschenka). Of course, she worked in pavilion 15, Jekelius appointed her to ward sister. I was there, nursing in the gallery wing, only for a few, fairly short periods and I thank the Lord to this day for being spared. My post was in pavilion 17 and even though both belonged to the same clinic, in practice there was little contact. It was only at the time when Katschenka started to take on some of Sister Bertha's duties that I got to know her a little better and, I must say, I never resented her as many of the others did. I felt that she might well be one of the nurses who are said to live for their work. Always there when she was needed. Always knew what was missing or what should be done. Never lost control, never lost her temper. Why, I'm not even sure she had a temper. She got around at this slow processional pace, sort of queenly, and the way she moved drove some people to distraction. Oh, hang on, let me hold up your train for you, I once heard Hilde Mayer say behind Katschenka's back. There was a rumour going around that she had had an affair of sorts with Doctor Jekelius in the past and that she went for the Spiegelgrund job just to serve under him; the story was that when he was called up later on, only about a year after she started, and then the entire institution was restructured, her world collapsed around her ears. I don't know if I believe any of that talk. There were so many rumours I sometimes had the feeling people got by on telling tales about each other and finding fault, and passing it on, or informing on someone, you know, for failing to show the right degree of political commitment or whatever it might be. That was something the Nazis brought with them and it did create an atmosphere of distrust and constant begrudging. I haven't come across anything as bad anywhere else. Anyway, if it was true that Katschenka had a special place in her heart for Jekelius, I must say that she took his departure quite coolly. I never saw the slightest crack in the façade she maintained against the rest of us. On the other hand, I did have a feeling that she was always waiting for something. I don't know what it could have been. Perhaps she just expected that she would crack. Or that someone would *command* her to crack. I know that she was one of the few who stayed behind with the children after von Schirach had capitulated and the entire leadership of the institution scarpered. It actually doesn't surprise me at all. Would you like me to say a little more about the others who worked in the clinic? First of all, I should make it clear that the two pavilions had quite different functions. The children in number 15 were the ones selected for 'treatment'. Pavilion 17 was for patients under observation and was meant to be a transit station where the children would only stay for about a month, maybe a couple at most, until someone reached a decision about them, one way or the other. Even so, some of the children were kept on for a really long time or sent back and forth between the wards. Take Felix Keuschnig, who started out in 17, and then went to 15, then to 17 again. Of course it was totally forbidden to spoil the children. But it couldn't be helped, some of the ones who were around for a long time became favourites. Sooner or later, everyone picked a pet to make a fuss of. Even Sister Katschenka. She had taken a fancy to a retarded boy they called Pelikan (it might have been his real name), whom she had trained to open the door for her whenever she visited the ward. That was quite typical.

About Emilie Kragulj– a dog. That's all. I won't say any more;

About Nurse Kleinschmittger – spent all her time badmouthing people (I don't think I've ever met anyone so quick to abuse others);

About Nurse Bohlenrath – I barely knew who she was (she worked on one of the wards for bedridden little ones);

About Hilde Mayer – she was quick and got on with things, a real workhorse. Before, she had been a psychiatric nurse at Steinhof and it showed. There were those who thought she was brazen, always ready to speak her mind about whatever it was. But she wasn't a snooping, false bitch like Kragulj. They said that Mayer was a Nazi; I mean, an actual party member. But she insisted it was a misunderstanding and that she had signed up because they demanded it of her if she was to keep her job. Everybody says that, of course, but just in Mayer's case it wouldn't surprise me if it was true.

About Erna Storch – now, she was a Nazi. She married a German from Sudetenland. I think she ran away with him after the war. I remember that she used to go around collecting for Winter Aid. Storch was in pavilion 15 at first, then in 17.

Frank was another one, Marie Frank, I think. A nice girl as I remember, who had a very hard time when the Russians came.

And Nurse Sikora. She was one of the ones who ran away. Sikora worked in pavilion 17 for a while. Built like a barn and an out-and-out sadist, if you ask me. It seemed to me that she positively enjoyed tormenting children. She often worked herself up into such a rage she could hardly breathe. To be honest, I think there were quite a few of those at Spiegelgrund. They were drawn to the place because there you were given the opportunity. To torture people to death, that is.

The Piano Player There is a piano in the first-floor day room, pushed up against the wall to be out of the way of nurses and others who need to pass by. Felix Keuschnig sits at the piano and plays for hours every day. He sits so straight you can see the tense tendons at the back of his neck. He strikes the keys unhesitatingly, with full force, and always plays incredibly fast: as if the music were already composed within him and he is in a hurry to make his hands execute the essential but clumsy mechanical movements. Nurse Blei stands or sits by him, listening. Sometimes, she suggests a song for him to play and they sing it together. Simple rhymes or songs for children, like 'Fuchs du hast die Gans gestohlen' ('Fox, you've stolen the goose'). Or 'Alle Vögel sind schon da' ('All the birds are already here'). Often, she needs only to hum the words and he picks out the melody on the keys, with the proper chords, and then sings along. His voice is breaking and sounds rough and hoarse (at least when he speaks) but he never misses a note. When he plays, he uses only the black keys. The white keys are dangerous, he says. You'll drown if you touch them. For him, playing is constant vigil, to keep safely on firm ground. Felix can play for hours on end without a break. If he is interrupted and someone attempts to make him think of something else, he howls like an animal, and he has been known to go for Nurse Hedwig's face and scratch it. That is why she sits by him, ready to catch the twisting, unwilling body that alternates between rigid, harsh resistance and slack, leaden weight. At these times, it becomes necessary to pilot him with cunning and gentle force out into the deaf, white, toneless world again, and preferably to do it quickly before Sikora or Storch or one of the others starts up the usual line about *never seen such an awful lot of fuss* and *why does she waste so much time on that good-for-nothing*: remarks also made within her hearing in kitchens and staff rooms, whispered behind doors that slam shut as soon as she comes near. On Sundays, Felix's mother visits him. Felix knows and counts down every week, starting at seven.

Now it's just four days to go, he will say, holding up the right number of fingers. But even though ahead of every visit he is buoyed up with expectation, he becomes cross and contrary on the day and, when his mother actually arrives, doesn't want to talk anymore. He cringes and fools around, rolls his eyes until only the whites show, climbs and clings onto whatever is at hand. Now and then, he emits loud howls, rather like mating calls, which embarrass all of them and his mother in particular. Blei observes his mother's hands as they keep sliding over the boy's body, caressing, protecting and attempting to cover it up, all at the same time. Felix's mother explains, explains away. Felix caught polio when he was one and a half, she says. The illness seemed to fade by the time he was four. For several years, he was a perfectly normal child who sang a lot and played like everyone else. The discipline problems began at puberty. He found it increasingly impossible to sit still, began to say things he didn't mean, lost concentration quickly and could become bad-tempered abruptly and unreasonably. Reluctantly, his mother agreed to register him with a Biedermannsdorf specialist children's home that ran support classes. When what they had to offer didn't help, he was taken in at Pressbaum. That's how it was these days: all children with something out of the ordinary about them had to be reported to the authorities, who made all the decisions about how to proceed, even if it was just something like certain learning difficulties, as in Felix's case. At Pressbaum, he contracted an inflammation of the gums which was left untreated for so long that the entire jaw area of his face became swollen and he had to have an operation. All this did Felix no favours, he got worse in every way and, in the end, it was decided that he should be transferred to Spiegelgrund. Felix's mother had no complaints about the care her son was getting here, she wanted to assure Hedwig Blei about that; but mightn't it have been better for the lad to stay at home or, at least, come home for Christmas and Easter? This was a matter she had raised in letters to the institution's board but no answer had been forthcoming. One of the secretaries in the office had told her in confidence that she didn't have hope. They wouldn't let go of Felix until he was fourteen. She then turned to the Gau-Jugendamt, the regional youth authority, even applied for an audience with the Reich Governor himself. Wherever she turned, she was cold-shouldered. But why shouldn't Felix be allowed to stay in his own home, when it is obviously good for him? Take his feet, for instance. At home we saw to it that he wore good shoes with the right kind of insoles, to help him walk properly. But at Pressbaum, they took the shoes away from him. They said that shoes were for well children and that if Felix couldn't walk normally he should stay in bed. But he must exercise his muscles to strengthen them, his mother said, how on earth can he ever get well unless his muscles are built up? And then she burst into tears. When she entered the day room, she had been walking ahead firmly and resolutely, and had used the German greeting. Now, this grown woman weeps because she isn't allowed to be with her son. Between the tears, she says that Felix isn't an idiot. Why, he can count and read and write, and has anyone ever heard a child sing and play so angelically?

Case Notes Doctor Gross had been duty doctor when Felix Keuschnig was admitted to Spiegelgrund and carried out the statutory medical examination. Gross had weighed and measured and assessed, and then made notes on his conclusions:

> *[. . .] intelligence appears structured as per average. Pat. can count and write simple words (capitals only). His behaviour is foolish – ludicrous. Doesn't reply to questions. Fairly good musical talents*

rendered useless by his other defects. Fundamentally unteachable and incapable of work. Probably a persistent post-encephalitic condition leading to mental decline. [. . .] The child's mother shows a tendency to hysterical reactions.

The last note had been added because the boy's mother had insisted on bothering him, Doctor Gross, with her silly insistence that Felix would be better off at home. There is a note in the margin recording that the mother is employed by the Wehrmacht which is followed by *(!)*, the exclamation mark intended to draw attention to the contrast between the mother's occupation and the fact that her child is unfit to live. Gross has also taken pictures of Felix, three in all, which show: one, the boy resists handling with his arms stretched straight out; two, he squints with his eyelids pulled back; three, he grimaces so wildly that his jaw seems dislocated, which makes him look imbecile. Felix behaves like this when making body contact with anyone, including his mother, at least initially. But of course Doctor Gross couldn't have known that.

There Is No Harm in the Boy Felix is one of the ward's bed-wetters. Still, he is dry during the day. Mostly, his state of mind is calm, at least if you compare him with the other children on the ward. As Nurse Hedwig writes in one of her day notes: *Felix is a kind and well-behaved child who calmly puts up with most things; his happiest moments are when he sits at the piano.* What Blei does not add is that Felix keeps himself to himself almost all the time when he isn't allowed to play the piano or his mother isn't visiting. He never plays with other children unless compelled and doesn't even talk with them. If you ask him for something he puts on the same stupid squint as when he feels disturbed or stressed. He gives gormless, irrelevant answers to even the simplest questions and can be crude and offensive. When a meal is served, he doesn't say thank you as he has been told but instead *Servos Kreutzer!* And he gulps down the food with incredible greediness, as if he hasn't seen food before or as if he could never be satisfied. There is ward time set aside for singing lessons, which is why the piano is there. But instead of leading the song herself and encouraging all the unwilling, half-witted children to sing along with her, though that admittedly only results in a distressing, baying noise, Nurse Hedwig allows Felix to sit down at the piano first and then tries to make as many children as possible gather around him. Felix accepts this. She whispers some of their songs in his ear and Felix plays and she sings and shows the children where to sing along or clap their hands, and they all sit around the piano, their eyes alight with excitement and hands raised, ready and eager to clap. And Felix plays song after song, all in the same safe key of C-sharp. When they've run through the songs, he starts from the beginning again. There is no end. Long after the other children have drifted away, he carries on hammering and crashing on the black keys. Then, a huge labour begins. She has to catch his resisting arms and make his entire oppositional body come to rest. At nearly fourteen, Felix is physically approaching adulthood. All the same, once he has calmed down, he curls up in her arms like a child. As if to show that that he might well have agreed to a temporary truce but that the contest has not ended, he often sits with his forehead pressed against hers and his eyes pierce hers like spears. All the same, the way he encloses her with his warm, moist breath is loving. She doesn't dare release him until they have sat eyeballing each other for ten minutes or more. *There is no harm in this boy*, she writes in her notes.

An Accident People from the country know how to look after themselves, Hedwig Blei had declared to Anna Katschenka. Nurse Blei had only failed once in her life to look after somebody else. That person was her younger brother, Nicolas. He and his older brother were as different as day and night. Matthias, like his father, seemed born to farm. He was slow to react but his mind was orderly and determined. By contrast, Nicolas was impulsive, proud, quick to anger and sometimes over-confident. Perhaps Hedwig loved him because she had been used to protecting him from early on (God knows, he did need a protector) but it could also be that she saw one side of her own personality reflected in his quick, fiery temperament, a side of her that at the time she couldn't or felt she shouldn't show. Ever since July 1936, when local and voluntary civil defence militias had been forbidden by the state, there had been flare-ups of trouble at the border with Czechoslovakia. Nazis, mostly Sudeten Germans, crossed the border at night to agitate and distribute flyers. Plenty of people in the area sympathised with them, but their father, Anton Blei, had no time for the Brownshirts. As far as he was concerned, they were criminals, the lot of them. When he saw young people march behind the banners of National Socialism, he would turn away and spit into the roadside dirt. Now, these people were suddenly around at night, even taking shortcuts across his own yard. The border guards never seemed to do more to stop them than they absolutely had to and whatever the insurgents were up to, they did boldly. Nico said that they smuggled arms as well. In the end, he and Matthias joined a handful of other local men in a voluntary Grünbach civil defence force. The men took turns to keep guard at night. It was illegal, of course, and a punishable offence. But who would stop them? The terrain was rough, a hilly highland that was hard to defend. Nico said he had an idea where some of the arms caches were. One suspect area was an old granite quarry where several insurgents had been spotted recently. The quarry had been abandoned long ago and had become overgrown. It was hard to reach unless you used the open road where you always ran the risk of being seen, so instead they decided to try getting into it from the back, down a narrow ravine. Nico, who was the slimmest and most agile of them, was roped up and four men took the weight at the top of the ridge. More rope, pay it out, more, Nico kept shouting. His voice grew fainter and fainter the further down he got. Then the rope went slack. An alarming silence fell. After waiting for half an hour, Matthias leaned over the edge and shouted his brother's name. The answer was a violent explosion. A cloud of stone dust and black smoke rose from the ravine. The explosion must have triggered a rockfall higher up on the mountain because they suddenly had to dive for cover from loose stones racing towards them and down into the smoke-filled ravine. Afterwards, no one could explain how it all started, or how the dynamite complete with blasting caps had ended up in the quarry. The newspapers reported the accident, if they did at all, in terms such as 'inexplicable'. When the emergency team reached Nico, he was still alive but both his legs had been nearly torn off at the knees and had to be amputated. He had a few weeks at home after the operation but was not the same Nico. He sat in his wheelchair by the window, staring outside with a distant look on his face. He never answered the questions about what he had discovered in the quarry, just turned his eyes away. Soon, he went down with a high temperature and the doctor thought that the wounds had become septic. They took him to the hospital again, but he had lost consciousness by the time he arrived. He died that night. Because Nico had been the younger son, he had left few possessions for them to inherit but Hedwig ended up keeping his best black shoes, bought for his first communion at thirteen. She brought them with her when she went to Linz to train to become a children's nurse, and again when she moved to Wien and took up a post at the newly opened clinic at Spiegelgrund. From time to time, she would pull the shoelaces out, polish Nico's black shoes and lace them up again. But dead people do not grow back into their old shoes, regardless of size. The enigmatic accident and Nico's sudden death made something inside Hedwig Blei freeze. She stands on the verge, watching the arrogant, insecure Hitlerjugend youths march past. In Linz, she sees the motorised Wehrmacht units roll across the bridge as joyful shouting fills the air and the local NSDAP cadres roar and sing so the streets echo with the noise until late at night. And she smiles, too, and the band of freckles glows on her blonde face. Those who don't know her well can never guess how she feels. She always comes across as easy-going, chatty and friendly, very much her older brother's sister. But behind the bright freckles, fury has hardened into a wall. Only those who have worked with her for a long time have tales to tell about the way her skin can suddenly pale to a chalky white, how the folds between her eyes deepen and her eyes cut like broken glass. Felix also notices when it happens. Then, the infantile spasms in his face vanish and he stands very still, as if listening for something.

Orthopaedic Shoes One morning, Hedwig takes Nico's old shoes to the orthopaedic workshop. The orthopaedic surgeon, Doctor Grieck, is doubtful at first. He wants a formal referral, he says, then he blames lack of time and, anyway, the shoes would be far too large and unwieldy for a child. But Nurse Blei is stubborn. She has been palpating the distorted ankles and arches of Felix's feet for weeks and is by now feeling quite sure about what is required. In the end, Doctor Grieck reluctantly agrees to try out a pair of loose insoles, and maybe also to strengthen the heel if necessary. Whatever else, she must bring the boy along. Doctor Grieck is a grumpy man with bushy grey eyebrows and grey hair in a spiky fringe around his bald head, which is crowned with a protruding, egg-shaped bulge. He sits on a low stool in front of Felix with the boy's left foot in his lap while Felix stands in front of him. The boy's eyes are glued to that smooth, shiny egg-shape. He looks as if he would like to touch it but doesn't dare. Just for once, he is on his best behaviour, doesn't grimace or resist the stranger's large hands that are touching his legs and feet. Perhaps the setting has silenced him. The orthopaedic workshop, with its high ceiling and long row of windows overlooking the old hospital garden, is a little like a schoolroom. It is a sunny, breezy day. The crowns of the trees are swaying in the wind and casting long shadows like pale curtains that sweep across the room's white walls and low workbenches. On the worktops lie finished or part-finished prosthetic arms and legs, and a whole hand with splayed rubber fingers. In the old days, Grieck and his team dealt with shoe lasts, strengthened soles and raised heels for people with club foot, when they had time in between making crutches and walking frames for elderly patients. But ever since the German *clinical experts* arrived with their lists of names and the hospital gradually emptied of the ill and the old, *that kind of work is few and far between*, Grieck says or rather mutters. Now, they mostly make prostheses for injured soldiers. Hedwig Blei stands nearby, watching intently as Nico's old shoes are adjusted to fit Felix's feet. She doesn't say anything. In pavilion 17, the doors at the back of the building have been opened wide so that children who are able to walk unaided can be outside. The area around the terrace is fenced off and nurses from the wards in the pavilion take turns to keep an eye on the children. Felix takes his first steps in his new shoes inside this enclosure. Like so many children damaged by polio, he has grown used to dragging and sliding his feet on the ground in order to avoid having to put his body weight on one leg only and now, when he really must move using his own muscle power, he hesitates a great deal and takes small, jerky steps as if wading in ice-cold water, while his posture is enough to express his resentment: one shoulder is pushed up close to the side of his face, his arms are bent and his hands left to dangle uselessly in front of his chest. Hedwig Blei watches from the day room window and sees him move towards the far end of the enclosed area, as usual trying to get as far away from the other children as he possibly can. *Paaah . . . !* the boy Pelikan wheezes. He has joined her at the window. Pelikan never goes outside willingly and prefers to creep from room to room, turn up in the doorways and listen along the walls, so he can keep tabs on what is going on, especially if it involves the other children; and next, *goodness, look at that boy, what's he up to?* Nurse Storch says. By now, she too stands at the window, watching the yard. Storch points at Felix. He has stopped and stands stock-still, looking down on his shoes as if in some mysterious way they have stuck to the ground. Nurse Sikora steps down from the terrace and starts to walk towards Felix. She seems agitated but determined and when Felix turns towards her – probably in response to what she is shouting at him – everyone can see the stain, roughly shaped like the African continent, which has spread across the crotch of his baggy trousers. The usual grimace disfigures his face as he turns to Nurse Sikora and, naturally, Sikora slaps his ugly face hard and then drags him, shoes and all, back into the building. The slam of the terrace door echoes all the way upstairs. *And what's the point, anyway,* Nurse Storch mutters, *giving* that *boy new shoes . . . ?*

Fatherlands The next day, she is called to the matron's office. Klara Bertha is at her desk and looks as if she has just bitten into something bitter and nasty. Sikora has clearly passed on the gossip. I hear that Nurse Hedwig has set out on her own initiative to supply the idiots with new footwear? she (Bertha) says. And Hedwig replies: they were my brother's shoes. Bertha: perhaps he had better have them back now. Hedwig: my brother is dead, he died defending his country. At first, Sister Bertha seems quite upset but she soon recovers her old, safe expression of patient goodwill. She keeps looking at Nurse Blei as if expecting her to explain just which country she has in mind or what, generally speaking, she means by 'country'. But Hedwig Blei doesn't elaborate. Instead, she says: Where I come from, we're not used to letting things go to waste. Bertha: and where does Nurse Blei come from, if you don't mind me asking? The amusement is back in her voice but also a hint of relief. As if Matron feels reassured now that any discussion of the country's defence has been dropped. She starts leafing through some papers, pretending to be preoccupied. You're good with children, Nurse, she says. Your colleagues recognise it. You will now return to nurse in the gallery. An urge to dress the children as you fancy is not quite so likely to arise there.

The Miraculous Births There is an outer and an inner world. The outer one is filled with unceasing clamour while the stillness in the inner world is like that of an early winter morning when the snow has just stopped falling. Hedwig Blei remembers such a morning. She was four or maybe five years old. They had just finished breakfast when a chorus of voices from the yard started to call to them. Outside, their neighbours and even folk from as far away as Grünbach were crowded closely together. Their frost-reddened faces seemed suspended inside a drifting cloud of vapour created by their breaths. They were on their way to Ratschnig's farm nearby, where a heifer was about to give birth to a monster calf. The words 'monster calf' stuck in her memory, as did the sight of all the bulkily dressed people stomping about in the thick layer of new snow, their shouting voices sliding across a silence that had been blown clean by the snow-laden wind. At Ratschnig's (once they got there), it was like a Christmas fair. Everyone was yelling and laughing, the dogs were barking and howling and tugging at their leads. The crowd was especially dense near to the cowshed door. Nico, who was bony and quick on his feet, had managed to squeeze inside and could report afterwards how the men had hauled the calf out (he didn't know if it was born alive or not) tied to a long rope, carried it out into the barnyard and set to beating and stabbing it with spades and bars while the farmer had kept shouting *spare the head . . . spare the head . . .* As the years went by, the monster birth was added to the many portents or local accidents that served as measuring rods sunk into the flow of time. This or that, people would say, happened the year the monster calf was born at Ratschnig's. It somehow added weight to the event. The episode stayed in Hedwig's mind, too. Not just because of the calf. After all, her childish eyes hadn't been allowed to see it. But everything that surrounded its birth seemed etched into her memory with unreal precision: the silence after the snowfall, the winter sky clearing into a nearly turquoise blue, and all their neighbours standing in the yard as if they had gathered to look for someone missing, a runaway or a suspected drowning perhaps (one of them had brought a hurricane lamp, though it was already light). And she remembers their elated eagerness, as if the local folk had already fantasised about the heavy tools they would use to beat the calf to death. And there was the thought of the calf itself: how it must have felt as it was pulled out of its mother's large, warm womb into a world of noise and shouts and iron bars that thumped and hit and, then, this terrible pain. There are no monster births, as her mother used to say: all living things born to God are miracles. This was how she had wanted to see the children in pavilion 15. But it was not to be. In the eyes of those who administered and managed the clinic, its patients were not actually children but specimens, living examples of neurological and physiological defects, or of various pathological processes, all conditions whose progress were worth observing. Nothing was real in any other sense, not even the convulsions and the pain that plagued some of the children continuously. If they were sedated, it was not to ease their suffering but to put a stop to their screaming. The doctors would arrive at regular intervals to study them, to select whose life should be taken immediately and whom it might be worth troubling to keep under observation for a little longer. Once the decision to eliminate had been made, they would return to take notes about the actual dying. In a group, always. For it would not do to look into the eyes of the newborn animal: the creature obviously has no idea about the infernal flaw that makes it unfit to live. It's easier to kill if you are part of a group. When you act with others, you don't personally kill a living thing but join a battle against a common threat. The staff in pavilions 15 and 17 showed absolute obedience to their superiors, not only because the strictly hierarchical order diffused responsibility so that no one individual took a life, but also because it reduced killing into an outcome of the order of things. It also followed that you must not allow yourself a second's inactivity. Standing around, crestfallen and empty-handed, gave you time to think. As Hedwig Blei admitted afterwards, it wasn't that there was such a tremendous amount of work to do on the ward. Truly, the daily routine was relatively light because most of the children were heavily sedated most of the time. But being constantly on the move prevented you from taking in how absurd the situation was: this was a clinic for severely ill children which did not specialise in making the patients better, or at least provide them with appropriate treatment, but, on the contrary, in avoiding any treatments that would make them harder to kill. The reason, it was argued, was that such children constituted a major threat against the Germanic peoples. Not that this was something you could discuss. The entire clinical unit operated under a duty of silence so total that it seemed like mental quarantine. But people had to talk about something, of course. Hence, the gossiping. No one escaped the wagging tongues, not superiors, not colleagues (when absent). The gossip offered one way, at least, of talking about what was going on. The clinic's staff included several former Steinhof employees, some of whom had been there long before the reorganisation. Like Hilde Mayer, who often spoke about when the so-called medical experts had turned up at the main asylum (most of these experts were Germans and members of the SS). They had walked around from ward to ward, always led by Doctor Jekelius because he was the one who made the final decisions. Later, the psychiatric nurses had been ordered to take the selected patients to the waiting buses and, though some of the elderly ones knew no better than to think that they had caused too much trouble where they were and that's why they had to be moved, the majority understood only too well, and wept and tried to hang on to whatever they could reach – beds, door posts, stair railings. By then, many of the nurses were in tears, too, although perhaps not always for the reasons one might have assumed. Naturally, some people were remembering their own old and ill, like I did, for instance, Mayer said, but the Lord be praised, my old folk were still mentally sound and, she added, I seem reasonably sane as well, at least as far as I can judge. Still, to be honest, most of the nurses were probably thinking of themselves and their jobs. What will happen to them, they worried away, now that the psychiatric patients are carted off and the hospital is to close? They might well be surplus to requirements. Jekelius gave a reassuring speech to the entire staff in which he said that there would surely be enough work for everyone. *Their* (here he meant his and his colleagues') work had, to the best of his knowledge, only just begun. When he had finished, there were no more tearful faces to be seen. When Hedwig Blei thought about Jekelius, she was often reminded of something her father used to say: you recognise the cock pheasant by his feathers. To her, the doctor was an embodiment of affectation: his gentle voice, so strenuously soft that one had to stand on tiptoe to hear what he was saying; his deliberately graceful movements, used to emphasise every word he uttered. Jekelius was seen, almost always, in the company of others. In his case, this was not because of some inner need to blend in. Somehow, Jekelius always managed to be a little behind, or drifting away from the group, as if wanting to keep his distance from those who were closest to him. It meant that it was always the *others* who had to turn to address him, while he never had to come after them. A man who behaves like this wants to be seen at any cost. Vain and self-assured, certain of his absolute power. Hedwig saw him only very rarely, though. His absences were due to his in-service travels or other tasks and, besides, he had no medical reason to stay at Spiegelgrund. The day-to-day running of the clinic was the responsibility of Doctor Gross and Doctor Türk, who were in charge of one ward each. The staff in pavilion 15 was working on a duty rota that meant Nurse Hedwig was on nights at least twice a week. According to the regulations, one doctor should be on call every night but Hedwig Blei had only rarely seen either of them. The rule was also that the doctor must only be called when a patient's condition worsened enough to require medical attention or when one of the children died and the doctor had to sign the death certificate. But it happened often enough that Gross, who, like Türk, had been provided with a house on site, took his time to 'come down', making the point that turning up twice was surely unnecessary. If he didn't come, the dead child was left lying until the morning. What was wrong with that? Overall, Hedwig Blei said, the lack of drama was striking, perhaps in particular when it came to the killing and the dying. Even though nobody had cared to state it openly, Blei had realised almost at once that the children's lives were taken deliberately. True, hints were dropped all the time. Don't you think these children are sleeping a little too much? Nurse Frank had asked rather rashly when she was new to nursing in the gallery, and Hilde Mayer had replied: Just practising for their eternal sleep! Give Mayer half a chance and she'd let her tongue run away with her. But, perhaps there was no need to speak out. The attitude of the clinic's leadership sent its own unmistakable message. They often couldn't be bothered even to begin treating a patient or to complete a treatment once it had begun. Why, they weren't even prepared to have the temperature on the ward kept at a comfortable level. Wartime scarcity was blamed, hence the need to save fuel. Nonetheless, the staff was ordered to keep the windows open at all times, even during raw, damp and cold days in winter, even though the children were in very poor condition and often febrile. Most of the severely ill patients stayed in the gallery for just a few weeks but, even so, many years later Hedwig Blei had clear memories of some of them. A baby boy, six or seven months old, called Heinz something (she no longer remembers his surname) had a tumour on his back, a fist-sized growth like a knobbly little rucksack. He could only lie on his side with his face pressed against the sheet. In this awkward position, he breathed like a wounded animal, his frail ribcage heaving up and down like the gill slits of a fish. A small girl in the bed next to him cried out all the time, as if something was slowly tearing itself to pieces inside her. No one tried to find out what caused the pain. She was prescribed huge doses of morphine and died within a week. Several of the children were tied to their beds to stop them from hurting themselves or eating their stools. Some of them had been strapped down for so long that their wrists had deep, infected gashes that seeped fluid and pus. A seven- or eight-year-old girl had initially been restrained but the ties had to be removed when blisters on her lips spread and turned into large, weeping sores. Hedwig Blei had asked Cläre Kleinschmittger for a little salicylic acid to apply to the girl's lips. Two days later, Kleinschmittger mentioned that salicylic acid had been taken from the medicine cupboard to Katschenka, who demanded to know the circumstances. Kleinschmittger told her that Blei had used the drug. A long time had passed since their meeting in the sluice room when Blei had asked Katschenka if she was married. Now, their respective ranks had been clearly established. I will never forget her coming towards me with that slow, processional pace of hers, Blei said. Katschenka had already caught my eye but because her whole face was so immobile, down to the muscles and bones, she always seemed to be smiling. It took an age for her to reach me. When I told her what I had needed the medicine for, she said that in this ward we never use anything unnecessarily. Soap and water would have been sufficient, she told me; that was all, no reprimand, nothing, only the gaze she fixed on me, so cold, as if I had done something disgusting, almost perverse. Afterwards, they had to apply the straps again because the girl wouldn't stop scratching. She must have been in utter torment but Doctor Türk just prescribed more morphine, and when Blei arrived the following morning, the girl was lying very still. Her swollen eyelids were closed and her hair stuck out in stiff, sweaty tufts around her head. No one had bothered even to disentangle her hair and comb it. Why should they, she was going to die soon anyway. When the doctors did their rounds, Katschenka always kept a step or so behind them. It was her job to summarise what the nurses had written in the day notes about each patient. Just two or three sentences, whispered into the ear of the medic on duty. Nothing more was required to indicate the child's condition and many of her short confidences were dismissed by the doctors before she had finished whispering. There was no telling whether that was due to plain indifference or whether everything had already been decided and matters were taking their due course, so there was nothing more to say. But sometimes Hedwig Blei felt sure she had seen an expression of distaste flit across Doctor Gross's face and *der kommt dran*, he would say. Blei says: I will always remember that phrase of his, *that's that, then*. Katschenka didn't bat an eyelid, just stood there, her grey face as impenetrable as always, waiting for Doctor Gross to move on to the next bed, but I'm certain that she understood the doctor's intentions perfectly and knew to whom and at what dose a certain drug would be administered in the evening. She was the perfect ward sister. Like a clock counting down the minutes to death. Meanwhile, she watched and waited and saw to it that everyone else was doing her duty. Not even Hilde Mayer, who would tell jokes and make fun of everyone, ever dared to stand up to Katschenka. The children died, one after the other, and later on, when Doctor Illing had succeeded Jekelius, the death rate was two or three every night. Once a child had finally given up the ghost and the death certificates had been filled in and signed, the body was wrapped in a simple shroud and sent off to autopsy via the back door to avoid any troublesome confrontations. By then, the child's parents would already have been informed but Katschenka insisted that no relatives must be admitted to the pavilion. If they wanted to see their child one last time, it had to happen somewhere else. Blei had, several times, witnessed incidents when upset relatives tried to force their way in. The porters had to be called and if they couldn't handle the situation, someone phoned the police. But there was never a word of criticism from the staff, not even after alarming, violent incidents such as these. What mattered was the clockwork running of the institution. In one of the secretarial rooms, Marie Kölbl was typing out the standard letters to the families of the dead children. The letters had been dictated in good time. The door to Kölbl's room was always kept closed and if the clatter of the typewriter ever stopped, it was only because she got up to open or close the window. Afterwards, the typing started again, sounding stronger or fainter, but it never stopped for any length of time.

> *Your child would probably never have learnt to sit upright or walk. Your child suffered from recurring convulsions, which no medical treatment could cure to any significant extent. Your child died from an attack of pneumonia that normal children with fully developed immune defence systems can deal with. Your child passed away peacefully and quietly without much suffering. It should be of some comfort to you to know that, for your child, death was a blessed release.*

But those miraculous young beings: what did the world look like to them, deep in the sleep of the drowned? Nurse Blei tells the following story: one evening, when she had just turned up for the night shift, the doors banged and strange voices were heard in the corridor. She went to look and saw Doctor Jekelius in the doorway to the main ward. He was dressed like an ordinary citizen in a coat and a hat. Two people stood next to him, a man and a woman, both upper-class types, Blei said, it was easy enough to spot. The woman's first impulse was to cover her face with her hand to keep the smell at bay and Jekelius put his hand protectively on her arm. *Now, now, don't worry,* he said. They had been drinking, the alcohol fumes hung like a cloud around them. *Where is the boy?* the man said impatiently.

Doctor Gross turned up shortly afterwards, so they must have phoned him. The smile on his face was the one he reserved for when he wanted everyone to know that he took no personal interest in what was going on but was present on professional grounds only. Jekelius said that Mr and Mrs whoever (Blei didn't pick up their name) had decided that they would bring their son home *gegen Revers* – with a consent form – and that he, Jekelius, had granted them their wish. Even later, after she had grasped the context, Blei couldn't stop being surprised that Jekelius had let her see him in that state, so obviously the worse for drink. However, Gross seemed not surprised in the slightest or, if he was, hid it well. He took the documents Jekelius gave him, started to look through them and said in an off-hand tone that Nurse Blei should go and dress the boy. The child weighed next to nothing in her hands and was so deeply sedated that he didn't wake up even when she lifted him close to her face. His thin breath smelled slightly of ammonia. In the morning, when Blei went off duty, the bed was still empty but if Katschenka took note of this, she never showed it. It could be that, to her, the child had died the moment it arrived. An empty bed would anyway soon be filled by another severely ill child. All according to Jekelius's orders.

The Drowned Just before Christmas, she is back at work in pavilion 17. As usual, Pelikan opens the door for her and, as usual, Felix is playing. But now he doesn't turn to her when she sits down next to him. He still takes no notice when she strokes his hair and bends forward to whisper in his ear. He just plays more loudly then before, crashing down on the black keys so that the bones in her face feel like shearing and Nurse Sikora shouts from the corridor *WILL YOU STOP THAT INFERNAL . . . !* Sikora is on her way into the day room but stops on the threshold when she sees Blei. A false smile spreads over her flat features. Nurse Blei's little favourite hasn't been a good boy recently, she says. Then, out comes a long tale of everything Felix has been up to while she was away. Spilled his food, made a noise in the day room, said very bad words to staff, even wandered around hitting other children in the face. All that is part of his routine now. Seems his evil spirit is getting out, Sikora says. One day, she placed him in solitary for a few days and it did him a lot of good. Isn't that so, Felix? she asks, and pretends to pay attention while Felix becomes very ill at ease, twists and bends, and finally manages to tear himself free from Hedwig's grip. Hedwig follows him. They sit together in a corner of the room. The boy called Pelikan listens, leaning against the wall. Can't you hear the row upstairs? he says. Who's making a row? Blei asks. The girls, Pelikan tells her. She can't reply because Felix struggles to get away. Finally, she manages to catch his legs between her own so she can grab hold of his face and inspect it. The boy has sores in his mouth running from the corners of his lips upwards to the nostrils. His breath smells badly. She tries to force his jaws apart to see if his gums have become infected again. Then Nurse Sikora is back in the doorway. We have to tie him at night because he can't keep his hands under control, he just scratches at the sores all the time, she explains. Perhaps it would've been better to cut his nails then, Nurse Blei says and holds up Felix's dirty, uncared-for hands in the light. But Nurse Sikora sees no fingernails. Only one thing preoccupies her: the ineffectual hatred that, for some reason, she feels towards her colleague.

Cancelled Leave The number of children in the pavilion has grown a great deal since Matron had dispatched her to serve time in pavilion 15. Erna Storch tells her why. The reason is that the reform-school side of the institution is constantly sending their 'hopeless cases' on to the clinic. Seemingly, Doctor Krenek thinks we're more likely to succeed with the tasks they can't manage over there, Nurse Storch says. They have also opened a new section for 'unteachable' girls on the second floor. These are the girls Pelikan is listening out for all the time. Most of the girls are there because they have failed to complete their duty-year, the *Pflichtjahr*, or tried to run away from foster families. Hedwig Blei's ward is by now so short of space that some beds are placed in hallways and corridors, which tends to make the already tense children even more nervous. One of these displaced children, a boy, just lies on his back, staring into the distance. He refuses to lift his hand to take the mug of water she wants to give him, despite having normal motor control, and fixes his eyes on the wall clock as if his gaze is stuck to the hands. A somewhat undersized nine-year-old with scabies sores on his head – his name is Otto Semmler – potters around the ward all the time, looking for an adult hand to hold. If he doesn't find anyone, or if Sikora or Storch slaps him or angrily pushes him away, he cries heart-rendingly. He doesn't want to stay in his bed. Soon, Blei realises that she is accompanied by Otto wherever she goes. It feels like existing with one hand permanently tied behind your back. She wishes that someone would look after Felix, but who would that be? Caring for individual children is not part of anybody's proper work. Whenever he is allowed to play the piano, he hammers the black keys as if they were nail heads and Nurse Sikora screams as if the nails were driven into her. One Sunday, Hedwig sees Mrs Keuschnig standing between the beds in the corridor, looking upset. She must have visited Felix, because she holds one of the black shoes. *What is this?* she asks, lifting the shoe by its laces with an expression of unspeakable disgust. *Are you preparing for his funeral already?* Mrs Keuschnig's face is long and thin, with marked folds on her cheeks. She gives the impression of someone who has spent her entire life exercising self-control. Now, when she bursts into tears, her eyes flood. With tears trickling down her cheeks, she says that she cannot stand watching what the clinic is doing to her son, their mismanagement means that he has lost ten kilograms in half a year and now she is told that it is Felix's own fault that he doesn't eat enough even though the doctor has made a note about a big sore inside his mouth which, it seems, has been caused by malnutrition. She says that she doesn't dare tell her husband about the bad treatment of their son for fear of how he will react. In letter after letter, she has begged Doctor Jekelius to let Felix come home over Christmas, at least for a few days. It surely can't be impossible? Just look at how crowded the ward is. Besides, Felix always gets better when he has been at home for a while. But Doctor Jekelius has not replied and every time she has tried to phone him she has been told that he is away on business or engaged with someone else. Hedwig Blei is tempted to tell Mrs Keuschnig that if she wants her son back, she had better be rich and, preferably, have a husband with a top position in the party – maybe her husband isn't enough of a high-up? Instead, she promises to try to put in a good word for her the next time Doctor Jekelius comes to the ward. But it takes a very long time before he visits pavilion 17 again. Meanwhile, the rumours about his out-of-office activities grow wilder and wilder. Several children, some of whom had already been passed for treatment, have been discharged between one day and the next, or else 'collected' from the clinic on unclear premises. One might even get the idea Jekelius is running another clinic on his own, Nurse Mayer suggests. On the side. Where he goes on all his 'business trips'. Another notion of Mayer's is that Jekelius was ordered to present himself to Professor Gundel, the city councillor, and that Gundel proceeded to tell Jekelius that his behaviour has attracted unfavourable attention in many quarters, all the way up to the Department of State in Berlin. Mayer claims that she has reason to believe they will 'see the back of Jekelius' before the year is out. But when Jekelius finally does turn up on the ward, he seems very far from a broken, haunted man. His movements have the usual, calculated arrogance. He progresses through the ward, followed by Sister Bertha, Doctor Gross and Edeltraud Baar, the psychologist, and if that smile had not been glued to the face of Gross, that exaggeratedly broad, jovial smiling at all and everyone in order to distance himself from his surroundings, one might have thought that nothing had changed. This time, the round stops for a long time at young Keuschnig's bed. Doctor Gross peers into the boy's mouth and the two doctors exchange a few brief sentences; but when Jekelius then turns to Blei it is not to explain a planned intervention:

I gather the boy's mother has been running around the ward. I expect Nurse Blei to keep her at arm's length in the future. For your information, Nurse Blei, from now on all leave for this boy is cancelled.

Doctor Gross, who stands close to his superior, looks as if the two of them together have succeeded in some great venture.

It's these marginal cases. If we give up on them we might as well admit defeat altogether.

This is that last thing she will ever hear Doctor Jekelius say as director. When she comes back from her Christmas break a few days into the New Year, she learns that Jekelius has been called up and has joined the army, and that Doctor Jokl is acting medical director until a permanent solution has been found. Meanwhile, Felix's condition has become much worse. The swelling that deforms his jaw is now so large he can hardly swallow. He lies on his back and breathes through his mouth, and the open wound inside his mouth must be dreadfully painful because he is whimpering and mewling, and rubbing the back of his head and the side of his face against the bed even though they have tied him down. She knows that they will try to transfer him to pavilion 15 as soon as possible and if he arrives there in the condition he is in now, he won't leave the place alive. On the Sunday, when she is on night duty, she phones Doctor Türk who is on call that evening to tell the doctor that the boy, whose health has declined rapidly over a short time, now has a high fever. She adds that it might be a symptom of sepsis. Half an hour later, Doctor Türk arrives, at first sceptical about the need to examine Felix at all. Have you managed to make him take any fluids? she asks. Not really, Blei replies. He can't swallow. Doctor Türk produces a spatula and a torch. While she roots around in the boy's mouth, Hedwig tells her about the jaw operation Felix underwent just before he arrived at Spiegelgrund, quoting his mother's description. It's all in his case notes, she points out. Doctor Türk glances quickly at the notes Blei hands her. Would it be possible to see if they can receive him in pavilion 3? One section of pavilion 3 is set aside for the reform school's casualty reception and sickbay. I shall have a word with Doctor Hübsch tomorrow, Doctor Türk says. I can't make that decision. Next morning, Felix is moved to the ward in pavilion 3. Two male nursing assistants carry him between them. Blei accompanies them, and carries the black shoes, the only things in his bedside table (apart from the regulation towel, soap and toothbrush). A nurse called Marie Darnhofer works in pavilion 3. Hedwig now knows that Marie had been at the special children's care home in Pressbaum while Felix was there. Felix recognises her at once and, for the first time in many weeks, a smile spreads over his swollen face. Two days later, Felix has surgery and when Nurse Darnhofer phones to say that he is out of the anaesthesia, Hedwig goes across to sit with him for a while. Most of his face is covered in a big bandage with only his eyes and the tip of his nose showing. He can't talk but no longer casts his head about to distract himself from pain. They stay silent. She plays with her fingertips on his arm. *Fuchs du hast die Gans gestohlen*, she plays. *Gib sie wieder her*. After a while, Felix plays along on top of his blanket, using his free arm.

Deserters The next time Hedwig Blei can take time off to drop in, two soldiers have been placed in the same ward as Felix. It looks quite strange. The small boy with his chin in bandages bedded down between two grown men who are far too large for their beds. One soldier is asleep with his back turned to the ward and snores fit to make the walls shake. Nurse Marie says that several of her colleagues have asked to be moved here to nurse war casualties. Their applications stress their patriotic zeal but secretly they all hope to find the right man. Marie laughs and Hedwig realises how wonderfully easy it is to talk to Marie. Here in the sickbay there is none of the hostility that makes working in pavilion 17 so grim, what with the busily gossip-mongering Nurse Sikora and Nurse Storch, her puffed-up companion who snoops everywhere and threatens with the sack anyone who doesn't donate to Winter Aid. Hedwig Blei now and then gives herself errands on other wards where the war-wounded men have been accommodated. Most of patients are young and have been diagnosed with various battle-induced neurotic conditions, which makes them, in the eyes of Wehrmacht officialdom, a bunch of defeatists and deserters, though defeatism isn't what first comes to mind when you see them, often covered in bandages, some with facial burns or shrapnel wounds. Two of the patients are in wheelchairs after having had both legs amputated. One of them, just a lad, with a wide face and chiselled features, reminds her of her brother. If Nico had lived with his legs blown off and his crushed pelvis, maybe he too would have been forced to stay here. The thought makes her feel sick at heart. The two wheelchair-bound men have been joined by two other patients, who have rigged up a card table between them. When she comes in, all four interrupt their game and their eyes follow her. She smiles at them but they don't return her smile, only stare as if their eyes can't quite take in what they see. On her way back, she spots Felix out walking in his black shoes. He is testing himself, all alone on the small lawn behind the pavilion, he takes one step forward, stops, then a couple of sideways steps, then one more forward. He reminds her of a chess piece moving on a very large board. Between black and white squares. Afterwards, when she sits by his bed, he points to his mouth to show her that he is hungry. Then he asks for his mother. And, then, for his piano.

Doctor Illing In the summer of 1942, six months after Jekelius's call-up to the front, a new medical director is appointed, a Doctor Illing. He is German. Everyone is making a big thing out of this: he comes *from there*, probably on direct orders from Berlin. Ernst Illing is Jekelius's diametrical opposite: a stocky, broad-shouldered, energetic man who stalks the corridors at a fast pace. He has a habit of sticking his head forward as he speaks, perhaps to compensate for being short or to make sure the other won't escape. Illing speaks with a marked Saxony dialect and the powerful tobacco he favours makes his breath smells sour and thick, and it stains the brief grin he bestows automatically on anyone who listens to him and does what he says. His domineering manner and sharp, piercing eyes make Hedwig Blei feel uncomfortable, and the new, stricter rules he enforces worry her. Already, on his first day, he states that visiting will be restricted from now on. No visits unless arranged beforehand with himself or, when he is absent, the acting medical director.

Visiting hours must be used to greatest effect and not to indulge the whims of relatives. Your work here is your contribution to the war effort, he announces in his loud, rather high-pitched voice. From now on, it is our duty to the Fatherland to maintain an unimpeachable front to the world. He also emphasises how crucial it is to keep the patient's case notes up to date. This is a medical establishment, he says. Every detail in the course of disease can become of the utmost importance to diagnostic assessment and the final decisions on treatment options. Illing seems to have recognised Sister Katschenka's usefulness. She is to act as Matron Bertha's deputy when the senior nurse has been required 'for other tasks'. Unlike Jekelius, who only leafed through the case notes, Illing wants to know all there is to know about every child. There is one boy in pavilion 17 who interests Illing in particular. The boy's name is Jakob Nausedas. He is eleven years old but looks about six. In the photographs Gross took of him, Jakob is almost alarmingly beautiful, with large, deep-set brown eyes, dark hair and delicately sculpted ears. Because he will not lie still at night, he has been placed in a netted bed but so far not in a straitjacket. He usually sits absolutely still in the middle of the bed with his legs crossed under him, staring straight ahead. He is very shy. If someone comes close, he pulls a blanket over his head. Even so, Blei has seen him up and about several times. Unlike many of the children, he seems to have no physical impediments. In fact, he moves like a little angel, leaping along with alternate long and short steps and, as he runs, he puts the front of each foot down first as if to use its arch to lift off. He seems fearful of being hit, holds his hands uncertainly in front of his face or upper body to cover himself, even when it is just Pelikan, on the alert as always, who is on the move to open the door for the caravan of white-clad doctors and nurses. By the time they are all inside, only the tip of

Nausedas's nose and one glinting eye peep out from underneath the blanket. The blanket was with him when he arrived, Nurse Sikora explains to Doctor Illing, who has already asked Blei to lower the side of the child's bed. Standing next to his chief, Doctor Gross gives an account of the patient's convulsions followed by paralysis, attacks that usually occur at night. Another characteristic of the fits is that Nausedas's voice grows deeper and somehow strange. Almost as if the boy was possessed, Sikora suggests. Doctor Illing impatiently skims the notes that Katschenka has given him.

Kaunas, now, isn't that in . . . ?

In Lithuania, Katschenka fills in.

And how come the boy has ended up here?

He's an orphan, Katschenka says.

He's actually circumcised, Doctor Gross says and turns away with assumed indifference, as if to say that he is done with this. But as far as Doctor Illing is concerned, nothing can be dealt with that quickly. He bends over the bed and rips the protective blanket from Jakob's grip. They hear the child's faint intake of breath; his body is already pressed up against the inside of the net cage over the bed. He breathes in gulps as he lies there like a wounded bird, with his arms and legs pulled up against his body. Doctor Illing pushes and digs with surprisingly strong, capable hands and when he has seen with his own eyes that Doctor Gross's information is correct, he just flashes his joyless, toothy grin and nods. Nurse Blei wants to let the boy have his blanket back but Illing waves her away, takes a firm grip under the boy's arms and lifts him upright. Jakob's head slips this way and that, his eyes roll, too, both pupils flickering like the quivering centre of a spirit level.

Can the little Jew boy be made to stand upright? Talk?

Blei shakes her head mechanically. Katschenka looks down at the case notes as if waiting for a new command.

Doctor Gross, would you see to it that by Monday next, this boy can stand? If you have to, why not give him something to perk him up. Just make him capable of *standing upright*. I would like to demonstrate this case at my lecture next week.

Nausedas's Song Marie Darnhofer told her a story about the man who had come to the door of the office in pavilion 1 and asked if this was the place that took in children. He had looked as if he was sleeping rough, unshaven and dressed in a large, worn coat that smelled. The boy he had brought had been standing a few metres away with his face turned to the cloakroom, as he wanted nothing better than to hide among the coats and jackets. The man stated that he was not the child's father and not any other kind of relation. But he had been given the child in his charge. That was the phrase he used. *In his charge*. For how long, or who had given him this responsibility and why, he could or would not say. Instead of answering Doctor Gross's questions (Gross was the medic whose job it usually was to assess the child's *status somaticus*), he produced a creased piece of paper on which someone had written down the boy's name, date and place of birth – born in *KAUNAS*, it said in large, wobbly capitals. The man said that the child was healthy and, at first, had not presented any problems but, of late, had started to behave very strangely at night, so he didn't dare to keep him at home anymore. By then, someone in the office had started to smell a rat, phoned the gate porters and asked them to notify the police. When the man saw a policeman come upstairs, he took fright and ran away. The boy also tried to run but was restrained. That's all. On examination, Doctor Gross was able to confirm what had been suspected by any thinking observer: this was a Jewish child who had been hidden from the authorities. How the boy had come to end up in Wien (if it was true, as the note said, that he was from Lithuania) was beyond investigation. Nor did it seem possible to find out who had protected him and hence if these persons, too, were of Jewish extraction and also in hiding. Whatever was the case, the boy seemed quite unable to provide answers to these or, indeed, any questions. He just stared at you with his large, frightened eyes and, if approached too abruptly, covered his face with his hands and curled up like a scared animal. Because he showed clear signs of debility, he was placed on the ward in pavilion 17 until further information could be obtained. It soon became only too obvious that Nausedas *made a row* at night. When Hedwig Blei heard him for the first time, she thought that the squeaking noise was from a dormitory window that had been left open and was swinging on its hinges. She opened the door a little and listened into the dim realm of subdued night-light and sweaty, sleepy breathing. If these children slept at all, they were usually restless. In the bluish light, she thought she saw the shadow of someone, presumably Pelikan, slip along the wall. Now, the sound grew stronger and came from inside Nausedas's bed-cage. If it hadn't been so loud, she would have assumed that the boy was grinding his teeth, but it was rougher and louder than that, a little like pulling a nail out of warped wood. It gradually became deeper but at the same time began to slide up and down, with a quality more like a vibrating saw-blade. Words emerged from the wavering tune: harsh, angular words, incomprehensible but unmistakably words from a song which formed part of an ever more distinctive melodic line. After a while, she became used to Jakob's alien song. The children did, too. When she was on nights, she would make her way past from time to time, look through the peephole in the door and see everyone lying nicely and quietly in their beds even though Jakob Nausedas was 'singing'. One night, there was a tremendous crash from the ward followed by loud shouting and howling. Jakob's bed was empty, the mobile children had got up and were running around. Pelikan was the liveliest of the lot. His shadow swept up and down along the long wall like a crazy minute hand and he was shouting:

Thunder!

Thunder!

And the song that came from somewhere sounded like distant thunder, short barking pulses as if the swaying melody had stuck in the boy's throat and had to be coughed out. Little Otto Semmler, who lived in a permanent state of fear, tugged at her hand and pointed to the corner of the room where Nausedas crouched with the blanket over his head. Someone must have let him out of his cage and he had gone to ground in the furthest corner of the room while he ejected his thunder clashes at an ever-madder tempo. Come to think of it, that such a small creature could emit so much noise was just about incredible. She wanted to know who had opened the net cage on Nausedas's bed? Her question was of course never answered. Pelikan, panting a little, was ready by the door when she left. He sings because he misses his mother, he explained helpfully.

The Living Dead It is said that when a human being dies, the soul leaves the body. But the soul might leave the body long before you die. If that happens, you get to look like Katschenka, Hedwig Blei said and went on to speak about that so seemingly calm, pale face and those eyes, which gazed at her with an expression of deepest benevolence despite the cutting criticism she, in her role as acting matron, was just about to deliver. These days, Sister Katschenka worked from Sister Bertha's office, although she had never formally been appointed to the post of matron. It was irrelevant, since Sister Bertha could be away for months on end. Besides, as Blei put it, Katschenka was 'made for the job': efficient, unswervingly loyal and invariably sensible. Now, she wanted to know how this kind of chaotic situation could ever be allowed to erupt in a ward that was under strict observation around the clock. And, has Nurse Blei found the culprit yet? Who was responsible? Katschenka looks at her in silence, still with that distant but kindly expression. In my opinion, Nausedas got out of his bed by his own efforts, Blei says. Katschenka doesn't contradict her, just shuffles some papers and remarks that Doctor Illing has decided to X-ray the child's skull. Just as well to have that done in good time. Good time, before what? But there is really no need for Blei to ask or say anything at all. He's just a Jew boy, isn't he?

Encephalography While Jekelius was in charge, 'puncturing' children was done only occasionally but, as soon as Illing took over, these interventions became practically a matter of routine. The great majority of the children, including many who were very ill, underwent lumbar puncture followed by cranial X-rays. Hedwig Blei hadn't grasped the extent of this practice until Miss Block in the office explained that Illing used the encephalographic evidence in a research project he had begun long before he took up the post as Spiegelgrund's medical director. His goal was to perfect a clinical method for the diagnosis of severe neurological disease, notably the incidence and manifestations of tuberous sclerosis complex. TSC is a rare genetic disorder that leads to small, dense tumours forming in the brain and many other organs. The symptoms are complicated and often contradictory because the tumour locations are so scattered. Illing was keen to record their distribution in the brain and in the cerebral cortex in particular. Miss Block said that she daily spent many hours corresponding with hospitals on Doctor Illing's behalf, asking for information from case notes and autopsy reports.

He has himself found two *proven* cases of the condition and displays them, not without pride, in his lectures to the medical students in the pavilion 15 auditorium. One of the patients is a boy of about thirteen or fourteen called Julian Eggers, and the other an epileptic girl who is an inmate in the girls' section of pavilion 17, even though the Berlin department decided that she was to be 'treated' and should have gone to the gallery. However, Illing insisted on 'saving her up' to let him follow the development of her TSC. Her symptoms and signs were near perfect and, for a start, her face showed the characteristic distribution of small, pale nodules. But the boy also has spots on his face, little leathery patches, and has had quite a few epileptic fits lately. It all adds up to a real monster for us to tackle, Doctor Illing explains to his audience of young clinical students who listen in breathless silence to his expositions of the illness his specimen patients are suffering from:

> *With regard to racial biology, tuberous sclerosis shows an almost alarming predictability. If only one parent has this disease, which is possible as that person may well be symptom-free, the likelihood is that one or several of his or her children will also acquire it. But its manifestations are treacherous in the sense that overt symptoms may remain dormant so that the condition only emerges in full force in later generations. Because the tuberosities may occur in several organs other than the brain, such as lungs, heart and kidney, and thus cause the symptomatology and course of the disease to vary markedly between individual patients, it is not uncommon for it to be confused with practically every other severe form of paediatric neurological disease. Unless the diagnostic methods are radically improved, we will remain defenceless against this enemy which threatens to undermine our race from within.*

Nausedas had also been brought in to model illness in one of Doctor Illing's lectures. That was why Illing had been so keen that Doctor Gross should get him to 'stand upright'. That TSC was never on the cards in Nausedas's case was neither here nor there. In order to determine the incidence of the disease, and its varied forms, whoever seemed a potential case should be included as a useful addition to the control group. Besides, all the children who had undergone encephalography were examined post-mortem and that meant you could compare the results of the investigation with the actual situation in the brain. Hedwig Blei lifts the lid of Nausedas's cage and frees the boy from his blankets. It won't hurt, she says. She is lying but knows that the boy won't understand her. Or perhaps he does, after all, just as an animal understands that its life will soon end. Unusually, he doesn't resist her, doesn't even bother to hold his hands in front of his face. She is not allowed to come with him into the X-ray suite but knows from experience how the children are treated, how the nurse undresses them brusquely and straps them down, even children with fevers so high they can hardly sit up, in the same painful position where none of their muscles are at rest: not sitting or even half-sitting, but bending over forward to expose the lower back; then, the long lumbar puncture needle is eased between the lumbar vertebrae and into the space around the spinal cord to extract some of the fluid that circulates around the cord and the brain. It must be carried out very gradually to let the body get used to losing the fluid. And the child's skin blanches and turns bluish, as if slowly suffocating; then, just as suddenly, the skin blushes and the eyes bulge and roll upwards, white with terror as the pain slashes the child's head like a thousand sharp knives. Because the child is immobilised, the nurse holds an enamelled basin in readiness for when the stomach contents come spraying out and the child tries to scream though the sound is dampened by the acid matter which continues to flow uncontrollably from its mouth. All the body's organs lie exposed, like stones rubbing against each other; and the air flows into the spinal canal and rises into the cranial cavity to surround the brain that is no longer suspended in its protective fluid; then, the light goes as white, reality seems as if corroded away from the world. From that day, Nausedas sings no more. She tries to give him the blanket. He does not react. She has never seen anyone look so vulnerable, like a featherless baby bird. His eyes sometimes stare unseeingly, sometimes hide behind closed, quivering eyelids. The next day, his temperature is very high and he doesn't respond to being touched. They take him to the gallery in pavilion 15 and there he dies a couple of days later.

Certified as cause of death: pneumonia.

Black Keys and White A couple of weeks pass, perhaps a month. The memory of Nausedas fades. After all, new children to care for arrive all the time. One afternoon, Hedwig comes by when Felix Keuschnig is thumping on the piano keys. She decides to tell him to play more quietly but before she reaches him, the chaotic jumble of notes fall into a rhythm that carries a vaguely familiar melody. She stops. It is Nausedas's song. Felix is running through the chords again and again but can't keep hold of the sequence. His hands keep slipping off the black keys and onto the white ones, as if the keyboard were slippery, covered with a film of soap. A wave of anger flows through her, so strong it surprises her, and she grabs Felix's arms to pull him away from the piano. Felix, who knows all the tricks by now, slithers out of her grasp, dashes into the dormitory and runs around slapping the sleeping children's faces. Fierce slaps. And with every blow, he laughs sharply, triumphantly: *Ha!* It sounds as if he is imitating someone. She comes after him but he has already found new victims: *Ha!* Otto Semmler screams, red flares on his face. Other children flee in fear and hide wherever they can, under beds and chairs. Felix runs jerkily and drags his feet as if about to make himself fall over. Finally, she manages to force him down in a corner of the room and calls for help. It is the corner Nausedas fled to when he got out of his bed-cage. Felix, she says. And she starts to sing, as if she knows she has to. It is their song: 'Fuchs du hast die Gans gestohlen'. Then he hits her too, with astonishing strength, right across the bridge of her nose. It hurts so much that tears spurt from her blinded eyes. *Ha!* he laughs and is quickly back on his feet. Of course, such behaviour must be punished. Off Felix goes to solitary confinement even though everyone knows that in his case, at least, it's pointless. He only sits on the bench in there, staring listlessly ahead. He doesn't try to hit anyone, but won't speak either. Instead of answering when you address him, his body twists and his face contorts in his usual elaborate grimaces. There he sits, his face working, for ten days. When he comes out, he asks for his mother. Asks and asks, because he has missed one of the statutory visiting days. Hedwig Blei tries to distract him and leads him to the piano but he sneaks away without playing a single note. She wants him to draw but his rough strokes with the pen rip the paper. He draws coarse figures with lines for limbs and large mouths full of sharp teeth. When Illing does his round, she tells him that Felix Keuschnig is showing hopeful improvements but when Doctor Illing glances at Katschenka she simply shakes her head. Children classified as *vollständig pflegebedürftig* – completely care-dependent – or, as in Keuschnig's case, just *Arbeitsfähigkeit nicht zu erwarten* – suitability for work not expected – are welcome additional subjects for Illing's clinical experiments. Sure enough, one morning Katschenka announces that Illing wants Keuschnig for lumbar puncture followed by pneumoencephalography. They come for him early one morning. By four in the afternoon, she removes the black shoes from his bedside table and places them next to her own in the staff cloakroom. An hour later, Felix is returned to the ward. He is conscious but very weak. She can't make eye contact with him. He is febrile and complains of pains in his head and the back of his neck. He lies in his bed and worries that someone is trying to throw him out of it. She tells him there is no one. Soon afterwards, he starts vomiting. He throws up again and again until the evening when he becomes feverish and agitated, casts his body from side to side, and waves his arms about as if fighting an invisible enemy. Doctor Türk is on call and Blei asks her to come. She isn't sure whether Illing has already decided to have the fatal dose administered or whether Türk is just giving Felix the usual sedative. The boy's eyes look glassy and his face is as white as chalk but he is much less restless, then seems to sleep easily, breathing too lightly but evenly. Anyway, she is going off-duty. Everyone goes but nobody comes, Pelikan says to her as she leaves the day room. She meets Nurse Sikora in the corridor, taking her coat off, ready to start the night shift. Sikora beams sunnily at her. When Hedwig returns to the clinic two days later, Felix has already been transferred to the gallery in pavilion 15. The next day, she asks Sister Katschenka to be allowed to nurse in the gallery again. Katschenka looks up with her usual expression of bland concern. There is no need for additional staff in the gallery at present, Nurse, she says. Besides, I must say that I believe it to be in Nurse Hedwig's best interests to stay here. When Hedwig goes off work that day, she visits the gallery on the way. Felix is already dead. The end came quickly, Hilde Mayer says. Perhaps that's just as well. No one wants to see a child suffer. Mrs Keuschnig is waiting on the gravelled path outside. A pale moon hangs in the evening sky. It could be that Mrs Keuschnig has already received information about her son's death or maybe she felt a premonition of something serious and has turned up here on her own initiative. What have you done? she asks Hedwig. A group of women are standing a little away from the two of them and follow their confrontation with tense faces but neither say nor do anything. Mrs Keuschnig has been standing in the shadow but now she takes a sudden step into the moonlight and her face gleams white as she raises her arms in a disconsolate gesture and asks, her voice sliding into a scream:

What have you done?
Do you feel no shame?

Two porters come at a run from their cabin. They take hold of the screaming woman and propel her off the site. The porters know the routine, well-used to incidents of precisely this kind. The watching women have turned their backs and started out for the tram stop. Nurse Blei returns to pavilion 17. The Pelikan lad opens the door for her and then closes it quickly to prevent anyone from slipping away outside. In the dormitory, the numb childish faces turn to stare at her as if they expect her to say something, but she can't think how to bring herself to break the silence or, anyway, if there is any silence still to be broken. All that is left now is a white sea. It covers everything.

VI

Guardian Angels

The War Moves In There were of course no angels standing guard at the summit of Gallitzinberg. The old viewing tower stood there, though. The Nazis took it over immediately after marching in and renamed it the Adolf Hitler Warte. It was the highest point in Wien and, from the tower, radio cables ran down into a concrete bunker some ten metres underground where young women wearing headsets received reports about Allied flight patterns, which they then summarised and displayed on a large screen of milky glass that covered the wall behind them. Of course, I heard about all that much later, Hannes Neubauer explained. I mean, no one let on that the mountain with its guardian angels watching out for us was in fact an armoured defence establishment – *Gefechtsstand Wien*. Lots of concrete-lined rooms dug in deep and linked by long passages, some so wide you could drive loaded vehicles down them. The story went about that Baldur von Schirach fled into the mountain during the last days of the war. Unlike the rest of us, he never once had to stick his head above the parapet. There was a safe tunnel ready for him to scuttle down. Thinking about it now, this much later, I think it was almost offensive, Hannes concluded. At Spiegelgrund, people had started to practise evacuating everyone to air-raid shelters long before the first Allied bombs fell on Wien. Every so often, the children had to line up in pairs, in *Zweierreihen*, on the path outside the pavilion, just as if marching off to school. When Mrs Rohrbach blew her whistle they were to jog along at *Laufschritt* and, without breaking formation, run as quickly as possible past a few pavilions and enter a building which had been equipped with a bunker-like basement room, where they were to settle down side by side with their knees close together while Mrs Rohrbach hovered in the doorway, timing them on her watch. All of which was rubbish, of course, Hannes said. Lining up in formation when an air raid is due simply isn't on. And no one thought of stocking up with food or even water in the shelter, there were none of the things we'd need if we were to stay for any length of time, days or weeks – not to mention years, as I figured we might. Sure enough, when the bombers did come, the whole evacuation plan went to pieces. It happened in mid-morning on a day in September 1944. Adrian Ziegler was no longer at Spiegelgrund, but Hannes was and so, inevitably, was Nurse Mutsch. Hannes saw her stand with her back to the staff room when the cuckoo call came from the radio that was always on in there. *Cuckoo, cuckoo*, it went. It was a signal to switch to shortwave reception. At the same time, the phone started to ring and Nurse Mutsch answered of course, it was her duty to report phone calls to the ward staff. When she at last had managed to make her trembling fingers link the radio to the telephone jack as instructed, Mrs Cuckoo's weirdly ethereal voice was already well into her account of the positions of enemy planes. *Ooost!* she said, extending the *o* in the word for east. Normally, there would have been an interval between the end of the broadcast and the air-raid sirens starting up but as far as Hannes can remember, the angels were screaming already. Suddenly, the pavilion doors opened wide and the rooms and corridors filled with nurses and porters rushing about, shouting and screaming so wildly it was impossible to work out if they were just trying to avoid bumping into each other or if they were calling the children together somewhere or if they simply had to speak at the top of their voices to be heard through the infernal noise of the sirens. It actually was insane, this screeching, wavering noise that penetrated walls and roofs and floors, made bottles and bedpans jump off the drying racks only to fall rattling into the sinks below and the corridor windows vibrate on a frail, resonating note as if each pane was about to explode out of its metal framework (later on, Hannes said, I asked myself if the Allied pilots up there in the milky glass sky didn't know that the city's air defence capability was lodged just there, inside Gallitzinberg. It seems obvious that they would have. But did they know that the pavilions scattered everywhere in the shadow of the mountain were full of unwanted children, like piggy banks stuffed with damaged or discarded coins? Or was that perhaps the very reason why the authorities picked just that location for the institution? Their first move had been to tunnel into the mountain and install the defence equipment. And then they brought the children in. As living shields? But, if so, why move us out again? And when the angels on the mountain started off their unholy noise, what happened to the idiots in pavilion 15? Were they, too, moved to special shelters or left behind? After all, they were meant to die anyway). And now the war moved in with them. It arrived promptly, from one day to the next, when the large ambulances with Red Cross signs on the rear doors lined up on the central path that linked the pavilions. In the lesson that day, Mr Hackl spoke in a trembling voice about the heroic sacrifices made by the soldiers who risked their lives on the most forward front lines, and insisted that the Spiegelgrund boys must show themselves *worthy* of such bravery. He picked six or eight of his pupils and had them stand in an orderly formation outside the schoolroom. They marched off to pavilion 12, lined up neatly again, this time by age and height, and sang for the soldiers, songs in praise of the infantry like 'Infanterie du bist die Krone aller Waffen' and

'Graue Kolonnen'. They had been instructed by Mr Hackl not only to march on the spot as they sang but also to push the fists forwards and back as if holding a rifle with a bayonet:

Ruhlos in Flandern müssen wir wandern
Weit von der Heimat entfernt
Graue Soldaten
Im Schrei der Granaten
Haben das Lachen verlernt.[2]

To the soldiers shaking with shell shock, the *Kriegszitterern*, the amputees and other wounded and sick men who lay dazzled by the light-bursts from the flares and dazed by the noise of the multiple rocket launchers that boomed all night long, the sight and sound of these stupidly stamping boys, singing in voices that were either childishly thin or hoarsely breaking, can't have been anything but a drawn-out agony, like a nightmare that came back to plague them long after waking up.

Ybbs Off and on for several weeks, Nurse Mutsch's face would take on an odd expression, as if she knew something very important but mustn't tell anyone. As usual, her fat cheeks bulged with menace but her wide-open eyes would gleam with secret knowledge. Looking meaningfully at Zavlacky and Miseryguts, she might say something about a *big clean-out* that was on the books, while she hinted to Jockerl, who had been in a constant state of fear ever since all that with Julius Becker, that he had better mind his manners if he was to come along or else he'd be left behind with the idiots. *Come along,*

2 Restless we must wander in Flanders / So far away from home / The grey(-uniformed) soldiers / While the shells scream past us / Have learnt not to laugh.

to where? Jockerl asked pleadingly but Nurse Mutsch said no more, only surveyed the group of boys with a glum expression on her face as if she couldn't but regret the fate that awaited them. One morning in September, the mystery was cleared up. Mrs Rohrbach stepped into the dormitory, complete with whistle and clapper, but instead of intoning her usual orders to get up and dash to the washrooms, they were told to dress at once and line up in the corridor. There was a big, grey bus waiting outside the pavilion. Nobody told them where they were off to. They weren't allowed any luggage except the few items of clothing and the pair of indoor shoes they had been told to pack in their rucksacks. As they boarded the bus, the boys were handed a small food parcel each. In it was some crispbread spread with margarine and topped with slices of cured ham. Many boys were scared; Jockerl drilled himself into one of the rear seats like a small woodworm. Hannes Neubauer thought about the Mountain and about his father, worrying that he couldn't let his father know where he was because he hadn't been told. The bus unloaded them after a short drive to Hütteldorf station where they boarded a train standing at the platform, as if it had been waiting for them. Adrian and Hannes, the tinker's lad and the officer's son, sat together with their faces pressed to the window and read out the names of all the stations they passed. Hannes tried to memorise them: Tullnerbach-Pressbaum. Neulengbach. Böheimkirchen. St Pölten. Melk. They were told to leave the train at a station called Ybbs-Kemmelbach, where Mr Hackl and the assistant teacher, Mrs Bremer, did a head-count. They lined up afterwards and marched off when Mrs Bremer blew on the whistle she wore on a string around her neck. As they walked for something like two kilometres, maybe more, hardly a word was said. After perhaps another kilometre, about an hour's marching, they arrived in Ybbs. The hospital looked like a quayside fortress, a cluster of low buildings by the river with rendered walls painted yellow. The buildings were linked by long stone arches which led to a series of internal courtyards. The boys were ushered into one of the courtyards and told to wait. On the other side of the yard was a large building that looked like a store or an oversized tool shed. Shouts came from inside it. Some of the more courageous boys, led by Zavlacky and Miseryguts, went closer and realised that it wasn't a store but a kind of enclosure. The doors had been removed from the wide gateway and the opening blocked by iron bars. The windows that ran along the wall, at least a man's height above the ground, were also barred. In the partial darkness on the other side of the gate, they glimpsed the pale faces of hundreds of men, most of them old and spent. Some sat on the cold stone floor, others lay curled up as if asleep. Yet others were standing with lips and foreheads pressed close to the bars, empty eyes staring into the dusk. They were all wearing baggy institutional clothing, a hospital uniform rather like what the mental patients at Steinhof used to wear and in the same blue-grey colour, only tattered and dirty. The place smelled badly: like mould or old compost mixed with the harsh saltpetre stench of urine. It seemed that they had to void on the floor where they sat or lay. The road to the building was closed off with a heavy iron chain. Obviously, access was forbidden; a sign hanging from the chain said as much: *Überschreiten der Kette streng verboten.* Jockerl, who was small enough to slip in under the chain, went to the gate and pushed his saved-up piece of bread between the bars. A man's trembling hand reached out for it. The man wasn't left alone for long. Seconds later, he was wrestled to the ground by two others who fumbled for the hand holding the bread, by now clenched into a tight fist. More men joined the confused mayhem, some screamed in desperate voices, others ran around aimlessly. An armed guard suddenly turned up and pushed the children away with the barrel of his rifle and then Mr Hackl and Mrs Bremer came along. Both looked upset. Clearly the boys had not been meant to see what they had just witnessed. They were pushed across the yard in a hurry, into the nearest stairwell and then up to the first floor where a large dormitory, at least three times the size of the Spiegelgrund one, waited for them with its double rows of already made beds. All night they heard screams and raised voices from the courtyard until, suddenly, the noise stopped. Silence. When they had had breakfast in the morning and were dispatched into the yard again, the chain and the barred gate had been removed.

They've taken them to Hartheim. It's probably for the best.

That was as far as Mrs Bremer would go. She turned her face away, pressed her lips tightly together and would say nothing more.

While the two supervisors were on their midday break, some of the boys, with Zavlacky still out in front, managed to get into the old store building. One wouldn't have believed that people had been in there if it hadn't been for a few torn rags of clothing and odd things scattered on the floor, objects like small wooden crucifixes and tobacco tins, some shiny copper coins and hand-carved toys that no child would have thought of making. Hannes Neubauer found a doll made of three sewing-thread spools with bits of thread stuck into the top one to mark eyes, nose and mouth. Light entered through four windows that faced the courtyard. The windows were filthy, and against the crumbly, grey light they saw that someone had begun to scratch his name on one of panes. The letters were angular and leaned markedly forward. The attempt at writing was followed by a date:

A . . . losa . . . 19 IX 1941

Don't know about the rest of you but I'm not waiting around to be slaughtered, Miseryguts said later, and the next day, he and

Zavlacky and a boy called Peter Schaubach were gone. They had made their way out during the night unhindered. The long, winding stairwells and many archways between the buildings and the linked courtyards must have baffled even the Steinhof staff. The boys spent the rest of that day and night locked in the dormitory. All they could do was sit and listen to the barking dogs and the rough voices of the Wehrmacht soldiers who had been recruited to catch the runaways though no one was found, at least while the children were at Ybbs. For some time afterwards, they talked a lot about what had happened. About the boys who had got away. About the mad old men and what might have been done to them. And the idiot children in pavilion 15. Would they be brought here? Or were they to stay on the old Steinhof site? Some of the boys were convinced that Spiegelgrund would be made into a slaughterhouse, which was what Nurse Mutsch had meant when she spoke about the planned *big clean-out.* Surely, they argued, the only reason for transferring them to Ybbs was that Jekelius, Gross and the other doctors didn't want the healthy children to 'watch' while they finished the other lot off. On the other hand, there were those who believed that they were the ones led to slaughter and that they were still alive only because the hospital staff was busy killing each other off. The day passed without anything happening at all. So it went for months. Autumn arrived. Chilly mists rose from the mighty river below the hospital walls. In the stairwell leading to their dormitory, a wide window overlooked the river flowing in all its grey, powerful grandeur, swollen by the rains, between banks hidden in unchanging swathes of fog. The river always seemed to flow fastest in the middle, as if the currents there were too impatient to wait for the massive volumes of water idling along the banks. Always, even though muffled by stone walls and sealed archways, you could hear the roar of water on the move, slowly but unceasingly. Whenever the flow slowed, Adrian thought he could pick up the faint rustling of the wings of the birds that came floating on air currents down to the glossy surface of the water and, as he lay in the darkened dormitory full of boys, some asleep and others not, he imagined animals wading at the water's edge, perhaps a stag raising his crowned head in the thick, creamily white morning mists over the banks.

Otherwise, nothing much had changed. Mrs Rohrbach woke them in the mornings with her whistle and her clapper, Nurses Mutsch and Demeter continued to discipline them during their quiet hour, and Mrs Bremer and Mr Hackl to struggle with teaching them to spell, count and praise the Führer and the German army's unbroken success in the field. They were even visited by Doctor Gross a few times, once to examine a boy who had a sudden attack of stomach cramps at night. On Christmas Eve, Doctor Krenek arrived and gave his usual speech about how, in these hard times, the children must forgo, even sacrifice things. Then they were told to queue for a seasonal gift: a paper bag containing a few rather dry pieces of cake and an apple. And that was it. No prettily glittering tree, no singing. The gloomy Christmas reinforced their suspicion that they had been sent here to hibernate, to survive some crisis. Then, one January morning (Adrian remembers the thin layer of powdery snow on the courtyard), they heard the coughing noise of the bus engine. Next, they were ordered to pack their toothbrushes and felt slippers and get going. This time, they went by bus all the way back to Wien. As Mr Hackl told them, as he swayed along the narrow aisle, hand over hand: they were going to Steinhof.

The Devil's Claw They had stayed at Ybbs for a total of 148 days – more than four months. On day 149, they were in their Spiegelgrund pavilion again as if nothing had happened. Pavilion 9 was just as when they had left it, with piles of books and drawings stacked in the day room. In the washroom, small, cracked bits of soap were still stuck in the drain covers under the showers. The floor under the beds was covered in a fine layer of dust. The idiots on the other side of the path were in place, and their moaning and shrieking travelled far in the crisp, clear winter air. Nothing had happened here, so why had they been forced to move? In the weeks that followed, excursions and walks in the surroundings were organised. Boys from other sections took part and each group was marshalled by an appointed group leader, responsible for organising the line-up outside the pavilion entrance according to regulations. The group leaders were entrusted with the football and also the obligatory bowling balls that gave everyone a collective bad conscience because nobody knew what to do with them. The excursions were usually led by Mrs Rohrbach but she was sometimes relieved by another *Erzieher*, like Mrs Krämer, who always turned up dressed in in knee-length woollen trousers and a tailored suit jacket with an NS-Frauenschaft pin on the lapel: a black shield with the hooked cross symbol in the centre like a small drop of blood. They often marched along the Steinhof wall, up over Wilhelminenberg to Kreuzeichenwiese, where they were to sit on the grass and eat their packed lunches. If there wasn't enough time for this, as was frequently decided, they went left immediately after the old fire station. By going that way, their excursion followed most of the old asylum wall, as if the point was to measure and once more fortify it, and so make the wall appear even more impossible to scale. In Adrian's memory, the late-winter sky always lowered above the landscape, dark clouds massed within the grey haze and swelled, growing into the misty sky until its greyness turned into true darkness. A sharp smell of woodsmoke always hung above the allotments in Rosental where the hollow rattle of utensils for cooking and laundry was mixed with the sounds of dogs barking and voices calling to each other, with long pauses in between. All of which induced a strange feeling in Adrian of being pulled into a fast-running stream that was carrying him off against his will. Unexpectedly, the excursions transformed Nurse Mutsch. She laced up her thick-soled, practical walking boots and stepped out briskly. As she walked, this otherwise uncommunicative woman talked a blue streak. As they followed the Steinhof wall, she would tell them that it was even longer than the old city wall that once protected the heart of the city, the Innere Stadt, and that the cathedral and the Hofburg and the *whole caboodle* could easily have fitted in behind this wall, and when she said *whole caboodle* she even laughed a little, real laughter and not just a lip-tightening smile. Mostly, Hannes Neubauer was picked for the special place next to Nurse Mutsch and he was the one to whom she directed her out-of-character chatter. Mutsch detested Hannes much less than the other boys in the section. It might have been because of his seemingly harmless round head and the upturned, somehow smiley corners of his mouth or perhaps simply that he never talked back, only walked along muttering to himself. But on one occasion, Adrian happened to be at Nurse Mutsch's side. She didn't seem particularly bothered one way or the other (the exercise rather than the company made her talkative) but Adrian felt hot with pride. If only he had dared to, he might have reached out for her hand and held it, at least for a little while. It would have been an attempt to hold on to the curious, unusual feeling of freedom that belonged to this day, to the sounds of their feet on the frost-hardened ground, and their breathing in and out in the cold air, and the deep, rising and falling notes made by the wind in the bare crowns of the trees high above their heads. To get all the stone blocks needed for the wall, Nurse Mutsch went on, they'd had to blast until they got so far down into the quarry that the sky couldn't be seen any longer. But there still wasn't enough stone and they carried on until they hit the Devil's Claw, right at the bottom of the hole. *The Devil's Claw?* The boys gathered around Nurse Mutsch, their mouths gaping like big *o*s. Nurse Mutsch's eyes had opened wide and were so pale they looked transparent. You see, she explained, the Devil's Claw looked like the black, curving root of a tree, but no matter what they did to try to get it out of the way, this black thing stayed where it was. And the men who attempted to shift it by heaving or pulling turned rigid, like stone, and shook feverishly for days afterwards. They tried to blow it up with dynamite but before they even got the blast caps in place the ground shook like in the worst earthquake. *Now, now, Nurse Mutsch, you're telling the boys an awful lot of nonsense*, Mrs Rohrbach interrupted, but she didn't look quite as angry as she usually did. Nurse Mutsch seemed to feel quite pleased with herself but a little anxious at the same time. Perhaps she realised that by giving way to her eagerness to tell stories, she had made the boys pay keen attention to her, much more so than with her normal disciplinary methods. A dubious victory, perhaps, but a victory nonetheless.

The Green Cart The worthiness of working hard was constantly preached. It was imprinted in their minds that they must at all times strive to be useful, to deserve being fed. The boys were divided into two teams: one made up of the older ones, who were to carry the heavy food containers that the small, red hospital tram brought every afternoon, and one for the littler ones, or *the left-overs*, which was how the bigger boys referred to them, who were to lay the table with plates and cutlery from the ward kitchen on a rota that Nurse

Demeter organised. Boys told to join the table team were thought to be favoured. Nurse Demeter called the names of the select in her hoarse voice: *Blaschek! – Hauser! – Neubauer!* A bit away from her, Nurse Mutsch was ticking off the food trays as they arrived against the list of names. The system broke down quite often due to the brisk turnover of children: a portion too many was delivered, say, or one was missing. One day, Mutsch turned and stopped Adrian by gripping his shoulder as he passed, carrying cutlery sets and glasses:

> *Ziegler, run over to the kitchen, tell them there's a portion missing this time and bring one back here.*

Normally, she would turn to Hannes with these requests. Nice little Hannes with the ball-shaped head, innocent eyes and little self-contained smile. But now *the tinker* had been given the go-ahead. Adrian would remember that moment for as long as he lived: Nurse Mutsch's hand on his shoulder, her face high above him, all glassy eye-globes and tightly stretched lips. Why was he granted this privilege? Was it because they had got *on speaking terms* during that walk, when he had even been tempted to hold her hand? Was she testing if the understanding between them was to last? Or did she know already what was likely to happen next? She produced a bunch of keys with strict instructions as to where to go and what doors to unlock and lock, and which key fitted which door. The keys that she had handled so easily weighed heavily in his hand. Children who were sent off to the kitchen on some errand were told to use a small door at the back of the building. Then, you went up a wide cement staircase and along a narrow corridor with a serving hatch at the far end. The frame of the hatch was lined with a sheet of tin, ice-cold when you leaned your bare arm on it. Beyond the hatch, the hot air was full of the heavy smells of cooking and of sour steam rising from the washing-up, and fat women in aprons hurried about with rattling trolleys stacked high with trays and glasses. You had to shout at the top of your voice to be heard above the noise and, when you had been shouting for a while, one of the cooks in a white uniform would come to the hatch, wipe the sweat from her face and, in a cross tone, ask something like *where are you from then?* but without bothering to listen to the answer. Adrian just pushed the chit with the order that Nurse Mutsch had given him into the cook's hand and she twisted the piece of paper this way and that as if she found it incredibly tricky to make out what it said. Then she sighed, disappeared and returned with a tray. On it usually stood a plate covered with a metal lid to keep the food hot. How proud it made one to be *allowed to carry the tray*. This time, there wasn't just one plate on the tray but two, one large and one slightly smaller, also with a lid on top. It was drizzling outside. Adrian lifted the tray closer to his face to try to smell what was on the plates. The large one smelled pungently of meat stock and overcooked vegetables. The other one didn't smell of anything at all. Adrian fancied there might be a piece of cake on that plate or maybe even a cream-cake made with real cream. He couldn't remember a single instance of the children being served a dessert or even given a sweet since he had arrived at Spiegelgrund. There were stories about boys who had were given nice things to eat, like a boy who had refused to open his eyes, and came and went quickly, but had been offered a small slice of apple pie with cream. Or, at least, Peter Blaschek claimed he had seen this: Nurse Demeter sitting on the edge of that boy's bed and urging him to have another spoonful of cream. Could the smaller plate be for some special thing like that? Who was to have this extra portion? When, much later, Adrian tried to remember what had really happened that afternoon, he was struck by the chilling insight that *perhaps there never was another plate with a lid on it.* Could it be that he had imagined the whole thing? Or rather: had the memory of the events of that afternoon made the second plate materialise, as it were, although there had only been one plate on the tray, as per normal. But if there hadn't been another plate, how come he remembers with such clarity that he spent ages in the increasingly heavy rain looking for a suitably out-of-the way place where he could put the tray down? Why had he suddenly become so troubled? He was innocent, after all. All he did was to walk somewhere carrying a tray. But he had chosen an odd way back. The obvious route went from the kitchens and then at the back of pavilion 13, the very same one they followed every day to walk to and from school. Instead, he crossed the central path and carried on, past the front of pavilion 13 and then towards number 15. Just as if it had been waiting for him, the green cart stood just on the edge of the steps leading down to the back of the pavilion. The cart had a thick, arched cover, painted green, and at one end, a pole for pulling it. The pole handle was resting on the grass because the labourer who pulled it around was urinating against the pavilion wall a little bit away. He was dressed in the usual institutional uniform, a grey jacket and trouser set that was far too small for him. Adrian stopped, unable to make up his mind what to do next. Still nothing to put the tray on. In front of him was that inexplicable green cart, so close that anyone who was looking out from behind the barred windows in the pavilion (if anyone was) would instantly have seen him standing by the cart. A voice spoke inside his head, sounding as powerful as the wind in the trees, and it said *don't do it don't lift the lid off the plate*. Afterwards, he was quite sure that when the voice said *don't lift the lid,* it had meant the metal lid on the smaller plate but, for some reason, he had put the tray down on the gravel and moved towards the mystery cart. Of course, it had a lid, too, with a handle on the lower edge. The man in the hospital uniform was still busy urinating. The pavilion windows glistened in the rain. He could see the trees along the path reflected in the panes and realised what he had thought were movements behind the glass was only the swaying branches of the trees. No one seemed to be watching. The strong, arched lid on the cart reflected nothing. The raindrops stuck to its painted surface before narrowing into tiny streams that ran along his fingers and down over his wrists when he finally closed his hands on the handle and pulled. The lid swung up and over surprisingly easily, as if an invisible third hand had supported his elbow and helped him lift. Inside, he saw the corpses of three children, stacked at odd angles to each other as if they had been thrown in any old how. They were naked. Their skin was a dull yellow, like old wax, and their faces were not really faces anymore. At least, this how the boy on top looked. His mouth was a gaping cavity and the pulled-back lips exposed rows of teeth as discoloured as an old horse. All he could see of the other two bodies was a slightly curved spine, part of a shoulder blade, and an arm that lay across another body, as if for defence or comfort. Where did the dead children come from? From pavilion 15? He glanced at the rain-streaked windowpanes. In that instant, something peculiar happened. It was as if he was up there, looking down at the green cart with the opened lid, and himself staring at the corpses of the dead children, already getting wet in the rain and, up there, other children came along to stand next to him at the window so that he was part of a crowd of warm, sweating bodies who, like him, wanted to see out. It made no sense, of course. How could he be himself and another himself at the same time, both inside and outside the pavilion? Where was he, really and truly? And could he trust that it was himself he saw, that he *was* himself? He cautiously lowered the lid over the bodies, picked the tray up from the ground and, without turning to look, followed the path back to his own pavilion. The park was completely silent apart from the sound of the wind dragging its hands through the trees and the crunching of damp gravel under his feet. Not another sound, not even from the idiots in number 15. When he reached his pavilion, he pulled out Nurse Mutsch's keys, found the right one, put it into the lock and entered. The corridor was full of dust and shadows. He walked along with the tray, past the ward kitchen and into that day room where the children were still seated at the table. But all the trays of food had been taken away. The boys sat as they had to sit during quiet hour, with both palms resting on the table, and Nurse Mutsch eyed him from her place at the top of the table, then glanced at the clock and said *where have you been all this time?* But she was smiling, her real smile, the one he had seen on her face when she had turned to him during the walk. And the fact that she was smiling at him *as if nothing had happened* even though it was only too obvious that everyone had finished their meal and was sitting there only to watch while he was punished suddenly became too much for him. His arms and legs grew long and heavier than they had ever been. Now, he had to hand the tray over but it slipped out of his hands and struck the floor, lids and all, in a wave of deafening clatter that broke all around him.

The Prisoners in the Trees He is locked up in the cell where Julius Becker had been held. It is equipped with a bench screwed into the wall, a blanket but no mattress, a washbasin, also fixed to the wall, and a bedpan to do his business in. There is a window but placed very high up on the wall and covered by a grid to make it even more difficult to look out. Resting one foot on the edge of the bench, he can swing himself up and jam the fingers of one hand under the grid bars. Then it becomes possible to glimpse the gravelled path and the trunks of some of the trees along it. And he sees legs walk past. Some of the legs don't move, as if they were rooted to the ground; other legs push and strain, as if supporting a person carrying or dragging something heavy. Then, once more, he hears the slow, rasping noise of the tall wooden wheels. The green corpse-cart slides into his field of vision at a majestic pace. Out of the narrow ventilation slit at the top, the stench of death wells in a dense wave. All around, the labourers in their institutional uniforms run away and climb the trees to escape. Adrian bends over the basin to throw up. But when he tries to drink afterwards, the thin dribble of water hardly reaches his lips. In the next moment, keys rattle in the lock and Nurse Mutsch enters. *Wipe your mouth*, she says. *You have visitors*. Doctor Krenek follows her in and, after him, Mrs Rohrbach, then an older woman he recognises as one of the psychologists, Mrs Edeltraud Baar. Mrs Baar is clutching an open folder to her chest. All four lean against the wall as if it couldn't stay upright without their support.

DOCTOR KRENEK: We gather that you don't appreciate the food we serve here.

MRS ROHRBACH: He did it on purpose. Threw the tray on the floor as soon as he came in.

DOCTOR BAAR: You perhaps feel that the food isn't good enough for you.

NURSE MUTSCH: He's always up to this kind of thing. Nags and ingratiates himself, but if you give him a bit of responsibility he ruins it every time. Not just for himself but the other boys as well.

He feels he must sit down and fumbles for the bench behind him. But he has hardly had time to let his legs buckle under him before Mutsch is there and hauls him upright:

Stand up you stupid boy, we're talking to you!

The whole cell sways around him. He wishes that he had a tree to hide in like the others. But there are no trees here, only Doctor Krenek, a gigantic figure towering up in front of the boy. The doctor's face is bulging with rage:

From now on, you stay here. No food.
And you will stay until we've burnt the idleness out of you and you've learnt to appreciate the food you're given and do what your superiors order you to do.

They leave and, exhausted with sheer relief, he collapses on the bench. But only for a few minutes and then he is back, clinging to the cell window. The corpse-cart is gone but the park maintenance crew is still up there in the trees. They perch on the branches with their heads drawn down between their raised shoulders and their knees bent against their chests, looking like great, brooding birds. They are everywhere, in all the trees he can see. Keys rattle in the lock again and Nurse Mutsch enters, alone this time. She places a plate with two thin slices of bread in front of him on the bench, and then looks at him. What does she expect? Probably an apology. He can't make himself apologise but must say something. So he says that, in the park, the idiots from the asylum have climbed up into the trees. Her glassy eyes fix on him. *They have done what?* she asks. And he says it again: the loonies have climbed the trees. He can see in her face that she doesn't believe him but feels uncertain at the same time. Especially as he doesn't turn round but keeps trying to look out through the window with his neck and body still twisting in order to hang on. She steps forward, curious. *Where?* she asks. He points: over there. She is about three times his size, so it is naturally much harder to twist her body and neck into the angles that allow her to see out through the window. She raises one leg, he pushes from below at her solid thigh and somehow manages to make the nurse's white-clad, massive body stand just as he did, one foot balancing on the edge of the bench, left hand around the grid and her face pressed against the wall. *Where?* she asks again and again; and, *there* he says and tries to squeeze a pointing finger between her face and the grid: *there, there, there* – if he smiles in that moment, it isn't because he feels pleased at what he has made her do but because he is frightened. Frightened, because he knows exactly what will happen in the next moment but can't stop. And then their roles are reversed. He is squashed against the wall and she leans her huge body over him. *You lying little swine!* she says, and once she has started beating him up she can't stop. The blows and kicks rain over all the unprotected parts of his body and even though he curls up on the floor with his hands alternating between trying to protect his belly and genitals, and his neck and head, he is struck everywhere all the same. This punishment isn't in proportion to what he has done, or to what he tried to say to her or show her. No matter. He has betrayed her trust, and everybody else's too. For that offence, no punishment is hard enough.

Shelter Outside, the air has become warmer and damper. The small ventilation pane is propped open on its safety catch and lets in noises, dead or half-dead sounds from the night outside. Strange birds race out of the leafy trees on clattering wings; car engines start with a roar somewhere on the road; and, like a dark backdrop behind or above or below these sudden noises, the drawn-out, pained wailing of the children in pavilion 15, interrupted now and then by a shrill scream or a howl as if from someone fighting for survival. In the cell, too, a treacherous angel-light is kept on through the night and feels, if possible, even stronger because the walls are that much closer. He is tired but his hunger won't let him sleep. Awareness, as light as a feather and as fragile, rests on his half-asleep body. Alien human faces emerge from the walls, somehow squeezed out from inside, as if from a tube. He reaches out with his arms to push them away. Hannes Neubauer had said once that dead children were led into the Mountain. Are they trying to get through the walls, back out to the living? Anguished, he wants to press the dead faces back where they came from. And discovers that the walls aren't there anymore and that the bench that was screwed into the wall is now in the middle of the cell, like a throne. A chandelier hangs from the ceiling suspended from three chains. The chains run together into a knot above his head and continue to a point on the floor under the bed where a hole opens, like the drain in a tub or a handbasin. It seems there must be an exit below as well. He had always believed that the cell was situated as far inside this repulsive prison as it was ever possible to go, that the only way to get out was to move backwards out of time and somehow render undone all that had been done but, then, who has such powers? Now he realises that if one could just become small enough, the hole under the bed would be an escape route and, as he thinks that, the hole grows wider. All that supported him from below has vanished and he must hold on to the cell walls to stop himself from slipping and falling straight down into the void. But soon his feet touch something solid, there are high, firm steps under his feet, a staircase that leads down into the shelter. He descends all the way to the bottom step where a passage begins, so low and narrow he can only get in by bending his neck. This, he realises, is because he is inside the Mountain. Although the glow of the angel-light can no longer reach this place he senses that the rock chamber is continuously widening around him. The sounds of his footsteps on the gravel create a chain of echoes inside a greater echo and when the breaths come out from inside his chest it sounds as if thousands of people were breathing. And now he sees them: the boys from his section. They are seated on two long benches pushed up against the walls and each one of them has his knees pulled up against his chest just as Mrs Rohrbach has told them to. Right at the end, he sees Julius Becker with the scissor handles sticking out of his belly. He smiles with teeth coated in black, clotted blood but he still frees up a place next to him and signals to Adrian to come and sit down. Where they are, they can clearly hear the streaming, running flow of water below. It is not like at Ybbs, where you sensed the presence of the river as a slight, whispering noise on the other side of the thick stone walls. In this place, the water is so close that he can feel its cold breath against the side of his face. Becker points to a hole that has opened up in the stone floor between the rows of benches. It would normally be covered but the massive wooden lid with black iron strapping has been pulled off and placed to one side. Below, the water flows so fast it seems to stand still. The boys take turns to go to the hole. First up, the boy at the end of the left-hand bench. He sits down on the edge of the hole, near the lid, and lets his legs dangle. Next, the boy seated at the end of the right-hand bench moves forward and crouches behind the first one, who pushes off and slides into the water. Just briefly, his head is seen above the surface and you sense how the water must be tearing and tugging at his body.

With a measured, almost gentle movement, the second boy places his hand on the struggling head, pushes it down and keeps it there until the body has been flushed away completely. Then he sits down on the edge himself and, already, one of the boys from the left-hand bench is there, standing next to the wooden lid and about to push the second boy's head under the water. And so it goes. The seated boys move along to fill the gaps in the rows. *There is only one way out*, Julius Becker explains. Soon, it is Adrian's turn. He stands near that lid and watches Jockerl who is in the water. The little head fights against the current to stay above the surface but, at the same time, his eyes look up at Adrian. Jockerl's gaze is full of fear but also pleading and trust. All the same: *do it now do it do it . . . !* the Mountain whispers and it is Julius Becker's dead voice he hears all around him. But Adrian can't lift his hand, it is as heavy as lead. A door opens suddenly, a hand stretches out past him and Jockerl's head vanishes under the swirling, black waters. He stands up and wants to scream but can't because his lungs have no air in them. Then, in the blue angel-light, he sees Nurse Mutsch's shadow. It must still be night. Behind the grille over the window, there is only a faint glimmer of daylight. Hidden in the darkness, Mutsch is leaning over him. He thinks at first that she has come to push *his* head under the water. But, instead, he realises that she is holding out a plate with two slices of dry rye bread. You eat this, she says. Then you can come out.

Pototschnik In September 1942, a new boy arrives in their section. He is called Karl Pototschnik and if what his notes state about him is true, he is a child embodiment of all that is evil and degenerate. He is idle and cares for nothing, servile and work-shy, false and manipulative, dishonest and a 'bad comrade' who respects nothing and nobody and who, instead of lining up with the others in good order and doing as he is told, starts a row and shouts abuse. Pototschnik is the same age as Adrian and Hannes but his shapeless body and placid manner makes him seem quite a lot older. His body appears to be just hung on his skeleton like a coat that is almost too heavy for its weak hook. On top of his bulk sits a head with a high forehead, and cheeks so childishly plump that the folds of skin leave only two narrow slits for his eyes; it is topped by curly blond hair that looks like a cauliflower. One might assume that his was a face that would be limited to one expression but in reality Pototschnik's features can at short notice shift into every kind of expression. If one of the staff comes in, with a hand raised to strike, his face goes white with fear. When Nurse Mutsch starts to pull at one of his long arms, Pototschnik's body contracts like a prodded mussel, and if someone gives him a row, his lips stretch like rubber bands, the corners of his mouth begin to twitch and quiver while real tears are flowing from his eyes. His exaggerated play-acting, which no one can quite fathom (*is* it play-acting or is it real?), maddens the staff. It is clear to all that Pototschnik cannot be controlled by the usual means. One day, there was a much-discussed development: Doctor Krenek came along to beat some sense into the boy. Krenek didn't take the trouble to march Pototschnik off to somewhere more private but went straight for the rotten little toad in the day room, which meant that everyone had a ringside seat. Memorably, Pototschnik appeared not to be bothered in the slightest by the thrashing he was given. True, he screamed and crouched under the swinging leather belt, and his hands and arms became gashed and streaked with blood because he tried to shelter his face, but after a more than quarter of an hour's energetic flogging, which took the two of them across and back over the day room floor in long, intricate patterns as if in a dance, Doctor Krenek was the first to show signs of weariness, his shoulders drooping and the striking arm lifting with less and less vigour while Pototschnik's lips were shiny and red, and his eyes gleamed with defiance.

You can't hurt Pototschnik, people were saying afterwards.

And to be invulnerable is to be powerful.

Of course, power is not only based on strength and resilience. Real power will only come to those who see the submission of others as an aspect of the proper world order and who don't waver for a second from their belief that all is well in a world where they are seen as the unquestioned rulers.

If Pototschnik thought that someone was made for this or that, then this was how he was to behave. Because Adrian was, once and for all time, *the tinker*, he was left alone for as long as he behaved as was fitting for a tinker, cringed and grovelled the way tinkers are expected to. The same line of thinking meant that Jockerl, who was short and fast on his legs, must serve as Pototschnik's fag every minute of the day. For as long as Jockerl folded towels and blankets, tied shoelaces and ran errands for Pototschnik, he was tolerated. But the day came when Jockerl didn't fancy any more servitude. He was in one of his dark periods when he hung his head and felt that everyone was out to get him. Pototschnik reacted forcefully. He lifted Jockerl up in his arms and then gripped the smaller boy's body between his thighs. His next move was to place his arms crosswise around Jockerl's neck and began to twist, with long, alternating turns, as if turning the handle on a mill. At the same time as he was grinding away so hard his big body shook, there were small bubbles of saliva hanging in the corners of Pototschnik's mouth and an unearthly, bellowing noise emerged from his nose and lips: *uuh-uuh-uh-uhhhh . . . !*

Hannes Neubauer was the first to register the danger signals and ran off to alert Nurse Mutsch. Not even Mutsch managed to undo

Pototschnik's stranglehold on Jockerl's neck. Two more asylum nurses had to be called by Mrs Rohrbach, who stood with her back turned and her hand cupped around the mouthpiece whispering *he's killing him, he's killing . . . !* and together they broke open the appalling grip, wrestled Pototschnik to the floor and freed Jockerl, who was unconscious and had to be revived with oxygen. And from that day, Hannes Neubauer became Pototschnik's Sworn Enemy, according to the logic that defined Adrian as everybody's Doormat and Jockerl as the eternal Footman. Hannes's and Pototschnik's beds stood just two beds apart in the dormitory. The two boys often ended up side by side in the march to school and the queue for the midday plate of soup. Now and then, Pototschnik would try to wind Neubauer up. *Why do you need to be here, you little turd? Your father's an officer!* he might say. Or, for example, *a real German officer doesn't dump his son in an institution!* But Hannes refused to be provoked and only went on muttering quietly to himself. Gradually, Pototschnik with his fat paws, vice-like thighs and slitty eyes welling with false tears became part of the ever-growing narrative that Hannes constantly told himself and which would be revealed in its full greatness first when his father came and the prisoners were released from inside the Mountain.

Visiting Hours What would once and for all decide the power struggle between Pototschnik and Neubauer was that Pototschnik had regular visitors while nobody ever came to see Neubauer. Also, Pototschnik's visitors came in large, busy groups, and they all laughed a lot in the corridor and banged the doors when they left. At least, that was how it seemed to the other children who were sitting quietly in the day room, waiting for their *special moment*, as Nurse Mutsch put it. The visiting hours were surrounded by more rituals and regulations than any other recurring event in the pavilion. The rules demanded that the children started the preparations by cleaning the washrooms and toilets and scrubbing the floor in the corridor. After the midday meal, the children were locked in the day room while the pavilion's staff stood guard outside. When the visitors started to arrive, the guardians suddenly underwent a near-total personality change. Names and titles were exchanged in voices laden with pretence and the children occasionally even heard the nurses laugh and joke. In the day room, the air was thick and sticky with sweaty expectation. *Shush-shuush!* The children who were standing with their ears pressed to the door wanted to try to understand what was being said in the medley of voices, the nurses' fluting tones mingled with the bassoon notes of the male visitors. Then the day room door would be unlocked, opened ever such a thin crack, and in the gap between the door and the frame either Nurse Mutsch's or Nurse Demeter's face would peep in, grinning as delightedly as if its owner had been sainted; yes, there might even be a modicum of breathless excitement in Mutsch's voice as she called out the names of the children who were granted the happiness of stepping outside to receive their visitor and, always, Pototschnik's name came first in the list:

Pototschnik, Rusch, Wild –
You have visitooors . . . !

And so Pototschnik stood up and left; next, Rusch and Wild: tight boys' backs, stiff with hope. Every time the door closed after them, Adrian told himself that he would never behave as soppily just because his name was called. But why sit there and hope for something that would never happen and, anyway, if, against all reason, it ever did, what good would it do? You thought all this if your *special moment* didn't arrive. Perhaps Hannes Neubauer thought just the same. Or else, perhaps he thought about nothing of the sort: his *special moment* was of course due in another world, another time than the present. But then, one day, the wondrous, unimaginable thing happened: the door opened, Nurse Mutsch popped her head in and smiled:

Zie-eegler . . . ! Visi-tooor . . . !

Adrian couldn't believe his ears. Seemingly, Nurse Mutsch didn't quite believe it either because when he came forward on trembling legs and bowed to get underneath the nurse's arm that held the door open, she glanced at him with an expression of such deep distrust that he at first thought that the visitor was some person from an authority that had come to take him away to some even worse place. But it was his mother. She wore the same tatty, collarless coat as usual when she went visiting and stood squashed into a corner at the far end of the corridor. She had put on lipstick and when she smiled, her lips expanded into a big, bright red flower. But she wasn't looking at him when she smiled but at Mrs Rohrbach who was just passing, sagging under the armful of folders carried pressed against her chest. Mrs Rohrbach returned the smile with an expression indicating that she had little time for that kind of thing. And: *thank you, don't worry, it's alright, alright, not to worry*, Mrs Rohrbach said to Adrian's mother, who had leapt to her feet to try to open the door for the busy lady. By then Mrs Rohrbach had smartly freed up an arm and produced a key, and now the door opened and then slammed behind her without any assistance from Adrian's well-meaning mother, who was left standing with hanging arms and pathetic flower-lips. This was the first time in four years that mother and son had been in the same room but Adrian's mother seemed hardly to see him or, if she did, had no time for what she saw. She behaved as if her made-up lips and her coat added up to a kind of disguise which might be exposed for what it was at any moment, so she had to say as much as she could before it was too late. Her first subject was Adrian's father, who had been sacked from his job at the locomotive factory after giving in to the temptation of sharing a bottle with a mate and who probably had to join the army unless there was some civil defence work to be done. Next, she spoke about Laura, whom she had managed to contact. Laura was in good hands but she had heard nothing about Helmut despite having been told that he was to be moved here, to Spiegelgrund, but now someone called Doctor Krenek has informed her that they have no record at all of a boy of that name and, she asked, has Adrian seen his brother or heard something about him? At this point, something thick and warm wells up inside Mrs Dobrosch, who can't keep it down and then her entire face bursts into tears. Actually bursts. Like a stone, perhaps, that cracks from inside. And his mother stands there, helpless, her face broken to pieces and everything just pours out. She doesn't even hide the mess in her hands. And inside Adrian, something changes. He wouldn't have thought it possible but now he is ashamed of his mother. And, worse: a mute, quite useless rage grows inside him. How can he go on to tell her what he really wanted her to know? How can he speak about this institution where they kill children and the doctors choose which children are to die next and show it by popping a sweet into their mouths? And the chosen ones are taken to a pavilion where they are injected with poison or maybe get poison in their food and, when they are dead, their corpses are dumped into a body-cart with tall wheels and a green, arched roof which is pulled by Steinhof patients in grey asylum suits who perhaps don't even know what a terrible load they are hauling along. But how can he speak such things to her drained and grief-stricken face that weeps for a child who is nowhere to be found? Adrian is reduced to helplessness and, when she opens her arms and takes a step forward to hug him, he feels even more helpless. The embrace she seems to offer him is no more than a pair of quivering arms and more sobbing. His *mother* looks to *him* for comforting, not the other way round. And her coat smells badly of damp and engrained dirt. She can sense how stiff he is and that he can't help becoming still more unyielding, which of course makes her cry even more. Then, *at last*, Nurse Mutsch approaches with a look of uneasy concern on her face, places an experienced and protective hand on the back of his neck, leads him away with firm, determined movements and deposits him in the day room where a wild fight has just broken out. Nurse Mutsch stands in the doorway and roars *you will stop this row at once, remember the visitors are still here!* Everyone obeys until the door closes again. Finally, Pototschnik stands in the middle of the room with his arm triumphantly raised. He lowers it slowly, opens his fist one finger at a time and shows the empty bullet casing in his palm and they all scream,

. . . I want it I want it I want it . . .

Hannes Neubauer stands by himself. No visitor today either. He desperately wants that cartridge and Pototschnik sees it in his face. It's a real Mauser cartridge, Pototschnik says. From an automatic pistol. And he comes closer, holding out his broad palm where the cartridge rests as if on a tray with its sharp end pointing straight at Hannes's face and then he says:

Do you know why your mum never comes to see you, Hannes?
It's because your mum is a whore, Hannes, a whore whore whore . . .

A WHORE! WHORE! WHORE! everyone in the room screams, Adrian is the loudest of the lot. His face goes red with the sheer thrill of saying a word like that out loud. Then Pototschnik suddenly turns and gives Jockerl the cartridge.

You take it, he says,

(and then, with his back turned to Hannes)

I don't want it anyway.

A Secret Weapon It is late in the autumn now. To stand in for Nurse Demeter, who is on sick leave with a hurt ankle, Mrs Lauritz has been moved to their section. Mrs Lauritz is older than Mutsch and Demeter, and her face looks stitched together, like a patchwork. One part of her face might smile while another part looks scared or tense. But Mrs Lauritz's body is slender and energetic, and it follows that she is very keen on outdoor activities. From the moment she arrives, they are to keep their rucksacks packed and always have at least one change of dry clothing ready. If, against all her plans, the weather really is so bad there can be no talk of open-air exercises, she makes them sit in the day room engaged in what she and Mrs Krämer call *kit cleaning*, which means that you take the laces out of your shoes, shine them and put the laces back, and keep repeating the task until Mrs Krämer feels you have spent enough effort on it. Adrian Ziegler is pleased to have these things to do because he has hidden the cartridge at the bottom of his rucksack. It's of course the one Pototschnik gave Jockerl. Adrian has stolen it but nobody knows about the theft. Jockerl doesn't. Obviously, Pototschnik doesn't either. Jockerl is surely content to think the cartridge is still with the other worthless precious things he has collected and hidden in a space behind the drawer in his bedside table. Jockerl never pulls out the drawer to check his treasure because he knows that it would give away what he keeps there. That wouldn't do, because nobody in pavilion 9 is allowed any treasures. Everyone remembers what happened to Rudolf Ortner. The first thing Rudolf did when he arrived in this place was to spread out his shell collection on a table in the day room: lots of differently shaped mussel shells that were beautifully ridged on the outside and bluish-white inside, or else coated in shimmering mother-of-pearl. Nurse Mutsch came along to admire it, too. When she'd had enough of the display, she swept all the shells onto the floor and trampled on them. The shells were crushed to fragments under her cork heels. *In this section you can forget about personal belongings*. Adrian Ziegler could only too easily imagine her face lighting up in a cold smile the moment she caught Pototschnik out for secreting real ammunition in some hidey-hole. Which was of course why Pototschnik had handed over the actual storing of it to Jockerl. Power-mad as Pototschnik might be, he was also a cautious, not to say cowardly operator who took no unnecessary chances. But they had failed to take Ziegler into account even though it's well enough known that tinkers can't resist anything that gleams and glitters. One night, said tinker slipped out of bed, gently eased the drawer in Jockerl's bedside table out of its seating, pulled the cartridge out and then sat with it in his hand, twisting and turning it for several hours. Being up and about at night is risky because now and then the duty nurse comes past to check the boys through the peephole in the door. And the night-light is treacherous. It seems feeble but is in fact very revealing. So Adrian carefully bundles up his coverlet under the blanket to make it look as if it covered a sleeping body and sits on the floor in a place he knows is safe because the bed-ends block the sightline from the door. He sits there night after night, grinding the point of the cartridge against the heel of his boots. Of course, in itself the cartridge is useless, but just to hold it gives him an intoxicating sense of space and freedom, of being in control of his life, and reminds him of what Hannes feels when he guards the entrance to the Mountain. In these moments, they can both say: I know where *you* are but you know next to nothing about where *I* am and what *I* am doing. Sometimes, Adrian replaces the secret weapon in the drawer, sometimes not. If not, he sleeps, coolly holding the cartridge in his hand, even up to the time when Mrs Rohrbach comes along with her clapper to wake them up. One day, he goes as far as to hold the cartridge in his fist and say to triumphantly to Jockerl:

This is the last night you see me lying here,
you had better believe me, you little shit
(everyone calls Jockerl 'little shit');

and Jockerl looks in terror between Adrian's clenched fist to his face, worn by lack of sleep, and doesn't have a clue what kind of secret weapon Adrian has got hold of, is clueless about everything.

And the days pass, and the daylight takes longer and longer to arrive in the mornings and disappears ever earlier in the evenings. The rain that falls during the night collects in deep puddles on the gravelled paths between the pavilions and the puddles are still brimming when the morning comes. The morning wind sweeps through the tops of the trees in the hospital park, carrying the sour smell of damp stone dust from the old quarry. The boys in pavilion 9 have lined up, rucksacks on their backs, for a new day excursion. They shiver in the cold. This time, Adrian Ziegler has brought his weapon, stuffed deep in his rucksack, concealed like a riddle or a treasure trove or perhaps just something that sets him apart from the others and gives him a glimpse of colour in the greyness. This morning, it seems to Adrian that they are not so much walking as rising: ever higher towards the sky that slowly becomes brighter and clearer as the sun climbs up behind

Gallitzinberg, like a sharp needle of glass. Level with the fire station, a horse-chestnut tree leans over the asylum wall, its leaves burning beautifully brown and yellow when the sunbeams strike them; a mighty, dangerous tree that, when the winds stirs its branches, leisurely scatters scores of small, angrily clattering chestnuts all over the place. The hard little fruits hit the boys on the path, too, and suddenly someone calls out about the chestnuts that are hitting his head. Before Mrs Lauritz has had a chance to respond, the boys have run off in every direction. Normally, no one would of course have dared to break the rules quite so flagrantly but Mrs Lauritz is new and not properly initiated into the strict routines introduced by Nurse Demeter and Nurse Mutsch, so even though Lauritz blows on her whistle . . . *tweet-tweet-tweet!* . . . no one takes any notice and she has to run around herself to try to sort out the boys, who are chasing chestnuts on the path. As ever, Jockerl is the first to spot imminent danger and self-sacrificingly runs up to tug at Mrs Lauritz's sleeve:

It was me, Mrs Lauritz, it was me who . . . !

But Mrs Lauritz will not be diverted. She feels sure that she has seen 'with her own eyes' who is guilty, and acts before Pototschnik has had time to get out of the way. She grabs at the cauliflower head, gets hold of an ear and twists until the boy's entire body is dangling from her hard, determined thumb-grip.

So far, it is all part of the traffic of dormitories and closed day rooms, a straightforward routine move of the kind that happens many times daily. But as Mrs Lauritz gets on with chastising Pototschnik, an older woman carrying a rough string bag full of shopping comes walking along on the other side of the road. When she catches sight of Lauritz with Pototschnik, who is screaming his head off, she puts her bag down and moves across the road while waving her arms in the air and shouting:

You leave that child alone! Have you lost what sense you ever had, woman,

going for a poor helpless child like that . . . !

Mrs Lauritz still holds on to the grimacing Pototschnik while she tries to get to terms with this utterly baffling situation: a complete stranger who dares to challenge her authority! But the woman won't back off. She would like to make it clear that her husband is personally acquainted with the institution's director, and Mrs Child-Molester had better state her name and employee grade so the husband can make sure that she is appropriately reprimanded. By now, many more people are joining in. Adrian notices that two boys are coming towards them. They look like brothers. The younger one pushes a bicycle and the older one walks at his side, looking a little doubtful. By now, Mrs Lauritz has clearly scented a potential threat because she goes bright red in the face, puffs her chest out like a bird and says:

I bring these children up in the spirit that my Führer has chosen and commanded!

Later, Adrian often speculates about what would have happened if he had legged it there and then. He was carrying enough for his short-term needs in his rucksack: dry clothes, a thermos of hot tea and the unopened packed meal that had been handed out that morning. And he had the cartridge, his secret weapon, as well. Still, he probably wouldn't have got away with it. The road was long and straight, and all around were houses on sites surrounded by tall fences and walls. He wouldn't have been able to run very far with his heavy pack before Lauritz or Krämer would have been snapping at his heels. Add to that the fact that Mrs Lauritz was furious. Still red-faced, she ordered her charges to turn round and start walking, leading the march at an exhausting pace. But Pototschnik was even more upset. As soon as Mrs Lauritz had turned her back, he jumped on Jockerl and stage-whispered so loudly that everyone, even those well away, could hear what he said: *when we get back I'll shoot your head off, you little shit*. Only this time, Mrs Lauritz was on the alert and hit Pototschnik with her walking stick until, temporarily cowed, he made himself small and took his place in the line.

Jockerl's Punishment The news about the incident must have travelled ahead of them because, when they got back, Doctor Krenek stood waiting at the door to pavilion 9. They were ordered to go straight to the day room without hanging up their outdoor clothes and stand at *Habt-Acht* – to attention – by their seats while Krenek lectured them on the subject of discipline and, more specifically, how they, whenever they were outside the walls of the institution, were to behave with the utmost propriety and, above all, never speak to any strangers. The fact was, of course, that none of them had addressed any strangers, or vice versa. It was their *Erzieher*, Mrs Lauritz, who had had words with that lady. But Doctor Krenek didn't waste time on the finer points and, anyway, no one protested. Mrs Rohrbach stood at his side with the register open and read out their names. As soon as yours was called out, you had to step forward and empty the contents of your pockets for Doctor Krenek to inspect. He was patently satisfied when the odd innocent chestnut landed in front of him, or a pretty stone or bottle cap, but then it was Jockerl's turn and, as Jockerl bent forward to show his empty pockets, Pototschnik started shouting in his familiar loud, shrill voice:

Hand back the cartridge you stole!

Jockerl showed no sign of hearing what Pototschnik was shouting. He stood still, as if glued to the floor, not moving a finger until Krenek irritably shoved him forward and they could all see how

Jockerl's legs were shaking. Had he already checked his secret bedside store? Did he know that the cartridge had gone? Did he guess who had stolen it? The next name was called and Jockerl returned to his place. Pototschnik turned round to glance murderously at him. Jockerl said nothing, just stared straight ahead. And then, what they had all been half-expecting happened: a bubbling sound that fused into a faint but sustained trickle while the sweet, warm smell of urine filled the air. Mrs Lauritz fixed her stern gaze on Jockerl, who tried to hide the dark stain on his crotch by putting one leg across the other. Doctor Krenek had of course also taken in what was going on but only turned to the window, his hands clasped behind his back, and pretended to look outside, presumably in order to spare his poor staff further humiliation. Mrs Lauritz swung into action, walked swiftly along the line of tittering boys, grabbed hold of Jockerl's arm and marched him out of the room. Doors were pulled open and slammed shut, then came the familiar sound of water splashing against the hard, enamelled sides of the bathtub. Jockerl was to have the *water treatment*. His screams echoed between the tiled walls but the sounds were unusual, with a tinny echo. Until, suddenly, silence fell, as if someone had put a lid on the tin. After that, nothing happened except that Doctor Krenek, who had stood by the window without moving, suddenly cleared his throat and walked out. A little later, Mrs Lauritz entered. Something had made the stitching that held the bits of her face together come apart but she didn't say anything, just sat down to keep an eye on them as if nothing else had happened. Because nobody had told them anything different, they all kept standing. Dusk darkened the room until they could barely make each other out, and Mrs Lauritz even less. Adrian was preoccupied with his rucksack and the best way to get rid of the cartridge. Finally, he mustered his courage and asked to be allowed to go to the toilet. Mrs Lauritz shuddered as if her deep thoughts had been shattered and, perhaps because she wanted to avoid any more painful incidents, she unlocked the door, told him to go on his own and knock when he wanted to come back in. Then she closed the door and left Adrian alone in the long corridor, so dark by then that all he could make out was the clock hanging from the ceiling, but only its blank face and not its hands. He heard a rhythmic drip from the sink where the tap must have been carelessly turned off. Then he caught sight of Jockerl standing in the cocoon of sodden towels Mrs Lauritz and the nurses had wrapped around him. Jockerl looked so peculiar, frail and tense at the same time. Long, shivery shakes ran from his thin legs up to his neck, extended like a hungry bird's. He seemed frozen to the floor. His head, hanging like a stone suspended from his angled body, looked different, no longer sad but transformed into that of a very old man whose skin has crumpled into stiff folds around his nose and mouth and whose unseeing eyes are hidden by half-closed eyelids. At first, Adrian thought Jockerl might be dead already but somehow still upright. Once he had thought that, another idea took over. Perhaps there was sly cunning, almost hatred lurking behind that rigid stare. Adrian slowly went over to the rucksacks that they had dumped in the corner, found his own and took the cartridge out. Then he gave way to a sudden impulse. The remorse for what he did would not give him any peace for the rest of his life. He bent close to Jockerl's shivering, old man's face, held the cartridge only a few centimetres from those dead, yet cold and condescending eyes and said:

Here you are. Look, arsehole!
See what I nicked from you?
One single word from you and I'll poke your eye out with this!

As he said it, he pushed the sharpened tip against Jockerl's left eye. Jockerl didn't even blink. His little old man's face with its corpse-like pallor was like a mask. Brief waves of shuddering kept running through his body. Adrian didn't know what to do and wandered off towards the washroom and the toilets. The showers were lined up along one wall, opposite a row of washbasins, and behind them was a screened-off area with toilets and urinals. The doors to the toilet cubicles couldn't be locked. The windows in the larger, lighter part of the room were different from the other windows in the pavilion in that their lower panes were made of milky, opaque glass. Two ventilation panes at the top stood open but were so narrow not even an infant could have pushed through them. For the escapist, the best thing would be to concentrate his efforts on the fastenings at the bottom. Zavlacky had showed him once how to attack them. Both window latches were attached to their hooks with a metal fastening that could be cut if one had a tool that was sharp enough. That was why Adrian had been sharpening the tip of the bullet casing. At best, the edge could function as the teeth on a saw-blade. He tried but hadn't had time to make more than a faint score mark in the polished metal when he suddenly heard steps approaching in the corridor and then Mrs Lauritz's voice: *Ziegler . . . !* He hid inside one of the toilets, crouching next to the seat with his back pressed to the wall, and prayed that Mrs Lauritz wouldn't open this door. If Jockerl had decided to tell on Adrian he would have done so long ago. But Jockerl was not like the other children in the pavilion. He was never out to gain advantages, didn't even seem to understand what was best for himself. Thoughts of revenge were utterly alien to him. Adrian felt ashamed. Now Mrs Lauritz was in the washroom, her voice echoing in there: *Zie-eegler . . . !* Then the telephone in the nurses' room rang, Lauritz responded to the sharp noise and hurried off down the corridor on thudding cork heels. He attacked the window fastening again with renewed energy. And now it was giving way, the latch shifted a little on its hook and the milky pane moved a fraction outwards. He went for the other fastening, which was easier to break. All that remained now was to climb up on the edge of the basin, force himself through the tight gap between the window and its frame, and he was outside. He landed with a faint sucking noise on the wet, muddy grass, broke the fall with his knees and arms, and then ran across the gravelled path and towards the Steinhof buildings. If only he had known how easy it was to get out, he would have brought his rucksack, which was still in the corridor, and for as long as Mrs Lauritz stayed on the phone no one except Jockerl would have seen him. Then it struck him that because Jockerl hadn't said anything, the likelihood was that he would have to take the punishment (again) once they realised that Adrian had escaped. Shame almost overcame him. He had a vision of himself holding up the stolen cartridge in front of Jockerl's unmoving eye, *here you are, arsehole* and, suddenly, he simply couldn't run fast enough. They had walked along the outside of the asylum wall on their excursions so many times that, although it was almost completely dark by now, he knew exactly in which direction he should run to get to the large chestnut tree where they had stopped earlier today. From the inside of the tall wall, the tree didn't look as proud and huge as it had from the outside but he knew he could trust its long, strong branches. It was hard to clamber up the slippery, mossy trunk but he managed to climb to the first point where a strong branch joined the trunk, about four metres above the ground. From there, he had an open view of the entire hospital site. He saw the colossal mass of the Steinhof asylum and, further away, the group of gardening sheds near to where the blank surfaces of the greenhouse walls floated in an inky blue, shimmering light at the edge of the parkland, which looked black in the evening gloom. In the opposite direction, he could just make out the brooding bulk of the anatomy building and the subdued lamplight from some of its windows. He climbed higher up. He had no idea of where the wall was below him and tested the toughness of different branches. The most solid-looking one took off upwards rather than sideways but he followed it as far along as he dared. Leaves, damp with evening dew, whipped his face. The branch swung and dipped under his weight, deeper and deeper. He could hear the showers of torn-off chestnuts pattering against the cobbled pavement. It meant that he must be clear of the wall by now. In that instant, he saw a dazzling light further away. It didn't come from a stationary source but bopped about like torchlight. From below he heard a dull rasping noise, like sandpaper rubbing against smooth wood. Were they about to catch up with him after all? His heart was thumping inside his chest. Should he hide inside the canopy of the tree or take a chance and let go? The branch made up his mind for him. It suddenly swayed and he slid down it as if poured out of the tree. He fell blindly and crash-landed with his hip and shoulder hitting the edge of the pavement. In the same instant, there was a screeching sound of bicycle brakes. Another body rolled heavily over his. Then the bicycle came down on top of them both and the handlebars slammed into Adrian's stomach. A pair of frightened eyes took him in and a voice said:

It's you!

It was the boy who, together with his older brother, had stopped to watch when the marching group had scattered and then stayed to listen while Mrs Lauritz and the shopping-bag lady were having words. Adrian recognised him by his broad smile and the beret he wore pushed well down over his forehead.

You're from in there, aren't you?

He said 'in there' in a deeply impressed tone.

I've seen you lots of times.

Adrian didn't know what to say. The boy's grin grew even broader.

You won't get far, at least not in that kit!

Adrian looked down at his short trousers and dirty sandals. The boy was tugging at the front wheel of his bike which had partly jammed under Adrian. It was a good bike, with a sturdy frame and wide tyres. It didn't have a light in front but the boy had a phosphorus lamp pinned to one lapel on his half-length jacket. In its pale light, the boy gestured to Adrian to jump on. They took off, Adrian perching uneasily on the handlebars, with the bell pressing into a buttock and his legs sticking almost straight out, while he heard his young benefactor sometimes singing behind him, sometimes panting as he pushed on the pedals and they zoomed downhill along Flötzersteig. He could just distinguish in the dark the allotment gardens they had marched past so often, then another place he recognised, the Wilhelminenspital's towering façade. As they swept down the long slope towards Ottakring, the wartime blackout meant that all he could make out at the bottom of the valley was a jumble of roofs and chimneys, but it didn't take long before he saw, rising out of the dark, real buildings with proper frontages facing real streets with cars driving up and down and on the pavements people walking about, real flesh-and-blood people, not half-dead prisoners. A wild happiness filled Adrian's mind. He was free.

VII

The Bleeding Führer

On the Run To escape is one thing but to stay alive on the run is another. While Adrian had been sharpening his secret weapon in the institution, he had made no plan, only known that he wanted to get home to his mother. Now he had to face the fact that he had no idea how to find her, that he didn't know where she lived or what she did. Maybe he would aim for the 11th Bezirk, he thought. Someone in the old house on Simmeringer Hauptstrasse might be in touch with her or at least know where she lived now. Or he could try to look for Uncle Ferenc; but even if Ferenc hadn't been called up (Adrian suspected that he had been) there was no guarantee that he or any of his friends would be able or even want to help Adrian. The elation seeped out of him and was replaced by worry and indecision, and after spending some time aimlessly walking the streets around Lerchenfelder Gürtel, he returned to Ottakring station by midnight. He tried to find a suitable house where he might sleep for a while but, by then, most houses had locks on their street doors. New regulations made it obligatory for all property owners to ensure that no 'alien elements' were present in their buildings. The radio broadcasted warnings about the danger of Bolshevik spies. He had heard Nurse Mutsch speak on the subject. Like flies, she had said, they follow you around. Finally, he managed to get into a tumbledown house on Roseggergasse where part of the attic was used for drying laundry. The drying attic was no more than a bare, rough stone floor under a tall wooden roof. At the top of the stairs, the attic was protected by a rusty iron grille into which a wooden door had been fitted. He found a couple of dirty log-sacks and wrapped himself in them but they did next to nothing to stop the cold that rose from the stone floor. He breathed on his hands, clenched and unclenched them to keep some sensation in them and fell asleep after making himself as small as possible, with his knees pulled up to his chest and his hands tucked into his armpits. In the morning, hunger drove him out to look for food. In the daylight, everyone could of course see where he came from and what sort he was. People turned to glance at his bare feet in muddy sandals and he could almost hear them whispering to each other:

. . . *one of* those *children* . . .

He dived behind rattling trams, crossed one street, then another. He managed to snatch two apples from a stall at the corner of Ottakringer Strasse and Neulerchenfelder Strasse and ran with them under his shirt towards the big brewery on the other side of the street. The wide gateway was blocked by a barrier but he waited around. When the man in the guard hut started a shouted exchange with someone he knew who was on the other side of the street, Adrian sneaked past into the brewery yard. Near the factory building, a pair of dray horses stood waiting, ready to pull their broad wagons. The horses chomped hay from jute sacks and dumped a load of dung now and then. The rich smell of malt mingled with hay and horse manure reminded him of all the times Mrs Haidinger had made him haul radio batteries all the way to Schwechat and back. Again and again, he was almost clipped by lorries that came into the yard loaded with clunking empties. The sound gave him an idea. The empty bottles must be stored somewhere. If he could take just a few of them he could try to cash in the deposits. No one would think twice about it. There were hordes of boys who did their bit by collecting deposit money on bottles. If he came home with a pocket full of money earned in a respectable way, maybe his mother would write to the board of the institution and tell them that she was going to keep him this time. He managed to get into the huge brewing hall and ended up in front of an imposing machine spitting out endless rows of dark-brown bottles onto a conveyer belt. The bottles whizzed past strong metal arms ending in claws that lifted each one, turned it in the air and put it down again. Workers rushed up and down along the moving belt, hollering and shouting, but the noise of the machine was so overpowering that their voices were dulled as if calling out from behind a glass wall. He came back to awareness with a jump when a hard hand squeezed his shoulder. A man in a foreman's grey coat loomed behind him and a large face hung over the boy like a lamp. The face might have asked *what are you doing here?* Or it might have mimed the words. Adrian didn't actually hear anything. *Waiting for my mum*, he tried to shout or mime, because he had to answer something. The words were sucked into the clamouring, thumping giant machine that at the same moment grabbed hold of the necks of another half-dozen bottles, tipped them upside down and dumped them back on the belt. *Wait outside then.* The grip on his shoulder changed into a firm hand on his back that pushed him towards the door. The foreman apparently believed him and, as soon as they were back outside the large hall, past the packing shed and the garage for the large lorries, he completely lost interest in the young intruder. He just let the boy out and shut the factory door behind him. Adrian retreated to the corner of the yard where the drays had been waiting. The horses had left, leaving only the dung heaps and scattered remains of their hay. He crouched down and watched as the dark slowly deepened and moved up the fronts of the buildings. Soon, only the top floors were still lit by reflected sunlight. Adrian felt as if the lower, unlit windows secretly observed him. Then the dark swallowed even the attics. He might have been in the bottom of a well. All around him, walls rose to the sky. Closest to him, the tall factory walls around the brewery. Beyond them: the frontages of the buildings around the marketplace. Not one of them showed a single light. Just as in Ybbs, these buildings seemed to have no exterior: all were part of a system of inner courtyards and narrow, interconnecting paths and passages. Like a prison, but in the outside air. The shadow had by now reached the roof of the factory and, as if that were a signal, the workers walked out into the yard in clusters, five or six at a time. Most of them were men, but there were women among them, too. He wished that one of the women really was his mother and that she would see him waiting and call to him so that everyone else heard it, and then he could run to her. Some of the women pushed bicycles and had already pinned the little phosphorus lamps to their coats, ready to leave by the factory gate, climb onto the saddle and wobble along on the star-shaped network of unlit streets. For by now there was no light anywhere except for a pale, faintly green, reflected band near the horizon. He walked to the house on Roseggergasse under that green, darkening ceiling of sky and climbed upstairs to the attic where the warped wooden door still hung open. At first he thought he would never sleep, what with the grinding hunger in his guts and the raw cold that rose from the stone floor and settled in his bones, but he did fall asleep quite soon after lying down. In his dream, his mother appeared in front of him. She hadn't stopped at just putting on her red lipstick but was also wearing Mrs Haidinger's red dress. And I who thought you would help me, she said as she bent over him. He felt terribly afraid because he knew this wasn't really her. When that face came close to his, the red lipstick-smile cracked and behind it were rows of teeth.

Hard, bony fingers reached for his hand that clutched the cartridge, tried to force his fingers back one by one and, when he wouldn't give way, she lifted his fist to her mouth and bit it with her pointy teeth, as sharp as a shark's, cutting his knuckles. He screamed, woke and sat up with his heart hammering in his chest. All around him shimmered something icily white, which took him some time to realise was only the frozen vapour from his own breaths. He sucked on his hand and tasted the metallic flavour of the blood that stuck his fingers together. He must have clenched his fist so hard around the cartridge that its point had cut him. He was dreadfully cold by now; the shivering began down by his ice-cold feet and carried on all the way up to his teeth, which were chattering uncontrollably. To exercise his legs or wrap his arms around his body didn't help at all. He tried to make some sounds, moans or whimpers, just to stop shaking, and rolled helplessly on the floor until he hit the wall. Then he heard a man's voice, quite near:

. . . and someone's been up there, you take my word.

Before he had time to react, the door was pulled open and in the dark above him torchlight sliced the dust-laden air, seemingly at random, into rhomboid shapes full of lit, whirling specks. He couldn't be sure where he was lying in relation to the jerky beam of light, or if he had been heard, but was aware that he had to stay by the wall. He pulled his arms and legs as close as possible to his body, and waited. A bit away from the sharp-edged light, another male voice called out but it was so harsh and deep it wasn't possible to separate it from the grating noise made by an iron blade against stone. The caretaker or whoever it was who held the unsteady torch shouted back that he *had to lock up first* and then, from nearby, came the sounds of chains rattling and a lock clicking. Someone tugged vigorously at the door. The beam of the torch slid upwards as if by its own volition, reached the roof, and then became absorbed into the darkness at the same time as the footsteps on the stairs grew more distant. Adrian stayed lying with his face to the wall as if he was what he had pretended to be: a lifeless object that someone had dumped there. Then he sensed the chilly stickiness between his thighs. He had peed himself. Like Jockerl. He wasn't the slightest bit tougher. He and Uncle Ferenc had picked up a bird once during one of the summers they had spent together herding cattle down on the flood-plain by the Hubertusdamm. The bird had been lying on the mucky grass and looked squashed, as if someone had stood on it. The wing that wasn't broken was flapping pointlessly in the air. When he held it, about to put it under his shirt, he felt the bird's heart tapping lightly against the palm of his hand. The sun had hung so low over the river its light was almost white. Now, too, he saw the whiteness. There had been an alcove where they stacked the logs, between the cooker and the sooty wall in the kitchen in the Simmering Hauptstrasse flat. Ferenc advised him to put the bird there, and he had, then settled down next to the bird to keep an eye on it. He didn't know what kind it was. Its plumage was speckled, its beak long and grey, and the downy feathers under its broken wing were brilliantly white. He had never before felt such a deep and terrible longing to get back to something or somewhere as he did now, when he remembered that sheltered place between the cooker and the soot-stained wall. When his mother had fired the cooker up, it was warm and he could lie there without being seen by anyone. Slowly, he would open the hand that held the trembling bird while, close by, Helmut was asleep on the floor, his sweaty hair sticking to his forehead, and their mother was getting ready to go to work. Then he'd hear her heels on the stairs and the door slam followed by the lighter sound of her feet on the flagged yard as she almost ran across it. The 71 tram came and went on wheels that rattled over the gaps in the rails. He opened his eyes and saw that the dawn light was already strong enough to pick out the shapes of the roof beams in the dark above him. When he made his arms relax their grip on his body, cold cut him like many knives. He breathed on his fingers and the back of his hands until he could move them normally before going to check the wooden door and actually see what he already knew had happened. They had locked him in. The padlock stuck through the hasp had been reinforced with a chain that had been threaded through the iron grid on both sides of the door. He pressed both palms against the upper part of the door. It swung a little on its worn hinges but didn't shift more than perhaps a centimetre. Pushing his finger between the bars, he could just touch the lock with his fingertips. There was only one thing he could do: dig the hasp out of the warped old wood of the door frame. Sooner or later, it must give way. He gripped the cartridge between thumb and index finger, pushed it out between the bars and began to dig into the wood with its tip. His fingers were soon bleeding again. Then his hand contracted with cramps and he had to massage it, and warm it between his thighs before setting to work again. The light had moved from one end of the attic room to the other when he heard the thuds of the street door open and close several times, and shouts between people who came and went, their shouting multiplied by the echo in the stairwell. One of the voices was the caretaker's, he felt sure of that, and he quickly backed away to be close to the wall. Too soon, darkness fell again but he had managed to gouge a big pile of woodchips from the door and made it possible to jiggle the hasp about. After a few more hours, it was completely loose. The padlock went with it and the door opened a little but was stopped by the chain that became taut when he tried to push his body through the crack between the frame and the door. The gap widened higher towards the top because the chain had been placed quite low down so, by clinging to the grille, and climbing up it, he succeeded first in getting an arm out, then hauling his body through the gap. By then, he was so exhausted by cold and hunger that he no longer had the strength to stay upright as he tackled the abyss of the stairwell. He crawled backwards down the stairs instead, negotiating one step at a time and holding on to the rail. The white-limed wall looked adrift in dark. The doors to the flats were all locked. No voices, not a sound came from behind them. By the time he had reached the bottom of the stairs, any guiding light from above had disappeared. He fumbled his way to the street door, which thankfully could be opened from the inside, and entered a world of shadows. There was no sky up there. Only a faint leaden sheen reached the street. Adrian kept close to the walls as if afraid that the pavement would give way in front of him if he walked too far out. Now and then, he heard the quiet swishing sound of tyres against cobbles but there would always be some time before he could see the dancing phosphorus glow from the cyclist's lamp. He looked for lost coins in the telephone boxes but the small metal bowls for returned change were always smooth and empty. Actually, it was meaningless to look for money because food was only available in exchange for coupons and where would he get any coupons without a fixed address? And even if he had coupons and money to pay with, who would give him anything to eat? All you needed to realise that he didn't belong to anything like a respectable family was a quick look at his face and his clothes. Slowly, the sky grew lighter and the buildings once more emerged from the murk with their closely spaced windows and strictly ordered patterns of panes. He was lying curled up in one of the telephone booths when a uniformed policeman spotted him and dragged him outside. Several passers-by, looking pale and upset, stood about on the pavement. No one stepped forward to kick or hit him. One man actually brought a blanket and spread it over him. The man wore an armband and a lamp on his forehead. He put his hand on Adrian's shoulder and said in a kind voice that he was to lie still and wait. In the end, an ambulance arrived and he was stretchered into it. The sunlight filtering in through the opaque windows of the ambulance told him that they were on their way up the mountain but, when they stopped, he realised that they had pulled up outside the real hospital, the Wilhelminenspital. He was allowed to spend the rest of the day there, in a bed of his own. A nurse brought him a glass of milk and asked if he was hungry. Then a doctor, a proper doctor, examined him. When Adrian told him where he came from and what he had done, the doctor turned to the nurse and said:

He'll be staying with us for today. Let's wait before we inform the institution up the road about his whereabouts.

Then they took him to a large ward where several children were bedded down and put him in a bed, too. The sheets smelled clean and fresh and Adrian fell asleep there and then, an untroubled sleep as if the world no longer existed. The next morning, they came for him and took him back to Spiegelgrund.

The Bunker Naively, he had imagined that his escape attempt would lead to an inquisition session conducted by Mutsch or Rohrbach or one of his other usual tormentors. He was mistaken. Instead, after he had showered, they took him straight to the punishment block in pavilion 11, down into the basement, which seemed to consist mostly of narrow corridors criss-crossed by bulky tin pipes that gave off burping or gurgling noises. One of the corridors ended with a wide iron door closed by massive bolts. His male nurse escort pulled the bolts back and pushed him into a large room, as low-ceilinged as the corridor and lit only by an unshaded bulb in a wall socket. This was the Bunker. And there they all were: seated on one of the benches fixed to the wall he saw the master escapist himself, Zavlacky, next to Peter Schaubach (another Ybbs runaway) and, naturally, Miseryguts, whose head was sagging between his shoulders. None of them seemed particularly surprised to see Adrian turn up. Miseryguts was the only one who spoke but only to state the fact that it was *totally insane* to run away as Adrian had, in the middle of the night without food or water or warm clothes. No further comments were made. As Adrian would put it later, once you got as far as the Bunker, you were on your own, no one gave a damn and all bridges were burnt – *jeer der duchbrennt muss sich um sich selbst kümmern*. Even so, being a Bunker detainee brought a certain status. Once you had done time there, no one would try to get the better of you or make fun of you. Evening came. Two male nurses – or were they *guards* now? – carried a cauldron of soup downstairs. Because all the others had their own bowls, he had to be content with two slices of the dry rye bread that was handed out with the soup. No one offered to share their soup with him. Once the meal was cleared away, the guards returned to take them to their cells on the floor above. Adrian's cell looked exactly like the lock-up one in his 'old' pavilion, with the one difference that here, two benches were fixed to the wall, not just one. When he realised that the other bench had no one assigned to it, it also became clear that his 'treatment' was not yet complete and, once that had dawned on him, he of course couldn't sleep. He spent most of the night speculating about what they would do to punish him. In the morning, he could hear the guards walk along the corridor, unlocking the door to the dormitory where the other boys stayed, then the sounds as they got going, emptying their swollen bladders noisily into the pans, then running water into the basins. His cell remained locked. By mid-morning, they finally came. Doctor Gross and, after him, two nurses. Both ex-asylum nurses, that was easy to see: the same solid build as Nurse Mutsch and the same flat, gormless features. Adrian expected Doctor Gross to acknowledge him, not exactly with a greeting but perhaps with some sign that he had seen Adrian before. But Gross seemed not to recognise him and didn't address him at all. The older of the two nurses told Adrian to lie on his back. When he didn't obey instantly, they pushed him down on the bench with practised hands, and then shoved both arms behind the back of his neck. It hurt horribly. The humiliation felt worse still. They manhandled him like an animal. Gross sat down on the edge of the bench and placed the palm of his hand against Adrian's chest. He held two syringes in his other hand, both about ten centimetres long, but with short needles. Adrian instinctively tried to twist his body away but the quick hands of the nurses had already gripped his kicking legs in vice-like holds while Gross administered the injections, first in one thigh, then in the other. One of the nurses swabbed the needle marks with a cold pad. That was all. What are you doing? Adrian asked pointlessly. Doctor Gross didn't bother with an answer, just got up and left the room, followed by the nurses. Adrian stayed where he was for a while, feeling slightly nauseous. Nothing else. When he stood to walk over to the half-open door his head spun a little. In the corridor, a little further along, one of the guards stood looking at him with a watchful, worried expression. Because he didn't want to be on his own in the cell but had no idea where else he would be allowed to go, he turned to walk towards the basement stairs. He saw from the corner of his eye the guard walk into his cell and come back with the institutional clothes he had worn the night before. With the clothes neatly arranged over his arm, the guard followed Adrian down into the basement and along the passage with the oddly slurping pipes. The iron door stood open this time, as if the Bunker welcomed him back. Inside, some twenty boys were waiting with their eyes fixed on him. I hardly felt a thing, he said cheerfully and, to prove it, took a couple of dance steps across the floor. Suddenly, a hideous, icy pain shot up from his legs, all the way into his pelvis. All the blood seemed to be sucked out of his head and he fell, face forward, with both his legs locked in cramp. For a moment, he had a vision of himself as the others must have seen him: his mouth gaping, his eyes staring blindly. He crawled around with his face against the floor, like an insect you have trodden on and almost crushed, and the pain was like nothing he had ever felt before, as if a rusty bolt was being hammered through both his legs to fasten them to the boards. The crowd of boys followed his torment with blank looks on their faces. They had seen it all before. The guard briefly stopped in the doorway before he quietly put down the bundle of clothes on the floor and left, as if he, too, had had more than enough of this spectacle and didn't care to stay on for more. He barred and locked the door behind him.

Among the Punished With time, he would become familiar with the range of treatments that Doctor Gross and the institution's other medics would apply to suppress any resistance. He had endured the sulphur cure, generally regarded as the worst. For two weeks afterwards, he could barely support his weight on his legs. Even when lying down on a bench, the cramps could start in his thigh muscles and spread into his hips and lower back. It made resting on his back impossible. As soon as he moved even very slightly, the contractions became so intensely painful that the tears streamed from his eyes. Helplessly, he screamed and flailed about, striking the cell walls as if desperately drawing attention to himself so that someone would come and help him. For several days and nights, he fought the pain as if it were a wild animal. He couldn't sleep but sometimes went into inexplicable semi-comatose states. Finally, the pain died down a little. It didn't go away but rather seemed to have retreated back down into his legs where it created a numb, unceasing ache. He still couldn't stand. As soon as he tried to get up, his legs gave in as if made of rubber. Zavlacky and Miseryguts took turns to bring him food in his cell. It's important that you keep eating, Zavlacky said with the weary assurance of someone who has endured most things. It was strange to see how much both boys had grown. Miseryguts had powerful shoulders, and Zavlacky, who looked more like a weasel than ever, had an Adam's apple as prominent as a grown man's. Whenever he raised his new voice, nobody doubted that he was in charge. He could stand, arms akimbo, and say things like *has everyone here understood what I'm trying to tell you?* or *any questions?* After a week in the isolation cell, Adrian was allowed to sleep in the same dormitory as the others. The boy who slept in the bed next to his was known as Gangly, and looked weird, with his long legs, skewed shape, strangely shifty eyes and yellowish horses' teeth that showed when he smiled. Gangly moved just like Jockerl, in a jerky, evasive way as if any time expecting blows and kicks from every direction. Adrian tried to ask Gangly questions when the two of them were on their own together, but Gangly never replied. He only spoke when there were several people around and then compulsively, in long, incoherent orations. Gangly's idea was apparently to distract his audience *away from himself*, as if the flow of words formed a wall he could shelter behind. And he kept smiling while he talked: a weird smile with his lips stretched over his teeth and a dull, submissive look in his eyes. *Please don't hit me,* his eyes pleaded. All the same, Gangly was the one who made sure that Adrian got up in the morning and helped him wash and dress while the effect of the treatment meant that he couldn't stand or walk. It was also Gangly whom Adrian had to thank for being taken down into the Bunker each morning and, when the guards unlocked the big door in the evening, it was Gangly who offered his shoulder for Adrian to lean on as he limped up the steep basement staircase. It was odd, the way we were left to our own devices, Adrian said later when he looked back on these days. As if running away once and for all turned us into a special category of boys. No longer ordinary inmates in a care home but not exactly prisoners, either. I never figured out what we were seen as. The male nurses or nursing assistants who looked after us behaved above all like guards, even though they wanted the title 'Tutor' – *Erzieher*. He remembers two of them especially well. Kohler was the one who had followed Adrian down into the basement after the sulphur injections and brought his clothes. The name of the other one was Sebastian. Because they had the same rota, they were often talked about as the collective *Kohler 'n' Sebastian*. The boys were given daily tasks by Kohler 'n' Sebastian. One morning, they might be told to scrub the basement stairs, or clean the kitchen and the dormitory, or make the beds. Everyone made their own first, of course, but then Kohler, or perhaps Sebastian, would rip everything up and order them to start again. It could go on for hours. If anyone objected, he had to stand in front of his unmade bed, as if in the stocks, while the others, boys who knew what obedience meant, were excused the rest of the bed-making. Then again, they might be divided into labour crews, and one crew left behind to carry out Bunker chores while the rest marched off to do straightforward jobs like ditch-digging, or sawing and stacking logs. It was usually Zavlacky who decided who belonged to which group and, for as long as he did it, the allocation of jobs went smoothly and without any conflicts. Adrian would later recall an occasion when one of their so-called tutors (someone who was *neither* Kohler nor Sebastian) had turned up in the Bunker to row them for not cleaning tools and returning them in good order to the shed, and then Zavlacky had stepped forward as if to physically defend his group. He went with the man to the tool shed and came back an hour or so later, looking as calm as if nothing out of the ordinary had taken place. No punishments were meted out either. In their previous pavilion, the situation would have been unthinkable from beginning to end because justice there bore no immediate relationship to the offence, but was no more than a device for maintaining a pre-determined, abstract order. Why this approach to discipline did not apply in the Bunker, Adrian never understood. Unless the fact that they were in the Bunker at all was seen as punishment enough.

The Women's Pavilion One early December morning, Adrian's crew had been assigned to ditch-digging around one of the outlying areas of the hospital's gardens. Frosty nights and an early fall of snow had hindered previous attempts to complete the work. By now, only a few weeks left to go before Christmas and, if the new vegetable plots were to be drained and dug before the serious cold set in, all who could had to help. Adrian was grateful to get away. He was fed up of the stench of stale sweat and old urine that hung around Gangly wherever he went, and after only a few hundred metres' march in the preferred army-style ranks, he was amazed at how much light and open sky you could find even here, in obscure corners of the walled-in hospital site. They worked for three hours before midday and then sat down to eat the meagre rations they had been given. The place that was to become part of the gardens was a low-lying meadow between two intersecting roads. Pavilion 23, the so-called women's pavilion, stood behind tall trees on the other side of the meadow. It looked like their own pavilion, Adrian thought, but perhaps a bit longer. It would have seemed abandoned but for the smoke rising from one of the chimneys. When they had been sitting with their spades across their knees for some twenty minutes, two female guards came out and stopped just outside the main entrance. Their clipped voices resounded under the frost-white sky. Soon, twenty-odd young women, in some kind of prison outfits, came outside, stood to attention – *Habt-Acht!* – and then received an order delivered at screaming pitch, turned and came marching straight towards the boys. Who just stared. The women marched briskly, two by two. When about half the line had passed, one of them suddenly turned to the boys, ripped off her prisoner's cap and exposed her clean-shaven skull. A little later, two of the other women did the same and raised their arms triumphantly in the air. It enraged the guard in front. She blew her whistle and then walked along the line, slapping the prisoners as she went. The boys were fascinated and kept staring:

Zavlacky, *you want to stay away from women like that lot*
and Adrian, *wonder where they're off to*
and Zavlacky, *if they're not off to labour camp it's their lucky day*
and Adrian, *what kind of labour camp?*

but by then Zavlacky seemed not to listen anymore, only smiled as if at some sudden inner vision. And then he spat between his drawn-up knees into the grass. Instead, Miseryguts had to step in with missing information:

it's what they do to punish them for being brazen
they flog the shit out of them

and the entire crew naturally burst out laughing so it was no good trying to find out more. But once they had returned to the Bunker that afternoon, Zavlacky sat down next to Adrian and said that he had better not expect to be allowed to stay. The punishment bunker was a transit station, just like everywhere else. Sooner or later, they would all be called to appear in front of the commission. Adrian didn't even know what the commission was all about. The commission, Zavlacky explained, is the authority that decides if you're smart enough to be sent to labour camp or if you're to join the idiots. And, when Adrian just kept staring at him (Miseryguts: *don't say you fancied that punishment meant sitting around in a heated bunker all day long . . .*) Zavlacky went on to say that he knew of several Bunker inmates who had been sent off to labour camp. Some said it was like a concentration camp though they didn't treat you like the Commies or the Jews. For a bit, Adrian kept staring at them (Miseryguts: *hey, are you to join the idiots or what?*) and then asked, was there really no other choice? Zavlacky suggested: try to sell it to the commission that you're too stupid to be in a camp but just smart enough not to end up with the idiots, it's not easy but some people make it, nodding towards Gangly who was sitting a bit further away but started at once to chatter and grin as if he couldn't agree more.

A Parcel From that day on, Adrian expected to be called to appear in front of the commission. He wasn't. Instead, he received a parcel. It was two days until Christmas Eve. His mother had written his name on the parcel in large letters and, to prevent any mistakes, drawn a ring around the number of his old pavilion. So, she hadn't been informed about his failed escape attempt, nor where he might end up next. The parcel contained a box of dry biscuits (Adrian shared them at once with Zavlacky and Gangly), a sweater and a pair of socks knitted in thick, grey wool. He couldn't recall ever having seen his mother knit. She wouldn't have been able to afford the yarn, didn't have the time, what with four young children to look after, and, besides, had she had no time to spare, there were other more important things to do. Where did that yarn come from? And was the sweater even meant for him? He tried to put it on and when he saw his bare arms sticking out of the far too short sleeves, the lump forming in his throat swelled and, in the end, even Gangly looked away. The sweater must have been for Helmut, or did his mother truly think he still was that small?

Christmas At this time last year, they had been housed at Ybbs and all Adrian remembered of that Christmas celebration was tired apples being handed out and the booming sound of the river on the other side of the thick, ice-cold walls. The river was heard so distinctly then, as if there had been no other sounds to listen to that freezing winter's night. It was as cold this year. On the morning of Christmas Eve, they had to scrub their section of the pavilion. Kohler opened all the cell doors and organised two bucket chains: one lot of boys dealt with the buckets and basins full of hot, soapy water from the kitchen, and the other with the buckets of clean rinsing water. Within a few hours, the section was awash with floor-soap foam and water and, because the pavilion wasn't ever properly heated, the floors soon turned as slippery as oiled glass. It was particularly bad just inside the front door, propped open by Kohler. Inevitably, someone slipped on the wet floor, a frail-looking boy called Felix Rausch. He was on the hot-water team, so boiling water washed over him and he had to be carried, screaming with pain, to casualty. The outcome of this incident was that they were late for the hospital board's specially arranged Christmas party that every ward and section of the entire institution were under strict orders to attend. The talk was of a *Weihnachtsfest*, but actually, everything to do with Christmas was forbidden. Not even Christmassy words, so glitteringly light and heart-warming, like *Weihnachtsfeier* or *Weihnachtslieder*, were allowed. You're to say 'Feast of Light', Kohler told them, no argument. But there was not much light to be seen in the snowy yard in front of pavilion 3, where the punishment-block boys were lined up to wait for Felix, the burns patient, to come outside. And there he was at last, a strange-looking figure leaning on Kohler. Felix's head had been bandaged so generously that only the tip of his nose and half of one ear stuck out. Now that their number was complete, they marched off across the creaking layer of snow. Large banners with swastikas on them had been hung from the second floor windows of the institution's theatre and, outside its entrance, Hitlerjugend youths formed a guard of honour. They held large flaming torches that gave off a sour smell of oil and smoke. But inside the theatre it was dark – and so silent; an almost tangible silence, like in a crypt. Adrian craned his neck to try to catch a glimpse of some of the children from his old pavilion but all he could see was a sea of stiff backs, slightly bent as if for a beating. There was a large podium set up on the stage and on it all the nurses and other members of staff were on parade, their faces turned to the audience. A little to the left of centre, he spotted Mutsch and Demeter, neatly attired in starched uniforms. There was a lectern, too, with swastika flags placed on either side of it. The board members as well as the administrative staff, including accountants and secretaries, stood around the lectern and Doctor Krenek himself stood behind it, speaking from a large bundle of notes. But although he spoke loudly and enunciated clearly, it was as if the words wouldn't quite take off from his mouth but instead hung on like large bubbles and, all the while, even more word-bubbles were pushing forward from wherever they were created. *Unser über alles geliebter Führer* – the leader we love more than anyone and anything – made one bubble; *der Endsieg* and then *der ewige Tag eines grossdeutschen Reiches* were other bubbles – the final victory, and the eternal day of the greater German Reich – and all the while more saliva-sprinkled bubbles kept being produced, now about the soldiers who fought in snow and ice for their German homeland, and as he spoke, he stroked his head with his hand, again and again. Had something had got stuck in his hair? Adrian was just going to point this out to the boy next to him when he – it was Miseryguts – said:

A LARGE BIRD SITS UP THERE AND SHITS ON HIS HEAD.

He whispered but articulated every syllable very clearly. A wave of subdued laughter ran through the row of boys. In the next moment Doctor Krenek inevitably lifted his hand to his head again and Zavlacky followed up with:

MAYBE IT'S THE FÜHRER HIMSELF WHO SITS THERE AND SHITS IN HONOUR OF THE DAY.

The whisper was just as quiet, almost inaudible, but impossible not to hear. By then they couldn't keep their laughter down anymore. It fizzed and fermented with such irresistible force that the only way seemed to be to bend forward and try to strangle it between your knees. Adrian just had time to see Kohler's alarmed face turn towards them from the row in front. Just as well that it grew no worse, as far as the anxious Kohler was concerned, because when the laughter was about to spread to the rows in front and behind them, everything was drowned out by the enormous roar made when the entire audience stood as one man and shouted:

HEIL HITLER . . . !

Doctor Krenek had just that moment produced another huge bubble with *Heil Hitler* inside and stood with his right hand stretched up and out. All around him and the lectern, and all over the podium, where the doctors and nurses and allied staff were standing, either in professional whites or in their best outfits, arms were raised in the German greeting. In the audience, the model patients in their grey institutional uniforms aped everyone else, held up their arms and shouted *Heil Hitler!* in their hoarse voices. All joined in, except Miseryguts who muttered *Grüss Gott*. But by then Kohler had already got the group moving. Because they had been among the last to get in, they were let out early. Even before the singing had had time to erupt inside the theatre, they were ordered to line up in *Zweiereiher* and run back to their pavilion. They truly sounded like chain-gang prisoners as they jogged along, breathing heavily, the cold prickling around their eyes. When they arrived, they were not even allowed to go into the Bunker but were told to undress immediately and go to bed. Adrian slept with the ugly, far too small and roughly knitted sweater jammed between his legs, and went to sleep wondering if being *brazen* might be something as seemingly innocent as to take one's cap off to show one's shaved head. When he got down into the Bunker the next morning, neither Miseryguts nor Zavlacky was there. Adrian asked around to find out where they had gone but nobody knew. Gangly only showed his yellow teeth in his usual grin and talked wildly. Felix Rausch, the boy whose face had been scalded, had vanished and his destination was also unknown.

Facing the Commission Four days into the New Year, on Monday 4 January 1943, Adrian Ziegler finally appeared in front of the commission. The interrogation took place in pavilion 1, the same pavilion in which Doctor Gross on another January day two years earlier had measured and described all Adrian's unseemly flaws. Half a dozen people were seated behind tables placed in a semi-circle around the central area of the room where he was told to stand at *Habt-Acht*. The director of the reform school Doctor Krenek, occupied the middle of the semi-circle as the would-be leader of the inquisition. To Krenek's left and right, grimly concentrated men and women sat behind piles of documents and folders. Many of them he had never seen before but he assumed they must be the providers of 'expertise' – pedagogically trained staff from the social services department who had been called in to attend the questioning. He did recognise the psychologist Edeltraud Baar and one of the teachers from the school pavilion, a Mr Ritter. The usual Führer portrait hung on the wall behind just behind Ritter. One of the experts, who seemed to function as some kind of secretary because he was writing all the time, addressed Adrian without even looking up from his notes, telling him to state his name and when he was born, and then, because he obviously wasn't speaking distinctly enough, demanded that he repeated the answers several times. When at last everyone was satisfied, Doctor Krenek opened one of the folders and started to read aloud in a declamatory, almost indignant voice from what seemed to be an official compilation of various reports, all about Adrian.

DOCTOR KRENEK: [*reads*] Adrian Z has shown himself to be a degenerate, ingratiating character, which stems from his depraved and filthy home conditions and his upbringing

by an alcoholic father and a frivolous, flighty mother with unmistakably limited gifts. [*Leafs through the pages.*] *Erbbiologisch ist die Sippe sehr minderwertig* – the family's biological inheritance is of very low quality. On the father's side, a long history of work-shy individuals and drunkenness; on the mother's, of debility and imbecility. One of the mother's brothers was kept at Steinhof for a considerable length of time. Adrian learnt early to use cringing as his approach to life. His nature is essentially frivolous, obsequious and full of tricks while on the trail of personal advantage, otherwise he is idle and recalcitrant.
One care worker has reported that A. Z. occasionally finds it so difficult to concentrate that he seems barely aware of his surroundings and, thus, only *physical* means serve to make him conscious of his situation. The veracity of this observation is confirmed by several other, mutually independent witnesses:
[A. Z.] has a certain ability to think on his feet, an expression of fast reflexes rather than of intelligence. He is well versed in deceit, 'hardened' and, in his 'gang', assumes a leadership role but is ready to submit when challenged.
When told to write a school essay on the subject of his aspirations for work in the future, he stated a wish to train as a waiter because his father knew somebody who could take him on. In other words, the degenerate pattern is repeated in the youth's dreams about the future. To him, work entails *pretending* to oblige, the aim of service is to *steal* and so forth.
The disciplinary issues pertaining to Adrian Z add up to a formidable list:
On 22 March last year, he was entrusted with the task of fetching an additional portion of the evening meal from the institution's

kitchen but skulked in an unknown location before returning from his errand. When required to explain the delay, he threw the tray on the floor in a fit of rage. His punishment was to be isolated from the other children for a brief period but, instead of spending the time in reflection about his severe misdemeanours, he enticed his carer into the cell on the pretence of having 'something to show her' and then attacked her 'with blows and kicks'.

Adrian Z's character traits emerge clearly from these notes. Ostensibly, he gives the impression of a well-behaved boy – although far from gifted. However, behind the quiet surface lurks a manipulative intelligence worthy of a ruthless criminal. Thus, for example, immediately prior to the escape attempt on 22 October this year, was a period of reasonable calm. Day-notes entries include:

06/10   A. Z. causes no trouble, well-behaved; pays attention to his work and completed it . . .

14/10   A. Z. works hard; offers to help with doing the dishes . . .

16/10   A. Z. replies politely and shows interest . . .

In fact, throughout this period he had stealthily planned the escape that he executed on 22 October: A. Z. asks leave to go to the toilet, then breaks the window locks with a tool he must have had in readiness to this very end. Later, he is picked up in a very poor state and taken to Wilhelminenspital where he is cared for overnight.

Even though his attempt to run away was a pathetic failure and clumsily executed, it had obviously been planned for a long time with the help of at least one, if not several, helpers or conspirators.

EXPERT 1: [*interrupts his note-taking*] Doctor Krenek. In my opinion, this youth isn't paying full attention to the proceedings. He appears to be laughing.

DOCTOR KRENEK: [*irritably, to Adrian*] What are you looking at?

ADRIAN Z: Nothing . . . at our Führer.

DOCTOR KRENEK: You're to listen and look at me, and speak up when you're spoken to.

ADRIAN Z: [*stares straight ahead*]

EXPERT 1: As a matter of fact, he was laughing.

DOCTOR KRENEK: Do you have any understanding of why you're here?

ADRIAN Z: [. . .]

DOCTOR KRENEK: You might begin by telling us who helped you to run away. Then we'll have that matter out of the way, once and for all.

ADRIAN Z: [. . .]

EXPERT 2: [*leafs through documents*] In my view, it's high time to go to the root of the trouble. Now, as far as I can see, the youth spent three years in the Münnichplatz primary school and was, even then, a knowing rebel. He failed in most subjects. Despite being urged to, he refused to join in the *Heimabend* programme of home get-togethers for the young.

ADRIAN Z: I couldn't go to any of the *Heimabenden* because I had to look after my brother.

EXPERT 2: That's a lie. He didn't attend any *Heimabend* because his father had been deemed of inferior racial stock. Hence, he was unfit for wartime service.

ADRIAN Z: That was before, when I was with the Haidingers.

DOCTOR KRENEK: Quiet unless spoken to!

EXPERT 2: Can this boy tell us anything he has learnt in school? Anything at all?

EXPERT 1: Describe a right-angled triangle.

ADRIAN Z: [. . .]

EXPERT 1: Name the three longest rivers in Europe.

ADRIAN Z: [. . .]

EXPERT 2: The date our Führer was born?

ADRIAN Z: [. . .]

EXPERT 2: He has no idea. Obviously an idiot.

DOCTOR KRENEK: What was all that about your brother?

ADRIAN Z: I couldn't go to any *Heimabenden* because I had to look after my brother. Besides, no one wanted me to be there.

EXPERT 2: For good reason.

ADRIAN Z: Mrs Haidinger always liked Helmut better and if she bought things or had clothes made up, it was always for him. So *he* could go to those evenings because he was blond, but Mrs Haidinger didn't think I should be there because I wasn't and it didn't look right.

EXPERT 1: Being present at the at-home evenings is a duty for everyone.

DOCTOR KRENEK: And now, can we return to the agenda? [*Looks sternly at some of the experts who are chatting, some even trying to hide smiles behind their hands.*]

ADRIAN Z: There's nothing wrong with Helmut, there's no need to kill him. Dad always used to say that Mum must've got him with someone else because he . . . [*Bursts into tears.*]

EXPERT 2: [*gets up, approaches Adrian Z, close enough to slap him hard across the face*] You speak when spoken to. Is that understood? And you can cut out that pretend-weepiness at once.

DOCTOR KRENEK: [*speaks with surprising gentleness*] Where did you think you were going to run to when you got out of Spiegelgrund, Adrian?

ADRIAN Z: [*mumbles something*]

EXPERT 2: Speak up when you're spoken to!

DOCTOR KRENEK: Home, did you say? But you have no home. You had a foster-home but you didn't want to stay there either. Where did you think you'd stay?

ADRIAN Z: [*mumbles*]

EXPERT 1: But the person you call 'mother' is a racially inferior woman, a depraved and work-shy parasite who hasn't the slightest notion of the responsibility and strength of mind required to bring up children nowadays.

DOCTOR KRENEK: [*bends forward, raises both hands with the palms inclined upwards*] You take a look at these hands of mine, Ziegler! They are large and strong and white and always clean. When they strike a blow, they remain clean and pure because, when they hit out, the blows are for justice. I wish that your hands were the same as mine. But instead of showing your hands, you hold them hidden behind your back. You use your hands for deceitful things, to steal and to conceal. Now, there are many places where we can send boys like you to teach them what working with their hands is like, like a *Jugendschutzlager* where you might have to work twelve hours a day.

ADRIAN Z: [*still speaking almost inaudibly*] I don't want to . . . to go to a camp.

DOCTOR KRENEK: Then you must take the opportunity to stretch out your hands, straightaway, and say: 'I have done what is wrong but I will improve from now on.' He who has nothing to hide, has nothing to fear, Adrian. So, begin with naming the boys who helped you escape.

ADRIAN Z: Nobody helped me.

DOCTOR KRENEK: You're a hardened miscreant. You disobey me out of sheer defiance. Camp is the only place for you.

ADRIAN Z: I did it on my own.

DOCTOR KRENEK: Had you only had the wit to spend more time pulling your weight, actively work as best you could for a healthy, forward-looking community, then you wouldn't have been standing here in front of us. Indeed not. Now, had you thought about that? As things stand, you have obviously chosen to make a virtue of your sins.

ADRIAN Z: I don't want to go to a camp; all I want is –

DOCTOR KRENEK: All we want is to cure you.

ADRIAN Z: [*weeps*] Cure me of what . . . *what* will you cure me of?

Mr Guido And so he was dispatched to Mödling again, just as he was when his foster parents had thrown him out. Only, this time, there was no father who stepped out of the director's cupboard to save him. Only Mr Guido mattered. Guido's view of Mödling, as he put it to Adrian, was that you were there because you deserved to be, that Mödling was something that had grown out of your own head and, if you wanted to be released from there, you first of all had to rid yourself of whatever was in your head. There was nothing else for it. Guido's surname was Peters. In this institution, almost all the staff were men and everything had a military flavour. Clothes must almost be immaculately looked after and time was even set aside for kit maintenance. To get from somewhere to somewhere else, like the dining hall or the gym hall, the boys had to line up and march. When floors were to be scrubbed or toilets cleaned, jobs carried out by teams according to a rota, a foreman-type always came along to force the pace and shout, beat and kick those who were too slow. Guido Peters was one of the worst slave-drivers. When they marched, he walked alongside to keep an eye on everyone, yelling things like *get a move on* and *back straight* and doling out slaps. But later in the day, when it was time for kit cleaning or at bedtime in the dormitory, he might jokingly grab somebody by the shoulder or say something jolly to show that all that yelling meant no harm after all. His gait was curiously soft and elastic, so you easily missed that he had come to watch you. He told Adrian that he, Guido, had worked with young people for twenty years and knew how they thought and felt. Take yourself, now. I know what you're thinking, Guido said. His round face was somehow rubbery, without a single wrinkle and looked younger than he actually was – which was late forties, maybe, or early fifties. You're thinking that you want to escape from this place, he said. Adrian kept looking at Guido because he didn't dare not to. Relax, Guido said, I'll look after you. People who work here believe that only fear can make boys like you learn to obey but I know what boys need and that's simply someone to trust. I might pick you to be a leader, a *Gruppenführer*, he added. All you've got to do is behave yourself. It was the first time that an adult had ever spoken to him in this way, as if Adrian was not only grown up enough to understand but also as if there was a bond between them. Day in and day out the eyes in that large, rubbery face kept watching him, during the gymnastics lessons, in the dining hall, on their marches across the yard from the auditorium to the dormitory, but Guido showed nothing; on the contrary, he often came along to shout *move on, you lazy arsehole* and slam his whole hand into the back of Adrian's head. But from the day of their talk, he knew that, even if Guido hit him, he wasn't to take it seriously. In fact, slapping was Guido's way of reassuring the others that Adrian wasn't given any special treatment. The trust between them was not affected. Sometimes, when Guido was on night duty, he would patrol the dormitory after lights-out and, although his movements were soundless, Adrian would hear his voice as he stopped occasionally on his strolls between the beds to say something in confidence to one of the boys. And Adrian would think, please come to me, too, Mr Guido, come to me. Then, one day, it happened. Mr Guido stopped to talk to him. He had brought a whole ration of bread as well. He said that he knew what was on Adrian's mind just then. Girls, right? Guido said. That's what boys think about. Young things with soft breasts and wet little cunts. Right? he said, as he probed underneath the blanket for Adrian's sex and touched it. Adrian, who was lying flat on his back, didn't dare to move a millimetre. I know what boys think about, Guido mumbled while his treacherous hand stroked Adrian's penis from root to glans, until the terrified limb reluctantly stiffened. *Tell me, am I right or am I right?* he mumbled and bent forward, still holding Adrian's penis, to whisper into his ear with warm, moist lips, *don't be afraid, despite your shameless behaviour I'll help you to get out of here. Guido always keeps his promises.* Adrian wriggled uneasily because by now his sex had gone painfully hard and pulsating in response to Guido's insistent rubbing. Guido laughed. I'll make you group leader one day, he said and then let go. It soon became obvious that Guido had several favourites among the boys and one of them, who was called Roman, was especially select. He was blond, blue-eyed and heavily built, with a broad neck and shoulders. Roman's back was always the straightest of all when they lined up and his deep, powerful voice the loudest and most resounding when they sang. Roman was also the first to call out the correct answers to the questions their teacher asked the class. The trouble was that he had instantly identified Adrian as the tinker's lad he was, an alien exiled to the great Mödling community without having done anything to earn his place and, consequently, someone who should be excluded, one way or another. It began imperceptibly with the odd push from behind when they were lining up for a march, or roughing up Adrian's bed when he had finished making it, or hiding one of his shoes just when they were ordered outside into the exercise yard. The mornings in the washroom were worst, when dozens of legs twisted themselves between his to make him fall to the tiled floor that was slippery with soapy water. Once, they succeeded and when he leapt furiously at the boy closest at hand, Roman immediately put his arm around Adrian's neck and wrestled him back down onto the floor. In that instant, the usually unruly crowd of boys split itself into two groups, one on each side of the two entangled fighters, and rhythmically called out their names, on one side *Roman!* and on the other (laughing madly) the name that had become Adrian's:

tinker! tinker! tinker! tinker!

None of the carers intervened, not even Guido, whose rubber features Adrian had glimpsed clearly, sometimes behind but sometimes in among the wildly yelling but, by now, scared boys who surrounded him. Guido, who was holding a towel and a piece of soap, stepped forward first when two other carers had detached Roman's sweating, terrified body from Adrian's grip. All around them, the echo of the whiplash sound of water from the showers hitting the tiles was overlaid by the shrill screams of fifty-odd boys, a layer of sound that floated on top of the hollow, slapping noise of the water. Guido stared at Adrian as if he realised exactly who he was looking at for the first time. And he shook his head. Do you think you'll get away with it? he said. Do you think tinkers and half-Jews like you end up here by chance? Any idea what they do to Jews nowadays? (He didn't seem to expect answers to his questions.) I'll tell you about Jews, they're turned into soap. He held out the bar of green institutional soap to Adrian. Two hundred and fifty of them, at least, go into a bar this size. Adrian washed himself with it. I'm not a Jew, he said. Guido scrutinised him from top to toe, then knocked several times on his round, hairless skull with his knuckles. I'll help you get out, he said. His rubber face stretched itself into a large smile. You'll see, you'll get out of here in one piece.

A Degenerate Character From that day on, Guido came to him at night. Adrian lay awake, waiting. Mostly, Guido touched him but he would sometimes insist that Adrian would do the same for him and Adrian obeyed as he knew he must to be left alone and finally be allowed to sleep. The beds looked like ships in the bluish, shimmering night-light, all of then sailing off towards the same distant, grey horizon. He imagined himself standing at the bow of one of the large Donau ships that his Uncle Ferenc used to fantasise about captaining. The journey went upstream but, because it was dark, one couldn't see the land towering up on either side of the river, and the further he travelled the more powerfully the currents tugged at the boat's hull until the water grew so violent it felt as if the ship moved backwards and down rather than forwards. He was woken by someone holding his head in a vice-like grip but it was only Guido, whose hot breath swept over the side of Adrian's face while his small hands fumbled underneath the blanket. Adrian was told to *stay completely still* and hold the round, hairless skull with both hands while its lips and teeth were busy nibbling and biting his nipples and then moved on to lick and suck at his penis as if it were an udder. He wanted to push the large head away or, at least, to the side, but Guido shoved a hard, determined finger up Adrian's anus and when he was about to scream, Guido covered his mouth with his other hand and swore at him to shut up. The next morning, it was as if nothing had happened. Guido stood in the changing room, as upright and strict as always, handing out towels and soaps to the boys, and when they lined up, he didn't even glance Adrian's way. Adrian realised of course that this was how Guido wanted it. Clearly, if you wanted to stay in favour, you had to be prepared to show willing at any time. Adrian tried to look elsewhere, to make his face neutral as if he didn't even know who Guido was. The game of pretence between them went on like this for a few days. Guido apparently loved this game, because when he came back for his night-time visits, he brought substantial gifts, like extra slices of bread and a little package of margarine that Adrian was allowed to spread on the bread, and sometimes also apples and sweets. There was of course a price to be paid for all these delicacies and while Adrian carried on chewing and sucking on all that Guido stuck into his mouth, his body was subjected to every kind of obscure exploration. Some nights, Guido was at it for so long that the hours of the day and night seemed to shift. Even when Guido did not come to his bed, Adrian stayed wide awake and waited all night. During the day, his seat in the schoolroom transformed into a freight barge cleaving the long swells in the shipping channel of the river while, on the upper deck, he was slowly rocked to sleep as he rested on the loose metal hold-covers that had grown warm from the heat of the engine. Because he had at this stage become used to people constantly doing things to his body, he didn't even realise that his teacher had bent over him and was trying to shake him awake. Behind the teacher, there were others, all serious men and women wearing white coats. Doctors and psychologists. They accompanied him back to the dormitory and watched as his bed was given a thorough once-over and his treasure trove discovered: a pillow case full of bits of bread and wrappers of margarine rations. Adrian confessed immediately the source of these offerings. Strangely enough, he was never punished for his confession. The white-clad delegation withdrew after exchanging quick, meaningful glances. That night, and for a few more to follow, Adrian slept almost normally. No Guido loomed into sight. Two days later, there was more upheaval. In the middle of a lesson, a secretary came into the classroom to call Adrian to the director's office immediately. At this time, Mr Heckermann no longer ran the institution and the new director didn't have a bird-like beak and high, pointy shoulders like a bird's, but the swastika banner was the same and so was the portrait of the Führer that had hung on the wall when the director had walked from his desk to open the door to the magic cupboard at the back of the room. No such miraculous intervention would take place today. Adrian realised this immediately when he entered and saw Guido Peters standing in front of the director's desk. This was another Guido Peters than the man Adrian had come to know. The sunny smile had been wiped off his lower face and his back was as straight as if his lumbar curvature had been hammered flat. His eyes were narrow slits and his lips so firmly pressed together that the saliva sprayed from his mouth when he, gesturing with an index finger that trembled with indignation, gave an account of the *perversities* that Adrian had tried to tempt him into carrying out. Not only had Guido himself been a victim of the youth's lewd acts but Adrian had tried to inveigle other children into sodomy in the shower room. The bits of bread found in Adrian's bed were clearly blackmail payments that this depraved delinquent had received from other boys in return for not telling on them. When Guido had finished, the director turned to Adrian and asked him in a stern voice if there was any truth in what Guido had said. Adrian did not dare to meet Guido's eyes. He looked down at the carpet and shook his head. In that moment, he knew that no one would believe him. The director told Guido to leave and, once the door closed behind him, ordered Adrian to go into the room where the secretary was sitting. Adrian watched as one specialist after another came and went. At one point, there seemed to be as many as four or five of them in the director's office and their voices sounded upset.

Either, he's seriously disturbed or else he's like that himself, he heard one voice say. *How else could he have put up with it for so long?*

The Bleeding Führer In the end, he was told to go back into the office. The Führer looked him in the eye but the director did not, so Adrian decided that it was better to stare at his Führer. While the director held forth, Adrian kept his eyes fixed on the Führer and observed how one wound after another opened up on the great commander's face. First, a small wound in his cheek, just below his left eye, and then another one a bit further down, by the cheekbone. And a third one, by the chin. At once, blood started to flow from all of them. His first thought was that Hannes Neubauer had been right all along and that the Führer was actually an air force pilot in disguise. But he changed his mind when it came to him that the Führer was bleeding for him – for Adrian. He carried on watching the face in front of him to see if its expression would change now that the wounds were opening up everywhere. It did not. How could it? Bleeding or not, it was the Führer's unyielding face. The only thing that happened was that the blood ran down over the white institutional wall below the portrait. Outside these walls, the car that was to take him back to Spiegelgrund stood ready and waiting. It delivered him to pavilion 17, section Bu – for *Bildungsunfähige*, for the severely retarded, the unteachables.

VIII

Reflections on Monstrosities

The Female Escapees Afterwards, the talk was that Doctor Jekelius's downfall had been brought about by two madwomen on the run. Anna Katschenka knew that this was untrue. Jekelius had come close to the abyss long before the affair of the two girls who escaped from pavilion 17 had emerged as final confirmation of the gossip that was already circulating: he had lost his grip, Councillor Gundel had lost confidence in him and no longer thought him competent enough to lead the work of the institution. Anna Katschenka assumed all that wasn't entirely true either, but what would the assumptions of a lowly ward sister matter? In the trial that followed much later, she was to state that, in her opinion, Jekelius had been the victim of a conspiracy. That was all. The two girls who escaped were a Gertrude Klein and a Marie Tomek. In December 1941, Gertrude was eighteen and Marie fifteen years old but both had already acquired reputations as unrepentant rebels. A couple of months before their first escape attempt, they had broken into a cleaning cupboard and stolen a large can of undiluted Lysol. They had made a suicide pact to kill themselves by drinking disinfectant. Actually, only Marie drank it. Gertrude sat next to her and urged her on: *Drink more, Marie, drink the lot . . . !* Their relationship had been like that from the start: Gertrude was the one who had the insane ideas and drove them to completion, while Marie was the meek one who agreed and followed. If Nurse Storch hadn't caught sight of Marie Tomek's unconscious body in the corridor and managed to call a doctor in time, the girl's life would soon have been past saving. Miss Tomek was taken to pavilion 3 and had her stomach pumped. Afterwards, the two rebels were put in the same isolation cell. That turned out to be an awful mistake. The ward sister had hardly locked the door behind her before she heard heart-rending cries from inside and, when the cell door was opened, they found Marie on all fours on the cell floor with Gertrude sitting on top of her and whipping her like a horse with wet towel-rags. *It's your fault, you fat whore!* Soon afterwards, the girls carried out the first of their two escape attempts. Gertrude managed to steal the keys to the front door of the pavilion from the nurses' office and, the same night, the two girls slipped unseen past the guard's hut at the main gate. It took several days and nights before they were found, frozen to the marrow and desperately hungry, waiting for a tram at the Brunnenmarkt stop. By then, everyone was clear about Klein's role as the instigator. After two weeks in an isolation cell, she appears in front of Doctor Jekelius. This time, she is on her own. Marie isn't at her side now as she and Jekelius confront each other. As always, when facing censure, Gertrude pretends to be dejected and submissive but her gaze hovers at floor level full of barely suppressed hatred. Doctor Jekelius is restrained. He doesn't raise his voice and shows no other signs of being upset. He asks Gertrude Klein if she feels any remorse about her pathetic, meaningless attempt to escape, especially in view of its consequences. Miss Klein repeats a previous accusation: Jekelius is a *killer-doctor* who intends to poison not only her but all the girls in the section. Also, that he has deliberately prevented her parents from visiting so that nobody will find out what is *really* going on here. And it's the same for all the girls in the section, she adds. The idea is to keep them all locked up in this hellhole until they go insane and die, or else the killer-doctor and his gang will put poison in their food. Whatever happens, they're all doomed to die. To this tirade, Doctor Jekelius replies that what the institution offers her is not imprisonment but actually an opportunity to reflect in peace and, without disturbing influences from the outside world, make her own decisions about what she wants the rest of her life to be. Either she learns to do as she is told by the staff and leave the other girls alone; or she continues to instigate rebellions, to misbehave and harass others. The decision is up to her, no one else. To prove his goodwill and emphasise that he has no goal other than her welfare and good health, he intends to give her one last chance. Christmas is four weeks away. If she shows that she can behave properly until then, he will arrange for her to be allowed to begin her 'duty year' sometime after the New Year. If she misbehaves, he will have her moved to a youth labour camp, a placement which, as Miss Klein is surely well aware, is much less desirable for a young woman. The choice is, and will be, entirely her own. Young Miss Klein nods in her browbeaten, seemingly servile way but, of course, has no intention of turning over a new leaf. Only two weeks after her talk with Doctor Jekelius, she engineers her next escape attempt and this time, as one of the nurses puts it, it is *total war*. Not only Marie Tomek follows her, but another four girls who join in the breakout: Edith Holtemeyer (15), Friedrike Roth (16), Margarete Schaffer (14) and Stefanie Wolfing (16). While Schaffer and Wolfing set about breaking the windows in their dormitory, the other four ambush the nurses who come rushing in to investigate the noise. Erna Storch is on night duty again but so is Nurse Erhart, who runs downstairs as soon as she hears the sound of glass shattering against the flagged area outside the pavilion. Presumably, it is because two members of staff are on the scene that they get away without serious injuries. Nurse Storch already has Margarete Schaffer's arm across her throat when Nurse Erhart enters and is met by the sight of Gertrude Klein's face, its features stretched and bloated by madness, as she leaps up from behind a bed wielding a shard of broken glass. The hand holding the piece of glass is already smeared with blood. At the last moment, Nurse Erhart knocks the weapon out of Miss Klein's hand. Together, the two nurses control Miss Schaffer. Nurse Storch locks both her arms across her back in the so-called Steinhof-tackle while Nurse Erhart manages to grab hold of the hem of Miss Wolfing's nightdress and pull her to the floor in a corner of the room. However, the other four get away, including the clearly deranged Gertrude Klein. Later, Erna Storch declares in a witness statement that several things had been stolen from her earlier in the evening, namely a watch, a small metal box of sewing materials, and forty marks in cash, all of which had been kept in the handbag she always carried with her. At some point that day, one or more of the girls must have gained access to the wardrobe where the staff locks up their clothes and other belongings. The girls must also have been able to steal the keys with which they opened the pavilion front door, although how and from where was not easy to work out. Now, wild, furious screams come from the paths outside and then, again, the sound of breaking glass. Inside one pavilion after another, outraged nurses and caretakers stand holding telephone receivers into which they speak of being under attack. Hordes of youths, they say, are roaming in the dark outside and throwing stones at the windows. These 'hordes' are the four, not yet captured escapees from pavilion 17 who, led by the blood-spattered Gertrude Klein, next turn up at the main gate. The guard, who has run out of his hut, is struck to the ground by young Miss Roth, who uses for that purpose a spade left by the door to a tool shed. However, the girls' attempt to instigate rebellion in other pavilions has delayed them. In pavilion 17, the nearest police station has been alerted by telephone and their escape route has been cut off by the police before the girls have had time to cross Hütteldorfer Strasse. They are brought to the police station for identification and interrogation, and then delivered to Spiegelgrund. Doctor Jekelius meets them. It is early dawn. He has been waiting since receiving the phone call from the duty doctor in pavilion 17, who told him about the upheaval. Doctor Helene Jokl is at his side, as are two male asylum nurses, ready to intervene should any of the girls try something again. Facing them in a line are the dishevelled, dirty runaways. Once again, Gertrude Klein is keeping up the pretence of submissiveness, her gaze drifting along door frames and table legs. Her right hand is bandaged, and the swellings around the cuts on her face make her look grotesque, more like a wounded animal than a human being. Jekelius speaks first. I entrusted you with a decision, he says. But you betrayed me. Gertrude Klein, who hasn't even listened, takes one step forward, pushes her chin out as she always does and screams:

Murderer!

All those present catch their breath, awed by her recklessness. A moment passes. Then Klein starts laughing hysterically. She folds herself double, squirms, kneels and, with her hands raised in supplication, entreats the doctor . . . *please, please* . . . and, before Jekelius has had time to react, the other girls start laughing, too. Neither doctor says anything at first. Then, Jekelius orders the two nurses to hold the newly submissive Gertrude Klein steadily and asks Doctor Jokl to give him the scissors. Klein tries to pull free but Jekelius has already grabbed a bunch of hair at the back of her head and started to cut. Klein shrieks like a stuck pig and her three companions burst into tears. Jekelius drops the scissors to the floor as if struck with weariness and tells Jokl to carry on. Don't leave a single hair on their heads, he says, then turns away and leaves the room. The last they see of him is his back in his doctor's white coat. The shorn Gertrude Klein carries on screaming as if she could make floors and walls – indeed, the entire building – tumble down on top of him.

Reflections on Monstrosities Members of the clinical staff were given a gratuity for Christmas that year, a bonus on their wages. The size of the sum was between one and two hundred Reichsmark depending on grade; Anna Katschenka received one hundred and fifty marks. During a brief ceremony, Jekelius had explained that the money should not only be regarded as compensation for their testing, occasionally painful work, but also as recognition of the care and devotion to duty shown by the institution's employees as they go about a task that was of *crucial importance* to the Reich. You are fighting alongside the men at the front, he told them. Thanks to your steadfast fight, the sick and unfit for life are made to retreat and make room for the sound of mind and body. He did not need to add that the gratuity amounted to an insurance premium: the authorities needed to make sure of their loyalty and silence. It was only too obvious. To Anna Katschenka, for one, speaking about her work to outsiders was unthinkable. Her mother wouldn't have endured hearing about any of it and her father would have found it incomprehensible. Twenty years after qualifying as a nurse, Anna Katschenka still stayed with her parents in the old Fendigasse flat, where she slept in her girlhood room. Her mother never left the flat so Anna or her father had to cope with day-to-day business in the world outside. Father and daughter had entered into an unspoken treaty: at any cost, her mother must be protected from anything that might distress or offend her. This pact was especially critical now, when Otto, Anna's brother, had been called up and sent eastwards as part of the big offensive against the Soviets. He was in the military engineering services and had so far seen little of the fighting, or so he had said in one of his rare letters to his family. On the other hand, his unit had been on the move most of the time, often in armoured vehicles but sometimes on foot. The only roads were forestry tracks. One day, he wrote, they had been forced to do a thirty-kilometre-long march with full load. After Otto's call-up, his father spent more and more of his time by the radio in the sitting room. It was always on, though at low volume so that Otto's mother wouldn't pick up any troubling news. As if to signal his lack of interest, he mimicked 'just happened to pass' by standing near the radio and never sitting down on the nearby armchair to listen. He could stand there for hours with an unvarying, awkward smile on his face that just made him look anxious and tense. He and his wife never spoke about their son or about the war or anything that might be at all upsetting. The quiet mumbling of the radio in the sitting room reported new German advances. One morning in December 1941, it announced that German forward units had reached a line just thirty kilometres short of Moscow. During the month of December, the temperature in the interior of Russia never went above minus thirty degrees centigrade. Anna Katschenka imagined her brother ploughing steadfastly through the Russian snowdrifts, as if swimming through tall, rolling waves, but he sometimes disappeared and dissolved, encapsulated in snow and ice. Even so, from time to time, the ice melted, and all that they were forbidden to talk about, or that they forbade themselves to mention, penetrated the surface. At night, she could wake up feeling that her mind was terribly crowded. She saw images of ill-proportioned and malformed children, who jostled for her attention, saw their distorted limbs and huge, helpless eyes as they filled her head with their noises, the crazy babble of high fever or the heart-breaking, helpless songs they sang as if begging to be let out. Because they were all inside her, she had no face that could be turned away from them. She also had no hands to hide the face that she didn't have. She had no defences against these moronic, monstrous children who pushed and chafed and fed on her, and she knew that if she made the slightest attempt to rid herself of them, the crowding and painful chafing would only grow worse. And so the monster children merged with the terrible devastation of the war. She carried it all inside her, aware of a guilt that couldn't be redressed just as it couldn't be dismissed, and nothing ever changed because nothing must be allowed to change. At such moments, she felt just as young Anna had felt when blood was flowing out of her: as if she was falling and, as she fell, she or her surroundings acquired a kind of weightlessness. Because she was weightless, the fall itself seemed to lack momentum. She *was* her own fall. Weightless, she fell day after day – for weeks, months and years – but didn't have a sensation of time either since time, like her falling, had neither space nor direction.

A Flash of Lightning from a Clear Sky Nurse Kleinschmittger stands by the linen cupboard. She pretends to fold and sort facecloths and towels. Seemingly, we'll have to manage without your doctor for quite some time ahead, she says and her face looks strenuously buttoned up as if to prevent a sour smile from reaching her lips. Anna Katschenka doesn't move, just turns Nurse Kleinschmittger's word *your* over in her mind. *Your* Doctor Jekelius. He has received his military call-up papers, she says. Yes, Nurse Kleinschmittger replies, it was like a flash of lightning from a clear sky for us all. In an instant, Katschenka makes a quite instinctive decision. By not revealing with the slightest word or movement what she thinks or feels, she is refusing to give any part of him away to anyone else. She will not even offer them her own consternation at the news that he has left. But the truth is that, from then on, an empty hollow yawns inside her. Later, she will speculate that this void is at least one of the reasons why she is seen to receive the news so impassively. From then on, she has not the faintest idea why she is in this institution, a potentially fatal thought that must be repressed, come what may. It did indeed take her several days to find out what had really happened, apart from the basic fact that Jekelius has been called up, that is. And it would take several weeks before she learnt the full story of the four runaway girls from Edna Block, one of the head-office typists. The mother of one of the girls had lodged a complaint against Jekelius and Jokl for shearing her hair, claiming that the two doctors had exceeded their rights to order and administer physical punishments and, according to Block, several members of staff, notably Doctor Krenek, felt strongly that a case should be brought against Jekelius so that a court could establish once and for all what kind of principles applied to the institution's work. What's the use of a young girl without hair on her head? Edna Block demanded to know, rhetorically of course. Who would ever employ girls looking like that? And surely there is no hope of them ever marrying? Or taking up positions in domestic service. Which is what everyone is going on about, is that not so? It's not in the end about how the girls have been behaving, or what they might have been guilty of, but if they can cope with the tasks set for them once we've let them out. Miss Block types away with restrained energy and, behind her quivering eyelashes, her eyes fill with tears. Anna Katschenka remembers her day away with Doctor Jekelius, when he spoke of Miss Block as a safe haven. Miss Edna would go through fire and water for me, he had said and jealousy had flapped its black wings inside Katschenka. She knew that Block, on behalf of Jekelius and the other doctors, handled the notifications to the Berlin committee. She also sorted and prioritised the documents that the clinic received in return. Perhaps it was one of these forms she was working on as she wound a fresh sheet of paper into the typewriter and whispered confidingly across the roller: one might have thought there were other things to make a fuss about in this clinic than a few delinquent girls having their heads shaved, right? Don't you agree, Sister Anna? And the doctor isn't even here to defend himself!

In the Field of War There are ways to fend off adversity or personal loss. But how to fend off slander? Malicious words get under your skin and stay there like invisible wounds, oozing blood long after the hurt has been inflicted but inadmissible because, if you admit to bleeding, the inference is that the blow hit home (*Your* doctor, Sister Katschenka!). During the months that went by after Doctor Jekelius's departure, she learns just how feeble and fragile her authority is. Nurse Kleinschmittger increasingly looks away impatiently when Anna asks her to do something and Hilde Mayer waddles past looking indifferent, hiding behind her large, self-absorbed smile. That smile of hers signifies a hold on certain higher insights of a nature that does not permit her to utter a single word of what she knows, but *should* she do so, her utterances would be such that, at a stroke, entire careers would instantly crumble to dust. So, despite the fact that no one knows anything for certain, the talk does incessant rounds in corridors and sluice rooms. About Jekelius. About how, already in the autumn, the *very highest authority* had expressed displeasure with his approach to managing the tasks demanded by his post, and how his use of a staff car for his trips has been cancelled and even expenses that have already been authorised are now rechecked and gone over with a magnifying glass. Anna

Katschenka feels ashamed. *So, it might be that he wasn't the man we, or at least some of us, thought he was,* she suddenly hears Hilde Mayer say from inside her greater understanding of things and, of course, with address to Anna. *Possibly a swindler, or what?* In pavilion 17, the boy called Pelikan stumbles or shuffles past on his twisted, inward-rotated legs. He presses his face against a window to watch two asylum patients in grey institutional clothes try to push a cart loaded with dirty laundry along a path lined by glacial ice ridges and long, murky snowdrifts, and she thinks of her brother Otto, the swimmer, who just in the same way struggles, striking out with both arms, to cross one wall of snow after another to reach Moscow. They don't know their luck, she thinks as she, too, watches the two miserable laundry labourers who have, by going mad, found asylum and so been excused from having to fight for their country and their dignity. The Pelikan lad stands next to her with his face so close up against the window that his face is outlined in the condensation on the glass. Crossly, she grabs at his twitching arm and hauls him back into the day room, but Pelikan whimpers and resists, then tries to reach around her with his other arm, which she throws to the side again and again as if it were a lifeless object,

for heaven's sake stop clinging on me all the time.

In the dayroom, the tinkling piano-playing stops and the child sitting at the piano, it's that Felix Keuschnig, turns to stare at her with his mouth hanging slackly open. Nurse Hedwig, who sits on a chair next to Felix, looks at her with her wide-eyed, clear gaze but all Hedwig can see is the shame that Anna tries not to show and she thinks,

if you hear this, dear Doctor, please come back, just come, come, come.

Then it is suddenly February and Anna Katschenka cuts across the Gürtel to catch the number 6 tram at the Westbahnhof stop. At the back of the last carriage, she stands face to face with Edna Block, the secretary, who tries to hide behind her handbag when she spots Sister Anna. But there are no free seats in the front of the bus and Anna has no choice but to stand at the rear. And then she sees that Edna Block is crying behind her propped-up handbag. The passengers on seats nearby stare intently ahead or out of the windows, obviously disconcerted by this stranger in tears.

Sister Katschenka, you don't know this. I've only just heard: Doctor Jekelius has been wounded in the field, he is paralysed. He's in a military hospital and perhaps he'll never be able to move again.

And the two windowpanes seem to join into one and she is back in pavilion 17, standing next to Pelikan while the boy rubs his face against the moisture on the inside of the pane and she sees once more the laundry workers hauling the big sacks of dirty laundry from the pavilion towards the last of the three carriages pulled by the institution's little train engine that has stopped just outside, and she observes both men slipping on the hard, rough ice and, as they fall, lose their grip on the sacks which open, scattering dirty bed linen on the ground and allowing the wind to tug at the bloody sheets and blow them up into the trees so that, for a little while, the entire institution seems draped by soiled linen and she thinks that these lost souls should be content, happy that they're still alive and able to stand on their own, helpless legs, watching as the outcome of their mistake flies away in the wind. She steps off at the next stop, unable to stand the presence of the weeping Miss Block any longer.

Letters

Herr Doctor Erwin Jekelius
The Lemberg Veterans' Hospital for Reservists,
University Hospital, block II,
Room 4

Wien, 23 March 1942

Most Esteemed Sir,

Should you find it improper that a previous inferior should take the liberty to write to you, I humbly beg you to destroy this letter immediately. My intention is simply to wish you a swift recovery, as I have learnt from Miss Block, your faithful secretary, that you have been wounded in a field of combat. Miss Block has entrusted me with the address of the field hospital and also shared with me the essence of the reports you have sent her concerning your state of health. I understand that even a man armed with your strength of soul and body might feel lonely when so far away from family and friends and hence, with these few lines, I aspire to reassure you that many of us wish to send you our warmest good wishes as we know you are fighting on the most forward front line. As you will surely be fully informed about the recent notable events at the clinic, above all those of an administrative kind, I will not elaborate here. I must tell you that, many times in my thoughts, I have debated with you about how the clinic is currently managed and run. And however much is being said, I would like to assure you, Doctor, of my continued loyalty. At a time when I felt the courage to live had failed me, you did what I had thought was impossible and gave it back to me. As you have often said yourself, that courage to live is the most important gift that one human being can give another. With this, as ever, in my mind, I remain your grateful and eternally faithful,

Sister Anna Katschenka
Heil Hitler!

She had not expected an answer and felt alarmed when a letter arrived for her. At first, she could not believe that the letter came from him even though his name was on the envelope. It was written in large capitals in a hand that was not his. She thought that he might have died and someone had written to inform her. She made herself read several sentences, filled with a numbing cloud of anguish, before she recognised his inimitable way of expressing himself:

Most Esteemed Sister Katschenka,

Your kind letter arrived in the afternoon today. I cannot write as I am totally paralysed since several weeks back. My condition is the outcome of a war injury. However, I have now 'borrowed' someone's hand: a kindly soul has agreed, for a reasonable fee, to write down as I dictate. As I remember once telling you, I was originally a member of the evangelical church and, according to its teachings, faith is central. Paul the Apostle insists that my hand and my foot, my spirit and my soul, and all that characterises me would not exist unless I believe that the Lord watches over me. To lose the sensation in one's own body and mind is, given these premises, a hard challenge to one's faith but I hope that this letter to you is proof that I have won through. Even though I may not have the hand and tools needed to write, yet I will write! Thus, once again, and as always, the human will proves itself stronger than the powers that set out to defeat it. In the same way, war constantly tests all our strength and capacity to endure. New challenges will and do face us daily, but only in such a furnace can our souls be toughened and our wills forged to steel. Just as Paul once saw it as his mission to help people to find the true faith, so I regard it my task as a doctor to ennoble and toughen the Aryan race until it is ready to fulfil its ultimate destiny. Thus, now as before, I must endure and defy adversity so that I can, with due strength and resilience, succeed in this task I have set myself.

Your kind letter has strengthened my conviction that my work has not been in vain. Soon, I will once more rise from my bed and I will then reward you, Sister Katschenka, for your loyalty and hard work.

You have, with your words, shown to greater effect than ever, that you are worthy of my trust.

Heil Hitler!
Dr E. Jekelius

Another Life A strange time began. She seemed to lead two lives, one in the pavilions with the monstrous children, and one with him. She carried on with the first life despite the shame she felt as all eyes followed her. She had never been one for trying to evade work or responsibility, not even to make a short private telephone call or to share a cigarette in the smoker's hidey-hole behind the back entrance. She had nothing but contempt for people who, as she thought of it, 'needed a break' from the demands work made on them. As if the capacity to endure physical and mental strain – precisely the trait that once made these women see nursing as their vocation – had been nothing more than a mask worn at work that only stayed put for a few hours before it slipped. She articulated thoughts like these when speaking with him in her head as she sat on the tram on her way home after another stint in the pavilion. Oddly enough, he was around in the Fendigasse flat as well, ever ready for a confidential chat. She would discuss Hilde Mayer's smile with him as she washed up after the evening meal and, even when she helped her mother with the ironing, he would sit at the narrow kitchen table, in her father's usual chair by the window where he would fiddle with the evening paper and look at the rain dripping onto the garden below. The sudden return of Jekelius in her life surprised and frightened her at the same time. It made her feel as if her earlier existence had been dull and mute, without either surface or inwardness. Now, every place and moment had another dimension in which new events or observations demanded to be described to him. Often, her conversations with him began with something he had written in a letter but her topics could just as easily have come from elsewhere. New letters constantly arrived for her at her private Fendigasse address. By now, he wrote them himself and although his hand still seemed a little unsteady, at least to her, he assured her that his health improved daily. The paralysis that had struck him down was now over, he wrote. He could sit up in bed and even eat without assistance. She sat next to him, by the head end of his bed. He had described the ward, so she looked around and saw a long narrow room with a row of tall windows along one wall and too little space for the nurses to push medication trolleys between the beds lined up on either side. One day in early April, he wrote to say that he was about to be transferred out of Wien, to Schloss Leesdorf in Baden, to convalesce. The Wehrmacht had just acquired the castle as part of the wartime hospital provision. Could she visit him there? In any case, it was clear that his period of convalescence would be short. He had already been told to await a new order to join up. His invitation stunned her at first. Would their intimate exchanges stand up to the cold light of reality? Would the sentences they had formulated, the lines of conversation they had spun between them while lying awake, he in his hospital ward in distant Lemberg where wounded soldiers cried out in spasms of pain or mumbled long, incoherent strings of words as the fever-frenzy raged in their bodies, and she in her bed, alone in the little room on Fendigasse, the very bed where she had lain as a young woman losing floods of blood and her sheer, unbreakable will to get up had been all that she'd had left to hold on to? But her life was still a matter of getting up and, unsupported, finding the strength and self-control to carry on. Then, one Saturday morning, she took the tram from the Opera House stop all the way to Baden. She found him on the garden terrace, resting on a reclining chair with a plaid blanket across his knees. He must have seen her when she arrived, escorted by the ward sister who had met her at the gate and briskly led the way along the corridor. He sat with his back to them but, even before the nurse had time to announce his visitor, he turned his head and asked: *Nurse Gertrude, would you be so kind and see to it that we get another chair . . . ?* That was all. She stood in front of him as she had decided to do. Facing him, so that he could see her clearly. And he did observe her for a long time, with his large, heavy head tilted a little to the side but without for a moment revealing what he felt. Then his eyes flickered and fixed instead on two stone urns, ornamental markers of where the steps went from the castle terrace down into the garden. From where she stood, close to the edge of the terrace, the garden looked like a sea of voluptuous greenery. Birds flew constantly in and out and, each time another lot emerged, their throats seemed fit to burst with subdued twittering. Further down in the garden, the wind was grappling with the branches of the firs that formed a high wall of trees, so compact that it hid all view of the road. A nurse came with a chair. Anna thanked her and sat down. The administration has just moved in here, he explained apologetically, making a gesture that included both the castle building and the two trucks parked below the terrace where two men were unloading a batch of folding beds. As he twisted his body to point, she noticed that his right arm stayed immobile on the armrest. Apart from that, he looked remarkably unchanged. The large head was somehow heavier, perhaps, as if more effort was needed now to keep it upright. His speaking voice was as it had always been, soft and gentle and strangely rich. He had begun to tell her about Leesdorf's earlier wartime designation as a reform school for girls. He had visited it while on one of his professional trips. Of course, such institutions are superfluous by now, he added. His arm stayed in its old position on the armrest. She wanted to ask about the paralysis, find out what injury had caused it and if he was still in pain; anything personal, to reduce the distance between them, a distance that had been increased by the way he had pronounced the words *reform school.* Still, it was obvious that he had prepared himself for what he talked about now, as if it mattered greatly to him not only to say it but also to say it in this particular way. They are conducting a court case against me in my absence, he said. It appears that they feel my presence in court isn't needed, as if they could bring the case against anyone, because all that matters is that it is conducted at all. He had turned towards her (his right arm still immobile) while he said all this and the expression on his face seemed to demand a response from her. She thought that the set of his mouth was stern, some might say bitter, something she hadn't noticed before. She looks down at her hands on her lap. Doctor Krenek . . . she begins. Doctor Krenek has been plotting against me for years, he interrupts her. Krenek is an upstart.

Nothing he attempts or plans has any inherent originality or vitality. That man never does anything except in simple imitation or obeisance of what others tell him. I don't know if Sister Anna has ever experienced, he says and, for the first time, there is something of the confiding note in his voice that she recognises from their one day together. The sensation, he continues, of once in your life facing something so immense that your soul or thoughts cannot even encompass it. I will give it its true name, he says. I will call it . . . love. And now, wide-eyed, he fixes her with his large, dark eyes. She stays still, fearful. She doesn't understand what he is referring to, with whom (or what) he is in love. She registers a swift, tingling glimpse of the possibility that he is talking about her but that of course can't be true and his absent gaze, lost in mid-distance, contradicts any such notion, as does the set of his mouth, once more reserved and stern. They know nothing, no one knows anything, he says and now she must do something, change her rigid posture or at least swallow or breathe out. She unintentionally moves one hand and, at once, his 'paralysed' right hand lifts from the armrest and takes her hand in a firm grip while his eyes, with their mild, penetrating expression, are again meeting hers, and he smiles:

You really must continue to write to me, Miss Katschenka;
do promise me that, your letters have meant so much to me!

On the return journey, she feels mystified. She looks out over the bare fields that seem alternately to approach and to retreat from the train; sometimes station houses flit past, or lowered barriers behind which the odd vehicle and other road users are waiting, men and women on bicycles with their hands resting calmly on the handlebars. She sees all and everyone, as if reduced to gazing, and hardly dares to move for fear that the light she carries inside her might be extinguished or lost among shadows. What might do it? Throughout the train's shuddering progress runs an uncertain, misty trail made by a slight suspicion that she might have been used, that everything he had said, even that obscure remark about love, has been part of a scheme. At whom, if not at her, had his words been aimed? Was he perhaps using code to refer to something quite different – to some greater duty? Or was it about the land, the same land above which the swallows are whirling now, as she watches them and observes their blind trust that each beat of their wings will lead on to the next; she sits very still, too fearful to move a single millimetre in case her frail certainty fades into something else, and she remains still and stiff until the Traiskirchen stop, when a large group crowds into her carriage and the conductor comes hurrying along to check everyone's ticket.

Healthy Children and Other Kinds In June 1942, she is finally able to write to Doctor Jekelius that the Spiegelgrund board has found a replacement for him: a German doctor called Illing. Perhaps Doctor Jekelius is already familiar with this gentleman, at least by reputation? He is said to be excellent, she writes, and adds that Illing has brought his entire family with him. Not even Hilde Mayer has managed to find out the precise number of family members who have moved into the medical director's residence on Baumgartnerhöhe but a nanny seems to be part of the establishment. Only one day after Doctor Illing introduces himself to the staff, members of his family are seen out on a brisk walk in the hospital park: in the lead, a young blonde nanny in a blue uniform and a neat apron, who carries the smallest child in her arms. These two are followed by three children, keeping in line as if pulled along on a string. At a guess, there is little more than a year between each one of them: a girl of about three, another of four or so, and a boy who looks between six and seven years old. All of them carry garden tools: hoes and spades and buckets. As they pass the pavilions, work practically stops and everyone who can runs to a window to watch. Under the nanny's supervision, Illing's children spend the entire long and lovely afternoon near the top of the slope below pavilion 15 where they bravely dig a large vegetable patch, which they plant later that summer with potatoes and winter cabbages, all of course to contribute to the household during this time of scarcity and self-denial. With time, people develop a habit of stopping by to admire their monument to hard work and utility. The nurses battle to gain favour with the doctor's steadily working children and become especially shameless when the nanny, a kind-hearted German woman, happens to be out of listening range. From inside pavilion 17, with its day room's windows facing the garden, the activities of the new children are observed with endless interest. Look, Nurse Blei says, and lifts the dribbling Otto Semmler to a window. Look, the doctor's children are playing outside again. Pelikan stands next to Otto and has made four fingers into a square on the pane. First, he presses his lips against the glass and then his whole face, as if the power of wishing could transfer the healthy little boys and girls, running and jumping, out of the garden and into his ever-confused mind. Anna Katschenka could easily have written a few lines about young Pelikan to Doctor Jekelius. She can't help connecting the lad to their 'excursion'. Which, incidentally, is likely to be the reason why she puts up with Pelikan despite all that, in her heart of hearts, she detests about him: his eager, busybody habits, like dragging himself along to open the door for her every time she visits, and his way of pressing his hot, wet mouth against everything, and of panting as if about to burst with animalistic, obscene excitement; she is repulsed by the voracious appetite that makes him devour any food in sight and by his small, clinging hands, always with sticky palms, that she has to keep smacking and brushing away but which somehow always find other bits of her to attach to. But, when all that was said, she cannot but feel some pity for him and look at him as one of God's creations that *almost* turned out well enough. He behaves as if the people and objects he seeks out so greedily are always just out of reach and he can't stop himself from trying to get to them, to grasp his chances with big gestures as if ready to embrace the whole world. None of this ever amounts to much more than a staggering gait and imprecise, flailing movements and, sometimes, meaningless vocalisations: that repetitive, panting *Katsch Katsch Katsch* which greets her when Nurse Blei has put him in a wheelchair to push him along to the main lecture hall. These occasions are another Illing novelty. He gives weekly lectures for medical and nursing students about different physiological and, specifically, neurological defects and malformations, and analyses their causation in terms of racial biology, which means that he requires a steady supply of children to display. Pelikan has to put up with standing as straight as he can, in all his naked frailty, on the podium Doctor Illing has had constructed in the middle of the hall. Despite the unmistakable pain it causes him to have to stand upright, the boy carries out his task with the same beaming enthusiasm that he devotes to everything, smiling not only towards Doctor Illing, who keeps poking at his back with the wooden pointer and shouting at him to *straighten up*, but also towards the embarrassed female students who wriggle uneasily where they sit and pretend to listen to Illing's hectoring voice, although Pelikan's well-meaning, almost ingratiating smile begins to fade towards the end of the teaching hour and gradually becomes a grimace of pain so profound that his childish face is pared back to knotted muscles and visible facial bones around his helpless, sucking mouth and always pleading eyes. When the lecture has ended, Anna Katschenka, who has managed to find an unrelated errand to carry out in the auditorium, busies herself with getting the boy into his clothes as quickly as possible and then back to the day room, although Hilde Mayer is ready with a comment, as always:

How nice that Sister Anna has found a small charge to look after . . . Sister Anna who is usually so cold-hearted.

Of course, she doesn't say that last bit. Not even Nurse Mayer would dare to be quite so rude but it is only too obvious that the thought hovers, fully formed, behind her grudging face and frosty, pale and ever-questing eyes. For sure, as soon as Katschenka has turned her back, the judgements on her flow freely. What else could they possibly be talking about in their spare moments in pavilion 17?

Intrusion One morning when she arrives at work, a man is waiting for her outside pavilion 1. He looks relatively young, perhaps about twenty-five, and is carelessly dressed in a worn grey jacket and muddied trousers. He holds his hat like a beggar would, upside down. *Sister Katschenka!* he calls out before she has had time to pass him by. In response to her question, he explains that he is there because he is waiting for a decision. *What decision is that?* she asks. *About what has happened to my son,* he replies and then, apparently having taken her question as an admission of interest, he unfolds, with fingers that tremble with tension, several documents that he tries to press on her. She refuses to take any of them or to be involved in this matter at all. She opens the pavilion door and hears how he follows her with stumbling steps.

Sister Katschenka? he calls again.

She is already on her way upstairs to the office. How does he know her name? Now, he follows her along the corridor. Around them, the typists' constant clattering stops, one room after another goes silent, and the only sound is his coarse voice that insistently and shamingly repeats her name. Next, people stream out into the corridor and he is soon surrounded by agitated women's voices talking across each other.

Decision? she hears Matron Bertha say. *For goodness' sake, man, can't you grasp the situation? Either your son is dead or else you never had one!*

After that, the man finally slinks away. Later the same day, Anna sees him standing among the mothers who gather daily at the tram stop across the road from the main entrance. They are the hard cases, the stubborn ones, who never take no for an answer but, day after day, persist in trying to deliver food or clothes to their children, or enquire about their letters to the board, letters in which they invariably demand information or make complaints. They mostly respect the ban on entering the hospital site but Anna Katschenka is always on guard. Sure enough: two days later, when she is in pavilion 17, Pelikan, clearly upset, tugs at her apron and when she turns round, the man stands there, only a metre or two away. It is the same man, wearing the same worn clothes with mud dried onto the hems of his trousers. The first thought that comes to her mind is indignant: why is this perfectly fit-looking young man not at the front? That is all she has time to think before he jumps at her. She hears the collective scream from all the children on the ward. Then the man's heavy body is on top of her, his hands gripping her throat. She hears nothing and senses nothing except Pelikan's moist lips sucking on the side of her face. She tries to push the boy away but it is no good, he goes on panting his *Katsch Katsch Katsch* in her ear until she finally gathers enough strength to throw them both off, the anxious boy as well as the appalling male weight on her chest and neck. By then, the intruder has already been seized by two of the asylum nurses, who bend and trap his arms behind his back. The face still suspended above hers seems as large as a horse's head and, like a horse, his lips are pulled back from his teeth. *Has Sister Katschenka no heart?* he says. It occurs to her first much later that he never said which of the children was his. And then, that nobody bothered to ask.

A Letter

Dear Doctor Jekelius,

I want to tell you about a dream of mine. In it, I was standing inside a narrow room with walls so close and a ceiling so low that it was impossible to straighten out any part of my body. There was hardly any space at all. At the same time, common sense reminded me of the likely reason for the ache in my shoulders and back: I had spent the whole day bending over beds and, even on the tram afterwards, I had been forced to stand crookedly, crammed in between strangers while the carriage incessantly rocked and leaned this way and that. But in my dream, the cramped posture had grown permanent and, when I looked at myself, I had become a cripple. Nurse Sikora had been to see Doctor Illing that day. Her mission was to accuse me of neglect of duty. An unknown man had made his way into the pavilion without permission. However, in my dream, they had put me in a cage. While inside that cage, the ache inside me made me burst internally, as when the rendering cracks on a dried-out wall. But it hurt so terribly. I remember telling you about my husband, Mr Hauslich, the fake doctor. He complained once about how dry I was inside and how I wouldn't open up to him. In my dream, I then asked you to help me, and your hand entered the cage, dear

Doctor. Only your hand. I sat holding your hand in my lap. I was able to lift it to my face. I kissed it and wet it with my tears and pressed it down between my legs. But I couldn't make the hand move, which frightened me terribly and, when in the end I woke, I feared that something had happened to you and that the hand somehow was a sign.

Tell me please, dear Doctor, is there any cure for me?

The Great Silence In September 1942, Otto comes home on leave. She and her father meet him off the train at Südbahnhof. Her brother has changed since she last saw him. His massive swimmer's shoulders still bulge and stretch the uniform material but everything else about him avoids the two of them, or turns helplessly away. Even his face, once so fierce and determined, looks vague, almost dissolute. When she steps close to put her arms around him, his cheeks are still stiff from all the coarse, simple-minded banter he has been trading with the soldiers who were his travelling companions and who now walk off in different directions, waving to each other. Otto waves energetically back. Later, he sits at the table at home, a large stranger, and thoughtlessly eats the food his mother urges on him. Anna watches his hands as they move from plate to mouth to plate, and realises with obscure but total certainty that these hands have killed and that he has made up his mind to give nothing away, by pretending that these hands have nothing to do with him. He has decided to ignore them, just as he has decided to no longer use any words that would let him express what has happened to him. He doesn't even know what such words mean anymore. And so, the great silence enters into all of them. It happens almost imperceptibly. Nonetheless, day by day, it is *hugely* invasive; on all fronts. Take the fact that, on the ward, Erna Storch turns the radio off as soon as the newsreader starts holding forth about the courage and will to sacrifice of the Fatherland's armed forces, and about the tactical retreats and realigned front-line sections and, of course, the preparations for a great, decisive, final push that is allegedly soon to go full steam ahead but which will never take place, as everyone knows. And then there are the losses: the dead who are left behind but also the ever-growing stream of wounded men brought back home. After all, it is impossible to be silent about them. Some of the pavilions with even numbers, on the east side of the site, have been requisitioned to provide reserve hospital beds. In the darkness of night, severely injured or ill patients are brought in by military transport. The acrid smell of engine fuel still hangs in the chilly morning air when Katschenka and a small group of other nurses from the children's clinic go there to help with the management of the new arrivals. Crowds of people mill around inside the refurbished pavilions. Screens have been rigged up in front of the windows to protect the patients and prevent rubber-necking but they can't stop the noise, the sounds of fevered raving and screams of pain and despair, as if the men were close to a huge wound that has burst open just next to them and they can't cry out loudly enough to make all these blind people see. It is almost a relief to return to pavilion 15. For one thing, the children are small and so much easier to handle. Doctor Illing has been insisting throughout that these children should be regarded as so many abscesses turned critical and that their 'treatment', as prescribed by Berlin, is nothing but a kind of hygienic intervention, part of a natural disinfection process. But however hard she tries, she can't see the children in those terms. They are victims, she thinks, just as everyone else has become a victim of this dreadful war. Just as the war has ripped arms and legs off the young soldiers, and ruined their faces, so it has sliced the children's nerve connections and caused their odd bone fusions, spasms and paralyses. The same agent, the monstrosity of this insane war, is the explanation for everything. She is convinced that if only the war would stop, the world would return to normal. Her brother's former face would be back in place and the terrible cage in which she is forced to crouch, day after day, would explode and the bars give way so that she can straighten her back again. However, nothing stops. The children keep coming and so do their persistent mothers. She sees them every morning as she steps off the tram. There they are, waiting on the opposite pavement: more of them, it seems, for every passing day. And because they apparently have nothing to do all day except spread hatred and envy, they also chatter recklessly to passers-by.

One morning, a transport arrives. A little boy with oddly large, protruding ears and a scared look in his eyes. Only one guard is there to escort him. After the child has been picked up, she spots the guard having a smoke while chatting with the mothers.

This must be the place where the children get the injections then?

My wife has a friend whose son they killed that way.

She and Nurse Kleinschmittger are walking past. It is just after their midday break. Both nurses stiffen but it is Katschenka who turns quickly and walks towards the man, who goes visibly pale and drops his cigarette.

How dare you say these things? This is a proper, respectable hospital.

She demands to see Doctor Illing, who makes a note of the incident. Then he asks her to describe as exactly as possible what the guard looked like. Can she remember his name? The child he brought in, what was its name? What did it look like? When Doctor Illing has written all that down, he shows his teeth in his notorious, tobacco-stained grin and, for the first time, directs it at Anna Katschenka.

It's very good of Sister Anna to be so alert.

Interpreting Signs At the beginning of October, Jekelius tells her in a letter that he will be moved on again. He does not say to where but she assumes that the censor has forbidden it and she takes for granted that he will be sent back to the eastern front. She has lived for so long with the thoughts of how he might be engulfed by the Russian winter that it takes a letter several months later, in which he mentions being paid in *Italian lira*, for her to realise that she has been wrong. Now she rereads all his latest letters and sees how often he has hinted at where he is and what he is doing. She has failed to notice. How could she be so careless? In one place, he speaks of a *donkey train* down the same narrow mountain road that he and his company are walking up and refers to the hollow sound of their hooves against the cobbles on a bridge. Do you really come across donkeys in Russia? Where are bridges cobbled? In Italy, or somewhere on the Balkan Peninsula. But hardly in Russia. Then he writes about the silence of the mountains, where he had camped with his company: a silence so profound that you can hear the melancholic notes of a solitary twittering bird ring out, all the way down from the sunlit western summits and into the dark, wooded valley, *without its song being disrupted by any other voices, from animals or human beings*. The otherwise scrupulous military censors have overlooked these little details. The letter is written on his usual lined sheets of paper. Even that time, the only one, when he first wrote to her with a *borrowed hand,* he had been using the same paper, which made her think that he carried a notebook with him wherever he went and tore out pages to write his letters. The thought appealed to her. In the letter that, from then on, she thought of as his 'Apennine' one, he also said that his years of running the institution, while still important to him, were retreating more and more into the background:

> I have a feeling that, during my existence so far, I have led many different lives but also that the others – the earlier ones – become ever more irrelevant, shrivel and fall. Perhaps all that is old must shrivel until it is gone, in order that we should be able to discern what we are *truly* intended to do.

A few lines further down, he added that he lately had been able to go back to *practising my old trade* and that it gave him satisfaction. At first, she couldn't think what he meant by his 'old trade'. Then it suddenly came to her and she didn't care to think about it anymore. Instead, she focused on the word *we* in the previous sentence. He had also written *on your behalf* about the necessity to look more intently at all that goes on around one – surely that was what he had intended with his story about the bird whose limpid song could be heard even at the bottom of a dark valley? There were periods when she was so preoccupied with interpreting all the signs in his letters and contemplating all the possible secret messages that she sleepwalked through her nursing duties. Meanwhile, nothing changed in the part of reality within which she was alone with herself. Even though Doctor Illing carried on killing children *like you'd be killing rats* (as Hilde Mayer put it), new ones kept arriving at an even faster rate than before, as if spawned by the war. Nature's power of perversion is endless. In Doctor Gross's ward for infants, there is a baby boy of three and a half months whom the nurses call Franzl (apparently he has no proper name), about whom Anna Katschenka knows no more than that his mother handed him over as a newborn, probably because she couldn't bear the sight of him. The shape of Franzl's cranium is strange, almost triangular, as it narrows to a forward point, like a fox's head. All his limbs show pronounced webbing between the digits: so-called syndactyly. An amphibian child. Doctor Illing palpates the angular skull with his thick fingers, then absently prods the joined digits while turning to the ward sister to ask her to arrange a time for pneumoencephalography as well as making the child available as soon as possible for an anatomical examination. A three-year-old girl called Marta Koller is in the next bed. Marta was born with an unusually strongly developed form of bilateral coronal synostosis that has caused the upper part of her cranium to form a protruding ridge. In sharp contrast to the grotesque, boat-shaped top of her head, the face below it is nice and ordinary, almost pretty, with alert brown eyes that follow Illing's exploring hands with anxious interest. When one of the doctor's hands inadvertently touches her cheek, Marta suddenly bursts into laughter. Her laugh is low and breathless, somehow secretive, but so infectious that even the usually grim-looking Matron Bertha allows herself a slight smile. The unteachables gather in pavilion 17's day room, where a fourteen-year-old boy called Felix Keuschnig plays on the out-of-tune piano. His repertoire seems to consist of only a few simple pieces that he plays again and again. Every time Katschenka has a reason to visit pavilion 17, she catches glimpses of these over- or under-developed, malformed children as they run or lumber about, shrieking or bumping into each other or the walls, as if the piano-player's tunes keep them and the world around them alive and the right way up, and so, if the song died, eveything would collapse. But even within the music, the world closes in on itself. It becomes tighter, note by note. The war is shrinking the world. The space of her own room at home, already circumscribed by domesticity, is dwindling, too. One day, when her brother was still on leave, he went along with his father to watch a football match: Rapid v. Admira Wien. For the first time in many years, Anna's father was to be away from home and stay out for a whole evening. His face was bright red with delight. But from that evening on, she felt that her father, too, began to disappear. He returned bare-headed and without his son, and had nothing to say about what had happened – not how the match had ended, not where Otto had gone to, not where he had lost or forgotten his hat. They never found that hat but, after searching for several hours, Anna came across her brother in a bar on Wiedner Hauptstrasse, surrounded by a cluster of lads still too young for army service and to whom he was speaking about something that made him fall abruptly silent the moment she stepped inside. He was so drunk he could barely walk but, behind the fog of booze, his face was naked and hard, as if the bones stretched the skin to breaking point. *You know nothing about what it's like*, his naked face said to her. This was the only meaningful thing she could recall her brother telling her for the entire duration of his leave. By way of duty, or perhaps atonement of some kind, the institution's children had been ordered to sing for the wounded soldiers in the reserved hospital pavilions. She endured one such 'concert' in pavilion 12: a gaggle of scrawny boys with stupid faces and hoarse, breaking voices who sang patriotic songs. The 'upstart Krenek' gave a speech in which he praised the soldiers for their courage, and their willingness to act and sacrifice themselves although everyone knows that they all are so-called psychiatric cases – that is, soldiers who either refused to rush ahead in the first wave like sheep to slaughter, or else were so shocked by the enemy bombardment that they cannot force themselves to speak a single word or stop their hands from shaking. Anna Katschenka, who is a calm, practical person with a strong belief in loyalty and hard work, has never been able to stand hypocrisy and affectation. She observes first the clumsy, delinquent boys trying to sing, then the bedridden human wrecks who once were soldiers, and then the nurses and nursing assistants who are crowded into the doorways, trying to look as if they enjoy the performance and feel proud at the same time, while all that is truly on their minds is agony about the unending misery and the fact that, soon, there will be nothing left to eat. She goes on night duty afterwards and administers the last dose of the scopolamine Doctor Illing has prescribed for the amphibian boy. She checks the little patient a few hours later. His breathing comes in bursts and his lips, still full and red, are going pale. Then his eyelids retract slowly and he dies. She notes the time of death. It is 3.55 a.m. on a close night in June when all the windows are open, the air outside is buzzing with insects, and the radio announcer speaks of enemy air raids over Sicily and the Italian mainland. After the news, the radio plays marches, as if at a wake, and she holds her breath as she prays, something she hasn't done for a long time, to the God she is convinced has long since turned his back on mankind: please save us.

The Victory of a Healthy Mind over an Unhealthy Body *Isn't this by him, you know, your doctor?* Hilde Mayer asks one morning after unfolding a crisp copy of *Neues Wiener Tagblatt* on the desk. She has been looking at the patchwork of advertisements and points helpfully at the top right-hand corner of the page:

It's him, Doctor Jekelius, isn't it?

Under the heading *Lectures*, she reads:

In Urania, at 7 o'clock
A lecture by Erwin Jekelius, Doctor of Medicine:
'The Victory of a Healthy Mind over an Unhealthy Body!'

For some reason it upsets Anna Katschenka even more that Jekelius turns out to be back in Wien than it did when she learnt that he was called up. It feels as if a secret agreement between them has been broken. At first, she can't think why he is here even though there are, logically, several possible answers to that question. He might be on leave or recalled for some consultation. It might be a family matter. Whatever made him not tell her in advance, she must now respect his silence. Unless, of course, the advertisement in *Neues Wiener Tagblatt* is his *very special way* of informing her. It is an idiotic notion, she knows that, but can't quite make herself reject it. She decides not to attend the lecture but ends up going after all. The title of the lecture had made her expect a sophisticated, well-behaved audience of perhaps older colleagues and educated non-medical men and women, but instead a noisy, unruly crowd of quite a different kind are pushing through the doors. Many are youngish middle-aged women, hanging on the arms of spouses who appear to be flushed and stiff-faced with embarrassment and try to hide it behind coarse gestures and over-jolly bursts of laughter. Among the back-slapping men, she catches glimpses of a few faces she knows from Steinhof, among them Doctor Hans Bertha and a younger colleague. Both look very uncomfortable. They must have decided to go for places further back in the hall than she has, because this is her only glimpse of them before the door to the lecture hall closes. The loud-mouthed audience gradually goes quiet and everyone turns towards the stage. Next, something very strange happens. The lecturer steps onto the podium, *but it isn't Doctor Jekelius.* Her first, confused thought is that he has employed the same device as he did in the Lemberg hospital when he 'borrowed' someone else's hand to write for him. Has he borrowed an entire person this time and is this person going to lecture on his behalf? This one looks very much like Jekelius, has the same facial features and the same body. But he moves quite differently, seems awkward and jerky, and also laughs almost all the time, or at least when he begins by telling some kind of humorous anecdote. She can't catch what he says and misses the point. Still, the rest of the audience must feel as lost, because there are only a few laughs and most people are shifting uncomfortably in their chairs. Then he asks in a tone that sounds slightly less actorly: *what are the requirements for being a truly good healer of souls?*

He launches into the answer to his rhetorical question:

In order to be good at knowing the souls of one's fellow men and women, one must above all have the ability to engage deeply with the lives of others. Thus, for instance, Goethe has said that he, too, must be capable of carrying out the horrendous acts that he makes his fictional characters commit. In that sense then, Goethe might have been a compulsive offender, had he not taken the opportunity to act out his inclinations in writing. Just as I might myself have murdered in the most terrible ways and acted like a madman, had I not become a doctor. Experience of life is essential if one is to comprehend the lives of others and I now believe that one must, in particular, have lived through three overwhelming states of mind – great love, profound suffering and debilitating illness. A great love and the misery that follows in its wake are both recent emotions that I have endured. And now, in the ongoing war, I have experienced severe illness. Therefore, I think that I can with conviction state that the man who now stands before you is exceptionally well-equipped to conduct a discourse around the subject set for us all this evening.

At last, the audience has fallen completely silent. All eyes are fixed on the lecturer who goes on to speak in his unexpected, almost unsettlingly personal way about how, on his way to Russia, he fell so ill his entire body became paralysed. He not only lost both the motoric and sensory functions of his body but the sight in both his eyes:

> *I lived as if immersed in an alien darkness; I was in enemy territory and unable to know for certain if those who cared for my helpless body were truly my helpers or intended to push me further towards annihilation. While in that condition, three letters were read out to me, all from women who in different ways had learnt that I had been wounded on the field of war. The first letter was from a deeply religious woman who wrote that she remembered me in her sincere prayers. The second was from someone with no religious beliefs. She sent me a few colourful pictures in the hope that they might stimulate me to regain my sight. But the letter that moved me most was from a third person. She sent me her good wishes and added just a few words: You are a doctor of souls, she wrote, and so need no eyes.*

She looks up. These are her own words, written to him. Now she suddenly recognises the *true* Jekelius behind the mask of a stranger. He is standing by the lectern, looking straight at her with his clear, open eyes. Of all the hundreds of people in the audience, he has picked her out almost at once. She can't cope with meeting his gaze and looks down at her hands, clenched into fists. *These words gave me strength*, he continues after a pause which, to her, seems to last for ever. He goes on to tell them about how one of the doctors at the hospital in Lemberg had let him know that there was another soldier in the same ward, much younger then himself, who was also paralysed from the shoulders down. Jekelius requested to be lifted onto a stretcher trolley and wheeled along to this soldier's bed:

> *When my stretcher stood edge to edge with the other patient's bed, I turned my face towards this stranger, concentrated all my strength and hypnotised him. Once he was in hypnotic sleep, I asked the doctor and the nurse, who had come along to be near us, to lift the patient upright. As he hung there between them, looking lifeless, I told him to start walking. And the sleeping patient began to walk with small, uncertain steps. Supported by the doctor's hand, of course – but he walked.*

Now uproar begins to spread among the members of the audience. *Charlatan!* somebody cries. *Cheat!* Katschenka turns and spots an elderly man in one of the rows at the back of the hall. He is waving his arms and trying to get to his feet but is prevented by somebody next to him. A few rows still further back, she sees Professor Bertha bending forward with his head in his hands. Up there on the podium, Doctor Jekelius holds both hands in front of his face in mock distress, then scans the audience as if to imprint it on his mind. *A soul,* he says. *Now, what is that?*

> *The soul can be defined as the sum total of our emotion, thought and will. The soul can also be defined as that which exists in the interval between desire and action. But then, ask yourselves the following question: does the soul cease to exist just because the body, for some reason, is paralysed and so temporarily out for the count and incapable?*

Once again, silence falls in the hall. She sees Doctor Jekelius smile. His smile shows his entire row of teeth, like the grin of a salesman or a thief. There is also something self-satisfied about it. As if he knows that he has the audience under his spell from now on.

You will by now wonder, full of utterly justified doubts, or indeed anger, how someone whose body was paralysed from top to toe, who could not use his eyes to see with or his tongue to formulate the words he thought – how can he act at all? How, you ask yourself, could such a person, relying only on the strength of his will, make another man rise from his sleep and walk as if he had never been injured?

You ask: can medicine create miracles?

You, who doubt what I have just told you, consider this:

Not even the most skilful medical man can heal himself but, then, the art and science of medicine has never been directed towards the self. The most important word in a doctor's vocabulary is neither diagnosis nor treatment, but . . . you. This single word means that the ill individual is seen and that a stronger soul can lift a source of suffering that has been too inaccessible or too daunting for the patient to touch. And, in that sense, a healthy soul will always be stronger than the most disease-ridden body. Perhaps the soldier whom I cured in that military hospital ward was suffering from one of the traumatic mental conditions that are such common consequences of war. One word was sufficient to loosen his self-applied fetters. In other cases, such as mine, perhaps the diagnosis will be different and other treatments used.

Nonetheless: you see me standing here before you and, once more, I can see; once more, I can move and I can speak. Ignorance and fear have made us think about illness in a way that is similar to how people during the Middle Ages thought about natural phenomena: as if illness was unchanging, and fundamentally incurable. But, for as long as the soul remains the stronger force, there will always be a way of healing bodily distress. The only questions concern the methods we use and how we regard individual human beings.

He turns to the part of the hall where she is sitting and, with a slight bow, indicates to the audience that the lecture is at an end. At the back, people close to the main door are on the move as if they couldn't exit quickly enough. Around the stage, a crowd that is almost as large has gathered to press the lecturer's hand and put to him the many enthusiastic questions they are bursting to ask. She finds herself standing alone in a sea of empty chairs. What should she do next? Leave the hall and seem to join his critics at the back? Or stay where she is until his ardent admirers finally let him go, in the hope that he will look at her and *mean it*, with a genuine smile that she knows is his own. As she waits just outside, she realises that her choice is already made. He knows it, too, and once he has allowed himself to be praised and questioned for half an hour, he comes to her in the foyer. By then, his face looks withdrawn and sombre again. *Sister Anna?* he says in a surprised tone that might be put on for her benefit or simply an affectation. *Have you, too, come here to denigrate me?*

The Blind During the years that followed, there were times when she could not, awake or asleep, visualise him in her mind. He might as well have made himself invisible to her or vanished into some sphere of reality beyond her reach. Sometimes, as she lay awake at night, her thoughts fumbled with the memory of him, as a blind woman would fumble with her fingertips on a familiar face, but without finding a single feature she recognised. His words, even the most significant and distinctive, were also gone. At least let me keep your voice, she said into the dark around her, but the voice that spoke in her mind had become indistinguishable from the crowd-pleasing tones of the speaker in Urania's large lecture hall. That evening, he had asked where she lived and, when she gives him the street address he must have known after a year of addressing letters to her, he suggests that they should keep company, at least for part of the way. Then he sets out on a route in almost exactly the opposite direction to her home: after descending the stairs in Urania, they stroll along the canal, first under the Schwedenbrücke and then Marienbrücke. She follows him obediently and, because he seems unwilling to speak, she starts unprompted to tell him about how things are going at Spiegelgrund. She mentions Illing's 'firm grip' that increasingly controls the work, how the children are subjected to lumbar puncture as a matter of routine, even in cases without the slightest indication of any relevant illness. Jekelius snorts and says: *so, it would seem that the institution has been transformed into some kind of experimental laboratory?* She doesn't comment and he anyway continues to speak, almost as if to himself:

Our people have never been faced with a more colossal task than at present but these career-mad medical men show themselves, as usual, to be more preoccupied with material status and greed for academic acclaim. Of course, all that is of minor importance. I had never thought that you would place such emphasis on trivial matters.

She puts her hand to her chest. She can't understand what he means with her 'placing such emphasis' – she had only told him what was happening. It doesn't matter because his thoughts are now elsewhere:

They had promised me a post as senior consultant on the condition that I left the clinical work at Spiegelgrund. Instead, they continue to persecute me. Many times, when I give my lectures, it has pleased them to turn up. Incognito, naturally. They always sit at the back and refuse to stand and be counted. For as long as I am in army service, they feel safe –hoping, no doubt, that they'll be rid of me soon – but at the same time, they watch my every step. It's fear that drives them. Fear that I will give their little secrets away.

He casts a sideways glance at her and realises that she is still at a loss: *By now, Sister Anna must surely know the full story?*

What story? she asks.

The story of the great love of my life, he says. *We would have become engaged. But he stopped it.*

He? she wonders.

Our Führer, of course.

And she thinks: he's out of his mind. She thinks it quite lucidly and soberly. His war injury (he still hasn't said anything about what kind of injury) must also have affected his sanity. He doesn't notice her silence and continues unconcernedly:

One single word from him could have rescued me. I wrote to his office and asked to be allowed to present myself in order to sort it all out but didn't even receive a reply. That, despite all I have done for him. Or precisely because of it. Do you know, Mrs Katschenka, I think that he is frightened of me, too. We doctors are of course the masters of life and death. And I have learnt from a close relative of his that he – yes, even he, the otherwise infallible – has a relation who was kept in an asylum. Perhaps he was afraid of what he had ordered us to do, of the consequences?

When she had been referred to him and they met for the first time in his Martinstrasse surgery, she had told him about her foolish marriage to the fake doctor, the repulsive Jew Hauslich. Jekelius had looked deep into her eyes and told her that she had behaved in a way typical of her. Again and again, you search out that which harms you, he had said. You do so, because you believe that the only cure for the pain you feel is a still more severe pain. Your have a large wound inside you but can't see it. He had said all that, precisely. Many times during the nights that followed their evening walk together, she would recall this and reflect that his diagnosis was right. Only, this time, he was her wound. What she had thought she had found in him was just what had driven her to fling herself to the ground, time and time again, expecting that the ground, at least, would support her. And this was why, since that evening in Urania, she could never again get a grip on him, however intently she probed his entire being with her gaze and her memory. For her, he was no longer firm ground.

She tells him that she must go, that she regrets having to leave him but she really must go now. He doesn't protest, just says a curt goodbye without holding out his hand. He walks away and turns right at the Gestapo headquarters on Morzinplatz. She notices that he limps a little on his right leg and asks herself if this is due to his war injury or if he puts on the limp because he knows that she stands there, looking at him.

IX

Gulliver

Otto the Stroker, and Pelikan, the General Adrian wakes because someone has stolen his hand. Luckily, the thief isn't far away. He sits on the edge of the bed with the stolen hand on his lap and gazes happily at its former owner. The thief is called Otto but on the ward, everyone calls him the Stroker. The Otto-Thief-Stroker creature is between five and six years old, and an idiot, for real, like everyone else on this ward. Odd, since they're all idiots, that they have such large heads. Otto's head is permanently tilted to the side which makes him look as if he were peeping at you sideways on, with a smile that is both pleading and guilty, the smile of someone who knows he is a thief but is quite pleased all the same. Adrian tries to pull his hand away but Otto tightens his hold and starts to caress the hand with both his thumbs as if it were an animal that could be calmed by stroking. By now, Otto is grinning broadly. Adrian hasn't the heart to disappoint him and lets the little boy keep his hand even though Adrian's skin is crawling and prickling with discomfort. He has no illusions about where he has ended up. This is the pavilion Zavlacky and Miseryguts and the other boys in pavilion 9 used to speak about as *the other place*, where the 'no-hopers' ended up. Just like all the pavilions he knew, this one has a dormitory and a day room. Actually, there are several dormitories. One of them is for idiots who can't walk on their own, and they don't need any day room, of course. The nurses' rules say that the dormitories must be silent. The day room for the mobile idiots is also meant to be silent but that just about never happens. There is a piano in a corner and a boy called Felix sits at it all the time and plays and, when he isn't actually playing, he nags the nurses to be allowed. Another boy, whom they call Pelikan, shuffles about, mostly along the walls. He spies on everything and listens out all the time. As soon as someone is heard in the corridor, he drags himself along the wall and makes a big show of opening the door, bowing deeply like some kind of servant to whoever is coming. This section consists of two wards or groups: one for girls and one for boys. The boys, both those who can and can't walk, are on the ground floor. The ward for girls is on the first floor. Regardless of where you go on the ground floor, in the dormitory as well as the day room, you can hear the noises made by the girls upstairs as they scream or cry or rattle and bang with things they have got hold of. Mostly, it is like a ghostly echo of the screaming and crying and rattling and banging in the boys' ward, but there are times when the sounds from above are enigmatic and frightening. It can be a dull monotonous whistling, as when a cross-draught sucks in winds through a room, or a long drawn-out grinding or chafing noise. Pelikan, who is an expert on sounds, stands with his ear to the wall for a while and then announces with conviction that they are constructing a ski slope up there. Or maybe a skating rink. Adrian has discovered that Pelikan is only able to express himself effectively and clearly if he keeps ramrod straight, like a general. When he does, complete harangues full of complicated, long words flow easily out of his mouth. When he sags, because he is told off by a nurse or the stiff leg he has to haul along makes him lose his balance, his store of words seems to empty instantly. Then, his face goes vague and confused, rather like a short-sighted person who has lost his glasses, but more than that, it becomes curiously mute, or somehow featureless. Adrian was a little scared the first time he observed this change. The upright General Pelikan, in his fine uniform of words, really wants to be kind. He wants to help, to please you. Dragging his crippled leg, he leads Adrian by the hand to the best wall, straightens his back and reports on what is to be seen and heard from up there. For Pelikan, concepts such as here and there, now and then or, for that matter, inside and outside don't exist. What is real to Pelikan is what happens to be in his mind at the moment of speaking. Now he explains to Adrian that the girls upstairs are decorating a Christmas tree. Pelikan is obsessed with Christmas trees. He asked Adrian straightaway if he had ever had a Christmas tree. Strictly speaking, the answer is yes. Adrian remembers very well when his dad took him to the market to buy a tree. His father was just going to see a business contact first, but as one quickie had followed another, the excursion ended with Eugen Ziegler reverting to type and staggering from one bar to the next. The money for the tree was soon gone. So Adrian shakes his head. He disliked Pelikan's Christmas tree fixation from the start. Here's where they put the Christmas tree, Pelikan says as they pass the piano corner. But now the Christmas tree isn't here, he adds and looks quite miserable for a bit. Then, he brightens. It will soon be back, he says. Such is the power of Pelikan's imagination that, for a moment, Adrian can almost see a large tree, hung with Pelikan's many words, making its glittering and imposing progress through all the rooms, just like a living being.

Night Thoughts and Day Thoughts Either Nurse Storch or Nurse Blei were in charge of the ward. Or else Nurse Erhart and Nurse Sikora. Sikora had mean, screwed-up eyes and Storch really looked like a stork. Her eyes were set close together and she looked at you in a sharply attentive way, as if she suspected you might sneak off any minute or do something bad. Blei was different. Unlike most of the ward staff, who handled children like bundles to be lifted and put away as quickly as possible, Blei had round arms and strong, gentle hands. Everything about her was soft and smelled nicely of soap and clean, freshly ironed clothes. Every time Adrian saw her, he thought that this ward would have been the right place for Jockerl. He thought a lot about Jockerl these days. Of Jockerl's face and how everything had frozen inside him as he stood wrapped in wet towels below the portrait of the Führer. Even Jockerl's teeth had taken on a dead, greyish-purple colour and his eyes behind the drooping eyelids had looked like the backs of spoons: unseeing and shiny. If there had been any justice in this world, Jockerl should have been lying in this bed, not himself. He chose not to think about what had happened at Mödling, or about Guido and what the pedagogues and psychologists had said about him afterwards, about how he was abnormal. It was not worth bothering with all that because he knew he was normal. It was people like Guido – and Jockerl, too, for that matter – who were freakish, and the only reason why he was brought here to be among the idiots was that he had been exchanged for someone else who *really* should be here. If there had been any justice in this world, that person would be killed and not him. His problem was working out how to convince them that he was who he was and not that other boy they apparently thought was him. Another thing that was different about the idiots' pavilion and the pavilion where he had been before was that this place was not the same in the day as it was at night. The days were long and uneventful. They sloped off towards the unavoidable darkness of the evening with mind-numbing indifference, as if even his own thoughts slipped away with the daylight. Nobody demanded anything from him. Even the psychologists were uninterested in his answers to the meaningless questions they asked him. During the day, the children around him seemed almost harmless, despite all the yelling and sobbing and groaning. They had no idea about where they were and went through their incomprehensible rituals, and ignored him or claimed him for their own mystifying purposes, like Otto the Stroker, who never let go of Adrian's hand once he had got hold of it and would quite happily follow Adrian wherever Adrian went. All that changed at night. Then, the idiots' enigmatic activities became intrusive and worrying, and they behaved as if something hidden had been set free inside them. One special case was a boy that nobody seemed to have a proper name for and was only called Thunder. He could walk on his own but hadn't been given a normal bed. Instead they kept him in a kind of bed-cage and placed it a little apart from the rest in the dormitory. Thunder would sit inside his cage with his legs crossed and stare straight ahead with unblinking eyes, although he often pulled a blanket over his head and peeped out from underneath it with one eye. Sometimes he disappeared completely. Thunder never uttered a single word but at nights he might start to roar. *Roar* wasn't the right word, though. What he did was produce a sound that was like no other made by a human being. Later, Adrian would say that it was like the cellar was rising up through the building, making a brutal, bursting and shearing noise. Next, another sound could be heard from inside the clamour. It started as a faint whistle that slowly grew into a whimper. At the same time, a dull, rhythmical thumping began. It took some time before Adrian realised that the thumping was Thunder's foot banging against the wall and the wailing, grinding noise was made by the bed-cage as it was propelled ever further across the floor by the powerful blows of his foot against the wall. By then, the main lights would be switched on and the terrified, confused children stood around watching as the duty nurse and a couple of assistants opened the cage and tugged at the blanket. For a moment, they saw Thunder's uncovered face, white and naked, and then a quick glimpse of a syringe. That was it. Just as quickly, the overhead light was switched off and only the bluish night-light would be left on. Then, a low humming noise would start up and it might be coming from Thunder's bed or not. Adrian was always certain that it was Thunder who sang or, perhaps more likely, that his lost soul was forlornly exploring the room and making this beautiful, unearthly sound. The doctors and nurses seemed to be fascinated by Thunder. He once heard Nurse Sikora say it was like a small demon was lurking inside that boy. The procession of people in white coats always lingered by Thunder's bed-cage. Once, doctors Türk and Gross turned up with Sister Katschenka in tow. She took notes all the time. But once the procession had left and the ward became quiet, they could once more hear the low, monotonous singing: it could be that Thunder was lying there, dreaming under his blanket, and all that was bright and shiny in the room was what Thunder's dream looked like when seen from outside. Adrian also dreamt a lot during the few mixed-up, anxious nights he spent in the main dormitory in pavilion 17. One dream was about his mother. This was the first time he had dreamt about her since they sent him to Mödling the last time. In his dream, his mother no longer has a face and is composed only of lines, like the drawings they keep demanding that he must do, either of her or whatever gets into his head. A pair of slack, very red lips hangs in the middle of the restless tangle of lines that is meant to represent his mother. The lips attempt a smile, just like that time when she visited him in his old pavilion. And just like that time, in his dream he isn't certain that she has come to see him. The reddened lips are swollen with humiliation and the mingled lines meant to be her limbs are twitching and waggling all over the place. Suddenly, it comes to him that his mother is here to look for Jockerl. The protruding lips even seem to pronounce just that name. Jockerl, they say. The pointy name seems to suit the lips. And then, suddenly, the dormitory doors open. Even much later, he is unsure about whether the doors opened in his dream or really opened just as he dreamt about it. But whatever might be the case, he is suddenly convinced that it isn't Jockerl they are coming to get. It's *him*, Adrian. Before the full meaning of this insight has become clear to him, he is up and about, moving aimlessly in the semi-darkness between the beds. Other children are milling about everywhere: whining, anxious, lost children who are bumping into bedside tables and beds. His mother is also on the move and he hears the lines that make up her arms dangle and flap, the way hanging branches of trees hit walls and roofs, and later he cannot think what it was that forced him into motion and even what he was looking for, but the movement seems to calm his anxiety. If he can keep this up, move from bed to bed, they won't be sure where to find him or even *who* they are after, and can't come for him at night to exchange him. And he keeps on the move, restlessly, until the early dawn begins to light up the floor's chequered pattern and the white beds become clearly outlined, and Thunder's bed-cage as well, where Thunder himself is enthroned, his legs crossed, wide awake and not hiding under a blanket, but now he can hear sounds in the corridor as the nurses come walking on rapid cork heels, their quiet voices calling to each other, the rattling of utensils in the ward kitchen and the sluice room, and he fumbles among the resisting, alien bodies to get back to his own bed but it seems useless so, in the end, he comes across one child who shifts in bed to make room for him. Then the door opens wide and Nurse Storch stands in the doorway, in full uniform. She draws breath, takes two long steps, reaches him and pulls him out of the bundle of sheets he has tried to hide under:

Are you out of your mind, boy?
Why go to other's children's beds?

The day has begun outside and now Mrs Baar, the psychologist, is there again. She takes notes endlessly. Whatever he does or says, never mind the context or whether it is innocently meant or not, she writes it down. It must be quite a long list by now.

The Black Shoes One morning, when he comes back from the washroom, he finds that Nurse Blei has put out clean clothes for him on his bed. It's all there: shirt, socks, and trousers with braces. By the end of the bed, she has placed a pair of black shoes that are at least two sizes too big for him. She tells him that they actually belong to one of the other boys but she has removed the insoles for now and he can borrow them. He and Nurse Blei walk out of the dormitory together, carry on down the corridor outside the day room (so far, he hasn't been allowed to be in there) and then down the stairs in the empty, echoing stairwell and out into the open air. This is the first time since Mödling that he has been outside. By now, spring has come. Despite the cloud cover, the light dazzles him. The trees are up to their ankles in muddy meltwater. When he drifts off towards the edge of the long, gravelled path, Nurse Blei reaches out for him and, for a while, he walks along with her freckled arm wrapped tightly around his shoulders. He senses the smell of her skin (do freckles have a smell?) and because only the two of them are there, he would have liked to say something nice, like how good it feels to be out walking together, but all she says is that he is to take care not to muddy his shoes. He looks down at the shoes. They are big and black and look completely alien in shape and appearance. Now, the insight comes to him. He knows where they're going. He is to be killed. That's why

Nurse Blei tells him to mind these shoes. It's because they'll want to use them for the next person who is made to walk this way. I don't want to, he says. It won't be any worse for you than for anyone else, she says and pushes him through the door. Pavilion 15 is smaller than 17, or perhaps it is just an impression caused by all the people everywhere. A flock of white uniforms and aprons pushing trolleys laden with sharp, clattering objects, and every time the doors open (and then slam shut) the harsh, sharp cries of children come from the dimly lit rooms behind them, together with a nauseating whiff of medicine and disinfectant. Nurse Blei wants him to climb the stairs to the upper floors but the shoes are so heavy and unwieldy that he has to strain his whole body to lift his feet and in the end Nurse Blei loses patience with him and slaps his face hard:

Hurry up, we mustn't keep the doctor waiting.

He has noticed this side of Nurse Blei before, seen her clear blue eyes narrow and the look in them become edgy and resentful. When Blei gets angry, her freckles pale and a kind of grin, all teeth, spreads across the lower part of her face. She directs it towards him now and he feels more frightened than he has been before in his life.

Upstairs, the layout looks identical to the floor below but is different in that there are no ill children around: only nurses dashing about, in and out through doors that seem to open and shut on their own. Nurse Blei shoves him through one of the corridor doors into a room where another nurse is waiting impatiently. She is older than Nurse Blei and looks fed up, as if she has been through this far too many times already. They pile into a very small room or cubicle, barely large enough for him and the two nurses. A wooden bench and a few hooks above it have been fixed onto one of the short walls. Here's where you hang up your clothes, the older nurse says. And your shoes go under the bench. He bends down to undo the laces but his hands are trembling so badly that Nurse Blei has to help him. His face is level with the broad ribbon of freckles across her nose but her eyes are expressionless. At the opposite end of the room is a door without a handle. Adrian hears sounds from the other side of the door: a distant mumbling on a single note, as when a lot of people talk quietly in a crowded space, and also a noise as if someone were pushing a heavy object across the floor. The people in there are presumably getting some kind of execution machine ready for him. What else could there possibly be on the other side of a door that is opened from the outside only? He starts to cry. Nurse Blei takes no notice. *You're to undress now*, is all she says and when he can't bring himself to do it, she and the other nurse together manage to get everything off him, his underpants and socks as well. When he is naked and shivering, the older nurse knocks on the handleless door. The last thing he hears before the door is opened from the other side is Nurse Blei's hissing whisper:

Remember, not a word from you while the doctor talks!

The Anatomy Lesson The space he enters is surprisingly large. In front of him are rows of expectant faces. All young women, sitting side by side on rows of seats that remind him of the classroom, except they are raked and arranged in a semi-circle, like in an auditorium, so that they can all see him when he comes into the room. He has never felt his nakedness *burn* like this before. The women's collective gaze starts off fires everywhere on his skin. He has nothing to shelter behind. Wherever he places his hands, in front of his sex or his face, he remains exposed. Not that the nurse who escorts him allows him any time for evasive moves. She shoves and drags him to the middle of the floor where Doctor Illing is waiting. Next to him is a wooden footstool. Doctor Illing is holding a long, thin pointer in his hand. It has a sharp tip, like a spear, and reminds him of a hooked implement Mr Ritter had used to pull down maps of foreign countries.

Adrian Ziegler is fourteen years old.
As you will observe, he is relatively well developed for his age.

He no longer knows where to look and so simply stops seeing. Somewhere else, beyond his closed eyelids, Doctor Illing's voice drones on, now and then interrupted by a well-rehearsed flick with the pointer:

Mixed race, second-degree Gypsy.
The father is a work-shy alcoholic.
The mother used to be a seamstress, now a daily help.
A low-grade type in terms of racial biology. She has a tendency to hysteria and keeps pestering us here with questions about her children.

For some reason, the last remark makes the audience laugh. Behind his closed eyelids, Adrian tries to recreate the image of his line-drawn mum, somehow enclosed in a bright red wrapping of shame, like himself. However, the angrily pricking pointer will not permit digressions. It draws down one map after another on his bare, burning skin and then slaps and prods busily at each one. Here is Franz Josef's Land with its high, terraced mountains . . . *as you can see, the cranial shape is what provides us with the most unmistakable indication: the long, partly deformed skull structure of marked Gypsy type* . . . the vertebral column that turns out to be the Andes, a landscape full of irregularities and marginal ridges and then deep ravines that he wishes he could merge with or disappear into but . . . *STAND STILL . . . !* smacks the pointer and then slides across the . . . *disproportionately elongated torso contrasts with the short, curved legs. I would ask you to notice especially the coarse vertebral curvature that accompanies these anatomical defects . . .* (New Zealand Tasmania South America) . . .

> *Other characteristics of the racial type include, in addition to the idleness and unreliability I have already referred to, a pronounced taste for sexual depravity that is reinforced by the miserable social and hygienic circumstances in which these people habitually live. In this particular instance, we have documentary evidence of incestuous relationships within the family. Although Ziegler has grasped, despite his near-retarded intellect, that he is under constant observation while kept in this institution, he has continued to behave with an indiscriminate sexuality that distresses even an experienced witness, as has been recorded in the nurses' day notes. On the face of it, he behaves in a helpful and friendly manner towards other children, often takes on the role of the older and more sensible boy, a knowledgeable mentor who will defend the younger and more vulnerable, only to, when left to his own devices, deviously stalk the youngest children's beds or try to persuade them to get into bed with him. When confronted with his deviant behaviour, he naturally denies everything. This, we should recall, is another characteristic of his racial type: a mixture of obedient servitude, devious cunning and moral degradation resistant to all disciplinary measures.*
>
> *Now, if the specimen can be persuaded to turn round a little, one leg in front of the other, just so . . . !*

A wave of blood-red hurt runs through the Pacific. Inside the Mountain, an echo lingers of what sounds like the noise made by Thunder himself. However, it is only Doctor Illing, who strikes at the shameful red suit with his pointer:

> *I must ask you to notice also the following details, which are also characteristic of this race: the curved ears, a Semitic feature; the low hairline, as well as the indistinct hairline just here, at the temples.*

That wasn't so bad, was it? Nurse Blei says when he is back in the small changing room again and he would have liked to be able to show with a gesture or a movement that, of course, it was perfectly all right. The trouble is that Doctor Illing has used his pointer to remove everything from him that he might have used for speaking. Hands, eyes, lips; and his tongue and gullet, too; all have been removed by that pointer. He is unable even to swallow the few words he might have found. Or, it seems, he might be unable to swallow at all. He just looks at Nurse Blei with eyes that he hopes will look pleading and despairing at the same time but Blei has no patience for those who can't speak when spoken to and is already off into the corridor on hard, tapping heels.

Gulliver He isn't dead yet. Though not properly alive, either. So, what is he? At least I'm not ill, he says one morning to Nurse Storch, who looks as if she doubts every word he says. He attempts another strategy. I'd like to read a book, he says. He fancies that his new status as exhibited specimen gives him some rights to ask for things. He tries this on the male nurse called Heinz who comes to help with changing the bed linen for the bed-wetters. What book would that be? Heinz asks dubiously. Because he can't think straightaway of a suitable title, he says *Gulliver*. He can't think why the name sounds so familiar. Instead of bringing a book, Heinz comes along with paper and coloured pencils. He tells Adrian to draw something. So he draws his bed: it's a huge throne. Zigzagging wires and lines radiate from the bed and join up at the other end of his drawing and meet in a small point which, with a little goodwill, looks like a crushed spider and which is all that remains of his mother now that he has heard what Doctor Illing has to say about her. Adrian might have been struck mute afterwards but he isn't stupid. If Illing's opinion of Adrian's mother is that she is *a low-grade type in terms of racial biology* who keeps pestering the staff with her *questions,* then it means that she has been here and that the doctor has met her, probably not just once but several times. It's a fact that lots of people who want to get into the pavilions aren't allowed to. He has this information from General Pelikan, who has observed with his own eyes that people have been turned away from the pavilion doors. Once, he saw male nurses jump on one of the visitors, wrestle him to the floor and use a police hold to keep him down. So, it could be, Gulliver thinks in his tall bed, that the nursing staff have orders to pack up and hide away all day rooms and dormitories every time an outsider comes along. Only on visiting days are they allowed to look around, and things like their day room and corridor are unpacked and then it's possible that the odd confused relative, who might have been looking for the right place for years and years, is suddenly welcomed with tremendous warmth by Nurse Erhart or Nurse Storch, who will then bring them that relative's *own* Konrad or Gustav or Roman or whatever they're called, all the dribbling idiots thought harmless enough to be on display. And now, it's a visiting day. Gulliver lies on his throne-bed and looks through closed eyelids so that he can squeeze a little red from the grainy light between the lids and eyeballs, and with the red he should with any luck be able to shape a pair of red lips. With still more luck, it might be possible to unfold and straighten the corridor so it gets to look like a real one and then, perhaps, his mum can be fitted in with her thin, stick-like line-legs. He works so hard at his eyelid gymnastics that his mother's face in the end looks more like a smear squeezed out of a tube. But whatever he does, he never manages to make rooms and corridors meet up with his mother in such a way that his mum can come through to him.

Thunderstorm Why is there never a visitor for me? he complains aloud to Nurse Storch one day. Not that he expects much of a reply. Nurse Storch reacts to everything he says by shoving it into the same old sack of angry silence and, should he ever dare to remind her of anything he has said, her eyes just draw closer to her long, resentful nose as she glances crossly and disapprovingly at him. But this time, something different happens. To his surprise, Nurse Storch comes back just a little later the same day and says that she has spoken with the doctor (she doesn't specify which one) and he has told her that Adrian isn't allowed to have any visitors because he has tried to run away once and if you've tried to do that once you might well try again, and that's a luxury they won't put within reach of a useless boy like him. Nurse Storch's voice sounds unusually kind. Judging by her stork's beak of a nose that moves rhythmically up and down, she is practically elated. On the other side of the hospital wall, his restless mother hurries past with a shameless smile on her blood-red lips. Gulliver, you mustn't be angry with me, she says. But Gulliver *is* angry. Gulliver is furious. Determined now, he approaches General Pelikan who is standing straight upright by a wall. He tells the general that he is no idiot, not at all, he can read and write and there isn't the slightest reason to keep him locked up in this place. Besides, he is very strong. With his Gulliver hands, he can tear down all these walls in seconds and fly away. Also, he can take everyone else along with him. Very well, prove it, General Pelikan says and straightens up some more. Gulliver stares at him, then pushes with his hands against the wall with such energy that his head swims. General Pelikan is not convinced by this kind of thing. You've got to let Thunder out first, he says and points to the dormitory where Thunder is sitting in his bed-cage with one eye looking blankly out from under the pulled-up blanket. General Pelikan is scared of Thunder. If it is possible to avoid coming close to the bed-cage, he keeps well away and sticks to his familiar routes. The Otto-Stroker, who shivers with fear if Thunder as much as moves about in his cage, behaves just like Pelikan. Of all the children on the ward, only the piano-player, Felix Keuschnig, fails to notice when Thunder is roaring and thumping. His noises simply don't reach into the bright space where Felix's long chains of notes ring out. (On the other hand, at times they hear Thunder hum some of Keuschnig's tunes, though only faintly, on feeble puffs of air between thin lips, and then the ward falls quite silent and everyone looks with trepidation towards the cage because when Thunder sings, an outburst will come soon. Everyone knows this so, by the evening, anxiety hangs over the dormitory like a suffocating, wet blanket and the younger children won't stop crying.) Just now, though, Gulliver has eyes only for General Pelikan. What's on the man's mind? However, Pelikan no longer stands by the wall, his face has slipped out from under its stern general's mask and has become as empty and expressionless as usual when he doesn't stand to attention behind his screen of words. This, of course, is a strategic move. Sneaky, smiley Pelikan can't be thought to have anything to do with fermenting trouble on the ward. He wants Gulliver to carry out his ideas for him. But what is Gulliver other than a far too large body in a too small bed? When he lies awake at night in the blue light, he hears his mother rummaging behind the wall. Mum is urging him on. Do it, Gulliver, she says. He thinks of the bullet casing he stole from Jockerl. If he hadn't stolen it, he would never have been able to escape that time. And Mum knows that. She has fixed her lips so they are large and red, and now she says to him: I'm here, Gulliver, I've been here all the time, though you never knew about it. And then, of course, he does it. He gets out of bed and walks over to Thunder's cage. In the blue light, the pale, flickering shadow of its grid falls on the white wall behind it. He has watched from his own bed several times when Nurse Blei bends over Thunder's bedside. The movements of her hands as she unscrews and lifts off the roof of the cage are so routine that he doesn't even have to search to find the right screws on the inner surface of the roof. Through the grid he can see the shadowy outline of Thunder's body under the blanket, pressed lightly against the side of the bed but as immobile as ever. He can't hear anything, not even faint intakes of breath. He loosens the nuts and puts the roof down, as he has seen Nurse Blei do. Thunder lies under an open sky, but inside Gulliver something has become knotted, like a clenched fist or like something bulky you've swallowed that won't go down properly. He walks back to his bed with short, uncertain steps and settles down at a safe distance to watch Thunder wake up. Then it begins: a dull, quivering rumble as when a loaded truck is driving past. Very slowly, the strength of the sound grows and you only grasp quite how powerful it is when walls and floor start to reverberate. Then comes a violent crack followed by dark, thumping thuds, as if Thunder were striking with his arm or leg against something hard. Now, he is ready for the thunderclaps. Adrian remembers hearing Nurse Storch say once how unbelievable it was that anyone human could make these noises but, then, Adrian is pretty sure that it isn't Thunder who is making the noise. It is as if he were placed at one end of something much greater than himself and has just triggered off an underground power source by accident, because that's truly what it sounded like (Adrian said later); that is, as if the underworld itself was heaving itself up through the pavilion, and everything on top and below it had to give way. By then, all the children are up and desperately searching for doors they can't find, or at least sanctuary in a bed further away. Adrian suddenly feels a mouthful of cold saliva pressing against the side of his neck. Of course, it is Otto the Stroker's wet mouth. Adrian is far too tired to kick the small, terrified body out of his bed. Suddenly, his mother comes and spreads her large red cloak over them both. He finally closes his eyes and drops off into Gulliver-sleep that lasts for seventy or perhaps seven hundred years. When he wakes, it's too late – inevitably. Thunder is gone. The dormitory is bathed in cold daylight and all the bedclothes have been ripped off the beds, which are left in irregular rows. Here and there, naked or wrapped in sheets, senselessly screaming children are standing about. He has just registered that Thunder's bed is empty when he hears Nurse Storch's cutting voice through the noise. Next, she is suddenly standing beside him holding his coverlet and, with her other hand, Stroker-Otto's hand. Around them, an increasing number of ward faces gather: Nurse Erhart and Nurse Sikora and, a little later, Doctor Gross with a contented smile on his face. He must have been called specially. Obviously, Adrian is in for it, because he has let Thunder out, but Nurse Storch seems much more interested in Otto-Stroker, who is still curled up in Adrian's arms with the dribbling mouth pressed into his armpit and all five fingers of one hand gently curled around Adrian's thumb. Have you no shame, boy, Nurse Storch says. It is unclear if she means him or little Otto. With one powerful tug, she succeeds in tearing Otto out of his secure place and forces him down on the floor where she wrenches both his defenceless arms up on his back in a prisoner's hold and, even though Otto screams like a stuck pig, doesn't stop banging his round, oversized head against the floor until a mask of smeared blood outlines the Stroker's nose, mouth and eye sockets. Meanwhile, Erhart and Sikora have grabbed Adrian and dragged him off to a solitary-punishment cell at the far end of the corridor. Once locked in there, all chances of flight or rescue have vanished.

Encephalography Since he obviously has no shame in his body, they have decided that the evil must be drained out of him, once and for all. Nurse Storch tells him this, pecking energetically with her nose-beak, now to the left, now to the right, as if to emphasise that a new order of things will start at once. Don't I even get any breakfast? he asks. She doesn't deign to reply. He is taken to pavilion 3, the hospital unit, where he is shown into a changing room only a little larger than the one next to the anatomy lecture theatre where he was on display for Doctor Illing's students. And, like that time, he is told to undress but is allowed to keep his underpants on. Two nurses march him into the examination room. He searches their faces frenetically for features he might recognise but it seems that he hasn't seen either of them before. Something that at first reminds him of a dentist's chair stands in the middle of the examination room. It hasn't got a backrest, though, and is more like a stool, surrounded by a steel contraption festooned with dangling leather straps. The structure is a little like the one he was put in when Doctor Gross measured his head on his first day at Spiegelgrund. The two nurses take a firm hold of his arms and place him in the structure, where he is to sit leaning forward on the stool. One of them keeps her grip on his arm, which shakes limply, as if all strength has drained away. By now, he is terrified. They lower the top of the steel frame down over him, fit two clamps to fix his head into place while a third is pushed against the back of his head until he is forced to sit with his head and the upper half of his body bent forward in a cramped position made even more painful by the forward angle of the seat. He feels as if he is about to lose his balance all the time but he doesn't fall, because of the leather straps that they are now busily applying to his arms and legs to keep him still and in place. They have pulled far too hard at the straps, which are cutting into the skin. He struggles a little to free himself. Stop fussing, someone says. The voice is a man's, but Adrian's head is clamped in that horrible tipped-forward position and he can't turn to see who is speaking. Someone pricks his arm with a needle. The sting causes something cold and white to spread under his skin. He feels drowsy, and nothing disappears but his consciousness splinters. When words, sometimes entire sentences, come his way, it feels like what you see when you scrape the paint off a window frame. Nothing makes sense. From now on you mustn't move, a voice tells him. This will take a long time but you must not move. If you move, it will be worse for you. They repeat this to him, over and over. Slowly, his mouth fills with something sweetish, a liquid with an unpleasant, metallic taste that he tries to get rid of by swallowing. But the metallic taste won't go away and it becomes harder to keep swallowing. He sees one of the white-clad ones approach him, holding a syringe that is the size of a man's fist and attached to a long tube. Now, sit completely still, the voice says again. Not that they have to remind him because he can't move a finger anyway. His jaws are numb and his tongue is like a gigantic lump in his mouth that stops him from swallowing. Something stabs at the base of his spine, as if a screw was forced into it. He screams but the scream doesn't leave his throat. The skull clamps that fix his head seem to press more deeply into his scalp. A painful stiffness spreads from his neck, like the sensation of spreading pain in his legs and buttocks after Doctor Gross's sulphur punishment. An intense headache starts up behind his eyes. He can't see any more. His whole body is awash with cold sweat. The pain in his head is too strong for him, too huge for his head, too much for his body to cope with and, however hard he fights to push it out, to heave himself out of it, he gets nowhere because they have already invaded him. He tries to find a way of puking it all up. But there is no longer an up and a down, nowhere to turn and get rid of what he throws up. He dimly glimpses a nurse who is moving around him. She holds an enamelled bowl under his chin. He can't feel it. She slaps his face with both hands but he can't feel it, neither her fingertips nor her nails –

wake up, wake up, wake, you must stay awake

– and, in the end, he actually does wake up. He slides back into an awake state that is infinitely greater than any awareness than he has experienced before. As if he existed in a different part of space or simultaneously everywhere within it, he watches as the white-clad ones move around him, hears them speak to each other although he can't make out what they are saying. He sees General Pelikan stand by the wall whispering, and it is as if he were close by, but on the other side of that wall. The whisper slides into his mind where it grows bigger and bigger, like an expanding bellows. At the same time, the thickness of that wall is reduced until it collapses into itself and becomes a small glass bubble, so thin-walled and fragile that by blowing on it you could make it crack and disintegrate. He understands that the wall isn't the real wall but the pain that increases and explodes inside his head. His mother is walking somewhere beyond the pain, her long spider's legs stretching, her red smile reddening. He screams to her,

mummy mummy mummy

but no one comes, the room is expanding as well, it is inside him and now there is nobody in it.

Line-drawn Mothers In every individual's life, the time will come when certainty about what happened earlier fades and at that point, stories take over. Adrian's time at Spiegelgrund had always been a gaping hole in his memory, and with what could he fill the hole except stories? As the years went by, he learnt to shape and exploit his narratives for his own advantage. His experiences inside the Nazi killing-machine made the normally tetchy and unapproachable Ziegler interesting in the eyes of his fellow prisoners. Adrian would tell them about his encounters with Doctor Gross and Doctor Türk, about the staff in pavilion 9, like Nurse Mutsch with her long dark hair and staring pig's eyes, Nurse Demeter with her bony chin and Mrs Rohrbach, lady of the clapper and the whistle. He was sparing with details about some of the aspects of his time there. If he did mention anything about the weeks he spent with the idiots in pavilion 17, it was only to get a word in about Illing, the murderous doctor. Illing was strung up, of course, he would point out; they hung him just after the end of the war. At the time, quite a lot had been printed about it in *Krone*. Adrian used to believe that he was pretty good at telling it like it was while never going on so much it made him seem too talkative. But not saying too little, either, or he might come across as a weakling, perhaps even vulnerable – a mortal sin for a prisoner, who is always at the mercy of the powerful inmates. The big black hole inside his mind grew neither bigger nor smaller just because he stuffed it full of stories. But then something happened, He was doing time at Stein then, so it was early in the 1970s and after his long stay in Italy. They were a team who ate the midday meal at a particular long table nearest to the canteen wall. Above the table there had been a window that had been covered with black sheet metal held by clamps mortared into the wall. Presumably the window opening had been bricked up as well, so the metal sheet covered a solid wall. An older prisoner used to sit at the table in a particular place opposite Adrian. The old boy's first name was Petter so he was naturally called Parsley – that's *Petersilie* in German. He was an exceptionally short man who looked even shorter in his worn prison kit. But inside the clothes, his small body was constantly on the move and, while they were all seated at their table, Parsley's buttocks and also his hands would shift about constantly on his chair while his lined, old man's face would stay turned to Adrian and not move an inch while he listened to whatever story was being told. Until, that is, one day, when he pressed the restless palms of his hands against the tabletop and interrupted the flow of words. *You're lying*, Parsley said. *You'd never be sitting here today if everything you try to con us into believing was true*. Adrian was taken aback. He knew what he had experienced. Still, he had never reflected on the possibility that what he was saying might be untrue. Anyway, if it was true, in what sense should one understand that? How to judge the actual truth in an account of events one barely remembers? But, as of now, he faces Mr Parsley, full of indignation, who insists that nobody should try to pump him full of fake stories, given that, if all these unspeakable things had really been done to a person, he couldn't possibly have survived for long enough to sit here and talk about it. And perhaps that's right. Perhaps it's like this thing with the blocked window with the fixed cover; that is, there might be a window just like it inside Adrian's head, a window no one can open and even if you managed to break through the outer covering, another wall would be all you found. But if there is nothing on the inside and nothing on the outside either, what is there left to talk about? Adrian bends across the table, looks in Parsley's eyes and says, well now. Let me tell you about my mother. Everyone has had a mother, he adds, everyone can identify with a mum. But mine was only an invented mother, he says. She was a pretend figure made up of lines which he had drawn himself on sheets of paper and then painted with a little red colour in order to make the mass of lines look more like his mother, and that drawing was the only thing he had to show when the other Spiegelgrund children were visited by their (real) mothers. But, believe me or not: one day, that clumsy bundle of lines with a little splash of red in the middle had walked from Erdberg all the way to Baumgartner Höhe in Penzing to see Doctor Illing because she (the line-drawn mother) had by some means learnt that her son had been moved to pavilion 17. Now, you might ask yourselves, what's so special about number 17? Well, the killer-doctor Illing had all failed children transferred to pavilion 17. Failed? Those were the children who hadn't managed to show that they were useful and willing to work. If a child couldn't prove his ability to work and so forth, the nurses straightaway stirred a deadly powder into the food they doled out. And that child died. It was ever so quick and easy, just like when you squeeze a poor little candle flame with wet fingertips and it goes out. But now this line-drawn mother stood in front of Doctor Illing and met his eyes in just the way Adrian had just met Parsley's eyes. She told Illing that she knew something he didn't, something her poor little son had told her one of the few times she had been allowed to visit him. The fact was (she said to Illing) that in one of the places where her son had been kept, there was also a boy called Julius Becker and apparently young Becker had managed to get hold of a pair of scissors. Obviously, the staff had been careless. One night, he stabbed himself in the stomach with the scissors and died. True, it was before Doctor Illing's time but the story of what had befallen Julius Becker, a keen, decent boy who in no way deserved to die, had already been doing the rounds among the mothers who usually clustered around the 47 tram terminal, and wouldn't Doctor Illing mind if something similar happened again; that is, would he care to deal with another boy (her son, for instance) who could no longer endure the conditions and decided to take his own life? The response was remarkable, in that Doctor Illing sat up and took notice. In his clinic, it was simply part of the routine to murder children (Adrian had himself seen the corpses being carried out and taken away in a cart) but the thought that one of the children should choose to take its own life was intolerable even to Illing because he was, after all, a *doctor* so it had to be on *his* say-so that someone was thought ill or well, fit to live or not. Besides, he had taken an oath that his section of the institution would be a model to all, and model clinics had no use for patients who try to control their own fate. So Doctor Illing called in a certain Doctor Krenek, who headed up the reform school part of the institution, where Adrian had been before, and made this Krenek extract the documentation on *Becker, Julius.* It turned out that the line-mother had been absolutely correct: scissors had been accessible on the ward and, mysteriously, ended up plunged into said young Becker's abdomen. That kind of thing really mustn't happen again. Meanwhile, Doctor Illing promised that he would check extra carefully the case notes of the line-drawn mother's son. That was how they came to decide to do what they did, Adrian says. They had already shone a light into his brain and found only useless rubbish in there. Next, my killer-dose of medicine had been measured up and was ready in the medicine cupboard but, at the very last moment, my mother managed to get me out after all. That, despite her being nothing more than a red blob in the middle of a mass of lines. Now Parsley, too, sits still and listens. Bugger that, he says. But he isn't referring to Adrian and his miraculous escape from the snapping jaws of the death ward. He is intrigued by the bit about Julius Becker. Now what I'd like to know is, he says, is that possible? Can you kill yourself with fucking scissors? Like that? Straight into your belly? And Adrian thinks about his mother. After the chaotic months immediately after the end of the war it would take several years before he saw her again. Laura had found a small flat for her in Meidling. Their father was gated (he had started to drink again). Adrian had also been told that he wasn't welcome, because in Laura's opinion, Adrian and his father were chips off the same block. Be that as it may, it was Christmas after all. She decided to be merciful and told all her brothers and sisters to come for a meal. Helmut joined them, too, despite no longer being in contact with his family. Laura had gone to his foster parents to find him, for her mother's sake. Helmut was constantly on his mother's mind and she never seemed to get over the fact that he had been taken from her. (It was obvious that Helmut was not really with them, though. In Laura's place, he just sat in the armchair by the window and stared out into the street even when they were trying to talk to him. Adrian sometimes wondered if his younger brother was all there. Or perhaps you got that way after a lifetime of strangers tugging at you this way and that.) But, with Helmut coming, Laura couldn't reasonably avoid inviting him and his father. Adrian can't recall which particular institution he was on leave from that Christmas but, in the end, there he was, smiling ingratiatingly into the mirror in Laura's hall. Laura had had a dress made for her mother as a Christmas gift. The material was thin silk crepe and all three of them were looking admiringly at it. Leonie wanted to try it on and he said that he would pull up the zip on the back of the dress. When he did, he saw how thin her shoulder blades were, as frail as an insect's wings, and remembered the line-drawing of his mother he had done while in pavilion 17 and then, a final touch: Laura took out her own lipstick to add a little extra *sheen* to her mother's lips, which meant that he suddenly saw his image of her completed: the mirror reflected the line-mother with her spidery legs and insect wings, and lips as red as sticky plaster. And then, the entire story flowed from him, just as he would tell it much later to Parsley and the other prisoners in the canteen. He spoke of Leonie Dobrosch, his mother who was made up of lines, and her visit to Doctor Illing and her announcement that, for sure, she would pass on what she knew about what was practised behind the reform school walls if the doctor didn't deal with her incarcerated son promptly. And then, silence fell. Inside the mirror, the woman with the red lips looked simply embarrassed as she always did when she didn't want to confront something that should demand her attention and, while Laura was clearing up cups and glasses in the sitting room, she (his mother) confessed that she hadn't really worried much about him:

oh, Adrian, I never worried about you
and he, *but what, didn't you ever meet him*?
and his mother, *who?*
and he, *Doctor Illing?*

And his mother muttered something about how she had found some doctor in the institution to talk to but she simply couldn't remember what he was called and

Doctor Illing! he shouted
and Laura, *don't shout!*

And in the mirror, he saw the red lips crack open in the same servile smile as the time she had visited him in pavilion 9, the only time she came to see him, and she had been so anxious to please that when Mrs Rohrbach had walked past with an armful of folders, his mother had responded to some deep-rooted instinct of domestic service and hurried along to open the door. At that moment, he knew that she would do everything she could to please him, too, never mind if it meant having to lie and pretend. But the truth was plain to see, namely that she couldn't remember a thing about any pleading on his behalf. So she told him, when everything is said and done, I never was that worried about you, Adrian, but your little brother Helmut, he was never as brainy as you. And when his sister Laura returns to the hall to lead her mother to the laid dinner table, his mother looks simply grateful: someone has come to get her out of the uncomfortable situation she has suddenly been landed in, alone with a son who has been kept away from her for so long. Much later, when he had been given access to his case notes, he realised that his mother had told him the truth. His notes record only one visit from his mother for the period between 1941 and 1944 and she apparently did not ask about him but about Helmut, who had disappeared around that time but was later found to have been adopted again by yet another family. It meant that the story about the line-drawn mother who had threatened Doctor Illing was a lie from beginning to end. There had been no visits. There hadn't even been a line-mother. If there was nothing to tell and nobody who was prepared to listen even if there had been something to tell, then – where to turn with all the unbearable things you remember? One has to be content that one survived, he said to Parsley as they got up from the table to return their trays and glanced one last time at the covered, bricked-up window that concealed nothing and led nowhere. And he thought that all he had done in his life was to stay inside the cranial cavity Doctor Illing had lit up for him, like a patient left sitting in the waiting room long after the surgery has closed but whom the staff have forgotten about for some reason.

Song without a Voice When he wakes up he is dead. At least, that's what it feels like. As if he were no longer inside his body but has been left hanging in an ether-stinking, hollow space criss-crossed by voices that have nothing to do with him or are even heard with his own ears. He observes an arm lying on a bed. It is his arm. There is something wrong. However much effort he puts into raising his arm it stays lying there, stiff and immobile. And because he is not inside his own body he can't raise his eyes either. He doesn't know where his head is. The place where his head should have been is occupied only by pain, ice-cold, smooth and relentless. It feels as if he is still held by the sharp-edged steel clamps that they screwed into his skull to keep it still, although he isn't aware of any screws. The dull ache in the muscles of his neck sometimes sends pulses of white, shooting pain straight into the back of his head. It causes a sensation of the cranial bone being about to break. He tries to wriggle just a little to move the place where the cramp might be starting but that only causes everything to slide and undulate and the nausea rises inside him like a wave of slurry. He would like to vomit but has no strength to do more than helplessly open and close his mouth. The nausea stays inside him, bathing him in cold sweat, leaving him in a sea full of shadowy bodies that move about somewhere deep below and then, from somewhere even further away, he hears a soft voice hum a song he vaguely recognises. It is a simple tune, a song for children, something about a fox that has stolen a goose but is told he must let go of the goose or the hunter will shoot him:

Fuchs, du hast die Gans gestohlen,
gib sie wieder her, gib sie wieder her.
Sonst wird dich der Jäger holen,
mit dem Schiessgewehr.[3]

Dawn is breaking, the moment has come when the light begins to take over the room but before it has acquired the weightiness of full daylight. Apart from the floating, white ends of the beds, he only manages to distinguish right-angled patterns like the white-painted grids over the windows and the chequered floor that disappears under the threshold and cupboards. The remaining darkness still swallows everything that is curved, like the bodies that must be lying there under the white coverlets. He is lying in the bed nearest the corridor wall. In the bed next to his, he sees a boy who he feels he has seen before. The boy is his own age or maybe a little older. He is lying on his back, staring at the ceiling, and his face looks strangely bird-like, with sunken cheeks and a sharp ridge of a nose. Even though the boy seems to hardly breathe, the song is emanating from him. His singing voice is low and only slightly modulated but clear enough for Adrian to hear how it takes off for each repeat – *gib sie wieder her, gib sie wieder her* – and increases in strength towards the end of the verse – *mit dem Schieeessgewe-ehr . . . !* When one listens intently to a song or just the sound of a voice, one's entire being is focused, wide open to the music. Even though he still can't sense his body, Adrian turns towards the day room at the bottom of the corridor where Felix Keuschnig is playing piano and watches how Felix's usually clumsy hands move across the keys on either side of his straight back. This is in pavilion 17 and the idiots are

3 *Fox, you've stolen the goose, give it back, give it back / Or else the hunter with his rifle will come and fetch it*

sitting about, on chairs or on the floor, surrounding Nurse Blei, lifting their hands and clapping and . . . *gib sie wieder her!* Nurse Blei sings and . . . *GIB SIE WIEDER HER!* babble the idiots and clap or try to clap at the same time or at least in the same way as she does. The very same Felix Keuschnig is now in the bed next to Adrian. Felix seems lifeless. How can this be? How can there be one Felix who plays and sings, and another one in that bed? Unless there are two of them, one in the day room and one here. It might explain why Adrian himself can't move his arms and legs. Actually, he is not here but in some other bed, in another pavilion or somewhere quite different altogether. From far away, he hears the sound of the medication trolley being wheeled along. The wheels rub and grind against the floor, the bottles and jars rattle and clank against each other when the trolley is pulled across the threshold. Soon the doors are opened to let in a whole horde of nurses in white. *His temperature is up again*, he hears somebody say. It is impossible to work out if they are talking about him or about Felix or perhaps someone else in a bed further away. Because he can't move or even focus his eyes, it seems to him that all voices come from every corner of the room simultaneously and that is too much for the heaving sea inside him: once more, everything tilts and the retching becomes uncontrollable and he finally feels he can't contain any more of this blackness without bursting and being ripped apart. *Hurry up with a basin, he's vomiting again!* He senses the surface of something hard and cold (metal, perhaps enamel) bump against his chin. *There now*, the voice says and out it comes, all that was in his stomach and then the stomach itself. He chokes on the thick, ripped-out, warm stomach lump, it suffocates him but he hasn't the strength to resist. And the hard enamelled dish is there again and presses against his chin and he heaves and cramps and finally succeeds in puking out the whole black lump, dripping with chewed food and after it comes everything that is joined to the stomach, the long, fat gut tube is hauled out of him like a gross length of sausage. He feels the pain inside his belly as one segment after another is torn off from its attachments and then the gut is followed by all his other organs: a slippery, fat-infiltrated liver, the slender kidneys, lungs squashed into two foam-filled bags and then, when nothing else is left, his heart. He can feel the sensation of it pulsating as it works its way up his body and into his throat, where it sits like a slimy egg that beats and beats. Then he vomits it out as well. He has no heart any more, and he lies back, scraped out and emptied, as if sunk to the bottom of the room. Only the angry hammering on the piano and the alien singing are left. The light in the room is large and white and open. Felix thumps on the piano keys as if the instrument were the only thing still keeping him here, in this world. The white-clad ones try to pull his fingers off the keyboard but he is ahead of them every time and off playing on new keys. They try to get a hold on his long, slender, straight back but he is too slim and too agile for them. Adrian sees them push a stretcher over to the piano and, heaving together, tip Felix's body onto it. But the piano has stuck to his playing fingers and follows him, tilts upwards and then falls to the floor with an enormous crash. Then, a sudden silence. A huge silence like a vast suffocation; he tries to scream even though he has no lungs left. He screams all the same and screams and screams. High up, somewhere near the ceiling, a door opens and a nurse enters. She comes walking down towards him, as if descending from the sky. It is none other than the ward sister herself, Katschenka. Her progress is slow, her movements measured and silent, as if she has all the time in the world. In the large white light, her face is expressionless and quite still. Nonetheless, she seems to be smiling at him and when she smiles, at the very instant her lips part to show her grey teeth, the room suddenly disappears and true silence falls.

The View from the Gallery He has no clear idea of how long he spends bedded down in the ground-floor gallery but at least it is long enough for him to get to know who is who of the different nurses that worked there. He keeps them apart more by the sound of their footsteps and the rhythm of their movements than by the expressions on their faces or the sounds of their voices, which still merge and separate again as soon as he tries to listen to what they are actually saying. Sister Katschenka's gait is unmistakable: slow and solemn, she floats along almost as if levitating. Nurse Mayer walks with a limp and breathes heavily when she has to bend down or lift something. In contrast to Mayer, Nurse Kragulj is utterly quiet and moves in little weaselly dashes here and there. Seemingly, her impatient fingers lack even normal sensation – they are hard and pointy and peck away at you all the time, like birds' beaks. In the mornings, it is usually Nurse Mayer who comes to empty the bedpan and wash his fevered, sweaty body. He hears her push one hip forward and then drag her leg along. Everything she does must, from some inner necessity, be followed by something she says. When she gives him food, she says *now eat up so you grow big and strong. You don't want to go the way of the rest of them, do you* and holds out the plate with the spoon on it. She smiles knowingly and seems well meaning but, behind her smile, her face radiates stern, single-minded insistence. He tries to twist his head away but the spoon gets into his mouth all the same. He believes that they put poison in his food. Surely they do. Why else is he lying here? They want him to die, that's why. He bites on the spoon. He turns his head. But Nurse Mayer knows her trade, turns the spoon and, one way or another, manages to make him swallow. *There, that's not so bad, is it?* she says in a contented voice that he has learnt to recognise. And the next spoonful is on its way. In the night, he wakes up because someone has covered his whole body with a tightly fitting sheet that isn't made of fabric but some kind of rubber-like material that adheres to every exposed part of his skin. His nose and mouth are almost sealed off, too, so he can't breathe properly. He has a vision of his face as it sticks to the inside of the rubber sheet like a mask. The rubbery stuff sucks the sweat out of him and it condenses into a cold, clear, metallic liquid that seeps into his mouth and nostrils and makes breathing even harder. He struggles to rid himself of the nauseating, elastic membrane, tries to spit or cough out the liquid as it reaches his gullet but every time he coughs it hurts and burns and the air he is fighting for doesn't seem to get into his lungs. On the other side of the sheet, many bodies are bending over him. He can only guess at their outlines but knows Nurse Kragulj's quick, impatient fingers the moment they touch his face. He hits out, again and again. An aimless fling of one of his arms must have struck someone because he hears a woman shriek. As he twists and turns, he doesn't just tangle his bed linen but knocks over everything on the bedside table. Glasses and metal objects crash to the floor. Then, briefly – perhaps the violent noise has brought on an attack of fever – he has a lucid vision. He sees the entire gallery space along its full length, the row of windows facing the garden, although now the curtains are drawn and let in only a dull half-light so it is impossible to be sure if it is dawn or evening or, perhaps, no time in the day since time might have been cancelled. He isn't clear about what is ceiling and what is floor, up or down, but distinguishes a long row of beds, placed closed together so that their iron legs form an abstract, brightly lit pattern, above or below which the children's weightless bodies lie. Felix Keuschnig's old bed is now occupied by a girl of about two or three. The bulging growth on her shoulders makes her look as if she has just been stopped mid-parachute jump. Or maybe the cancellation of time has meant that her fall has been halted. Below the unwieldy lump, her face looks glazed, sombre and blank at the same time, and her two wide-open eyes also look so glassy it is impossible to say if they are watching him or if they stopped seeing long ago. His weightless state lasts only for a little while. Perhaps he has managed to crawl in under the bed but, anyway, they have already got hold of his arms and legs. By now, the group around him has grown to four or five people, he is inside a cage of bodies that cuts him off from above and below. They are not all nurses, even though he feels nurses' hands on him. More firmly and distinctly outlined then any of them, he sees Doctor Illing's compact body leaning over him and, behind the doctor, Sister Katschenka's face rising like the pale, shining disc of the moon.

Well, some are stronger than you'd expect,
so we'll have to use other means to manage this.

He remembers these words but not who said them because, in that instant, something happens, something like a sudden shift of perspective. The change is as abrupt as it is inexplicable. He is no longer inside the room. He has become the room. Doctor Illing is not looking in at him from outside the cage. He is the cage and Illing is inside it. The cage is more than a room, anyway. It is expanding all the time. It grows into a cave, then a mineshaft into a mountain. Now he understands. He has moved into the mountain Hannes Neubauer was always on about. He himself is the Mountain and, far below him, the white-coated Doctor Illing is gesticulating and the words are streaming out of him but they don't reach Adrian because they dissolve into the great silence of the Mountain. The only clear sound is made by the water that trickles and flows through the cracks and hollows in the rough stone walls. Doctor Illing tries to fix his eyes on Adrian but he can't hang on to him, not even now. He is everywhere and nowhere, and *some are stronger than you'd expect*, Doctor Illing says, but to whom? *We'll have to use other means to manage this*, Illing continues but his voice does not echo and not a single one of his words reaches Adrian where he is floating, high up under the vaulted roof of the cave. He is that roof, he is the cave walls and floor on which they all stand, the doctors and nurses dressed in white. Or think they stand on. One quake, one tremor from him and they will all tumble into the abyss.

Final Diagnosis Next time he returns to consciousness, Adrian is in an ordinary ward, full of light and movement. Nurse Mayer stands rooting around in a linen cupboard near his bed. He recognises the broad hips under the nurses' uniform and her wheezing breath as she opens and closes the drawers in the cupboard. All around him, the idiot children are making their barking noises and drawn-out, drooling moans. Back to normal, sort of. No more the silence of the gallery. Now, Nurse Mayer stands up straight and looks down at him in his bed. We've been struck off the list, have we? she says with an expression of grim distaste, as if the mere fact that he has been transferred back to an ordinary ward contradicts everything she believed right and proper. Struck off the list. *Then*, her words had seemed almost meaningless. Later, he would repeat them many times, to himself and to others. I was struck off the list at the last minute, you see, he would say to Parsley and anyone else prepared to listen to him. But, what kind of list was it? He has been allowed to see almost all the relevant documents: the lists of patients; the day nurse entries about oddities in his behaviour and any punishments; the 'clinical' records from his stays in pavilions 15 and 17; all the medical and psychiatric assessments of him. He also studied the forms sent from the Spiegelgrund institution to the state committee in Berlin and how they were returned complete with a coded instruction to the doctors in Wien either to initiate or cancel a 'treatment': there would be either a plus or a minus sign in the upper corner. However, no such form with his name and personal details was ever found, just as his case notes make no reference to any visits by his mother. After the pneumoencephalography, his stay in pavilion 15, ward and gallery, is recorded only in the day notes, where the nurses comment casually on how his condition changes and grows worse, day by day:

> *16/03 Adrian puts hands constantly to his head and neck, also forehead and left eye; complains of pains in his head and neck. Slight fever, 37.7°.*
>
> *17/03 Possible bronchitis, coughing and rel. large quant. sputum. Temp. 38.3°; cough mixture prescribed.*
>
> *19/03 Febrile. V. restless, complains of feeling suffocated. Poor food intake. Temp. 38.9°.*
>
> *20/03 Febrile, temp. 38.7°; drinks too little. Still refuses to eat. Consid. weightloss. Still pats the back of his neck. Complains that 'someone lies on top of me'.*

Then, suddenly, the notes stop. He was sent to the gallery but has no idea how he escaped. He never found who or what saved him. It could have been a random event or the outcome of a chain of decision-making, but he can't prove anything one way or the other. Possibly, some documentation has been kept from him, or lost or, perhaps, destroyed. All he has to go on is Doctor Illing's last report, written after the authorities decided to use other means to eliminate him – dispatching him to a German youth concentration camp in Moringen:

> After completing a careful programme of medical and psychiatric examinations, it has been concluded that Adrian Z. has no symptoms indicating any psychotic condition, or any chronic/more profound mental disturbances. We are dealing with someone who has reached relatively normal mental development for his age but whose family background is of inferior quality in terms of racial biology and social morality. Judging by the boy's progress or lack of it so far, and taking into account observations and evaluations carried out in the institution, the good and caring efforts of the staff, as well as all attempts to influence his character and change it for the better, have had only minor or, at least, scarcely noticeable effects on him. Major inherited character defects tend to direct his behaviour towards misdemeanours of every kind. His offensive and irresponsible manner, repeated thieving, deceitfulness and self-assured mendacity – all these behavioural aberrations can be seen to originate in his almost monstrously impoverished emotional capacity. Adrian Z. lacks normal bonds to other people. He is immune to both praise and criticism, and instead exploits all that is said in his favour or against him in order to attempt to manipulate those around him and gain advantages at the expense of others. He is incapable of remorse, resistant to threats and, according to the nurses' notes, even demonstrates bad faith when learning of any defeats suffered by the forces of the Reich in the field, while also trying to turn other boys into fifth columnists by urging them to treachery. Thus, he has,

among other seditious acts, been heard to say to another boy: *When the Bolsheviks come we'll join the partisans . . .* With due regard to these severe mental (in the sense of character) flaws and his neglect of normal social rules, it is, in the experience of youth psychiatric expertise, not possible to give him a useful upbringing. The conclusion must therefore be that only borstal or youth labour camp should be deemed appropriate. When dealing with actively antisocial persons with inherited criminal tendencies, such as this youth, one must always expect recidivism.

The Mountain in His Head Two weeks later: the punishment bunker in the cellar under pavilion 11. He has been here before. This time, six boys are waiting in the stinking semi-darkness for their transport to take them away from the institution. They have all grown out of their younger bodies and some of them are almost unrecognisable. Gangly, for instance. He is now so tall that he almost hits the ceiling when he stands. A boy called Emil Furth, who was one of the smaller boys in the group at Zavlacky's time, has changed, too. Emil used to shy away from others and mutter to himself. Now, he still doesn't talk to anyone, but the withdrawn child has grown into a rebellious teenager who regards everything and everyone with eyes that are full of hate or scorn. Even though several of them have met before, few speak to each other. What's the point, when they're to be taken away from here anyway? They have all learnt to be on guard against each other as well as everyone else. Who knows what any confidences might be used for in the place they're going to? In the days of Sebastian 'n' Kohler, they had been sent off in teams to carry out simple gardening jobs like digging ditches and tending flower beds. This time, they just wait. The transport is said to be on its way every morning. After getting up and making their beds and packing their things, they are made to take their rucksacks outside and stand at *Habt-Acht* for a couple of hours. And then it turns out that there is no transport. The carefully rolled-up towel is flattened, soap and toothbrush are removed from their metal covers, and everything is returned to the right places in the bedside table. The rest of the day is spent polishing shoes or reading the copies of *Der Stürmer* that have been placed here and there in the day room and corridor for their edification. One of their guards, a young man got up like an Hitlerjugend Führer in a brown shirt and with a hunting knife on his leather belt, comes along every morning to lock them in the Bunker. He says he's called Pfalz. His job is also to see to it that they wash 'as per regulations' every morning and to distribute the meagre breakfast. Pfalz comes back later in the day, together with the cooks from the main kitchen who wheel the food trolley around. At about the same time, cleaners arrive to scrub and wash everything and change the sheets. Usually there are two of them: a blonde, plump younger one, and a sour-faced older one who is dark-haired and thinner. The bunker floor has to be sluiced down like a pigpen and, while it dries, they all have to gather in the day room. When the sullen Furth refuses to move for some reason, the cleaners have no choice but to start scrubbing away while he sits on his bunk. At that point, Gangly turns to them and calls out: *why don't you stay the night?* His lips as he speaks are nervously pulled back over his long, yellow horse's teeth, but when the other boys start laughing, he tries it on again. *We could play cards*, he says. *You could dance the rumba.* In Mrs Rohrbach's day, anything of that sort would've cost him at least four days in solitary, but this time there is nobody to stop the mischief, no other *Erzieher*, not even Pfalz, and the cleaners themselves obviously have no rights to say or do anything. The dark one looks as sour as usual while the blonde picks anxiously at strands of her hair to make them stay under her cap. Then they carry on scrubbing. That day, there has been a leak of information about the transport. Apparently the truck that was to take them to the camp has been in an accident on the road from Linz and spare parts are hard to come by, so hard that none have been located yet. What caused the accident, the dutiful Pfalz can't tell them. But at least they're allowed to be in the day room from that day onwards. This is when, for the first time, they become aware that the wards have been emptied, not only on their floor but on the floor above them as well. There are no children in the building. Adrian feels a strange mixture of dread and elation when it dawns on him that he can move around almost freely in this place where it used to be impossible to get more than ten metres away from the guards' immediate field of vision before being captured and punished. The rapid thud of cork heels against the floor, the rattling of bunches of keys, the hoarse shouting of *get up! Bed-wetters step forward,* Mrs Rohrbach's clapper hitting the beds and then *one two three four!* – all that is still hanging in the dull, dead air, ready to strike him down at the slightest rash movement. He walks slowly through the sun-lit whirling dust in the stairwell. Ever since they left the Bunker, his eyes fill with nothing but sunlight. It is May already and the warm light has brought with it a steady breeze high in the leaves of the trees lining the paths. The wind makes the branches of the Swiss pines swing majestically. The sound of cleaning comes from upstairs, the rhythmic swish of brooms and brushes, the clanking of galvanised buckets and the trickling flow of rinsing water. The younger cleaner is kneeling on the floor of one of the empty dormitories and is scrubbing the floor nearest the wall. The windows are wide open and the reflected flashes of light from the surface of the bucket dance along the walls in quick, glittering curves that make the whole room swing. He stands in the doorway and the young woman doesn't see him until many minutes later when she absently looks up from her work. Scared, she presses the wet cloth against her chest. It looks comical. The cloth leaves a large, damp stain on her apron. But Adrian doesn't laugh. The Mountain is in his head now. He realises how very careful he must be not to frighten her. So, he smiles humbly, almost shyly. The transport hasn't come yet, he says as if to explain. This is when she makes her first mistake. She asks where he is going. Now, the room is filled only with wind and glittering water. From her point of view, he must have looked as if he were gliding in and out of the swinging shadows of the trees. All he can see is that she is quite defenceless. That is why he tells her. He smiles all the time while he speaks. He wants his smile to inspire trust. And it could be that she, too, is pulled into the sense of safety that the Mountain offers because she suddenly says something about her brother, that he has been forced to go to some camp as well. They dealt with my brother just the same way, she tells him. Why she has decided to cast off the last vestige of the authority she could have sheltered behind is more than he understands. Clearly, she is no Nurse Blei. There is no hard armour underneath all that softness. Her body is young and afraid under her neatly ironed uniform with its apron and cap. He notices all that. She wants to carry on scrubbing but can't think how she could dare to tell him to go away. Then, he takes a few steps across the damp floor. He sees her open her mouth before she gulps down her scream. He doesn't have to make her stay silent. She is in the Mountain now. She walks to the windows to pull them shut. But he moves faster. He places his hand on hers, red and a little swollen from the scrubbing. Don't, he says. And he can't believe his eyes: his brown hand holding one of *theirs*. Her eyes are huge and round like balls and she strains to get away from his hands but there is something else as well, something that wants to give in to his heavier body and this other sense makes him weak at the knees. His mouth goes dry with triumph and excitement. That is when he lets her go, scared by his own daring. She opens her mouth and he waits for the scream that will surely follow. But she only adjusts her uniform with trembling hands. Then she picks up her broom and cloth and bucket, and walks out. Without saying a word. He is left, standing with his hand on the open window. Deep inside the rich greenery, he hears the thudding of a diesel engine. On the path just below the window, one of the park labourers in grey institutional clothes walks past pushing a wheelbarrow. He looks straight down at the shaved back of the man's neck below his cap. A group of men and women in white are discussing something a few pavilions further along and then they stop talking and everyone walks off rapidly in different directions. He leans cautiously out of the window. The drop down to the path is three metres, perhaps three and a half. If he succeeds, it will be his third escape attempt. Oddly enough – and even though he knows that it is highly likely that the young cleaner at that very moment is telling her superiors about him and a phone call might well have been made already to the relevant staff in pavilion 1, who will call in young Führer Pfalz to get on with it and stop that misbehaving lout – he isn't in a hurry. Later, he will say that someone helped me the last time I escaped. A young woman took pity on me. I had grown up by then. In reality, the enemy hadn't weakened at all. All that had happened was that the wall had retreated a few steps and the prison confines grown a little larger. He knew that, even as he let go of the windowsill and let himself fall. Ask yourself, what's the point of escaping when you have nowhere to go?

X

Upstream

Hasenleiten He thought he was on his own at first, lying low and trying to keep out of reach of the authorities, but it didn't take long to discover that there were many other boys who, like him, were homeless drifters and always looking for a lucky break. Some were his age, others older and already members of a gang. Then there were the boys who always seemed in transit from one institution to the next and were known as 'spooks' because you could never be sure which side of the fence they were on. Hans Blanker was one of them. He boasted of having escaped from four different Nazi camps where orphans and young people were used for slave labour. Several runaways sought out Blanker, hoping to find some kind of security by being with someone who had been through even worse things than they had. Then, one night when they were holed up in a cellar, the police arrived and arrested the lot of them. Afterwards, the word was that Blanker had been acting as the rat-catcher who lured the invisible children straight into the arms of the waiting police. Later, Adrian realised that he, too, had been suspected of being a spook and that he had been watched for a long time before he was contacted. During his first few weeks on the run, in May and early June, he stayed on the edges of the city, around Gerasdorf and Süssenbrunn, where he hoped to find jobs on the farms. During his time with Ferenc, he had learnt to handle a fork and a shovel, and knew how to make himself useful. He slept in stables and haylofts, and sometimes in the open air. The earth kept turning below him and star signs he had never seen before appeared in the sky. But however conscientiously he worked, in the farmers' eyes he would never be anything other than a shifty, unreliable type. They suspected him of stealing. One night, he woke when three men (one of them was the farmer who was employing him as casual labour) marched an unwilling policeman along the edge of a field where the rye was already waist-high. It was the bright beam of the policeman's torch that alerted him in time. He ran, slept for a few hours in an old linesman's cottage in Stadlau and then, in the dim light of early dawn when what was left of the crescent moon hung pale and exhausted above the still-dark Prater forests, he crossed the river first by the Stadlauer bridge and then by the Ostbahn bridge. The river flowed so fast and huge under the railway bridge that its banks seemed to hold their breath to let it through. The cold mist of water vapour above the river swept everything along with it, his body too, as he crouched on the bridge. Now, he was almost back home. The tall chimneys of the generating station towered on the other side of the canal and next to them, the large gasometers in Simmering. Hasenleiten, the site of hospital barracks from the days of the empire, was further to the east, on the other side of Simmeringer Hauptstrasse. When the hospital moved out, the buildings provided shelter for the homeless and other drifters. Adrian's father had often made his way there to buy cheap alcohol or just have a natter with his 'mates'. Adrian remembers the lanes well, bone dry and dusty in the heat of summer and muddy ditches when the rains came, but always crowded with people. Back then, the whole area was fenced off with a barbed-wire fence. There was only one way in, a gate wide enough for horse-drawn carriages and trucks. There was a guard's hut that would probably have a policeman in it now, so he couldn't risk the gate. Instead he climbed the two-metre-high wooden fence and got in at the back of the most distant row of barracks. They looked even more tumbledown than he remembered and some had collapsed. Once, the long, low buildings had small front gardens where some of the inhabitants grew vegetables. All had been trodden into the ground and not a trace of greenery was left. Most of the windows were either broken, the remains of the curtains torn, or covered with thick boards. Solitary figures moved about here and there. Some stopped and stared openly at him. He tried to walk purposefully, stopped at one of the barracks and pulled at the handle of a door before noticing the padlock. To his surprise, the door opened anyway. The lock had been tampered with. Someone had stayed there, or perhaps still did and had left only for a short while. Dirty crockery was stacked near the sink and clothes, both men's and women's, hung in the wardrobe. Other items of clothing were thrown over the backs of chairs and on the unmade bed. The property, if that was the right word, had three rooms: the kitchen, the narrow room where the bed stood and, on the other side of the main door, a store or, better, a workshop. A carpenter's workbench had been put in the far corner, with irregular rows of tools hanging on the wall above it. A low window to the right just inside the door was too silted up by muck and dust to let in much light. A kiln stood against the wall along from the window and its rusty chimney-pipe exited through a hole in the windowpane. The ashes in the kiln were cold but Adrian decided that he couldn't trust that this place with its workshop was actually uninhabited. He sat down on the road outside the house and waited for a long time until the last of the evening light had gone. Since no one had come to claim the place, he crept back inside, spread some rags out on the floor under the workbench and fell asleep. Next morning, he woke to find a boy of his own age crouching by the workbench and staring fixedly at him. The boy had the bluest eyes

Adrian had ever seen, so blue they looked almost transparent. Are you a Jew? the boy asked dubiously. Adrian must have looked shocked. Jews lived here before, you see, the boy explained. Can't you smell them? Adrian hadn't noticed anything special by way of smell, other than damp wood shavings, varnish and the stench of solvent-soaked rags. I thought you might be one of them, the boy said and the vague, guileless tone somehow went with his strangely luminous blue eyes. I mean, you might've come back to look for someone . . . or something. Who took them away, then? Adrian asked. The Nazis, of course, the boy said without blinking. Then he stood and sounded much more decisive when he spoke again. My uncle says, if you're not a Jew, you can come to our house and have something to eat. This was how Adrian came to meet Leopold and his uncle, Karl Brenner. Mr Brenner was a middle-aged man, short but powerfully built. He had a bushy black moustache and always wore the same things, including a light overcoat and a cap with a black lacquered brim. He might have been a city porter once, Adrian thought. The Brenners lived on Kobelgasse, very near the St Laurenz church. When he arrived, a woman was already making soup for them. Poor lad, you must be starving, she said and moved the heavy soup pan from the cooker to the table. You sit down and eat now. But she didn't bother to look at him and Adrian realised that they must have agreed on something between them, probably all three of them or at least Leopold and his uncle, because they didn't say anything while they ate, just stared into their plates and spooned up the soup. After the meal, Leopold took him down to where the Ostbahnbrücke crossed the canal. Just a few hundred metres after the railway bridge, the tracks turned a shallow curve. After crossing the bridge at speed, the large freight trains had to slow down almost to a crawl for less than half a kilometre. On the curve, the trains would move so slowly that if you managed to get up the high embankment, and if you could sprint quickly enough, it was possible to catch up with one of the coal trucks at the rear, grab hold of the lowermost rung on the ladder and clamber up. Then you would have a few more seconds to shuffle or kick down coals before the engine driver started to accelerate. But there's got to be at least two of you, Leopold explained. One who climbs into the truck, and another one who runs along on the ground to collect the coals and can warn of risks, like if the driver turns and sees what is going on, or if there is a guard on the train (it has happened more than once). Mostly, the driver doesn't notice or perhaps doesn't mind that much. The trains go past here several times every day. Of us two, who'd be the runner? Adrian asked, and Leopold said that he had to ask his uncle who supplied the buckets, but by then Adrian had of course already worked out what it was all about.

An Encounter from the Past At dusk, just as the light in the sky faded and the mists began to rise from the wetlands along the canal, they made their way to the Ostbahn railtracks again. Leopold walked in the lead with his uncle's wheelbarrow full of rattling tin buckets and Adrian followed, ducking all the time to avoid being hit in the face by insistent low-hanging branches. When they arrived at the embankment, half a dozen boys had already gathered. Adrian had thought it would just be the two of them but before he had a chance to say anything, Leopold had started up the slope. It was so steep he had to use both hands to stop himself from sliding back down. The train was already on its way across the Ostbahnbrücke. They could hear the slight clicking noises from the rail joints. Then, the engine's whistle sounded and the air vibrated with the shearing, grinding noise of the brakes. Adrian looked up and saw the engine approaching slowly, as if to show off its full grandeur. The last carriage hadn't travelled more than one metre from where he stood when about a dozen heads suddenly emerged above the top layer of ballast on the track and boys started running past at crazy speeds. Some were hanging on to the ladders and hauling themselves up into the trucks. Adrian saw four or five of them, moving as if in a mad dance, outlined against the inflamed evening sky. Chunks of coal were raining down and the boys left below ran about on the embankment to pick them up. Among the boys, he recognised one as easily as if all the others had been tarred and only that one painted white. Adrian stood as if frozen to the spot and just stared. *Get moving!* Leopold shouted, grabbed two of the buckets and started to pick up coals with his bare hands, just like the others. Unwillingly, Adrian took a bucket and began. It was only a matter of time before he and the white one would meet up. Then Jockerl looked up from his bucket and met Adrian's eyes. A shadow seemed to fall over his pale face. Then Jockerl bent again and carried on with the task in hand as if he hadn't recognised anyone or there had been no one to recognise.

The Silver Knife Jockerl had grown, just like the other children. His frame was as thin and frail as before but he was taller and almost reached Adrian's shoulders. On the other hand, he seemed to behave as he always had, still as jumpy when someone addressed or touched him. But at the same time, he couldn't bear being left out when something important happened and would wrestle or squeeze himself into any crowd regardless of who was in it or where. Jockerl didn't want to let on that he knew who Adrian was, even though they worked in the same team and didn't compete with each other, as Adrian had at first thought. All the runners and pickers – as they were known – were under the command of an older person called the Silver Knife. His hair was streaked with grey and he was always correctly dressed in a three-piece suit and hat. He wore the hat at an angle calculated to have the brim shade his scarred face. A deep cut ran from his left ear across his cheek and ended at the chin, almost like someone in an adventure comic. The Silver Knife was domineering but spoke in a weak, nasal voice and hardly stressed any one syllable so that everyone had to come close to him in order to make out what he said. From his mouth flowed instructions about which trains to run for and when to expect them. The coals or briquettes the boys scraped together were stored in a tool shed at the back of Karl Brenner's garden and in the cellar under his house, where several boys, including Adrian, also slept. Twice a week, late at night or early in the morning, a small lorry came bumping along on the potholed roads and then all of them had to work as a chain gang to load it with coal while the light was still low. Once the back of the truck had been covered by a large, black tarpaulin, they were allowed to troop into the kitchen where Gertrud or Mrs General, as she was also known, dished out potato goulash in deep bowls. Mrs General wasn't Mrs Brenner, as Adrian assumed at the start, but another of the Silver Knife's employees. When cooking utensils, crockery and cutlery had been washed, dried and put away, she walked to the tool shed that doubled as a coal store, hauled out her bicycle, carefully pulled on a pair of tight, white gloves and cycled away. It was the Silver Knife who decided who was to be a runner and a picker on a particular day and, for that reason, he usually turned up somewhere along the tracks about an hour before the train was due, gathered everyone around him and said *you!* in his dreary, whispering voice. Everyone held their breaths while the eyes under the hat-brim swept past their faces, the cowards trying to avoid his gaze and others meeting it anxiously until it fixed on the next chosen one. The runners were those who chased the train, clambered up and shoved coals off with hands or feet. The simplest and most effective way was by kicking but to stand made the runner's job extra dangerous even if the train was moving slowly. If, as often happened, the driver took it into his head to brake (presumably to shake off the boys who crawled all over his train like bedbugs) or if the train suddenly jerked or became unstable for any other reason, one could easily topple off the trucks. The drop to the track was at least two metres, followed by another three down the sloping side of the embankment. Even so, the boys competed and jostled each other to get to stand in the place where the Silver Knife's pointing finger would stop once his decision was made. *You!* signified that you had been moved to another, higher division, like a football player or a boxer. Adrian couldn't help remembering the time at Spiegelgrund when they had been ordered to line up in the corridor and Doctor Jekelius had given that speech about how they all were *the chosen ones* and Doctor Gross had produced one of the boiled sweets he carried about in the pocket of his white coat, peeled off the wrapper and popped it into Julius Becker's mouth and how, later, Julius had stabbed himself in the stomach with a pair of scissors and bled to death in the night. Adrian couldn't think why that memory returned to him just then and wasn't sure if he was alone in remembering things like that or if similar bits of the past came back to Jockerl sometimes. What did Jockerl actually remember? Anything at all? The days went by. They chased trains and searched for coal all along *die Ostbahnstrecke*. Now and then, the police came. Their orders were to 'scatter', as it was called, if the cops turned up, and then follow certain routines. They became steadily better at being in one place for a split second, only to vanish and materialise somewhere else. One June evening, they were getting ready to follow the narrow gravel path that made a shortcut up to Karl Brenner's house when the Silver Knife came to meet them. Leopold had just gathered up the shovels and spades, put them in the wheelbarrow and was about to grab the handles when the Silver Knife put his arm around Adrian's shoulders and said in his monotone, which this time sounded a little confiding:

I understand that you're a Ziegler.

Adrian was holding two buckets brimful of coals, one in each hand. Had he been found out? The sharp tin handles cut into the palms of his hands but he didn't dare to change his grip for fear of losing his balance or spilling the coals. The Silver Knife was moving off and all three of them walked through the little wood and up towards Brenner's house:

I knew a Eugen Ziegler back in the old days;
a fine man, easy to get on with;
is he your father?

Adrian kept staring at the Silver Knife's shoes, marvelling at how shiny and well polished they were despite all the muck and dust and mud they had to walk through every day but the real question was, how was he to understand the warmth that spread like a wave through his chest and into his whole body? He had done everything he could not to be recognised but the Silver Knife's appreciative words about his father filled him with a mixture of pride and shame unlike anything he had felt before. From that day, Adrian's position in the collective of coal pickers had changed. Karl Brenner showed a certain regard for him when they spoke together. When Mrs General placed the bowl of soup or goulash in front of him, there was a slightly respectful restraint about her movements and he no longer had to sleep in the damp cellar but was allowed to share an upstairs bedroom with the blue-eyed Leopold. In the evening, the

Silver Knife's trusted runners would meet up on the embankment. Some brought cigarettes and were keen to offer him one. Mostly, they just wandered about and smoked and told each other tales about a war that none of them had experienced. They saw themselves as real deserters by now, *Schimmlern,* or even as *Politische* (those were the ones the police were supposed to be after) and Adrian might fall back on his father's overused line about how *when Stalin and his boys come, I'll join the partisans* and although he had repeated that one to death and the words were meaningless, everyone laughed to show how they appreciated it. When the weather was nice, they went along to Simmeringer Haide to sit on the grass and watch the teams of local boys playing football. Sometimes they divided up into teams and played each other. Further out on the heath, between the football pitches and the canal, the Nazis had set up a prisoner of war camp. This was what some of the footballers had found out. As one of them pointed, Adrian looked at the high walls, the enclosing barbed-wire fence and the guards that could be seen coming and going. Strangely enough, he didn't feel threatened or afraid. It was as if it didn't have anything to do with him and didn't arouse any feelings. Many years later, Adrian could clearly remember the long evenings of summer dusk vibrating with full-throated birdsong, the air rich with the lightly acidic smell of wild flowers and newly mown grass, and how, in the gathering dark, everything dissolved except their faces and made them look like great big lumbering animals rooting around on the football pitch. In the end, only Jockerl was left running with his legs kicking out in every direction, white legs – *albino-white*, Adrian would say later – so white that someone might have deposited a layer of frost over his skin and made him freeze in the middle of the warm dusk, until someone formed their hands into a megaphone and *Jockerl! – fuck's sake, give over*, and then *Jockerl! Jockerl!* and Jockerl finally veered to the sideline and let his body slump on the grass and then sat with hanging head and his elbows resting on his knees while his white chest rose and fell like bellows, just as Otto Semmler's had when he was close to death and lying in the bed next to Adrian's in the gallery of pavilion 15: breaths far too heavy for so small a body. Adrian steeled himself and went to sit next to Jockerl. I'm really sorry about that thing with the cartridge, he wanted to say but perhaps he didn't, perhaps he only heard himself say it inside his head. It could be that all he did was to hold out a packet of cigarettes towards Jockerl, pressed him a little to have one, as the others did when they wanted to confirm with a mate that there was an understanding or even a pact between them. And he wanted to say something about the fact that they were both *outside* now, meaning that what went on *in there* surely didn't matter that much anymore. Perhaps it had also been best if Jockerl hadn't said or done anything except being pale and exhausted, and just carried on breathing with his body hanging limply between his splayed knees, but he didn't. He turned to Adrian and smiled, the same submissive, anxious, affectionate and despairing smile that had been on Jockerl's face when Pototschnik was in a really mean mood and went for him, and *Jockerl!* Pototschnik's voice was saying, *you sad sack, I'll kill you!* All the time, Jockerl smiled and smiled. After a while, Jockerl packed up his smile and walked away, and Adrian, too, walked back to the room where he and Leopold slept. That night, it started to rain. At first, it sounded like small fingers tapping on the roof but, later, an ice-cold draught seeped in through the unsealed cracks around the window frame and the rain hammered against the walls and the roof, sounding as if someone with large, thumping fists wanted to get in at any cost. Within the noise of the rain, they heard a diesel engine coming close, car doors open and shut, and hoarse voices shouting loudly and urgently to each other. On the ground floor, Karl Brenner was having words with someone and then came the sound of many hurrying feet in heavy boots coming upstairs. The smell of leather and wet uniform cloth that invaded the room when the door was opened told him this was the police. A torch beam swept the room. Karl Brenner's upset, breathless voice rose from behind the cops, saying *I told you, it's just my sons who're sleeping in there.* The door slammed shut again, there were more heavy boots stamping on the stairs and then they were suddenly gone. He stayed still, burrowed into his mattress, feeling like a frog at the bottom of a well. His heart was beating, fit to break the well walls down. Finally, there were voices from outside the house again. They seemed to be laughing, loudly and on a single note, though it might just have sounded like that because of the rain. The car doors slammed shut and, after a while, the engine noise grew fainter and faded away.

The Last Run It rains all night. It has stopped by the morning but the air is close and humid, as if the rain hasn't quite given up. The trees in the small wood they have to walk through every day to get to the tracks are striped with dripping moisture, under a sky as smooth and pale as an eggshell. As always, the Silver Knife is already at his post by the embankment. Somehow, his name seems more right than ever. The shadow cast by the brim of his hat seems to cut his face in two. His voice remains, but only just. Even though the Silver Knife doesn't mention the police raid last night, they realise that this will be their last run. Perhaps that is why no one steps forward when the pointing finger starts to move around the ring of tense, dejected boys and: *you!* Silver Knife is just about to say when Adrian steps forward and says *Jockerl could be a runner!* It's meant as a joke because everyone knows how useless Jockerl is when he runs. The boys laugh and the Silver Knife laughs most of all, and puts his arm around Adrian's shoulders and gives him a friendly squeeze. In that moment, all the laughing boys know that it is him, Adrian, who will be running tonight and he is taking it on to save everybody else but he will run so well that it won't matter that this is the last time. Leopold, who himself used to run at least once a week, has taught Adrian the ropes. Start the exact moment as the first truck comes by and then keep a steady pace with the train or run faster if you can. The best thing is to put more power in at the start of the run because it's when the engine driver enters the curve that he pays the least attention to what happens behind him. There's a short ladder on the side of each truck. The bottom rung sticks out below the side of the truck. Try to grip the ladder as high up as you can, then swing the lower part of your body up and place your feet on the lowest rung. You've got to let go with one hand when you take hold higher up and then you can heave up and over using your body weight. Once you've steadied on your feet it's just a matter of balance. When you're there, standing upright and the train is racing ahead, the freedom you feel is like nothing else, Leopold had said and Adrian, lying on a mattress next to him in Mr Brenner's house, often imagined that much-desired moment when he alone would be on the move and everything else left behind. But he knows it will be hard. His body is heavy, perhaps too heavy for his running speed. Still, if only he catches up with the truck he will have enough strength and stamina to hang on and climb up, whatever else happens. But once he is up there on the embankment, he has no time to think. The train is rushing towards him from the Ostbahnbrücke, as if shooting out from nowhere or as if it had been formed out of its own noise: the heavy, pulsating beats of iron against iron. A *body* of iron suddenly shatters the air with its howling whistle. Then, the shrieking noise of the wheels as the brakes slow them down: a sound like a huge iron ore crusher. By then he is already running, running like the wind, as the tall trucks roll past him in a strong current of dusty, oil-laden, burning-hot air that hits his face. He hadn't reckoned with this, nor that the wet and slippery ballast along the edge of the track would make it so hard to put one leg in front of the other. His right foot slips all the time, his back curves forward and his groin takes the strain. He reaches for the ladder but it is touch and go because it ends much higher up than he thought. Or is the ballast base settling or sinking underneath him? He stretches his arms as far as he can and grabs the bottom rung. Just then, he hears a cry behind him and sees Jockerl come after him at a run. The boy's pale face is stripped bare with effort and he holds out one arm, as if trying to catch up with Adrian to tell him something. By then Adrian is only halfway up and hasn't got a very good grip but he still reaches out his free hand to Jockerl. Despite his clumsy, uncoordinated arms and legs, Jockerl has managed the incredible feat of keeping pace with the truck and even hangs on to the bottom rung of the ladder, his legs beating like drumsticks under his swinging body. Adrian can't stop himself, he has to reach out with his arm as if to support the runner or at least offer a helping hand. At that moment, the entire train shudders but, instead of slowing down a little more, it *increases* its speed. Adrian sees the ballast rush past faster and faster. A wave of panic washes over him. He leans half his body away from the side of the truck and there, behind him but not all that far behind, Jockerl lifts his head and looks up at him. This is the first time their eyes meet. *Hold on!* Adrian wants to scream. *Don't let go!* But just as their hands are close, Jockerl turns his head away, his arm shoots straight up like an exclamation mark while the rest of his body hangs in the air like a white, flapping piece of cloth. Then the air current weakens and lets go of him. There is a short, horribly dull thud as his body hits the truck behind and what is left of Jockerl is tossed in a wide arc up in the air and then disappears out of sight as abruptly as if the ground had opened to swallow him up. Adrian is already on top of the truck and is trying desperately to gain a foothold on the mass of loose, slipping chunks of coal. When he can finally turn to look, the train is taking a slight bend and he sees the other boys come running from all over the place to gather at one spot on the edge of the road that runs alongside the railway. Adrian stands there, helpless, on top of a mountain of meaningless coal. He knows he must jump, but *where*? The train is still gaining speed and around him the track is widening, one set of rails cut into another and the buildings grow denser. Already, he glimpses behind the next curve what must be the roof of the station house in Simmering. He knows that if he doesn't jump now he will never get off this train. Flailing with his arms to keep his balance, he advances to the edge of the truck. Far down there is a chasm of shining rails. The beat of the wheels across the joints makes the side of the truck shake along its full length, and almost throws him off as he tries to climb over the edge. His feet are back on the ladder as the train gradually begins to slow down. At that moment, he sees in the distance an oncoming train. He stops hesitating and, with violent force, leaps away from the side of the truck. Instinctively, he curls up to make his contact area with the ground as small as possible but it doesn't help much: he hits the sleepers with the left side of his body just below the curving border of the ribcage. For a few seconds, everything becomes flickering lights and a bleeding, pulsating sound. He thinks that he will lose consciousness and be run over by the other train. He hears its screaming brakes as if the sound were coming from somewhere inside him but somehow pulls himself out of the pain that presses him down and, with one hand against the side of his chest, crawls off the deadly track with only seconds to spare before the other train rushes past in a cloud of hot, oil-soaked air laden with trackside dust. Hidden behind the seemingly endless freight train, dragging himself along with a slowly spreading, cramped stiffness along the side of his body, he starts the slow walk back to where he has just come from, one metre after the next, while shouting at himself: why go back? Don't do it, there's nothing there for you, get away while you have a chance! But he can't rid himself of Jockerl's face, now so close he feels he could reach out and touch it. Why was Jockerl allowed to run? Or had the Silver Knife sent him to tell Adrian to cancel the run? He knows that he will have no peace until he has found out. And so, once more, the gap between sky and ground grows narrower, a gap that for one dizzying moment had seemed truly to open up around him. He has a vision of walking towards his own mirror image that slowly but tirelessly advances along the track, as if he and it were pulled together by an invisible cord. Then the figure suddenly stops and starts waving with an object held in its hand, and Adrian realises that he isn't watching his own reflection but that it is Leopold who has come to look for him. The thing in his hand is a spade. He lowers it to the ground and then starts running down the embankment. Adrian sets off at a run, too, and stumbles, slips and slides down the slope. Leopold's face is flushed, as if he had been slapped or as if he is burning inside. Quickly, he says, we must get him away from here. He points at the road where a police car has stopped. Two officers climb out and set out towards the embankment. Leopold pulls Adrian towards the edge of the ditch. Jockerl lies there, half-hidden behind some shrubs. The contents of the top of his head have spilt, a sloppy grey mess coated with blood and gravel. The rest of his face is still perfectly recognisable, its features distinct as if painted on and its eyes staring as emptily and helplessly as ever. Leopold has left the wheelbarrow on the roadside and is now pulling at one of Jockerl's legs and signalling to Adrian to take hold of the other one. But Adrian can't make himself do it, just stands as if paralysed, staring down at Jockerl's strange miniature face. He can see the Silver Knife a little further down the road. He is turning round, a quarter-turn at a time. Like a weathervane: first a quarter-turn one way, then a quarter-turn in the opposite direction. Getting nowhere. Now the two cops have him in a firm hold with his arms twisted behind his back. Leopold lets go of Jockerl's leg. Just then, a train goes by and envelops everything in a cloud of black dust and flakes of coal. Its insane howling noise thunders and crackles, forcing the two policemen to bend over until the last truck has passed and the train disappears up the bridge approach and then across the river.

Borstal

> Adrian Ziegler's mental development is average and there are no grounds to assume any psychotic condition or mental retardation at the time of examination. His grossly delinquent behaviour must therefore be due to poor racial stock and having been raised in a criminal and markedly antisocial family setting. Judging by the boy's achievements in life so far, as well as by our clinical observations and assessments, it appears that well-intentioned and caring attention, as well as all attempts at forming and schooling his character, have had little effect.

Legally, one reached the age of criminal responsibility at fourteen. After having spent four weeks in the youth detention cells on Rüdengasse in the 3rd Bezirk, the court sentenced him in September 1944 to eighteen months in borstal for vagrancy, thieving and refusal to work. The sentence was based on the evaluation Doctor Illing had issued from the Spiegelgrund institution.

An ex-SS guard called Nowotny escorted him from the Rüdengasse police cells to the youth detention facility in Kaiserebersdorf. They walked all the way from Rüdengasse to the tram stop at Oberzellergasse and boarded the 71 tram together, the same tram that he and his little brother Helmut had travelled on once, accompanied by Mrs Haidinger who had picked them up from the Lustkandlgasse children's home. He remembered how Mrs Haidinger had bought Helmut chocolate from the kiosk at Zentralfriedhof when they were waiting to change to the 73 tram. Mrs Haidinger had told him that he was too ugly to get anything. Now the ugly boy was getting on the same tram, chained to the former SS guard like a beast led to slaughter. And, although Nowotny had already given what little he had to offer to his Führer and the great leader's army, he felt taking a prisoner from the police cells to the prison was a shitty job well below his proper status and so he shouted *prison transport prison transport!* as they were boarding and hit Adrian over the back of his neck and back to force him into the most remote corner of the carriage. It would have been hard to decide who of the two of them disgusted the other travellers more: Nowotny and his brutal treatment of the prisoner, or the prisoner himself, the deserter and layabout who had been lying low while decent people had obediently made sacrifices but now was hauled out from his lair to be properly punished. Deserters, wartime saboteurs and ordinary criminals were all incarcerated in the borstal institution in Kaiserebersdorf. Arguably, the saboteurs and other miscreants were in the majority, because all young people were regarded as deserters if they had failed to turn up for labour service or ignored the call-up to the Wehrmacht. It was tacitly understood that the prison guards could do what they liked with deserters. Adrian shared a cell for a while with a youth called

Viktor Zobel. Zobel had psoriasis, which meant that his arms, back, chest and belly were covered with large, red, scaly lesions that itched terribly and were made worse by the coarse, dirty prison uniforms they were forced to wear round the clock. Even though Zobel did all he could to stifle his whimpers, the guards heard him. One night, one of them dragged him into the corridor and beat him senseless. After that, Zobel kept back the small ration of margarine that came with their evening meal and used it as an ointment for his wounds, though if his tortured moaning through the night was anything to go by it didn't help much. The war will be over soon, he kept mumbling, as if the two phenomena were linked – the war and the wounds that gave him no peace. Adrian Ziegler spent a total of seven months in Kaiserebersdorf and all he saw of the sky in that time was a square grey area above the exercise yard where they had to line up in the morning, most of them wearing only wooden clogs. Sometimes snow fell from the square of sky and sometimes it did nothing but, as far as Adrian was concerned, it was just as cold all the time. In snow and ice and drifting rain, their bodies still stiff and sore after the damp chill of their cells, the prisoners had to stand waiting until everyone had been allocated work of some kind in a prison workshop or in the kitchen and its attached bakery. Adrian was sent off to the Hellhole, as they called the laundry in the cellar, presumably because it was the only place in the entire prison that was kept really warm. He and two other prisoners, Heinzl and Matthias, were supervised by a one-armed sergeant called Schwach. The other arm was left behind in Vitebsk, Schwach explained to the boys. Adrian's job was to see to it that the level and pressure of the water in the two high-pressure vessels were kept constant and to top up with coal or water as required. Bringing the coal twice a day was the heaviest part of the job: it meant carrying the twenty-five-kilogram coal buckets, one in each hand, and tipping the contents into the purpose-built coal bunker. Every time he did it, the memory of Jockerl came back to him, the memory of how he had reached out his hand to the running boy and how Jockerl hadn't been able to take hold of it or perhaps hadn't wanted to and then plunged from the truck. It seemed weird, but Jockerl hadn't even been mentioned in Adrian's sentence, as if he truly hadn't existed, or had once, but been erased from reality. All the same, Jockerl was always very much present inside Adrian. Like a second prison guard, he saw to it that there was no let-up from the memory, not even when dropping off to sleep because, as soon as Adrian became drowsy on his stool in front of the pressure gauges, there was Jockerl, his skin as white as ever, running along the train and Adrian was holding out his hand but Jockerl refused to take it. Over and over again, as if a film loop were running in his head. Unless the air-raid sirens went and he had to stop. The standing order on hearing the sirens was to put out the fires and remove all embers. As far as Adrian could remember later on, the bombing raids over Wien began at about the same time as his prison sentence, in September 1944. It happened that they had to douse the fires and run to the shelters several times a week. One consequence was that the piles of unwashed laundry grew bigger and bigger. One day, the boss of the provisions department at the army base turned up and demanded action. The soldiers couldn't wait any longer for their clothing: uniforms, socks and underpants. Sergeant Schwach stated that in case of raids, his orders were to extinguish the fires and have embers removed. The officer turned to the prison governor and it was decided to start up a night shift in the laundry. Everyone who worked nights would receive an additional meal consisting of the leftovers from the kitchen at the barracks. As a result, the laundry staff were given bread and decent food, delivered by lorry nightly and in good order. It made existence in the hellhole almost tolerable. Apart from keeping an eye on the fires and the temperatures in the boilers, Adrian was given the task of going through the mountains of uniforms and greatcoats before they were laundered, looking out for things like coins or faded pictures of women and children. Once, he found a wedding ring and, another time, a cigarette case engraved with initials. His finds were requisitioned by Sergeant Schwach, who let Adrian have big pots of marmalade to spread on the black bread. When the night shift began, Schwach would ask if everything was under control so he could withdraw briefly and Adrian always answered that everything was fine (what else could he say?) and so Schwach went off for a kip, in a small space behind the large laundry pans where he had fitted in a bed. He kept a small radio receiver on a bedside table switched on. During calm nights, Schwach snored in his quarters while the radio, turned down low, was chatting to itself. Sometimes, the cry of a cuckoo cut through the broadcast to warn of another raid and the sergeant shot out from behind the pans with his hair standing on end and his braces dangling at knee height, shouting *Feuer löschen! Feuer löschen!* – which gave Adrian just a few minutes to put out the fires under the pans and, once he was sure that the ashes were dry and free of any glowing embers, sprint the eight hundred metres or so to the exercise yard, then cross it to the building on the other side and down the long, echoing cellar stairs to the shelters where he sat down among the others, seething inwardly because now it would take at least two hours to restart the fires and get the pressure up in the boilers. Now and then, they heard the dull thuds of exploding bombs, sometimes far away but sometimes so close the ground shook. Then, at dawn after a night raid, when he had just got the fires going again, a guard ordered everyone out into the exercise yard for a line-up. Adrian was so tired he didn't know if he slept standing up. Every time he looked up at the square piece of sky, the light cut his eyes like a sharpened knife blade. A truck with armed guards in the back came to pick them up. For a short, senseless moment, Adrian thought they were all to be executed. Heinzl, whose face was ashen, sat opposite him, then a boy whose name he didn't know, who was so frightened his knees were shaking almost too hard for his arms to keep them still. Next to the scared boy, Jockerl was facing him as usual, smiling his terrified porcelain smile. This was in February 1945. He remembers the white sky and the new layer of snow on the fields on either side of the road. The truck bumped along towards Albern where he saw the river for the first time, like a black slash through the whiteness. They passed burnt-down houses, buildings that had been flattened, and there the ground, too, was black, as if a huge wall of flame had travelled along the road, leaving only ashes behind. The truck stopped at one of the grain silos by the harbour basin. It looked unharmed but the adjoining buildings were in ruins. They were ordered into teams, given spades and told to start clearing the site. As he set to work, he heard a diesel engine throbbing somewhere behind him. He couldn't work out why at first but then he realised that it belonged to a pump draining overflow water from the grain store via long hoses into the harbour. Though the guards were armed, they were not brutal: after digging for a couple of hours, Adrian's team was told to take a break. They were given bread and sausage and, after the meal, he was even offered a cigarette by one of the soldiers. Adrian looked into the kindly face under the helmet and realised this was a young man, not much older than himself, even though he tried to make himself look as solid as possible with gestures and voice. *It doesn't matter what they do, soon river shipping won't be possible anyway.* The soldier waved the barrel of his rifle towards the black river that was rushing along between the white snowdrifts. *The Americans have mined it all the way from here to Nussbaum*, he said, then puffed up his cheeks and rolled his eyes upwards until they protruded like two white balls, and *BAA-BOOM!* he shouted meaninglessly and flung his arms out as if to mimic the explosion of a floating mine and, all around him, the other guards and the digging prisoners turned and smiled, white grins on their dirty faces. They carried on hacking and shovelling stone and pieces of reinforced concrete until long after dusk. Then the trucks arrived for them and took them back to the prison. The digging teams' wet and filthy kits were waiting for him in the laundry. He had barely started throwing them into the boilers when the air raid began. In front of him, as if sprung out of the cellar floor, Sergeant Schwach rose up and shouted his *Feuer löschen! Feuer löschen!* in a voice that sounded as if large wounds had been ripped open inside his throat. This time, Adrian had no energy left to move out of the merciful warmth that enclosed him and nobody even tried to make him go anywhere. That night he dreamt about the river as he had seen it when he walked across the Ostbahnbrücke in the early light of dawn: like a huge wall of black water that grew taller and taller as if just waiting to come tumbling down over him.

Upstream The beginning of the end was an unmistakable bad smell. It stinks of cow shit, Heinzl said. It did. They had just finished yet another night shift in the laundry and from the other side of the ventilation grid they heard mooing cattle and something sounding like large wagon wheels grinding across the cobbles outside. From one of the windows in the stairwell, they looked out over the exercise yard and it looked like a marketplace, packed full of wagons loaded with every kind of furniture. Between them, cows, goats and pigs ambled about. Where the prisoners used to line up, someone had placed a fodder bin full of hay and a long tin tub that served as a water trough. They later learnt that Soviet companies had reached the edge of Münchendorf and the local farmers had spent the whole night trying to move themselves and their animals to safety. The decision to evacuate the prison must also have been taken that night. The order went from room to room: all prisoners were to line up in the yard. They had to stand along one wall, all three hundred and sixty-nine of them, hardly anyone above the age of twenty, packed so closely together that they had to contract their back muscles not to touch each other. The day was bitterly cold, with a strong wind driving rain showers that felt like hail against their faces. Above them, an armour-plated sky, covered with heavy, leaden clouds. After about half an hour, the prison governor, accompanied by two officials, came outside. He was in full uniform. Adrian had never seen him like his. It was hard to work out what he was saying, above the wind and the rumbling of the penned-in cattle and the shouting of the soldiers who were trying to inch two covered trucks towards the main gate (the drivers sounded the horns and hung outside the side windows screaming at the cows, who took no notice). Adrian picked up only a few words but remembers that the prison governor held a pair of black leather gloves and was slapping them nervously against his Sam Browne belt while he might have been speaking about heroic courage and the invincibility of the Germanic peoples and so forth. They had heard that kind of thing many times before. He also spoke of the delinquent prisoners who had shamed the native land. However, despite their evil deeds, he wasn't leaving them to their fate at the hands of the Bolsheviks but would transfer them to safety. To the last man, he said. Or, anyway: in so far as he was able. Or, he might have said something quite different because now the wind was fierce and strong enough to tear the fodder bin from its wooden supports and send it tumbling across the cobbled yard. The noise was so violent it hit the shaved juvenile necks like a blow. When the hand holding the gloves pushed the governor's hair out of his face one last time, Adrian noticed his cheeks, dark with untrimmed beard growth, were glistening with tears. The camp guard shouted *Attention!* and then they were made to walk back to their cells to pack and sign receipts for their possessions. Yet another convoy of army vehicles had arrived at the prison, and one of them brought the unit of military police detailed to escort them. They lined up again to be counted and, afterwards, the guards set about tying them together in pairs and then running a long rope from the front pair through to the last one. It took hours before all the names had been called and the ropes tied and secured. Finally, in the afternoon, the prison gates swung open and the prisoners marched off. They were like a manacled chain gang, bound by hands and feet, and guarded by a dozen armed men from the special police who walked along the line on both sides. For as long as he lives, Adrian will never forget this march and the journey on the river that followed. For one thing, he can't ever get his head round why their tormentors were so dedicated to taking them all along on this mad exercise. Was it because they regarded the risk of them falling prey to the enemy as a greater threat? Or, was it that they had no idea what to do with them but brought them along by default or perhaps because they were simply property, just as the farmers tried to take their goods and chattels with them? But the prison governor's face had been streaked with tears while he spoke. Could it be that he was convinced that even for lowlife like Adrian Ziegler or Viktor Zobel, the kind of people he and his comrades-in-arms had been trying to wipe off the face of the earth, there might after all be some freedom to find in the crumbling Reich? Or was the plan that they would all go down together, murderers and victims alike, still stuck with each other, the victims to their last breath remaining under the murderers' orders? Still in prison uniforms and bound together, they marched towards the city. At first, they stumbled continuously on the ropes because their guards tried to make them move at too fast a tempo. Of that part of the march, Adrian only remembers the furious shouted commands, and that some of the boys ahead of him fell and were dragged along by the others or were brought to their feet with kicks and blows, still with their arms and legs hopelessly tangled in the ropes. They followed the canal in the direction of the generating station and the gasometers in Simmering, then carried on under the Ostbahn viaduct where he once (how long ago it seemed) had run coal for the Silver Knife. He stared fixedly at the ground to avoid having to watch Jockerl tug at the ropes. Not even the wind that swelled and flapped above them like the sail of an abandoned boat could carry away the sickly sweet stench of rotting cadavers. There were dead cows and calves everywhere, in the fields and the muddy ditches. And in the canal, too, where dead bodies that had been stopped by rubbish or tree roots now floated in the water by the banks with their legs helplessly sticking up above bellies distended like fat balloons. The closer they got to the centre of the city, the more terrible the devastation. Near the slaughterhouses in St Marx, whole city blocks had been flattened to the ground with only the odd gable or chimney stack still standing upright, pointing stupidly towards the sky. A burning stench of fire, diesel and decay filled the air. They passed a few horse-drawn carriages that must have received direct hits from shrapnel bombs because the entire vehicle had burnt, including the animals. Some of the carbonised horse cadavers had no heads, others had spilt their innards on the street. Live animals, sheep, calves and pigs, were wandering among the torched ruins, paradoxically liberated by raids aimed at killing the lot of them. At St Marx, the column suddenly stopped and was then ordered to carry on over the Stadionbrücke. The wind was so strong at the centre of the bridge that those up in front found it hard to keep up the quick-march tempo or even to keep upright at all. The wildly impatient officers walked up and down, shouting, swearing and hitting prisoners with their rifle butts. As they crossed the Prater, along the full length of Meiereistrasse they had to move at a jogging pace and weren't allowed to stop once. They came to a sudden, involuntary halt on Handelskai, causing the rope to tighten so abruptly that Adrian almost fell. When he turned to look he saw that one of them, perhaps five or ten boys back along the line, had managed somehow to wriggle out of the loops of rope. His clogs were left on the quayside, looking sad and pointless. One of the guards pulled at the slack ropes. Then, very quickly, shots rang out: three sharp cracks in succession. Over by some harbour sheds, he saw the runaway, whose leg had been injured, struggle to sit up and drag himself behind the sheds. His naked, hopeless face was raised in desperation as two of the policemen ran towards him. One of them stopped just about a metre away, raised his rifle and shot once. The boy jerked and sank into a heap. Whispers flew between the prisoners in the column, giving the runaway's name, Adrian thought it was Alois Riedler, but before the name reached him properly, the officer in charge of the column started to shout at them. He was a large bulldog of a man with chins like car tyres stacked on his broad shoulders. Adrian, who was too exhausted to raise his head, didn't bother to look at him. They set off again, keeping closer together and moving with tired, shuffling, resigned steps. A tugboat was at anchor by a jetty just below the Reichsbrücke. It had two long barges attached, one at each side. The wind was blowing hard, making all three boats seem to fight to stay pointing in the same direction.

At the far end of the jetty, a tall, thin man in a light overcoat was waiting for them. The man would later introduce himself as Mr Rache, a schoolteacher. If that was true information or not, and how this man had come to take on the responsibility of three hundred and sixty-nine inmates from Kaiserebersdorf, Adrian would never find out. Mr Rache had a list with their names inside a folder, and proceeded to call them out in a loud voice while the pages fluttered in the wind. One by one, the boys stepped out onto the jetty. Adrian's name was called and Rache looked up from the rustling pages and glanced at him with empty, utterly indifferent eyes. Then he said a number to the guard, who pointed with his rifle at one of the barges. Near the barge, a young woman wearing a pale blue dress and white sandals was handing out a blanket and a small flask of water to everyone in turn. Adrian would later call this woman Miss Santer, though he was as vague about why as about using the name Rache for the man. With her white sandals and her long, tousled hair flying in the wind, Miss Santer looked as if she came from another world: maybe an actress, maybe somebody's secretary, but definitely not a prison guard. The cargo hold was unbearably hot and stank of stale bilge water, rotting ropes and diesel fuel. Mr Rache let down a large bucket at the end of a rope and shouted to the boys to secure it and use it as a latrine. The tugboat engines were thudding and pulsating below the waterline. He heard shouts from on deck and for a brief moment, the hatch framed the young woman's face, wreathed in her flying blonde hair. The barge was turning through a semi-circle and he had time to glimpse the Reichsbrücke under a swiftly sliding sky. So, they were going *upstream*. The woman's face vanished from the hatch as if the wind had carried her off. Heavy boots trod the deck above them and the hatch cover was shut and screwed down. The hold became pitch black. There were three loading hatches but while the barge was on the move, only one of them was propped open enough to admit a tiny strip of light and it wasn't the same hatch each time: first, aft and, later on, either at amidships or stern. Each time they stopped and the position of the ventilation slit changed, a wild tumult broke out because the strongest and most ruthless fought with hands and feet and whatever they could use as weapons (things like rope stumps, bailing-out buckets and old oil cans) to get themselves close to the only air gap. A fight to the death, if necessary, to gain a little fresh air and brief glimpses of the open sky. Adrian took one look, gave up the idea of fighting and withdrew to what he reckoned was a reasonably safe place by one of the bulkhead walls. A bucket fell over, it might even have been Mr Rache's latrine bucket; someone screamed loudly for a long time and a new fight started to shut the screamer up. Then for a while, the hold became completely quiet. Adrian could sense the bodies around him, the warmth of backs and thighs pressing against him. The original sickening smell of mouldy wood and rotting water was thickened by the bitter stench of urine and shit from the presumably overturned latrine bucket. He remembered Uncle Ferenc's stories about people who had been pulled along by river currents and drowned. Would he be one more of them? If that young soldier at Albern was to be believed, the river was mined, probably all the way up to Nussbaum. Or higher still. And if the mines were carried by river currents, they would be meeting them any time now. To distract himself from the mines, he tried to calculate where their barge was in the convoy by listening to the monotonous beat of the tugboat engine and the blunt waves slapping against the hull. He guessed that they were in the first barge. Sometimes, all the boats moved out into the main channel, which could be felt from the gentler, more rhythmical wave movement and heard from the steadier rumble of the engine. Now and then, the engine sound became slower and more uneven, then cut out and restarted on an odd, almost quivering note as the noise level sank until all that was heard above the coughing motor was the anxious splashing of water against the hull. He had a vision of the tugboat veering off mid-river and slowly making its way towards the bank. It was the first time they had stopped. No one in the hold had a clue why they were going towards land or what they might expect. Adrian fell to thinking about young Miss Santer, she of the blonde hair and white sandals and long, lovely legs. Then he thought of the bodies of the terrified boys crowded down there, where the air already stank of their waste and the hatch lids were screwed down like coffin lids. And suddenly, his whole body started to shake. To control the shakes, he pressed his hands flat against the bulwark just above his head. The surface of the steel plate was interrupted by two nuts. He touched them, then used his nails to scrape the paint off them while the barge carried on rocking on its own small waves. A ceaseless but faint buzzing sound was coming from somewhere far away. It rose and fell, as if reluctant to approach them. On deck, people were running. Suddenly, it felt as if a giant hand had grabbed the barge from below: it reared and there was a detonation powerful enough to drown the screaming in the hold. Was this a mine? He looked around but could see nothing except eyes and mouths gaping with terror. Viktor Zobel crouched as if in spasms at Adrian's feet. He bent down to try to help his old cellmate and then the barge rose again. Zobel was now no longer below but above him and vomit sprayed from his mouth like a fountain. Blinded and footloose, Adrian fumbled for something to hold on to but the bulkhead plate with the two nuts slipped away from his hands. There was a burst of firing from a machine-gun position somewhere close by. So they hadn't struck a mine, then? Adrian bent over to try to find out if they were taking in water and glimpsed, he thought, Jockerl's shiny porcelain teeth scattered over the filthy hull. Another powerful detonation tore at the barge and nearly upended it again. He had time to hear the swooshing sound, as massive volumes of water were pushed aside, and then the entire ship tilted until it pointed straight down towards the riverbed and he crashed against the bulkhead wall. The pain hit him at the same time as the icy certainty that he would die. It was not so much a conscious thought as his body's intuitive grasp of a reality that couldn't be perceived by his sight and other senses: this cold, stinking place was the final boundary and on the other side was death and beyond death there was nothing. It was as if the dreams about the Mountain that had filled his head all the years in Spiegelgrund had come true. This cargo hold was inside the Mountain. This was what they had been travelling towards all the time. Or, perhaps, towards the torrents of water that whirled past underneath the most remote cavity in the Mountain, which would be cracked open by the bombs falling on them or the mines lying in wait near the banks. And then they would actually have to do what they had already practised thousands of times in the dreams: help each other to sink into the dark, deep, swift-moving water that flowed so powerfully below. They had to push each other's heads below the surface, just as he had pushed Jockerl's head under in the dream, until they had all drowned. When they were all disposed of and the barge's hold empty, the journey could finally continue as planned. While waiting for this, there is only one thing to do: stay as still as possible. Try to stop his runaway thoughts. Concentrate on objects in the ceiling. A rope. A metal eye. Two nuts in the bulkhead, covered in thick white paint. The scratches in the paint made by his nails. Ahead of him, the back of a boy's neck, its tendons tense like a terrified animal's. Viktor Zobel's flame-red face, vomit dribbling down his neck. Someone gets up, slowly and cautiously. In that instant, the distant tugboat engines start thudding and the light slapping of water against the side tells them that they are once more on their way to the main channel. But now, it will never be the same again. Fear of death is lodged in the very walls and every bump against the side of the barge awakens it as if the hull were covered with living skin and the regular beating of the engine were the sound of their own pulse, slowing down and speeding up and slowing again as they make their way through the swift waters. When the hatch was opened again, twenty-four hours had passed and the convoy had pulled up at Stein. All he grasped was the place name that was passed on in whispers from one boy's parched lips to the next. The engine noise died down and Miss Santer's windswept hair could be glimpsed through the hatch against a fragment of clear blue sky. They were allowed out of the hold for the first time in two days and nights. All three boats had pulled up along the quayside and he was able to confirm, with eyes that stung and ached in bright sunlight, that his guess had been right and that his barge was the first of the two. The tugboat swayed on its anchor just ahead of them, swinging to and fro in the silvery, glittering light reflected off the waves. In the dancing light, he saw Mr Rache talking to a sturdily built, shortish man who was probably the tugboat captain. Along the quayside, special police in field-grey uniforms stood at the ready, their rifles pointing towards the barges. They weren't taking risks even though none of the prisoners could reasonably be in any shape to resist. They stood clustered together on deck in their stinking clothes. Mr Rache exchanged a few words with one of the guards and then picked half a dozen boys to help with carrying water and provisions from the prison. Around Adrian, several of the boys said they'd soon be joined by more prisoners. Stein was one of the largest prisons in the country and where would the inmates go from there? But when Rache returned a few hours later, he was still escorted by the policemen, who didn't bring any more prisoners with them. The boys who served as porters were hauling a cart loaded with large drums of water. Food was handed out: sausages smelling strongly of acetic acid preservative, and *Schwarzbrot*, the black rye bread. Everyone had to queue to fill the water flasks they had been given in Wien. For a while he stood close to Mr Rache, looked into his face and could have asked him where they were going and how long it might take, but their ferryman's face was reduced to a mask of contracted muscles and blank eyes. Then, the dull thud of the tug-boat engines started up, the exhaust fumes drifted across the water and they were ordered to go below. At least for a while, it seemed possible to travel in mid-stream. Despite the oven-like heat, the crowded, unwashed bodies and the increasingly evil stench from the latrine bucket, he managed to sleep a little, with his head pressed against the familiar bulkhead plate. Soon, though, he woke to the sound of running feet on deck (like blows with a club just above his head) and shouting voices that seemed to be answered from some-where on land. They pulled in to the bank again. The hatch was opened. Outside, night had come. Miss Santer's face flitted past but there was already a fight brewing at the open hatch. People were struggling blindly to get up on deck and at least steal a quick look at what was going on. He managed to get out by supporting himself on the shoulders of some boys who were squashed too tightly together to move and saw, as if in a nightmare, the fortress-like building of the hospital at Ybbs come drifting towards him out of the dark. The past, in this majestic shape, had returned to attack him. A heated discussion was going on between Mr Rache and the solid little cap-tain, who absolutely wanted the prisoners to stay in the hold. They compromised in the end. The prisoners were allowed on deck, but only so long as they stayed completely still. The cold up there felt biting and almost unreal in contrast to the hot, repulsive air below. He sat with his arms around his pulled-up knees, watching the long hospital buildings with their sheds and walls emerge through the hazy dark. Not a single light was visible in the main block, as if the whole place had been evacuated. But the hospital staff must have come from somewhere because here they were, their small torches gleaming like fireflies in the dark. In that ghostly, wavering light, he saw two boys carried off the other barge and stretchered up towards the huge, dead-looking hospital. Some of the prisoners were handed torches as well, but then the guards turned up and waved with their rifles to make them go back below. The hatches were screwed on again and, as the boats chugged back out into the river channel, something inside his belly turned over like a large animal and he had to shout out that he needed the latrine. A light flickered between the bodies and, from the uncertain shadows, a hand reached out to support him and usher him to the bucket. It was upright but had fallen over so many times it was surrounded by a grim pool of urine and faeces. The wavering torchlight picked out a boy squatting with his naked feet in the filth, his hands gripping his stomach with an expression of unfathomable suffering on his face. Adrian pulled his pants down, straddled the bucket and emptied his entire gut in one massive, disgusting rush. There was of course nothing you could wipe yourself with. Exhausted and still nauseous, he made his way back to his place by the bulkhead and lay there, probing the nuts in the plate, scratching the paint with his nails and trying to calculate the distance between Ybbs and Linz. So, if their speed was fifteen knots, how long before they arrived? If one included a factor for the speed of the current going the other way? He tried to hold the numbers in his head but couldn't even visualise the outlines of the figures. He fell asleep. Or thought he slept. But he was woken over and over by the same noise, a fearful coughing of the engines that then went back to quiet regularity. Twice, it was a false alarm. The third time, it was for real and panic had already broken out in the hold. He heard one boy screaming exactly like an animal, in long, stuttering howls. At the same time, someone tugged at his arm and a voice very close by was saying *please, please, help me*. The torchlight searched and then picked out the boy he had seen squatting by the latrine. A length of gut dangled between his legs. He stood and held that thing in his hand, trying to push it back in but fell over when the barge suddenly jumped against the waves. When the light found the boy again, he was lying on his side, curled up and with the loop of gut still hanging out. His face was a pale mask. Someone shouted from further along, *help help!* and hammered with what looked like a broom handle against the middle hatch cover. The hatches stayed shut. They heard the engines cough, then fall silent. The only sound was the splashing of water against the hull. The convoy had moved to the bank again. Fast footsteps passed above them. *Open up! Open up!* It was the same voice as before and the boy thumped at the hatch cover again. There was a violent crash and the entire barge made the same heart-stopping dive as before. It was followed by a long series of massive explosions that made the barge pitch this way and that, up and down in an insane dipping movement that slowed and then quickened again after the next wave of bombs. Across the racket he still heard the stubborn plead *please, help me*, but it was becoming fainter and more monotonous. Everyone hung on to what was closest at hand, a piece of rope, an iron stanchion. In the dark, Adrian could hardly distinguish his own body from all the others that were lying near or partly on top of him. He felt others slipping or crawling on him, their feet or sharp elbows pushing into him as they tried to get up.

Everything was becoming less distinct now, as if all the bodies in the hold were fusing into a single being. He was sinking deeper into foggy togetherness, ever more deeply as the shouting and movements died down and when he next opened his eyes, everything around him was quiet. At first, he thought he was dreaming. Not a sound from anywhere. No slow, empty engine sounds, no creaking plates below him, no trickling of the wake flowing along the hull. When he raised his head to look out over the dark sea of bodies around him, no one was moving. Then the hatch just above him opened. A shadow fell into the hold, sharply outlined by the light from above. Someone called something. He turned. In the slanting light he saw a hand lying, palm upwards, with its fingers lightly curled. The hand seemed to be cut off at first but then he realised that it was attached to an arm which was a single, large, bleeding wound. The blood had flowed and clotted in the pool that reached all the way to a head. It was Jockerl's head, the same mask-like bloodied face, the same staring, rolled-up whites of his eyes, the same pale porcelain teeth. *Seems there are some dead'uns down there*, he heard one guard say to another in a sober, almost indifferent voice. Booted footsteps. Someone fetched a ladder. The two guards clambered down, guns rattling against their belts. Mr Rache followed their heavy uniformed bodies, pressing a handkerchief over his mouth and nose. Above it, his eyes looked around, as pale and expressionless as before. Adrian sat stock-still next to the ladder, suddenly frightened that they would drag him away even though he wasn't dead yet. The guards tramped about and turned bodies over with their rifle butts. Some boys crawled away like crabs, one (perhaps the same one) screamed in pain, some cried for help. The dead bodies were pulled along to the hatch and then up on deck. Because he was so close to the ladder he saw that one of the corpses had his guts hanging out. The boy's body was stiff and lifeless but his naked feet with small splayed toes seemed almost touchingly alive. The corpse was hauled up the ladder and he heard it being dragged across the deck to the railing and tipped overboard, making a dull splash followed by a short but intense wave motion that caused the barge to rock like a cradle. Then, another splash. And another. He counted four, then five bodies. Immediately afterwards, the tugboat engine started up again as if it had been waiting only for the barges to be rid of some of the ballast. The journey continued. He had no idea of how long it took or how far they travelled but when he emerged from his semi-comatose state, the engine had stopped, the hatch had been opened and the ladder was in place. This time there were doctors among the guards patrolling the hold. Real doctors in real white coats. Somehow, the hold seemed more spacious around them. Their voices resounded more strongly. Or perhaps he just imagined it. He heard one of the medics, an older man with a white moustache, ask Mr Rache where these youths were meant to be taken. Someone else raised his voice and said that they should be hospitalised, the lot of them. Simply not *transportfähig*, the first one said, or maybe it was the second one. To the remarks, Rache replied (his voice was sharper, more piercing than Adrian had expected): that's none of your business. I'm just obeying orders. Anyway, they were all taken up on deck. The nurses helped those who couldn't climb out on their own. They had reached Linz. The quayside was packed with Red Cross staff manning tables and primitive sickbays. They lined up for food, a bowl each of rice soup and a piece of bread. He wolfed it down without being aware that he ate. They stayed there for a little more than a day and a night. Adrian watched as the crew loaded water and provisions. When they set out again, all the hatches were left open and groups of them were allowed on deck. Miss Santer was standing aft, watching the swilling water as the tugboat ploughed along. She was wearing the same dress and sandals as before but had put her hair up. The sky was overcast. They seemed to be pushing on into some alien, threatening part of the world, and the landscape reinforced the feeling of menace as it rose taller and closed in on them. By the end of that day, the mountain ridges were obscuring the sunlight and they travelled among darkening rock faces. The only sounds came from the engine, strangely harsh and choppy inside its own echo, from the water that splashed and rushed along the hull, and from the birds that rose above the racket and swept past under the dark grey sky in a lacework of white wings suddenly flung out into the gathering night. This is all he remembers. The next day, they chug past Passau and arrive in Germany. Here, or perhaps at some other stop, the medical people must have come on board again, because the ladders are back, lifeless bodies are hauled up, dragged across the deck and heaved overboard. By this stage, he is long past caring. Exhaustion has invaded his body and his mind feels as clear as water and utterly empty. Thinking is no longer possible. All he does is sit and finger the two nuts, following the crack that his nails have worked into the layer of paint. Except, by now, the crack has deepened into a cut. Then, one day (the seventh day? Or the ninth? Or the eleventh? He lost count long ago) they arrive at Regensburg. An officer materialises in front of him and yells at him to stand up. He smiles stupidly and leans against the bulkhead to steady himself. But however hard he tries, his feet seem to slip and his knees fold under him as if made of rubber. The man grabs him under the armpits and, with the help of someone on deck, he is dragged up through the hatch. On the quayside, Mr Rache stands around puffing on a cigarette as if totally unconcerned about the macabre load that is hauled or led out of the barges. Miss Santer is perched on a bollard further along, busy fixing her make-up. The reflexes from her pocket mirror dance on the oily harbour water. When she has put her mirror away and clicked her handbag shut, her lips are as red as his mother's once were. They are taken to the local state prison, though that was something he learnt much later. From that morning, all he remembers is a large, white-limed building with several wings, which towered over the railway station opposite. Inside it, he struggled to get up the steps in the large, dim stairwells. He remembers iron doors that opened and then closed behind them, the echoes of yelling voices through seemingly endless corridors and the large cells they were shoved into, twenty or thirty at a time. While he slept that night, he seemed still to be travelling on the river, as if the hard floor beneath him was rocking and swinging up and down. But it actually had. When he woke up next time, it was still night. Now, the floor shook and trembled, and his mouth was full of grit. Someone (he didn't know who) tried to pull him closer to the wall but it was shaking, too. Then, finally he realised that they were in the middle of an Allied bombing raid. Getting out was not worth thinking about. He looked out through the barred window and saw that station building on the other side of the square was burning. The freight train pulled up on the tracks further away was on fire, too, and inside the tall flames one could make out the dark outlines of the trucks. Black smoke was rising towards a spookily rust-coloured sky. His first thought was that the prison was on fire as well and they would burn to death locked up in it. But the cell door stood open. In the corridor outside, a cloud of stone dust welled forward like a gigantic, grey tongue. Soon, their cell was also filled to bursting point with dust that hurt your eyes and scorched your lungs. In the end, the air became unbreathable and they all sat with their heads between their legs, waiting for the floor to open under them like a trapdoor. Finally, the building stopped shaking. But the terrible clamour did not cease: the air-raid sirens were howling and from somewhere they heard a noise as if a large bulldozer were hard at work. It was only afterwards that he realised the demolition noise came from buildings that collapsed and burnt. The prison itself seemed not to be hit. Where the suffocating dust was coming from was a mystery. Viktor Zobel was the first to move. He took off the dirty bandage that he kept wrapped around the sore on his leg, the bad one that he used to rub with margarine, and tore the strip of cloth into pieces that he wetted under the tap and handed out to as many of them as possible. With the filthy, wet cloths pressed against their noses and mouths, they made it down the stairs and out into the street. The dawn was more unreal than any he had ever seen: inflamed and red behind a plume of black smoke still rising from the ruins of the station building. Further away, in the marshalling yard, freight trucks were also burning and giving off more black plumes. Sirens howled all the time, by now from fire engines and ambulances that kept arriving and spewing out firemen, nurses and soldiers. No one took much notice of them at first. It took several hours before a police officer ordered them to go back to their cells but he obviously couldn't be bothered with the gang of dirty, poorly clothed young men watching from outside the cordon. They were a distraction, no more. From then on, the guards stopped locking the cell doors. The assumption seemed to be that they might as well stay there for their own safety. One morning, the tray with bread and water that used to be placed outside the cell door was not there. The prisoners conferred for a while and then decided to send one of them off to reconnoitre. After a quarter of an hour or so, the scout returned, shouting and waving and very agitated. The Negroes are here, he shouted, the Negroes! The others followed him nervously. The prison seemed abandoned and there was not a guard in sight.

Outside the main entrance, a jeep stood parked, and inside it sat four men in unidentifiable uniforms. Only one of the four, a man sitting next to the driver, was actually black. The two in the back of the jeep were talking all the time but the black man in the front seat smiled and waved and handed out cigarettes. Adrian took one and the Negro lit it for him, protecting the flame with his cupped hand, which was white on the inside as if the blackness had been painted on. What's your name? he asked but Adrian didn't know, or perhaps he didn't understand the question.

XI

The Blind Ones

Under a Bombed Sky Fear infiltrated the sky, a sky either threateningly blue or else hidden behind pale, impenetrable winter mists, and the radio broadcasts of meaningless symphony concerts might at any time be interrupted by the official air-raid warnings of unidentified bomber formations approaching from the south, always read by a young woman whose cool voice, like the off-white haze in the winter sky, seemed to lack form and clarity. In February 1945, not a day passed without cuckoo calls sounding, and the well-spoken woman dutifully enumerating positions of the enemy planes, their direction of travel and likely destination, and sometimes Anna Katschenka could not get to work because everyone in the block had to hurry down to the shelters and then stay there for hours, waiting until the anti-aircraft batteries had stopped their devastating counter-attacks and the distant, diffuse buzz of the Allied planes was no longer heard. They sensed the hits only as bursts of low-frequency vibration in the ground but the smoke from the fires could linger for hours until the wind finally drove it away in another direction. Her father and brother had been ordered to join the civil defence force as part of the Volkssturm that Hitler had commanded as the last front against the advancing Soviet army. Her father's age and increasingly confused mind in no way counted as reasons for exemption. Her brother patrolled Südbahnhof as an air-raid warden and sometimes, when they were short of people, he was recruited to help with loading boxes of weapons, grenades and tank-gun ammunition onto the lorries ferrying goods non-stop to the front. Katschenka couldn't sleep during the nights her brother was on duty. She lay awake, listening to the steady ticking of the clock. Behind the blackout blinds, the night was like a single, huge structure about to fall apart. Everything was collapsing, even the everyday reality that had always surrounded her and she had taken for granted. The truth was that nothing seemed real to her anymore: not the wall in her 'girl's room', which was still hers though she now thought its striped wallpaper too colourful, too vulgar; not her mother's hysterical plea that they must agree on a safe place to hide jewellery and table silver now that the Bolsheviks were coming; not the patch of pale sky appearing in a previously solid row of houses one morning after another night spent in the shelter. The Allied bombing seemed to be aimed mainly at strategic targets such as factories, harbours and oil refineries but, more often than not, bombs also detonated in residential areas. Where whole city blocks had been hit and reduced to chaotic piles of splintered wood and broken masonry, the exposed areas of sky looked as cold and grey as if they had never seen sunlight. It could be almost impossible to make your way to work after a day-long air raid. The trams, when they finally turned up, would be crammed and some desperate passengers would cling on to the outside. On 21 February, after a massive bombardment, the trams didn't run at all and she had to walk to the hospital. The burnt-out shell of a 52 tram had been abandoned on Mariahilfer Strasse. On its scorched roof, bits of the trolley stuck out like the broken ribs of an umbrella. Opposite it, the entire façade of an office building had been ripped off and the shell that remained looked as if scooped out with a giant spoon. In front of the street-level row of shops, odds and ends of stock were mixed with other debris: crushed bits of furniture, lengths of fabric and torn pieces of paper. Sometimes, the debris from ruined buildings formed obstacles so massive it was impossible to get round them, and people on foot had to walk along narrow corridors inside the heaps. When it rained, or when darkness fell (there was no electricity), she felt as if she had left her familiar cityscape for another, countrified place where she had to find her way along cattle tracks made dangerous by hard tree roots and treacherous puddles of mud. Many of the hospital staff used the constant air raids as an excuse for not coming to work at all. Nurse Kragulj, for instance, was absent three days running and blamed it on caring for her sister who had been hurt falling down the stairs. Hilde Mayer was the only one who always punctual but it was easier for her who had been allocated a service flat on the other side of Sanatoriumstrasse when she nursed at Steinhof. Anna Katschenka kept a record of all lost hours at work and ran a tight ship generally. Shoes worn outside must be cleaned, dirty clothing kept in designated cupboards or hung up outside, and exposed parts of the body cleaned and disinfected. As both the electricity and water supplies often broke down for long periods, they had to get used to working in the light of candles and sooty paraffin lamps. The cold air inside the buildings chilled their joints and numbed their fingers but the worst deprivation was lack of water. The toilets hadn't been flushed for weeks and the stench was becoming unbearable. They worked together to carry water in buckets and basins until the bathtubs were filled, then pumped out the excrement and cleaned the toilets with floor soap. There were, Lord be praised, diesel-fuelled generators, but they couldn't supply enough for the whole institution, so pavilion 17 was closed and the remaining children transferred to number 15. This move meant that Pelikan's world went to pieces. Even moving away from a wall he had made his own troubled him. The new door he had to watch felt all wrong and, at first, he crawled around on all fours, rubbing his belly against the floor like an anxious dog. Anna Katschenka observed him with amazement. The boy had grown almost half a metre in just a few years and his movements were now so clumsy and awkward that he was a worse obstacle than ever. One morning, when Cläre Kleinschmittger simply could not get past him with the ward drug-trolley, she jammed her elbow in his midriff and then slapped his smarmy face. *Give it a rest, won't you!* she said. *They'll be here soon enough*. And so said aloud what they all thought but didn't dare to say. Although Nurse Kleinschmittger was trembling with distaste and anger, it was she and not Pelikan who looked beaten. *They*? Who were they? What would it be like when *they* came? Kleinschmittger was frightened. They were all frightened.

The Blind One afternoon in early April, one of the grey patient-transport buses from Gemeinnützige Krankentransport stopped in front of the institution and two social care workers climbed out, a man and a woman. They were followed by a large number of older children, all carrying small suitcases and neatly dressed in shorts or skirts, and grey or dark brown jackets. Some of the children stayed by the bus while others, seemingly confused, set out in different directions. Anna Katschenka couldn't understand why neither of the two carers did anything to gather them together. Then it came to her: these children were not normally sighted. Doctors Krenek and Illing had gone to meet the new arrivals and were talking to the carers. The children, not all of whom were blind – some were deaf or deaf-mute, and some could neither see nor hear – looked remarkably well nourished, at least compared to the children in the neurological clinic. They were almost all quite well, apart from a few cases of ringworm and a girl of eleven who had hepatitis and was brought later in a separate transport. The reform school was to take in the healthy ones and the clinic had to house the rest. Preferably, they should be kept together in the same ward, Illing decided, since it would make it easier to keep an eye on them. When Katschenka began to say something about the shortage of beds, Illing said that pavilion 17 was to be brought back into use and the new children placed there. Katschenka didn't know where the blind and deaf children came from, or what the point was of transferring them to Spiegelgrund. Though, as Hilde Mayer suggested, it wasn't too hard to figure out the answer to the last question – presumably, they were running from the Bolsheviks, just like everyone else. They cleared a former day room on the first floor and put the ill children there. During these last, desperate couple of weeks, wild and contradictory rumours started up everywhere. Some said the Soviets had been seen just ten or twenty kilometres to the south-east of Wien, some that the Germans were mounting a successful counter-offensive and had driven the enemy out. One day, Doctor Illing addressed all the staff. It was essential, he said, that they loyally carried out their duties, until the very last hour, as he put it. As he spoke, he kept pacing up and down with his characteristic swagger. His hands were clasped behind his back and the brown tobacco smile never left his face, as if to cheer them up and instil confidence, but something hard and knotted lingered in his face which contradicted every word he said even though he afterwards continued with his rounds and still issued orders about which children should receive the 'treatment' or stay under observation. But where would the staff come from? Kragulj simply didn't turn up for work now. Nobody knew where she had disappeared to. The next day, Erna Storch also failed to arrive. Katschenka eventually found out that Nurse Erna had gone off to join her husband in Reichenberg. They recruited staff from pavilion 3 and from pavilions that had been converted to care for patients from other hospitals which, like Rosenheim for instance, had had to evacuate part of their premises. Marta Fried, a young nurse of barely twenty, was recruited from pavilion 3. Nurse Marta knew perfectly well where she had ended up. She was as white as a sheet and her slender, pale hands were shaking but she didn't dare to say anything when Katschenka instructed her about the daily routines. Doctor Türk and Sister Katschenka went together to visit the blind children in one of Krenek's pavilions and were met by the bright, happy chatter of children's voices. Katschenka couldn't recall if she had ever heard children laugh in there. The carers had been given rooms in the same pavilion, and it was obvious that the children relied on these two for everything. If the weather was good enough, they were allowed to play outside for a few hours every day. They were always very disciplined about it and lined up in the corridor outside the dormitory, just as they did when they had to go to the shelters. One afternoon, when Sister Katschenka went into the empty dormitory, one boy of about eleven was still there. He couldn't see her and couldn't have known who she was, but he stretched his arms up to show her that he needed help to get his sweater off. Anna was reminded of the little boy in Totzenbach, whom Jekelius had lifted up into the pear tree where other giggling children already perched. That boy had made just the same gesture, helpless and trusting at the same time. That day, Doctor Jekelius had instructed her that reality had only two dimensions: existing blindly or exercising the will in order to control existence. He had gone on to say that it meant there were only two kinds of people, the rulers and those who submit to the rulers. But it came to her that there was a third kind, who gazed past you and everything else and seemed able to walk through walls. Pelikan had taken up a post by the door where he showed off and bowed, and beamed at the visually impaired children who were housed in his ward. Not that they would have looked his way even if their eyes had been functioning normally. They were living in a world of their own, enclosed and inaccessible to outsiders. All the time she spent in the company of the blind children, she had a feeling that their presence was some kind of omen. As if they had been sent on a mission. By whom, or with what message, she never quite understood. Perhaps, it once struck her, they were the seeing ones and she, Anna Katschenka, was blind. Then, the meaning of their presence was simply to remind her of this.

Extramural The jaundiced girl had been placed in isolation in one of the single rooms off the ground-floor corridor. The door was to be kept closed at all times and no one from the institution was allowed to visit. One morning, when Sister Katschenka passed the sickroom door, it stood open. People were talking inside the room, one in a childish voice that was the blind girl's and another a grown-up voice that the ward sister soon recognised. As she stepped closer to the door, she sensed that they had not heard her. The blind girl's bed took up almost all of the space in the narrow former cell. At the head end, Hedwig Blei was seated, leaning forward with both hands on the girl's, which rested on top of the coverlet. Nurse Hedwig was either speaking or singing – her voice was very low – and the girl was listening to whatever it was with wide-open eyes and a smile on her lips. After a little while, the blind girl startled and turned her empty, unseeing eyes towards Katschenka. The girl's smile grew rigid. Nurse Blei fell silent but didn't turn round. So far, only the blind child had 'seen' her. It made her feel distinctly uneasy. Why are you not on duty? she said straight out, very loudly, as if to shut up someone who had spoken out of turn. Nurse Hedwig stayed very still and didn't even look around. I can only assume that when you're really needed you will also be unavailable, Sister Katschenka said. She had intended it to sound mildly sarcastic though it came across as merely resigned. Blei noticed it. I have no intention to make myself unavailable at any time, she said in a low voice. Not for as long as children are here. Then she got up, still without a glance at Sister Katschenka, and left. Later that afternoon, Hilde Mayer revealed that they were busy burning documents – correspondence and patients' case notes – in the boiler in the office basement. Not long now before the Bolsheviks will be panting down the back of our necks, she added. A quite unreasonable fear for her family spread inside Katschenka. When she finally came home, several hours later, her father stood within earshot of the mumbling radio, as was his habit. Her mother sat on the armchair with the blue dustcover. Why so late? her mother asked and fixed her familiar, blank gaze on her daughter. Supper has been ready for a long time. Anna didn't know what to say. Her mother's accusatory, stony face and the incessantly ticking clock on the chest of drawers were both measures of the depth of the silence that filled the room.

The Queen of the Well Once upon a time, there was a little girl and her name was very pretty, just like yours, Imogena. There was a well in the garden of the house where she grew up. The girl used to sit by the well, resting her arms on the edge. Now and then, she threw a stone into the well and counted – one, two, three – to find out how long it took before it hit the water. Once, she dropped a big stone into the well, listened and counted, but this time she heard nothing. Instead, a strange creature appeared before her: a beautiful woman with long blonde hair. Her large eyes shimmered and glittered like water. She was the Queen of the Well. Every time you drop a stone into the well, a human being dies, the Queen of the Well told the girl. But because you're just an idle, disobedient girl who knows no better, I have bewitched that last stone you threw. Here, do you want to hold it? she asked. Imogena said yes and held out her hands. Hedwig Blei put her hands on the girl's. The Queen of the Well opened her hands to show not a stone, but a small bird, a sparrow. The girl held the bird in both her hands, feeling its tiny heart beat and beat. Then she parted her hands a little (like this, Hedwig Blei said and showed how) and the bird flew away, high up into the sky.

The March into the City They're here now, Otto says as he bends over her. She is lying on the bed, fully dressed. The first thing she thinks of is what Nurse Blei said when they last spoke, that she would go nowhere, *not for as long as children are here*. When she said this in the blind girl's room, it had sounded almost like a threat but Anna Katschenka doesn't doubt that Blei meant every word. And so she, too, must go to work. There is no other way. She puts her hand on her brother's arm but almost faints when she tries to get up. The cloth in Otto's overcoat feels rough under her fingers and smells sourly of sweat and smoke. When his unshaven cheek touches hers, something else is there that feels damp and sticky. Blood? Or tears? But from inside his strained, deeply tired face, her brother looks at her with dry eyes that seem as innocent as ever. Now, she registers for the first time that the rifle fire and heavy-artillery bombardment of the last few days has stopped. Silence must have fallen hours ago without her being aware of it. Her brother has carried a bucket of water up to the kitchen. She splashes a little water on her face, brushes her hair, pulls on her coat and steps out at Otto's side into the pale dawn. The air is heavy with the fatty, sickening smell of diesel fuel and burnt rubber. Margaretengürtel is transformed into an avenue of ash between overturned or abandoned army vehicles. A burnt-out German tank has come to a halt with its gun barrel pointing at the railway tracks and the marshalling yard. Everywhere, there are towering stacks of masonry and other debris from bombed houses. The stacks must have been used as defensive positions, because dead soldiers, lying on their backs or sides, are scattered among the ruins. Their bodies, like everything else, are covered by a thin layer of dry, grey ash. Anna Katschenka is amazed at how quickly the fighting has come to a decisive end, after all the uncertainty and waiting. At first, the story was that the Russians had reached Wienerberg, then that they had been pushed back to a line three kilometres to the south-east of the city. She can't remember who said that but it was probably Otto. A little later, a rumour circulated that Russian forward units had taken Südbahnhof. That same evening, the battle went on late into the night. They hadn't dared to go down to the shelters and instead curled up where they could on the floor in the flat. The sounds of grenade explosions and artillery fire seemed to come from every direction and, soon before dawn, there was what sounded like a very close bomb blast. She remembers the awful whistling sound before the impact, then the shell exploding with such a powerful detonation she thought that ceiling and walls would fall on top of them. The terrifying roar of artillery mingled with the tiny, helpless, squeaky voices of people who had been trapped underneath shattered masonry and were screaming with pain or shouting for help. No one dared to leave the shelters for fear of being shot, or buried under falling buildings. One rumour was that the Nazis tried to retake the railway station and, to make up their numbers, captured civilians and forced them to fight. Apparently, the Wehrmacht had put up roadblocks on all the side streets below Belveder, along Rennweg and also Wiedener Hauptstrasse, in order to stop the Austrian soldiers from deserting. But by the morning, the Germans were already in retreat and the roadblocks had been eliminated, Otto said, and when she insisted that she had to go to the hospital, he told her that their part of town was still reasonably safe but that nobody knew what the rest of the city was like by now. The first Russian soldiers they catch sight of look like men from a forward unit of engineers: two young men in padded, mud-brown uniforms, one bare-headed and the other wearing a kind of fur hat with earflaps. The bare-headed one is crouching, bent over a field telephone that he is trying to rig up while the one in the fur hat is unwinding a long cable across the street. In Margaretengürtel, she stops to watch a seemingly endless column of muddy army vehicles. A provisions unit with a field kitchen attached rolls along in the middle of the sea of motors. Next, the soldiers, thousands of them, on foot or crammed into lorries. Without a plan in her head, she instinctively starts walking, then jogging along the column. Perhaps she even shouts something to the passing soldiers because, without warning, a small four-wheel drive car stops at her side and a man leans out of the mud-spattered, half-open window and tries to say something. She comes closer to hear better. *Dolmetscher?* he seems to be saying. Then, the penny drops. They need an interpreter. He speaks in marked Austrian dialect and has a red and white band around his sleeve. It calms her down a little. In the rear seat, she sees someone who is clearly a Soviet officer of fairly senior rank. He looks just as keen as her countryman. She shouts back that she is a nurse but either they don't hear her or else they misunderstand, because the Austrian speaker has already moved back to sit next to the officer. She turns to them and repeats that she is a *nurse* and that she must get to Steinhof quickly. *Please, drive me to Steinhof,* she says. *There are very, very ill children there. They won't live if they're not looked after*. The Austrian nods at her to get in and makes a place for her but doesn't seem to hear what she says. The car starts the instant she closes the door. They all seem too impatient to wait or even listen to her. She begins to feel afraid and wishes that she were back with Otto but as they seem to be going the right way, she keeps quiet. So far, few civilians have dared to go out into the streets but lots of people are already gathering at windows or in gateways. Some of those on the pavements look elated, others scared or numbed. A few young women call out to the soldiers, others wave with handkerchiefs or shawls, whether from fear or joy is hard to say. The Soviet army officer seems to take no notice of the civilians and is constantly questioning the Austrian resistance fighter, who in his turn is trying to explain the way to the completely uncomprehending driver. Suddenly, the Austrian stretches out one arm, the vehicle makes a sharp right-hand turn and starts driving up Gumpendorfer Strasse. That is the completely wrong direction. *No!* she shouts and grabs the Austrian's coat sleeve. He pulls his arm free and continues to show the way with big gestures. They pass Esterházy Park, and the large anti-aircraft battery to which her brother and other 'voluntary' recruits have been so busy delivering ammunition. It now seems to be under Russian control. She has no time to see because they are going full speed up Mariahilfer Strasse. The Austrian points and waves his arms about until, after a sharp turn, they dash in through the gate leading to the Stiftgasse barracks. Presumably, this was their goal all the time. Anyway, the officer steps quickly and resolutely out of the car and the Austrian communist (she assumes he must be a communist) signs irritably to her to follow suit. Suddenly, they are all gone, the driver too, and in a moment of desperation she can't think what to do. The Germans must have abandoned the barracks in a hurry because commandeered weaponry as well as uniforms and greatcoats are stacked on the exercise ground, next to piles of ammunition boxes. The entire area around the barracks has been cordoned off and a convoy of

Russian troop-transporters are reversing into the compound, an exercise that apparently requires huge precision from the soldiers who are directing the event. Crowds of people are on the move around her, most of them young privates but also civilians with obscure tasks. Some of the soldiers grin suggestively at her but nobody blocks her way as she leaves, almost at a run. There are many more ordinary citizens walking up and down on Stiftgasse now, and on Mariahilfer Strasse large groups of men and women of all ages are on the move, silent but determined. She hears the sound of breaking glass when they start kicking in shop windows. Immediately behind her, a group of women is looting a shop selling dress materials. They are helping each other as well as themselves to rolls of fabric from the well-stocked shelves. There are Soviet soldiers nearby on the pavement but instead of intervening, they shout encouragement and laugh when some of the women stagger outside carrying huge bundles of goods. A large number of men have formed a protective chain outside the big store Gerngross, near to where the burnt-out tram still stands with its useless trolley and wiring like a perverse crown on its roof. The chain includes many with white and red ribbons on their sleeves, like the Austrian resistance man in the car. But, by now, many have brought implements and the mob is becoming restless. Her heart beats faster as she watches the scene. She can't think what to do and returns to the Stiftgasse barracks where, by some miracle, she finds the Russian driver in the milling crowd. He has returned to his car and is smoking and chatting to two young women. *Please, drive me to Steinhof*, she says even though she knows that he won't understand and that it is pointless to ask. One of the women takes on the duty of translating and the driver listens patiently but not a muscle moves in his face. The woman tells her in broken German that she is from Ukraine. Why she is in Wien and what she is doing at the barracks she doesn't say, but she smiles at the driver, who smiles back through the cloud of cigarette smoke. Anna Katschenka grasps that this might be her last chance of being understood. She comes close to the Ukrainian woman. Steinhof, she says. Then: The children. They are dying, she adds. And emphasises with gestures that she tries to make as persuasive as possible. The woman explains to the driver who listens, apparently still unmoved. Then he gets out of the car and walks away. Anna Katschenka's heart sinks. She thanks the woman and has turned to go when the driver comes back. He has brought three soldiers with him, the oldest of whom declares in stilted but very polite German that they have a car of their own and that she should come with them. Afterwards, she realised that it had been insane for a woman on her own to set out in a car with unknown soldiers, and enemy soldiers to boot. Their motives might well have been very far from helpful. But she has no time to plan another approach. The sky is ripped apart above them and a formation of German fighter planes sweeps in over the city. Civilians and soldiers run off in the same direction across the yard and she doesn't resist when her three soldiers pull her along to their car, another four-wheel drive vehicle, very much like the one she travelled in before (even the mud-streaked windows look the same). It is when they are driving off that she first realises that the fighting is not yet over and that the Germans might well be launching a counter-offensive. They pull into a backstreet behind Westbahnhof and the driver shuts the engine off, a cue for everyone to light up cigarettes (evil-smelling Russian ones) and for one of them to produce a half-bottle of vodka. The talk becomes noisier. She turns to the German-speaker, who seems to be an officer, and tries to tell him very carefully, street by street, how to get to the hospital. The officer translates but the driver seems more concerned about getting his turn with the vodka. When they finally start again, it is with a sharp jerk and an abrupt turn that almost ejects her from the car. The car speeds shakily off towards Hütteldorf. There are intermittent roadblocks along Linzer Strasse. They are waved past some of them, stopped at some, and at a few they stay on to chat to the soldiers on guard. She uses every opportunity to explain the route to the officer but he has long since given up on the finer points, and the men in the back behave less and less like escorts and more as if she were a prize possession to show off. Everywhere, they see looting, small-scale and large, and this is what seems to interest the men most of all. In Penzing, some of the villas are on fire and, here and there, men are carrying out furniture and stacking it on army lorries. She thinks that, unless the soldiers decide to stop her, she can walk to the hospital from where she is now. It would take her fifteen, maybe twenty minutes. Of course, it is unlikely that she will be safer there than anywhere else. The car stops again outside a villa where four men are struggling with an enormous grand piano. Many more items of furniture are already stacked on the pavement. The officer and the driver get out. The two men in the back try to march her into the villa but are stopped by the officer who has turned up again, blood-red in the face and shouting at them in their incomprehensible language. Possibly, all that was not about her at all, but in the momentary confusion she manages first to back away a little, and then, when no one seems inclined to grab her again, she turns and runs up the steep street. Three blocks further along, she stops and looks over her shoulder but can't see anyone coming after her. Dusk is already gathering by the time she arrives at Baumgartner Höhe. She has cramp in her legs after running, something she hardly ever does, and when she draws breath there is a sore, stinging sensation in her chest. The wind carries the smell of burning from somewhere and the slight haziness in the air lends a dream-like insubstantiality to the outlines of buildings and people. Steinhof looks as normal, though, except that the red Nazi flag no longer flies in front of the main building. The guard's hut by the gate is empty and instead a young soldier stands there with an uncertain hand on the strap of his rifle. I am a nurse, she says and holds up her identity card. Instead of giving it to him, she snatches it back. He looks shocked and calls something after her, but she doesn't respond and walks calmly and steadily towards the pavilions. He calls again, perhaps wanting somebody of higher rank to come to his rescue and, shortly afterwards, she hears running, booted footsteps on the path behind her. She knows that is someone who might take aim and shoot, and that everything could end forever now, but nobody shoots and the end doesn't come.

XII

The Mongols Attack

The Solitary Guard of the Mountain Hannes Neubauer has been keeping watch at the entrance to the Mountain for many years now. He has let no one pass, and has not tried to escape like some of the other boys. First, it was Zavlacky and Miseryguts who legged it just after they had been taken to Ybbs, then that thieving tinker's boy, Adrian Ziegler, went off and, not long afterwards, Jockerl disappeared. Though Jockerl didn't run away. He fell ill and then someone came to get him *gegen Revers*. To be discharged *gegen Revers* meant that the institution consented to hand back children they had agreed earlier to take on – usually for only too good reasons, Nurse Mutsch said, which is why it only happens in very few cases so that's nothing for you to be hoping for, Hannes. But Hannes hoped all the same, never mind what anyone said. He kept guard outside the Mountain, let nobody pass and if one of the others came to him with escape plans, he always turned them away like the brave warrior he was. He would stay at his post until his father came for him, whether *gegen Revers* or in some other way. Though it was true that Nurse Mutsch was a little less rough these days and less sure of herself when she harangued them about the war and the courage of the soldiers. Somehow, an inexplicable anxiety had sneaked into her mind. Hannes checked on her sometimes when she was holed up in the nurses' room and the radio was on. Usually it played music quietly while Mutsch pretended to be busy with something else altogether, but Hannes observed her keenly and noted how she held her head – a little to the side as if intent on listening – and that she would stop mid-movement from time to time. She was concentrating on the radio, that's for sure. And so it came at last, that sharp, piercing cuckoo-clock signal she had been waiting for, and Nurse Mutsch turned round and shouted *IT'S TIME AGAIN* and from all around the pavilion, white nurses' uniforms came running and gathered around the radio.

Right! Line-up! All children to the shelters!

Doors were pulled and pushed, shoes laced up at record speed and soon they stood lined up in front of the pavilion, ready to carry out the manoeuvres Mrs Rohrbach had practised with them hundreds of times: set out for the shelter at a regular running pace, keep in step and don't break formation, get down there and, in an orderly manner, find a place to sit on the benches. Meanwhile, Mrs Rohrbach locked the heavy door. They sometimes sat there for hours without anything happening. This time, though, they heard the bombs fall, or rather felt it, because the Mountain shook under them. Nurse Mutsch sat stiff and silent on her bench with her tightly clenched hands in her lap and her eyes staring blindly ahead. Hannes made an attempt to calm her. You mustn't be worried, Nurse, he said. The Führer is sure to come and rescue us soon. But, to Hannes's great surprise, Nurse Mutsch looked baffled, even shocked, as if he had said something offensive, bordering on very rude. The air-raid warnings come much more often now. It happens that they have to run to the shelters so early in the morning that they don't even have time to put their clothes on. One day, they had to stay down there all the time, a whole long day without food or water, just sitting on the benches or the bare floor wrapped in the blankets that were the only helpful things Mrs Rohrbach had had time to bring. That day, 12 April 1945, the detonations were very close. Hannes listened out especially for the heavy thudding noise of the anti-aircraft batteries. Now and then they would fall silent, but after a short while they started thudding and howling again. It all seemed endless. When Rohrbach turned the large, tap-like handle on the shelter door to let them out, he expected to see the hospital in flames but it still looked just the same, a grey backdrop against the cooling, pale yellowy-pink, early evening sky. The Steinhof rooks were flapping above them, excitedly raucous, as usual. But somewhere further away another light glowed, flickering and red. Nurse Mutsch, who always used to keep up an impassively stern, utterly unemotional attitude towards the children, suddenly turned out to have a great fund of information which she would share generously with anyone, colleagues or children. *The Opera went on fire*, she said. And *St Stephen's cathedral has also been hit* and *what shall we do?* she said, and then *what will become of us?* and *you poor children* and so forth, all incantations that she couldn't stop herself from repeating. From that day, Hannes takes on an extra stint of guard duty by the Mountain and stays awake, which is really hard, while the others sleep. By undertaking this, he actually witnesses several strange things. One night, Mrs Rohrbach and Nurse Mutsch come into the dormitory. The faintly bluish-violet glow of the night-light makes their bodies dissolve a little but he hears their voices well enough. Mrs Rohrbach says that the hospital board will act to stop the children ending up in the wrong hands, whatever it takes. There's talk of sending them to München or possibly Berlin. By bus or truck. This makes Hannes Neubauer realise that he must on no account leave the Mountain. In the worst case, he will have to follow Julius Becker's lead and use the scissors. Will he be brave enough? A few nights later, he dreams about his sister for the first time in many years. He knows he had a sister once but his father has told him that the children's mother took the girl away. Despite having no memory of his sister when he is awake, he sees her quite clearly in his dream. She has thick blonde hair braided into two plaits and is standing on top of a tall stone wall, quite near the edge. They must be about to demolish the wall because there are broken chunks of stone everywhere, and crowbars and pickaxes and lots of other tools are lying about on the ground below the wall. His sister is dressed in a simple, bias-cut dress that is tight around her upper body but swings like a sail every time she jumps from the top of the wall. She is laughing. Her laugh is happy and gurgling and it wells up from his own insides, too. But the dream behaves like a film that has stuck. Again and again, he sees his sister spread her arms, and her skirt lift as she falls, and he hears her quickening laughter. He never sees her climb up onto the wall. She just jumps and then she is back up there and, with each jump, the wall seems taller and the fall more precipitous until he is gripped by fear and he can't stop her because he never sees her climb the wall. But *come on, jump, jump!* the Mountain screams from everywhere around him. He opens his eyes. Everything is silent and there isn't a nurse in sight.

The Mongols Attack At first, he doesn't want to believe that it is true. The night-light is still on, even though sunlight enters through the crack under the blackout blind. It is so silent that, through the top-most ventilation pane that has been left open, he can hear the birds twittering. He lies absolutely still and tries to catch at least one of the *ordinary* sounds, like the echo when a door opens and slams shut, or the tap-tap of cork heels disappearing down the corridor or voices speaking to each other. Nothing. The towering silence, as compact as a wall, is nearer than the birdsong, and all the more insistent and lasting since it is not interrupted or undermined. He realises that he isn't the only one to lie awake. All around him, other children stir anxiously and their white, wide-open eyes stare into the darkened space. And then the silence is ripped apart by machine-gun fire. The firing seems to come from very close by. He climbs out of bed and walks towards the door and, in that instant, the machine gun starts rattling again and, when it stops, there comes what sounds like a shout and then a low laugh. He expects the door to be locked, as usual, but to his huge surprise, it slides open easily. Outside, the corridor is empty and abandoned in the glassy light. The ventilation panes have been hooked open and here, too, the birds are building their trelliswork of fleeting, insistent twittering. He walks on, his legs seemingly filled with water. Checks the nurses' room. Empty. Ward kitchen? Empty. The washroom, with its heavy enamelled tub and the row of showerheads that look like bent boys' necks? It is empty and the tiles shine with reflected light. Back in the corridor, he meets a boy from the upstairs section. He is called Rudi and is a driven soul who wanders restlessly whenever there is a chance. It is as if his feet have a will of their own and the rest of his body simply follows wherever they go. Hannes has never heard Rudi say a word to anyone. He doesn't this time either, just jumps nervously when he sees Hannes. The two of them stare at each other as if they were complete strangers. And then, Rudi's feet start to move on and Hannes returns to his own dormitory.

They've all gone, he says.

Twenty pairs of eyes are fixed on him.

What, have the Mongols come?

As always when Pototschnik speaks to Hannes, there is a hint of a sneer in his voice. But this time, Pototschnik is frightened. His roving eyes betray him. Pototschnik realises that Hannes has noticed and instantly reshapes his fear into a kind of desperate daring. He swiftly walks past Hannes and out into the corridor, then to the nurses' room where he picks up Mrs Rohrbach's clapper. With grimly stuck-out chin and strict expression, mimicking Rohrbach, he walks energetically from bed to bed, hitting the ends with the clapper, and shouts in a loud, shrill voice, *aufstehen!* or, alternatively, *raus aus den Betten!* Once he has roused the entire dormitory, he goes to the ward kitchen and sweeps all the plates and glasses from the shelves, pulls out all the cutlery drawers and tips the contents on the floor so that knives and forks and spoons scatter everywhere. Now the wall has cracked. Some of the boys try to hide under the beds but most of them join Pototschnik. They bang saucepans and lids against tables and chairs and whatever is within reach and nobody listens to Hannes, who calls out *wait!* and *hang on, they might be here any minute!* At least, Pototschnik doesn't listen. He leads a whole company of children into Rohrbach's office to pull down folders and books, empty cupboards and filing cabinets, and tip what is in her desk drawers onto the floor. The telephone, the only one on the ward, is torn down from its shelf and carried like a trophy by eager children's hands all the way up to the day room on the first floor. Here, Pototschnik finds a new use for Rohrbach's clapper. He breaks one windowpane after another and then, to huge acclaim, the telephone is squeezed out between the bars and lands, neutralised, on the lawn outside. From a little bit away, the bulging, unmoved gaze of an alien soldier follows their activities. *Shuush!* Hannes hisses and they all duck below the window sill. After a while, tips of noses emerge as they try to look outside. The soldier has a rifle hung with a leather strap over his shoulder and continues to ogle their window. *A Mongol*, Hannes says. Then the Mongol is joined by two other soldiers. He points out the telephone to them. It still lies on the lawn below the window with the receiver off. Hannes explains: they think it's a hand grenade. Pototschnik has flecks of foam around his mouth, either from fear or excitement. He starts to say something but interrupts himself at once. Now, they can already hear the clomping sound of the Mongols' heavy boots on the staircase and their coarse, strange voices are calling out to each other. They'll cut the throats of the boys down there any time soon, Pototschnik whispers nervously. But instead of howls from the dying, they hear a man's voice burst into loud, hearty laughter and then a chorus of children's voices trying to join in the laugh. The soldier's voice seems to be saying: *Burszuj . . . !* He says it again and again in an apparently jolly tone and the children on the ground floor keep laughing. They cautiously descend the stairs with Pototschnik in front, raising Mrs Rohrbach's clapper like a blunt lance. Three Russian soldiers, surrounded by a horde of wide-eyed children, are now standing guard at the entrance to their ward. The soldiers are much shorter than Hannes had imagined but they have broad shoulders and necks. Two of them wear fur caps with earflaps and, framed by the caps, their faces look small and fat. One of them really does look like a Mongol, with his narrow eyes, blunt nose, and straight black hair sticking out below the edge of the cap. The third soldier is different from the others in that he is tall and blond and wears high leather boots spattered with dirt and mud. When he catches sight of the small crowd led by Pototschnik, he holds out a packet of cigarettes: . . . *Vy kurite? Mogu li ya predlozhit sigarety?* A tense moment this, as the strange soldier in the boots – Hannes understands that he must be some kind of officer because, unlike the other two, he has a uniform greatcoat with insignia of rank sewn on – tries to persuade Pototschnik to accept a cigarette while Pototschnik looks anxiously around, wondering if he should continue the advance with the clapper or take a break and have a cigarette. The officer puts the packet a little closer to Pototschnik who makes up his mind, takes a cigarette and holds it between thumb and index finger as if it were a fragile insect. The officer has a lit match ready and takes a step forward to light the fag for Pototschnik, who leans forward and then straightens up, puffing happily with fat, round cheeks. The soldiers let out a roar of laughter. Obviously, it is all just a game to them but, no matter, they are full of goodwill and slap the boys' backs. More cigarettes are handed out and lit. Some of the boys don't know which end to hold and they cough and grimace with tightly closed eyes and it all ends with everyone laughing inside a cloud of smoke.

Riot Hannes Neubauer isn't able to recall with any certainty what happened next. Or, rather, he has a series of sharp, distinctly remembered scenes but he can't order them into a sequence or be clear about which role he had at any one time. Is he the one who is beating a nurse across the back with a broom handle or is he standing aside, watching someone else do the beating? In another memory tableau, he sees himself standing at a window, screaming at the top of his lungs into nothingness. The window is the one on the first floor in pavilion 9 that they broke to dump the telephone. The evening is drawing in but it is still light outside. The telephone lies untouched on the lawn but in the dormitory behind him all the beds are overturned and the floor is covered with blankets and mattresses. In yet another memory, Sister Katschenka is looking at him with her steady, calm eyes. He can't think how she came to turn up but knows who she is even though she isn't wearing her uniform. At the other end of the room, Pototschnik stands at the front of his company of about thirty boys, all armed with something: dustpans, pulled-off chair legs, broken bottles. From the start, Pototschnik plans the operation. After making sure that the kitchen has been plundered of anything edible (with limited success: all they found were dry biscuits and a few loaves), he leads his squad towards the main building. The plan now is to take the hospital kitchen by storm, find more to eat and then liberate the idiots in pavilions 15 and 17. Hannes isn't clear about exactly who is following Pototschnik. Some join the ranks because they really want to, thrilled by their leader's enthusiasm. Pototschnik's face is glowing with excitement under an imaginary helmet. Others, like Hannes, are coming along because they have nowhere else to go, or because they are afraid of what will happen to them if they stay behind. True, considering all that has been said about the Mongols and their cunning and capacity for evil, they do seem oddly indifferent to what the children are up to. While Pototschnik's company advances as per his plan, trucks are reversing in through the main gate. The Mongols are moving goods into the hospital grounds. In the garden in front of the old hospital theatre, soldiers are resting, some lying in the grass next to a pile of their packs. Members of the hospital board and a few doctors in white coats are conferring with enemy officers. From their gestures, it is obvious that the Bolsheviks are looking for soldiers' quarters and that the hospital board is trying to fend them off. However, when Pototschnik's small army reaches pavilion 17, it is already full of Mongols. An obviously retarded boy stands by the door and bows with a silly smile on his face and won't let up on the bowing and scraping even after all the soldiers have passed. However, he refuses to let Pototschnik through, makes an ugly face and then starts to cry with an irritating, hacking sound. Pototschnik hits him on the head with the clapper. That does the trick. The boy becomes servile again, bows and smiles. Pototschnik pushes past with his followers behind him. The boy is the first idiot they have come across but there are many more. Most of them stand pressed against the walls, some rock helplessly from side to side and others stare with open, wet mouths, whining or screaming heartbreakingly. Hannes isn't clear why they are so upset but it could be the upheaval as the Russian soldiers are pouring upstairs to claim dormitories and day rooms. There are nurses here. At least, there is one nurse, who rushes about, trying to get her patients out of the way as the soldiers take over the children's beds. One of the children seems to be paralysed. The nurse tries to move him with her hands under his armpits but he is either too heavy or else he might be resisting her. Hannes watches as the nurse sags under the weight. One of the soldiers, a tall, bony man with pockmarked skin, makes an awkward attempt to help. Then the nurse screams shrilly, as if someone has stabbed her, and the paralysed boy falls to the floor with a bump. The soldier makes another attempt to lift him but now the nurse is hitting out wildly with one hand while holding her other hand in front of her face. More men come along until the nurse and her patient are surrounded. Hannes sees the boy's eye-whites gleam nakedly between the broad boots that are suddenly tramping about everywhere. Meanwhile, Pototschnik is advancing. He and his company have gone upstairs and found that the upstairs rooms are swarming with Mongols. They have settled down with their cooking vessels between their knees among scattered hillocks of piled-up packs, while they drink and smoke and pass bottles from hand to hand. A group of staring children have gathered in the doorway. One of the soldiers has an accordion and squeezes it to produce long, wailing notes. Two others grab at the reluctant children, pull at their arms and legs to make them dance, but they don't understand, try to get away and stumble when the laughing soldiers trip them up. One of those who fall is a girl with her hair in two long plaits down her back. A Mongol grabs one of the plaits to pull her up again and the girl's face twists in pain. Suddenly Hannes understands what the Mongols should have understood long ago (or maybe they did and that's why they amused themselves with the dancing lark): the girl is blind. The boy the nurse dropped on the floor was probably also blind. The pavilion is full of blind children who have no idea of what is going on around them and can't work out who these strange people are, who smell odd and shout and yell without saying anything you can understand. At this point, Pototschnik steps straight into the noisy dancing circle and is greeted with great good cheer by the soldiers. A bottle is produced. Pototschnik takes it with unbelievable self-assurance and drinks a couple of deep draughts. The accordion player pulls the bellows out as far as it goes and twenty-odd alien male voices howl out something that later shapes up into singing in harmony. With crazy, swinging chords, the accordion player launches into a polka and Pototschnik dances. More precisely, Pototschnik staggers around the room, hopping on one leg at a time while the soldiers clap to the beat and watch him. Then – when he looks about to fall over – they push and pull at him to drag him back into the dancing circle. Pototschnik's face is bright red, and his thick cauliflower hair looks like a wig that someone will soon rip off his head. Hannes cannot tell how long the performance drags on. Nor is he clear about how many others, apart from Pototschnik, are forced to join in. All he knows is that he must get out of there. Suddenly, the walls seem to have closed in on him. Men with dirty faces whose uniforms stink sourly of sweat are everywhere, on their way in or out. They have taken over the corridor, too, and filled it with their things. When he tries to slip away, they reach for him or grab at him or hit him around the head with rifle butts. Their language is strangely boneless and seems to stick inside their mouths. The more there are of them and the more wildly they hit out, the more deeply he despairs. How can his father come and rescue him now? Does this mean that all of Germany is lost? What has happened to Mrs Rohrbach and the nurses? Have they slashed these women's throats, the way Nurse Mutsch always said they would? Just as he thinks that thought, time collapses and he loses several hours. Is that time lost only to his memory? Or has it been excised from reality? He finds himself again at the first-floor window, screaming out into the night with all the power that his young lungs can generate. The dusk is growing denser. He can see the last gleams of daylight as a faint line above the allotment huts on the other side of the road. The strangest thing is that, although he is screaming with all his might, no noise is coming out. It is as if he were screaming into a padded bag. Why scream at all? Something dreadful must have happened but he can't remember it. After another few lost hours that seem to have left no trace in his mind, he is once more himself but, by then, it is dark and he is in a quite different pavilion, in an unknown dormitory where the beds stand in orderly rows along both main walls. The beds seem to float in space. Even though he hasn't been here before and has not the slightest idea of how he got here, he is absolutely certain that this is pavilion 15. Like his own dormitory, this one smells strongly of Lysol but mixed with the bitter, stinging smell of iodoform and the sweet, nauseating odour of urine and loose stools, a combination so powerful and penetrating in the warm half-light that he has to swallow several times to stop himself from vomiting. Some of the beds are covered with grids or gates. Faces are pressed against the netting, their features dissolved in tears, or whining or grimacing. In other beds, he sees small bodies distorted beyond all understanding, some with undeveloped or malformed limbs, some with huge skulls and watery, blank eyes. Half a dozen soldiers have pushed their way into the room. Hannes recognises one of them, the officer with the muddy boots and the big, black-toothed grin who offered the children cigarettes. The soldiers have brought torches and the criss-crossing beams abruptly isolate a stretch of brown-painted wall, then a child's face (scraped as bare as a skull from a grave), then a pair of hands with partly bent fingers fumbling in the air. The soldiers walk from bed to bed with scarfs or handkerchiefs over their faces to keep out the stench while they talk agitatedly in their soggy language. One of them starts rolling a bed out into the corridor, probably because the officer has ordered him to, but a nurse suddenly comes running from nowhere, shouting *no no no no!* She is directly followed by another nurse, who tugs at the soldier's sleeve to make him take his hands off the bed. He seems taken aback at first, but then steps closer and hits her so hard in the face that she staggers and falls to the floor. *No!* This time, Hannes is shouting. But even though he stands nearby, nobody pays any attention to him. Seemingly, he is not in the room at all or else they can see straight through him. Two soldiers are trying to shove the nurse out of the way and when she struggles they do to her what his father has described other men doing to his mother. One of them grabs her arms, another her legs. They drag her into a corner of the dormitory, tear off her uniform and then the things she has on underneath. But now he can't see her anymore because the bodies of the men are in the way. Only a pair of thin white legs sticks out. The legs open and close spasmodically. Hoarse, rumbling laughter comes from the corridor and someone shouts in the Mongol language. Even if he understood some of it, he wouldn't have grasped anything because now the woman's screams and the idiots' loud wails are drowned by a terrific row in the stairwell. The door suddenly opens and the first thing he sees is that bowing show-off of an idiot boy from pavilion 17. Sister Katschenka lies on the floor next to him. She must have fallen down the stairs because she has a bleeding cut on her forehead. She is trying to get up and Hannes wants to help her. He wants to tell her that what is going on in here is against all law and all justice but she looks at him with an expression of such bottomless contempt and disgust that he can do or say nothing. The moment is only seconds long. Then the boy-army, with Pototschnik still out in front, comes stumbling down the stairs. Pototschnik's face is very red and there is more foam around his mouth now. He floors the bowing parrot-boy with a single blow from the bloody clapper. The boy curls up like a hurt insect, his limbs pulled up against his belly. The rest of the army trample over him to get to Katschenka, who has no time to stand before the blows start raining down on her. He recognises some of them: Jan Schipka, a big boy called Ewald, Rudi Steinhofer, Bruno Mayer. They all take turns to let her taste Mrs Rohrback's clapper. And before he knows how it came about, he is with them and beating her as well. True, he isn't sure whom he is hitting. It might be the yelling Pototschnik and his hateful, curly head, or the broad back of the woman who is collapsing under the burden of the children (he can literally hear her body sag, air whooshing out as if from a punctured tyre), or the flabby idiot who is still lying in a foetal position on the threshold of the dormitory and who, once the Mongols start to separate the boys, seems to be the only one left around for them to beat up.

XIII

Held Captive

Occupiers When Anna Katschenka finally arrives at the hospital, everywhere is dark and silent. Someone must have closed the ventilation panes because on a mild evening like this, distant echoes from the hospital wards are carried by the wind out under the trees in the park. You never get away from these noises: the screams and moans of the children that on some days can be as loud as the cries of rutting animals while, in a higher register, you hear the deceptively harmless-sounding chatter of the nurses against an accompaniment of rattling glass and metal objects. She realises as soon as she uses her key that the pavilion door is unlocked and, somehow, that frightens her more than any of the tangible signs of the otherwise invisible presence of foreign soldiers. The air in the stairwell smells of sweat and bitter tobacco smoke. From somewhere, she hears strange voices speaking, coarse ones. Male voices. Further away, a repetitive, dull thudding sound, a little like the diesel-engine generator they used when the electricity supply was cut. Are the Russians installing generators? She takes a step into the corridor and then, suddenly, Pelikan jumps at her. He doesn't utter a word, only presses his long body against hers. He is as wet and slippery as an eel. In her mind, the number of unlocked doors is multiplied, Lord alone knows how many times, and panic grows inside her as she tries to rid herself of the clinging boy. How has Pelikan managed to get here from pavilion 17? He refuses to let go of her, instead tightens his grip and won't stop his dog-like panting. With the boy on her back like a heavy sack, she gropes along the walls to find the door to the gallery and catches sight of a familiar figure in a nurse's uniform at the far end of the room. *Is Nurse Hedwig on duty here tonight?* She hears her own voice sounding so thin and unconvincing it might have belonged to someone else. A door opens upstairs and she hears men talking again, more distinctly this time. Definitely soldiers' rough voices. *Nurse Hedwig,* she says again. *Is everything in order?* Her question is patently absurd, as she realises the moment she asks it. Behind Hedwig Blei's white body, three alien men step forward, all of oddly short, stocky build, or perhaps they only look small against the white uniform of the nurse. One of them leads the new nurse, Marta Fried, with a hard grip around her arm. The other two walk towards one of the gridded beds closer to the corridor. She sees the whites of their eyes, the rows of teeth in their half-open mouths. She also spots a boy of about fourteen or fifteen who doesn't belong to this section but is vaguely familiar. His head is bald and as round as a ball. He stares at her with a leaden gaze. She tries to say something, perhaps to beg the boy to try to get the soldier to set Nurse Marta free. She would like them all to leave the pavilion. The incomprehensible presence of these men soils the space around them. She opens her mouth or perhaps makes a dismissive gesture with one hand. Instantly, Nurse Hedwig – who earlier stood stock-still, as if frozen to the floor – springs at the alien soldier and starts pulling at the hand that holds Marta. The other two shout indignantly and hurry towards their mate. She, too, wants to run to Marta's side but Pelikan stubbornly clings to her back and now he squeezes her sides with his heels as if she were a horse. This time, the boy is the stronger of the two. Or it could be that what she has witnessed has drained her strength. Like a determined rider, Pelikan steers her out into the corridor again and then upstairs. The presence of the intruders is if possible even more obvious on the first floor. Piles of kit and parts of uniforms are strewn everywhere and the air is heavy and turgid with smells of sweaty feet, tobacco smoke and alcohol. Once upstairs, Pelikan hurries off to the dormitory where some of the blind children are housed. The beds are in place but there are no blind children in them, only fully dressed Russian soldiers. Now Pelikan runs ahead of her into the room as if to demonstrate with his body the enormity of what has happened. His obvious eagerness, while still shying away from the beds, and his rather dog-like movements make the foreign soldiers laugh. Suddenly, a boot flies through the air. Pelikan ducks in time but can't avoid the kick that follows up the thrown boot. The tip of another soldier's boot lands on the boy's jaw with an oddly crunching sound and Pelikan howls with pain, then half-falls, half-crawls out into the corridor. Anna Katschenka looks around, utterly powerless. There are alien bodies in the beds where children should be resting, and hostile eyes are fixed on her. No officers in charge anywhere. And – where *are* the children? What have they done to them? She fumbles through the semi-darkness but it feels as if she is moving against a slow current. Wherever she looks, soldiers are coming and going. One of them stands on the landing. He is wearing a pair of shoes that are far too large for him. He holds one of those smelly cigarettes of theirs in one hand and draws on it with grandiose, exaggerated gestures. He sucks, and his cheeks draw in while his eyes bulge like large, white balls, then exhales with his eyes almost closed into narrow Bolshevik fissures and his lips stretched into a threatening grin. She understands that he grimaces at her, that he wants to provoke her for some reason. Then he suddenly says something, it could be *get 'er* or *go for 'er* and the moment she hears his slight, hoarse voice she knows where he comes from. They are on her in a second, fifteen or twenty of them at once. All are children from the reform school.

How have they got here? And where are the children who should have been here, the sick and the blind ones? She is asking herself this even as they knock her down. They are no stronger individually than Pelikan but much more determined about what they want. Some are carrying implements from the kitchen like knives and forks. She sees one of the boys grin delightedly and lift a pair of scissors with the tip pointing at one of her eyes. She lifts her arm to protect her face just in time. A powerful kick hits her in the belly and she tumbles helplessly down the stairs with the whole horde coming after her. The back of her head hits the railing with a hard crack, then one cheekbone. The pain makes her lose control. She believes, or maybe it is just fantasy, that someone is calling out *KA-TSCHENKA KA-TSCHENKA* in a loud, piping voice. What she is definitely not imagining is that the alien soldiers stand by and watch as the children either heave her or (when her knees fold under her) drag her along the corridor. Some of the soldiers are laughing out loud, and applaud encouragingly. But *none of them* intervene when the children shove her into the office, dump her on the floor and slam the door. Someone kicks at it as well. Then cacophony breaks out next door. She hears the boys rummaging about and coarse soldiers' voices talking across each other saying God knows what. Then more laughter, as someone inserts a key into the lock. She throws herself at the door. It is too late. They have already turned the key and the door doesn't budge.

Helpers in Need At some point during the night, Pelikan must have curled up on the other side of the office threshold. She even thinks she can feel the sticky warmth of his breath through the narrow gap between the threshold and the bottom of the door. Now and then, she hears him whimper in pain as he turns or tries to turn his body into another position. But he doesn't move away, not even when someone (one of *them*?) stumbles on him or, possibly, kicks him again. She wishes she could do something, anything, to help the boy but feels paralysed. As soon as she attempts to lift or just straighten her body, pain cuts like sharp knife blades through her head and the back of her neck. When she touches her head, her hand becomes smeared with blood. She wonders what Jekelius would say if he could see them now, her and the boy, lying head to head almost like conjoined twins, separated only by a locked door. If truth be told, she backed the boy up all these years only for Jekelius's sake. She has needed to keep the memory of him alive – which is bizarre since Jekelius himself would never have let a misfit like Pelikan stay alive. She thinks back on their journey together, and of the village church in Totzenbach where she waited for him and found the relief of the Fourteen Holy Helpers in Need. She tries to remember all their names but the only ones that come to her as pain pulses through her body are the ones in a memory rhyme that her mother must have taught her when she was little: *Barbara mit dem Turm, Margareta mit dem Wurm, Katharina mit dem Radl – das sind die heiligen drei Madl.* Barbara is the saint of the dying and also protects the imprisoned and incarcerated. Margaret watches over the wounded and over pregnant women, while Catherine helps all those who are struck mute and can no longer speak. There ought to be a fifteenth one, a saint who intervenes for those who abandon their duties and fail to protect the weak with whose care they have been charged, someone to heal those who stand back when the barbarians come and chop the heads and limbs of the helpless and vulnerable kneeling at their feet and begging for mercy. She must have fallen asleep, or perhaps consciousness was mercifully taken from her for a while. When she comes back to life and reason, it is still night. The silence is total. She listens for the breathing of the boy on the other side of the door but can't hear it any more. The next time she comes to, daylight fills the small office from the edge of the desk to the shelf in the corner with its rows of roll-top archive cupboards. She hears resolute steps in the corridor outside. And voices, not only speaking in that Russian babble. The lock rattles as someone tries out several keys. Meanwhile, a man bangs vigorously on the door and shouts in German: *Open up, it's an order!* She tries to pull herself together and reach the threshold but has no time before the door is pulled open and at least half a dozen men enter. The group is led by a senior Austrian police officer, an older, squat man with narrow grey eyes and grey stubble all over his cheeks and chin. He may or may not be in charge but, in any case, he speaks for the others. He gestures in her direction and, without a word, two of his men lift her upright. She almost faints with pain. The policeman comes close to her. His breath smells acidic, sharply metallic, almost like battery fluid.

Who are you?
What are you doing here? Why have you locked yourself in?

He yells the questions straight into her face. *The Russians . . .* she answers, or tries to answer. He looks at her as if he had never heard anything quite so comical. *There are no Russian soldiers here*, he says. *They're all quartered in barracks.* I was locked in, she wants to say but feels exhausted merely by knowing that now she has to tell him about something he really can't know, namely that the Russian soldiers helped the children to find the keys but it was the *children* who locked her in. The pain sends steady hammer blows through her weakened body. All she wants is to lie down on the floor and sleep. But where can she find a place to rest? The ruined room is full of people wandering in and out, opening cupboards, pulling out books and folders which they leaf through without understanding a word of what they read. And the policeman won't leave her alone. He pulls at her arms, slaps her face and shouts at her again:

Answer my question! Who were you trying to get away from? What is your name? Just tell me your name again!

She tries to say something about the children but gets no further than the word when he steps back abruptly and then: *the children*, he says, *they have been taken away and are now safe from the attentions of people like you*. She doesn't know what to say, except to ask: *what do you mean?* Or, perhaps she doesn't ask. Perhaps he only reads the question in her face because he smiles, a tired, slightly arrogant smile making her suspect that, somewhere behind that worn grey face, root fibres link him to an ancient family, to nobility or, anyway, to a class which deals with inferiors like this, with a slight smile and a dismissive gesture. *We'll stop you from carrying out any more experiments on these sad, useless creatures. Because, that's all they meant to you, isn't that so? Experimental animals, nothing more*. Someone carries a large cardboard box into the room and starts putting files with correspondence and address registers into it. Instinctively, she wants to stop them and demand to know by what right they expropriate other people's possessions. But her palpitating heart won't allow her to say anything. Anyway, she couldn't draw enough air into her lungs to pronounce the words. The officer turns to her. *Of course, we have no idea how much you have destroyed already. You've had all night after all*. He searches in his memory for her name. She has already told him innumerable times and can't bring herself to say it again. Then he straightens his back, as if her anonymity and her inability to answer him make him feel still more indignant:

Let me tell you, Sister,
sooner or later, justice will be done also to people like you.
Sooner or later . . . you can be quite certain of that.

A Letter (not sent)

Most esteemed Mrs Pelikan,

You have already learnt in a letter from the doctor in charge that your son Karel is dead. I write to you in no official capacity and with no wish in any way to make your already profound grief any harder to bear. I was previously Deputy Matron at Spiegelgrund but no longer, as the institution was dismantled and closed from the last day of June this year. Because so many malicious things are currently being said about its clinical work, I would like firmly to reject any such rumours, including the claim that your son lost his life as a result of deliberate clinical malpractice. I met your son for the first time when he was transferred from Bruckhof in Totzenbach and can assure you that during the years he spent at Spiegelgrund, he was given the best available care. Karel was a good boy. Even though mentally backward, he was always obedient and helpful. It is with the greatest regret that I admit that circumstances would not allow me to do more for him. Towards the end, I believe that he refused to take even liquid feeds and that there was little more anyone could have done. Much happens in our lives over which we can have no control. At another time, your son might have been offered a greater opportunity to lead his own life. I would like you to know that we did everything in our power to make his life at least tolerable, as we did for all the children who were placed under our protection.

With my highest regards,
Sister Anna Katschenka

The Burdens of Liberation During the first few months that followed the arrival in Wien of the Soviet army, it seemed that she couldn't move a metre without coming across foreign soldiers. Even though contrary to orders, they were constantly around in the streets. Gangs of them plundered and looted everything they could lay their hands on. There wasn't an intact frontage along all of Ringstrasse, and in the adjoining blocks, the shop windows were broken, and shelves and storerooms emptied. Some shop owners had attempted to protect their property by boarding up the windows and putting iron grilles or bars over the doors but their defences were usually forced, the padlocks cut and the boards shot through or chopped down with axes. Their food rations may well have been sparse, but the soldiers seemed to have unlimited supplies of alcohol. Even in the middle of the day, they were seen drifting along the streets in noisy, boisterous groups with their arms draped across each other's shoulders, making the most of what they obviously felt was their unassailable right to molest every woman they met. Katschenka always crossed the street when she saw them coming. Soldiers who against expectation managed to stay sober were mainly employed in repair work. Along Ringstrasse, trees were felled and the tramlines restored. One morning, the entire street had been closed off level with the Volksgarten and, on both sides of the cordon, people were waiting to be allowed to cross the street. Suddenly, two of the Russians supervising the work shouted commands and tried to grab people in the waiting crowds. The lucky ones got away but an older man in hat and overcoat, encumbered by a large briefcase, either wasn't quick enough or thought he wouldn't be picked in view of the superior position he no doubt held. He pulled handfuls of documents out of his briefcase and then pointed several times with an insistent expression in the direction of Ballhausplatz, where the Chancellor's office was. All that only served to annoy the soldiers. A fight broke out and the man got a blow from a fist in his face. Katschenka watched as his hat rolled helplessly across the dirty tarmac. Bare-headed, he was led to the edge of the street while the soldiers laughed at him. He was made to work, carrying branches to a chainsaw where they were logged and stacked in a waiting lorry. The last time she had seen anything like this was in March 1938, just after the Nazi takeover. The horrible Jew-chasing had started almost at once. It was different then, because the Austrians themselves did the persecuting and were the most enthusiastic plunderers, too. Now, the slightest incident made the ground swallow up her countrymen. Generally, the liberators lived in one city and the liberated in another. The other Allied armies arrived in June and the city was divided into zones of occupation. Law and order improved quite a bit, although Otto still claimed that the police were forced to recruit 'communists' who spent most of the time searching out former political opponents for punishment. She thanked her lucky star that she lived in Margareten, which had become part of the British zone, and because Hietzing as well as Margareten were under British administration, she managed to get out to the Rosenhügel hospital. She had no illusions about finding Jekelius there but hoped that friends and colleagues from the days before the war would back her up and help her find a post somewhere. There was really nothing she could be blamed for. She had never joined the Nazi party or supported their rule in any other way.

The air raids had left Rosenhügel in a dreadful state. One wing was almost razed to the ground. Scaffolding surrounded most of the rest where work on restoring the façade was underway. But quite a few wards must be open, judging by the traffic of doctors and patients. In the corridor leading to the personnel office, she ran into Hedwig Blei. The two of them had never got on. Blei treated her with a kind of suspicious guardedness, always stepped back away from her, and never really listened despite pretending to (after all, Katschenka was her superior). Now, something contracted in Blei's broad face and her pale blue eyes narrowed.

Katschenka . . . fancy you daring to show your face here . . . ! was all she said.

Blei had made an effort to speak in a light tone, almost as if joking. But her words were sharp and precise, and she stood still, without holding out her hand. Katschenka felt that an invisible line had been drawn across the floor between them, a line drawn to demarcate where shame and complicity began. Blei, so visibly proud and self-righteous, must have seen herself as safely on the other side of that line. Once the moment had passed, they began to talk, presumably because they both reckoned they couldn't walk past each other unless they at least pretended to be on speaking terms. It turned out that Blei, like everybody else, believed that Katschenka had locked herself into the nurses' office with some dark purpose in mind. That the children could have got hold of the key was something Hedwig Blei hadn't even considered. She had never left the hospital, Blei explained, and slept in the ward office for several nights. Most of the staff had absconded by then. Nurse Marta and a couple of other nurses and I, Blei went on, were the only ones there when the Russians arrived. What do you think would've happened to the children if the Russians had been given free hands? What did they do to you?

Katschenka wanted to ask but didn't have to. Blei answered the question anyway. I managed all right, she said. Nurse Marta wasn't so lucky. Later, she found out that she was pregnant. Katschenka felt a chill spreading inside her. Even though she had seen what it had been like, this was something she had somehow been unable to imagine. How has she . . . ? Katschenka began. Blei shrugged. Some people have useful friends since way back, midwives for instance, who might help. Or doctors who will prescribe Salvarsan against syphilis, or carry out the actual intervention if necessary. More wasn't said on that subject or any other. Hedwig Blei stood her ground and Anna Katschenka didn't continue past her down the corridor, only nodded goodbye and left. But she remembered what had been said and, a couple of days later, steeled herself, looked up Nurse Marta's number and called her. Marta's younger sister answered. She was apparently Marta's confidante. Anna Katschenka lied, claiming that she was in the same predicament as Marta, and the sister told her of an address in Leopoldstadt.

Death Certificate Stephansplatz looked worse than what people had told her; much worse, in fact. The cathedral itself had been saved or, at least, the huge spire was intact and pointed towards the sky like a giant's accusatory finger. One of the transepts had burnt and parts of the roof caved in. She had been told that the damage wasn't due to bombs that had missed their targets but to the activities of local arsonists and looters who had been carrying out acts of revenge around the time when the Red Army arrived. Nazi insurgents and saboteurs, the new Soviet authority had proclaimed. Katschenka distrusted everything about the Russian propaganda machine but was still uncertain. There could be no doubt that the fighting had caused the destruction she saw all the way along Rotenturmstrasse up to Franz Josefs Kai by the river. The city blocks had been turned back to nature, in a sense: now, they were fields of ash and stone, edged on both sides by hollow, burnt-out buildings. Here and there, an isolated gable would still stand and stare at nothing through soot-rimmed window openings. The canal bridges, including Schwedenbrücke and Marienbrücke, had been blown up by the Germans as they retreated westwards, and stones that had fallen from the broken-down spans and abutments were scattered in the water. People crossed on provisional pedestrian bridges resting on top of the ruined piers. There were crossing places where the bridge was almost level with the water surface and those who managed to get down to them had to climb up the bank or ask the soldiers on guard for help to get back up to the quayside. Russian army patrols were everywhere. The soldiers stopped passers-by for no reason, but Anna Katschenka didn't worry. She carried her identity papers and her nurse's certificate and also official permission to visit one of her mother's relatives, an elderly lady who lived out at Marchfeld, where it was still possible to lay hands on things to eat if you were prepared to pay cash. She knew that lots of inner-city inhabitants did exactly the same thing – made a case for going to see relatives in the country and then, by the way, acquired a little butter or cheese or fatty bacon or at least fresh vegetables. The flow of all sorts of people – soldiers, black marketeers, even the odd secretary or civil servant in hat and overcoat, who stubbornly went to work in bombed-out offices – was simply too large for anyone to control properly. Predictably, she was stopped by a patrol, but the young soldier who demanded to see her papers was apparently much more interested in swapping witticisms and black tobacco with his mates than finding out who she was. In the old days, before the war, a lone beggar used to stand playing the violin somewhere on the Marienbrücke. She remembered his emaciated figure, deep-set eyes and pale face. He had looked like the angel of the poor, and his bow flew over the strings on a violin whose body had hardly any resonance left. If he had stood here today – his sad countenance was far from unthinkable in this busy, ruined landscape – he would have been a guard at the entrance to another world, for Leopoldstadt was no longer recognisable. What she remembered from her youth was a messy, noisy, somewhat chaotic place, very different from the equally poor but still very orderly working-class part of town where she had grown up. The crowds on Taborstrasse and the streets of the blocks around Karmeliterplatz were like nothing else she had known. Most of the people were Jews but the most diverse sorts also seemed to have holed up here since the imperial era: Polish and Ruthenian workers, Gypsies, Bosnians wearing fezzes or headcloths. The local Christians must have had any amount of trouble to keep their end up. She remembered one morning, when her father was taking her and Otto for a day at the Wurstelprater amusement park. It was the Feast of Corpus Christi, and the schools were closed. They were barely halfway there when they were held up by the crowd around a procession that had just emerged from the Carmelite church. She caught glimpses of a priest carrying the monstrance and of colourful standards swaying like the masts of ships in a storm. But the closer they got, the more obvious it became that the crowd was not all made up of the faithful. On the contrary, they had been swallowed in the mass of people already there. Despite the support of choirboys singing and bells ringing out thunderously in the tower of the Carmelite church, the procession route was blocked by indifferent passers-by. Others who also wanted to be on their way were stuck, too: bicycle messenger boys ringing their bells impatiently, market traders pulling carts loaded with goods. The Chassidic Jews in their kaftans and strange fur hats seemed complacently unmoved by everything except whatever was a subject of discussion between them. After that experience, their father had taken them to Hotel Stefanie for a little peace and quiet. It was the first time she had been taken anywhere quite so famous. There were businessmen at the tables near them and fathers having breakfast or tea with their families. Everyone was wealthy, that much was obvious, and one couldn't but notice that everyone was also keen to show off. The men addressed the waiter in unnecessarily loud voices and rarely looked at the people they were with, preferring to catch sight of themselves in the mirrors or scrutinise other guests, as if confirmation by others was what they lacked to complete their image of what contentment should be. Also, you never heard a single word in German. Instead, these people were speaking Hungarian or Slovakian or some other incomprehensible language that often reminded her of what some of the Jews were using, which her father had said wasn't really a language but a dialect, a *Mundart* or something 'from the mouth', which made her think that their speech wasn't made up of real words but of half-digested stuff they held inside their mouths and then spat out. But this was not to say that they ever spoke badly of Jews in their family, only that it was agreed from time to time that Jews were *different*. Anna's brother knew lots of Jewish words, like *die Schmier*, which was what they called the police. It sounded like a German word but wasn't. It was something else and that was somehow typical of everything the Jews said and did. Still, on the football field, they were tough and showed real stamina. Otto's team had played one of theirs from Leopoldstadt, and Otto's side lost. Afterwards, they all shook hands like good sportsmen. Her father used to say that Jews were hard-working and clever people and many of them were just as good Social Democrats as he was himself. That was probably why he trusted them. He had trusted Hauslich from the start, even to the point of lending Hauslich money from her dowry and believing every single one of the lies he was told. He even believed that there was an uncle ready to hand over a flat in Leopoldstadt to the newly marrieds. The flat never materialised and, as likely as not, there had been no uncle either. Strange, that her father should have been so blind when she had seen through that awful con man almost from their first encounter. What was it about the Jews that always made them assume borrowed identities, always pretend to be something that they were not and to own things that weren't theirs and never would be? As Hauslich had. And now they were back, wearing uniforms and greatcoats given to them by the Red Army. Her father said that there had always been a disproportionate number of Jews among the communists and that was surely the case also in the Soviet army. Anyway, now they were returning to claim all that they had borrowed but come to regard as their own and to live in *their* Leopoldstadt. After a while, she found that orienting herself was really difficult. She had just passed the entrance to Hotel Stefanie. Two Russian army lorries had been parked outside. Nearby was Tabor-Kino, where she had gone to watch films when she was studying at nursing college. Judging by the colourful, new-looking posters, they showed only Soviet movies now. Propaganda films, presumably. Overall, there was something foreign, outlandish or distorted about the appearance of the place. She couldn't put her finger on exactly what, but it worried, even scared her. It had nothing to do with the destruction, with all the heaps of shattered masonry at every street corner. Nor was it to do with the strange Cyrillic characters on the over-bright film posters. Or even with the fact that everything was so dark. At first, she had thought that the electricity supply was down, but there were lights on in some windows, though dimly, behind drawn curtains. The streets, which at first glance had looked nearly empty, turned out to be full of people seemingly having emerged from somewhere without her noticing. Outside what looked like a bombed-out bakery, a queue had formed. People stood patiently in line, back to chest, even though the queue did not move and there seemed to be nothing to queue for. And the begging children, they were running around everywhere, groping for her hands or touching her coat sleeves but fleetingly, as if they didn't dare to stay in the same place for long. Everyone she saw moved in the same way, stealthily and nervously. She never got to look into anyone's face. She kept walking through this strange, shadowy half-world without knowing exactly where she was or whom to ask. The address she had been given was on Grosse Sperlgasse, and she knew that it ran somewhere just below Karmelitermarkt. When she got there, the street was as dark as a sack and blocked off at one end by something that, in the dark, she thought at first was a wooden board but on closer inspection turned out to be yet another pile of stones and bricks, this time mixed with the remains of what must have been an entire home: pieces of a kitchen workbench, wardrobe shelving, a bathtub, an intact toilet seat, its enamel shining white in the darkness. The yard opposite was used as a coal store. It looked isolated behind the rusty iron fence that closed off the space between the houses, but then she spotted a fire lit somewhere at the back. Exactly what was burning she couldn't make out but the firelight allowed glimpses of someone who clearly was tending the fire. The face was in shadow but the light reflected off a glistening forehead, strong upper arms and a pair of broad, bare shoulders outlined by a dirty vest. The man (if it was a man) was observing her unflinchingly from within deep eye sockets but didn't move towards her or say anything. The address was the building next door, if it had ever been there. It was practically gone, with only a basement left intact under the ruins. She would never have spotted it but for two women who came up the steps leading down to it, as if ascending from the underworld. At the bottom of the steps, a door opened into a long, unplastered corridor. On one of the raw brick walls, a long red banner had been hung. It had political slogans in Russian written rather carelessly on it. The Cyrillic letters had become almost undecipherable in places where the cloth was giving way. The line of words ended with two energetic exclamation marks, the hammer and sickle insignia of the revolution, and a picture of a smiling Stalin. Above and below the banner, someone had pinned up children's drawings of things like little dogs on leads and square, clumsily coloured-in houses with smoke curling out of the block-like chimneys. The nursery seemed to be open even though there was no house above the basement. Perhaps it had been here before the bombs fell and the children had nowhere better to go afterwards. The only door she could see in the semi-darkness was at the far end of the corridor. She opened it and stepped straight into a room that must have been used as a shelter once. A handful of women were seated on the long benches fixed to the walls. Their eyes stared dully ahead. Two of them had brought small children. Nobody spoke, but when she stepped inside, a few of them shuffled sideways to make a place for her. The room wasn't large, just an ordinary cellar space with pipes running just under the ceiling and coarse, flaking plaster on the walls. Nothing else, apart from the seating, a naked bulb in the ceiling and another door at the far end. Then that door opened and a woman in a nurse's uniform stuck her head out. Their eyes met and some kind of intuition (perhaps because of the glimmer of recognition on Katschenka's face when she saw the uniform) must have told the nurse immediately that Anna Katschenka was not another patient. Katschenka made up her mind at once, without thinking. She rose from her seat and walked to the door. The nurse tried to close it but Katschenka got her foot in. Beyond the door, in a smaller room, she had caught sight of Doctor Jekelius. The woman he had just treated was lying, naked below the waist, on a narrow table in front of him. A dark red mass floated in bloody liquid in the basin under the table. Jekelius slowly pulled off his gloves and met her eyes without saying a word. Her first impression was that his face looked grim, his features forbidding and sharp with tiredness. Later, when she tried to recall his face, she felt that he had looked worn-out rather than tired and that his expression had been more anxious than forbidding. For how long they stood like that, she couldn't be sure afterwards. She remembered it as an eternity but it probably wasn't long before Jekelius said *shut the door* and the nurse said *you have to wait your turn*, then pushed her back outside and closed the door in her face. She didn't stay long enough to see whether the door would open again or if it was ever opened.

XIV

A Respectable Life

Across the Border Adrian Ziegler would many years later have to give an account of himself in front of disbelieving police officers: how had he, who was always unwelcome, managed in the end to find his way home after the war? He had to tell them about how the long march from the youth detention centre in Kaiserebersdorf had been organised, who had been there to supervise it, for how long they had travelled inside barges on the river. And how long had he been in Regensburg? Only a short time, he replied. Maybe a week, at most. He had been questioned by the American military police through an interpreter. When he told them that he came from Wien, the interpreter had let the American policeman know, and both had laughed and said there were so many dead in Wien by now that they stacked corpses on street corners like piles of planks. This image stayed in his mind every minute of his long journey home. His father's and his mother's bodies, Laura's and Helmut's, all on top of each other like logs with their empty, dead faces turned towards him as if they were just waiting for him to complete the stack. When he had insisted on going home despite the bad news, the MP had turned his face away and the interpreter said that, at present, they let nobody cross that border. After he had left them, he spotted a bicycle leaning against a wall near the bombed-out station building. He took it. Nobody made any attempt to stop him, so he carried on cycling in what he fancied might be the right direction. A couple of kilometres south of Regensburg, a crowd of agitated people blocked the road. A loaded carriage had overturned on a sharp bend and tins of condensed milk, packets of sugar and cocoa powder, which judging by the stamps had been stolen from an American military store, were scattered everywhere in the road dust. One of the men had unshackled the horse. Now he turned to Adrian and asked where he was going. Passau, Adrian said, because he didn't dare say that he wanted to go to the border. The man started to tie sugar and cocoa packets to the parcel-rack behind him and gave him a folded banknote and a piece of paper with a street address on it. Go to the address and hand over this stuff, the man said. Adrian had become a fence within an hour of having been released by the Americans. Of course, he never said anything about this to the policemen who were questioning him all those years later. To them, all he said was that he had gone to Passau and then followed the valley of the river Inn southwards. A farmer's wife gave him something to eat, let him sleep in a barn overnight and told him where the best place was to cross the river. The following night was overcast and a light rain was falling. He knew that he would never have a better opportunity than this. He emptied his pockets, made a bundle of his clothes, held the paper from the US military police stating that he had been discharged from prison – *die Entlassungsschein* – between his teeth and waded out into the river. The water was cold, much colder than he had expected, the current was strong and, although it was May, the sky was hidden behind the high mountain ridges. Soon, the night around him grew as black as the inside of a cave, so black that he didn't know where he was going or was just allowing himself to be carried by the current. All of a sudden, Jockerl was riding on the back of his neck, sitting so high up that he could feel the flaccid white flesh of the inside of his thighs around his neck, at the same level as the line of cold water. *You're not forgetting about me, are you?* Jockerl said and pushed his head underwater. Suddenly, Adrian is back in the crowded hold again with water pouring in from all sides. Jockerl's head is already underwater but it doesn't matter because he is dead. *We're alone here, you and I*, Jockerl said and looked at him with his unseeing fish eyes and shiny porcelain smile. And so they were tumbling around in the currents, tightly entangled. Jokerl was pressing his dead lips against Adrian's who no longer knew where he was or what he was holding in his arms. One moment, he thought it was the blue material of Miss Santer's dress that was twisting itself around his fingers, next that it was Jockerl's hair. And then it came to him that he was clutching real, living grass. Rising above him was a long, grass-covered bank. He grappled to hang on, thrashing with his legs to find a foothold in the stony river shallows and then slowly began to haul himself up. He collapsed among the tall grasses, as if inside a huge head. But was he back home in Austria or had he just been swimming with the current and ended up on the German shore? When he turned to lie on his back, there was still no sky to be seen. The only sounds came from the mass of water flowing over the riverbed and filling every space that ground and sky should have occupied, a sound that was to him wondrously light and open. Or was it just because the night around him was so dark?

Gulliver Comes Back Home After that river crossing he decided to get rid of Jockerl once and for all. He had worked out how to go about it in Kaiserebersdorf, the day they had been driven in trucks to help clear up after the bombing of Alberner Hafen. He was going to smash Jockerl to pieces with a spade, or perhaps a shovel. He had landed a job on a farm on the outskirts of St Florian. It hadn't been at all hard. He had been picked up by American MPs on this side of the river as well and they had interpreters who spoke German. In

Grieskirchen, the interpreter advised him to present himself at the mayor's office and they had exchanged the provisional identity papers issued by the Americans in Regensburg for a new document in his own name and stating the names of his parents in clear typescript, with signatures and proper stamps underneath. He had also been told to go to a farm a few kilometres south of St Florian. They could give him a job there. The farm's owner was called Maximilian Gruber, a very affluent man. Gruber actually owned two farms. One was a major establishment, where the farm buildings formed a large square, a *Vierkanthof*, situated on the long slope above the village. His second, smaller place was a few hundred metres further down in the valley. The large farm also had a long, barn-like building where some thirty-odd labourers were housed. They were all kinds of people – milkmaids and tractor drivers and even a groom and a carpenter with his own workshop. The first floor in the house had been taken over by half a dozen bad-tempered Polish POWs who spent their time playing games with matches. Adrian is housed with these would-be arsonists who tell him that if they aren't let out of here soon they *will* set the whole shit heap on fire. Big-time farmer Gruber deserves to burn, they say, because Gruber was a Nazi and a prominent member of NS-Bauernschaft. The local people told them all about it. The only reason why the locals don't dare to demand that justice is done is that he employs so many people in the neighbourhood – refugees from the war, too, and old enemies like us, one of the Polish pyromaniacs says and strikes a match. Gruber has a twelve-year-old son who follows him everywhere as if joined to the big farmer's broad hip. The boy is as thin as a rake and his body won't stop trembling. It looks as if he suffers from the cold shivers even though it is June already. Adrian knows the type. One of those who at the time would have been picked for special treatment at

Spiegelgrund straightaway. Gruber must have had the authorities in his pocket or else he knew something about how to make children escape special treatment that most people didn't. When he lies awake at night, Adrian thinks about this. Generally speaking, he thinks a lot about what one might call, for wont of a better phrase, social justice. He thinks back on the time when he was Gulliver, large and powerful but tied head and foot at the same time. Everything is connected. That is why he thinks that it is high time now for him to break free for good from all that ties him down, and from Jockerl first of all. He is sure that if he doesn't do it now, he will be wandering about with that ghost on his heels for all eternity and never come home. Of course, he also knows that if he *does* do it, if he really kills Jockerl, then he still won't be free. If you murder someone, you will never be free. The next day is a Sunday and everyone on the farm, including the Polish pyromaniacs, has gone to church to celebrate Mass. The morning is lovely, with a high, clear blue sky and gentle tolling of bells that hangs in the air over the valley. One wouldn't have believed that there has just been a war on. Adrian looks down over the dirt road that links Farmer Gruber's two farms. It winds its way between the sunlit fields like a bright, white ribbon. Only the dung heaps behind the barn are still in the shade. Jockerl is lying on the grass, waiting for Adrian to come and kill him. He holds his hands over his head even though he knows that it is pretty pointless and the familiar Jockerl stench is spreading around him. Jockerl stench. Dung stench. Adrian raises his spade to strike. He goes on, one blow after another, gripping the handle firmly with both hands as if shovelling broken masonry. He only stops now and then to wipe the sweat from his forehead and shift his grip. Jockerl-sweat on the shovel handle. A pair of staring Jockerl-eyes rolls into the grass. A Jockerl-skull cracks and then the old Jockerl-brainstuff wells out and mixes with gravel and straw and dung. But the shovel keeps slipping in his hands, so he has to shift his grip again before he sets to and chops up the upper part of the body, the jaw with all the Jockerl-teeth, until not one single scrap of grinning porcelain splinters remains. Then he stamps on everything until it is buried in the dungheap, shovels and forks it all down, and scrapes soil on top. Even so, many more Jockerl bits and pieces are still around. So much more to stamp on and bury, all of that Jockerl-carcass, his cartilages and bones that will not break. Fingers that still fumble in the air. Adrian puts the fork down, wipes his face with the back of his hand and realises that blood is seeping from his eyes. He screams at that point. He isn't sure why he screams. Even though his head swims and his eyes bleed, he doesn't feel particularly angry or upset. Perhaps he screams because he should have done it long ago but now he has the strength and the lung volume. But his scream dissolves in the vibrating noise as the church bells ring out. It flies harmlessly up into the sky and vanishes unheard. When he lowers the fork he sees his father come walking up the road between the two farms. He recognises him straightaway. There is the shabby black hat his father always used to wear. Now he carries it in his hand and a bottle in his other hand. The way he holds the bottle, dangling somehow absent-mindedly between his fingertips, and his odd way of walking, teetering from one side of the road to the other, only to stop now and then as if he had hit an invisible wall – all that points to him being drunk again. His usual rambling about after a piss-up. He stops again, looks towards the big farm, and it must be that the booze has sharpened his eyesight because he smiles and waves at Adrian. And Adrian, who had believed himself to be out of sight in the shade that falls over the dungheap, suddenly becomes very busy. He can't think how to dispose of the rest of the body parts from the Jockerl-corpse but carries on digging and, thankfully, the soil is soft. He hides all the shameful bits of Jockerl in holes in the ground just in time before a cluster of folk from the farm becomes visible on the road from the church, and noises from the kitchen are heard once more. When he steps inside, he sees his father seated at the large, round table where they all sit every evening after the dinner bell has been rung, the big-time farmer as well as farmhands like himself or the Polish arsonists. His father looks bigger than he remembers him. Or, rather, he looks inflated, and his head and body look somehow *heavier*. When he turns to Adrian, he has to lean his arm on the edge of the table and move his whole torso as his face opens up into a big grin. I've come to pick up *that one*, he says and points at Adrian, who isn't sure whether the paternal finger is trembling because he wants to put extra emphasis on their relationship or if he is in the grip of some momentary excitement, and has forgotten his son's name. Adrian thinks the latter is more likely. His father is so drunk he can barely sit upright but he is still determined to do what he has come here for. Eugen Ziegler, the self-same Ziegler who once swore he'd kill his son if he had any dealings with the Nazis, is now doing business with an old Nazi farmer. The bottle that dangled carelessly from his hand now stands between the two of them on the table and, as the talk continues, he produces yet another bottle from what must be a sizeable store. And Gruber doesn't mind being treated. After all, Mass has been attended to. Every time an ever-more slurred and incoherent Eugen Ziegler gabbles another joke between gulps of drink, the over-loud Gruber belly laugh rings out obligingly. Meanwhile, the cardboard boxes that Gruber's wife puts on the table are steadily filled with every conceivable type and shape of cheese and ham and sausages, long strings of *Rauchwurst* and *Selchwürste,* glass jars with gherkins and cooked apple and preserved horseradish. All the boxes are packed in the rucksack and shoulder bags that his father has brought and any items that can't be packed, young Ziegler has to carry all the way to the station. His father is obviously very pleased as he lurches along the road with one arm nonchalantly draped across his son's shoulders. Just think about it, in Wien there are people who'd kill for just ten grams of this sausage, he says and pulls out a few curls of the dark red blood sausage from his rucksack. Adrian can look over the top of his father's head now and observes that his old man's hair is thinning. In that black mane, his father's pride and joy, always oiled at bedtime and protected by a stocking every night so it would keep its styling, and which Ziegler would later claim to be a dead ringer for the boxer Joschi Weidinger's hair, Adrian can now see the scalp with its short hairs, like pig's bristles, through the strands carefully combed back from the hairline. How sad it looks, how pathetically white. And how far his father must have travelled for the sake of his son. Or else, his father's travels had nothing to do with his son and everything with the satisfaction of setting up in business again. Now they are sitting on a crowded train and can't feel quite safe, his father explains, before they have been through Enns. The thing about Enns is that the Russian patrols take over there. Still, he – Ziegler – can deal with Bolsheviks as craftily as with old Nazi farmers. Just you wait and see, he says. Sure enough: a foreign tongue rings out in the carriage corridors, and the tramping of heavy boots and the quick slamming sound when compartment doors are opened and shut. Eugen makes no attempt to hide the blood sausage. On the contrary, he has wound loops of sausage around his neck. When the door opens, he holds a side of fatty bacon up in one hand, shushes with one finger across his lips at the confused young man in a private's uniform and waves to him to come in. The soldier looks quickly right and left, then stealthily closes the door to the compartment. They are alone and while his father gestures expressively and smiles and gabbles in the same crazy Russian that Adrian has heard him use before, the side of bacon and half the sausage are slipped in under the soldier's belt. A quick salute (both men salute), the door opens and shuts, the stationmaster blows his whistle and, as they watch through the window, the train departs from the platform and, shaking intermittently, rolls into the Soviet occupied zone. Several new passengers have come on board at Enns. Most of them carry rucksacks full of food and fuel, all so bulky that their owners can hardly find space for them in the narrow compartments. An older man has brought a cage of rabbits. When the train shudders, the passengers shudder too, and the furry bodies in the rabbit cage slide around. Large, terrified rabbit eyes are staring out between the bars. The rabbit owner opens his mouth, then gestures with both arms as if to apologise. Adrian notes immediately that this is a Jockerl-smile. A wrinkled strip of skin has been ripped apart to expose a set of porcelain-grey teeth. Adrian doesn't know where to look other than stare stubbornly at the floor with its covering of trampled fag ends. His father has produced another bottle. How much do you want for one of the rabbits? he asks the rabbit man. The bottle starts circulating and the atmosphere becomes jolly and loud. Adrian takes a drink from the bottle and the alcohol is at body temperature and bitter and, despite having gone round several times, still tastes of his father's strongly scented hair lotion. The rabbit man tears the skin flaps apart over his teeth and a raucous almost-song flows from his mouth, but his singing is chopped up by the shaking and rolling of the carriage. After a few more grabs at the neck of the bottle, he opens the cage door and hands over one of the kicking animals. As Eugen breaks the rabbit's neck with one practised twist, Adrian watches the reflection of his father's grimacing face in the window. *You haven't once asked me where I've been*. Adrian turns back to the floor, which rises up and slams hard into his face, like the deck of the river barge. The carriage swings and grinds against the rails and for a while it feels as if it straddles the track while the rails slip further apart. At this point the lights outside the window grow more numerous, the train passes an angrily ringing barrier signal and then a whole block of dark housing with emptily gaping windows. A station sign flicks past but Adrian has no time to read the name because his father has got up in his usual abrupt way and begun to collect his bags from the luggage rack. Here! he says and pushes the rabbit down under Adrian's collar. Something sticky and rubbery, excrement or clotting blood, drains from the rabbit's body and runs down his chest and belly. And then: here! his father says again. *Not once have you asked*. Everyone is trying to squeeze out of the door simultaneously. Adrian can feel the carriage lean over even though it is definitely standing still. The voice over the loudspeaker bangs in his ears. The text on something like a station sign reads *WESTBAHNHOF*. However, there is no station building behind the sign, only a small hatch at one end of a pile of masonry. Behind it is a barrier and, next to the barrier, half a dozen Russian military police have set up a kind of passport control with a sign written in unreadable lettering in red and black. You leave this to me, his father says and immediately starts walking towards the wall of uniformed police and passport officers. Adrian tries to walk after him but the ground still behaves like the river barge, toppling this way and that, and even though he does move forward he seems to be getting nowhere except into an ever-denser dark. The further he enters into the murk, the heavy, swollen taste of the drink seems to rise higher up his gullet and soon nausea wells up inside him. He tries to hold the rabbit's body in place just below his collar but it glides further and further down; the straps of his case are cutting into his shoulder, then slip off as his legs shake and give way until all of him slumps at the edge of the platform and a stream of acrid vomit gushes out of his mouth. The space between the rails is as dark as a grave, and it is dark once he stands up again. He wonders if all of Wien is like this or if there is something wrong with his eyes. Then he catches sight of his mother at the far end of the platform. Her shoulder blades protrude under the grey cardigan like a pair of wilting, powerless wings. He smiles at her in a way that she knows well because it is just as uncertain and guilty as his father's smile used to be, and *don't you recognise me?* he asks her.

His Father's Land From that day onwards, all inside him that might have responded to the name Dobrosch had died and his allegiance was to Ziegler. He had become securely rooted in his father's land. During the first few months after the end of the war, he worked as a bartender for a friend of his father's known as Count Frosch or just 'the Count'. Frosch ran a restaurant on Rotensterngasse in Leopoldstadt. Adrian turned seventeen that year and it was the first real job he had ever had. But the restaurant guests were thin on the ground and, often, the only ones sitting at the tables were waiting for people they had arranged to do business with. He usually had little to do behind the bar except wash glasses and stack boxes of empties. One day, the Count took him along to the store which was housed in a building across the street and consisted of a suite of several dark, dusty rooms. In one of them, crystal chandeliers lay on the floor like wounded birds. Two of the rooms were filled with sofas and couches, dressers and dining tables and lamps of many kinds, with shades of glass, or pleated or pretty flowery fabrics. The Count assured him that nothing was stolen goods but objects which he had rescued, often risking his life, when the Jews were driven out of the city, and which he then had to take care of again when the Nazis left. The Russians were in Leopoldstadt now and the Count's relationship with them was, to put it mildly, rather complicated. Only a few days after the 'liberation', a small gang of Red Army soldiers had come into his restaurant and demanded to be served schnapps. When he refused, they simply commandeered his entire stock of flour, sugar, sauerkraut and potatoes. The only things they let him keep were these items of furniture, probably because they hadn't realised that the rooms on the other side of the street belonged to him. Lately, he had managed to negotiate a cessation of hostilities with a senior officer in the secret police on terms that granted the officer all he could eat and drink a couple of times a week, and also to invite any colleagues he fancied to dine with him, at the Count's expense. Once he had finished the meal, the GPU officer would usually leave it at that, on the condition that he could take a few cases of German sparkling wine with him as he left. The Count would have the boxes in readiness for this eventuality. If he had only dared to, the Count said, he would have entrusted his store to this officer, too. However, he knew that in the Russian zone of occupation, the police crime squad had initiated a wide-ranging investigation into dealers in stolen goods, and in particular among restaurant owners. Also, it was well known that the zealous communists in the GPU did not take kindly to anyone who seemed to do too well at the expense of the others. So, the stored items remained where they were and the entire place was swelling and becoming sore, like a bad conscience, and would Adrian not care to help him dispose of these compromising things? Preferably in exchange for medicines, food, cigarettes and suchlike – things that people truly valued. He would earn a good commission on every item he managed to sell. Adrian didn't answer. He had reached a room crammed with shoes: from tall riding boots to rubber overshoes, from button boots to elegant women's pumps. Some looked as good as new, others were worn and dirty. For a long time after he had taken on responsibility for the store, Adrian couldn't think about anything except shoes. Nothing in which a human being clothes himself – or herself – could possibly be more humble than a pair of shoes, and nothing easier to wear out or get rid of. Perhaps his fellow prisoner Alois Riedler had known that when he, like a new Houdini, slipped out of the ropes that tied him to the others as they were marched to the river barges. The clogs he had so elegantly leapt out of stood on the quayside as if they had never had anything to do with the childish body that had been torn apart by rifle bullets just five hundred metres away. But, at the same time, there is surely no item of clothing that carries more visible and intimate traces of its owner? The movements of a whole life can live in the heel grips of a pair of much-used fabric sandals. Adrian Ziegler had become the administrator, responsible for other people's lives and property. But what of his own life? Officially, he is registered as staying with his parents, but because he can't stand being with his father, Count Frosch has agreed to house him in a small room, hardly bigger than a walk-in wardrobe, that is part of his restaurant. Adrian actually prefers to go home to one of the Count's friends, a man called Paul Schöner, who owns an allotment on Wasserwiese near the Prater. Schöner's piece of land is taken up by a vegetable plot and a tool shed. They move parts of the Count's store to the shed, and because someone should keep an eye on the goods, Adrian persuades Schöner to let him sleep there. It is a cold, draughty place but there is a small wood-burning stove and logs to feed it with. Water can be drawn from the pump next to the vegetable plot. He has survived in worse conditions than that. Paul Schöner works night shifts at the famous Ankerbrot bakery out in Favoriten, another part of the

Soviet-occupied zone. Because the large bakery receives earmarked consignments of flour from the Soviet Union, they have succeeded in getting production going already. For Adrian, it means that Paul comes cycling every morning with freshly baked bread, as a special favour from the bakery. Schöner has managed to sell several pairs of Adrian's black, ladies' evening shoes to Russian police officers who don't care in the slightest that the shoes might have been worn by Jewish women and happily send them home to their wives or give them away to prostitutes. Sometimes, Schöner is paid in vodka bottles and then lots of people turn up at the small shed on Wasserwiese. One day, the Silver Knife is there. *I know you*, he says, *you're the one who ran away from that madhouse*. And he smiles as if he had just made an amusing discovery. But Adrian hasn't got it in him to become really angry about the taunt. Since they last met, the Silver Knife has become afflicted with cancer of the liver. Below the brim of his hat, his face is, if possible, even thinner. His suit hangs on his emaciated frame as if on a scarecrow. At one get-together in the shed, he pulls out his wallet and extracts a newspaper cutting, which he hands to Adrian in a manner as significant as if it had been a banknote. Three of the doctors who worked at Spiegelgrund have been arrested and will be appearing in court. There is a photo of the accused flanked by armed guards: Doctor Illing is seated between doctors Türk and Hübsch. He stares at the three familiar faces and wonders: why not Doctor Gross? Has Doctor Gross been allowed to get away? To where? That is the only thing he thinks. Otherwise, the people in the photo might as well be complete strangers. He reflects on how he has rid himself of them. That is why he feels nothing now. He has excised the five years between the ages of ten and fifteen from his mind. It was a time he lived through without having to think or sense or miss anyone or dream about anything. But what will become of your life if you haven't even got a past? That night, they all drink Paul Schöner's schnapps, all except the Silver Knife who mustn't drink anything alcoholic ever again. As so often when he has had too much to drink, Adrian becomes disorientated and speaks about many things from inside the unrecognisable mask that is his face, and just because he can't make out who he is any longer, it seems all the more important to keep them reined in with long ropes of words and he won't stop letting out more rope until Paul Schöner shouts that he must fucking stop this crap. So Adrian slaps Paul in the face and then hits him again and again. He beats up Paul as he once beat Jockerl, slowly and intently, with a sluggish, heavy charge behind each blow. It is as if his aim were to completely annihilate this man with whom he had been laughing and joking just minutes ago. Only the swift, united intervention by the others stops Adrian from murdering his friend. It seems that's all the thanks I get, Schöner says the following morning when, covered in bloodied plasters, he mounts his bicycle to go to work. A few hours later, the police come for Adrian. If it is Schöner or someone else who has fingered him, he will never find out. This is in September 1946. They take him to the county court, the *Landesgericht*, and he is eventually sentenced and sent off to the youth detention establishment in Graz-Karlau to serve fourteen months for breaking and entering, dealing in stolen goods and causing grievous bodily harm. This is the next stop in what will turn out to be a lifelong progression from prison to prison.

In the Store It would take many years before Adrian Ziegler learnt to endure the sight of the children of strangers. Or any groups of strangers, whatever age. As soon as he encountered gangs of noisy children or groups of schoolboys with rucksacks on their backs, he would look away and cross the street. It troubled him especially to observe the unformed, thin bodies of boys who, ever anxious about where the next blow or kick was coming from, cowered in front of their mates, because he felt, back inside his own young, hunched body, as weak-kneed and frightened. He remembered the anguish in his belly; it had felt like a scoopful of scalding hot water always about to splash. The longing for obliteration of the self that he saw in the eyes of some children was perhaps still more frightening. He thought he knew it as an ingrained, unending plea to be *let off*, not to have to *be* here, or *walk* here and, above all, not to have to *pretend* all the time. Most of all, Adrian would have preferred to vanish entirely or become invisible to all these people who were messing about and crowding in on him. If only he could be seen by himself alone. His mother and father had moved in together again, just a few years after the end of the war. They lived in a large apartment on Kundmann-gasse which had been rented out to a Nazi family who had all left when the Red Army marched in. As with all such abandoned homes, the Russians first thoroughly plundered it of everything of any value before handing it over to the Wien city council. Because Ziegler senior had useful contacts among the Russians, he managed to have them register the apartment in his name. It is so sizeable – four rooms, a kitchen with a separate larder – that Adrian's sister Laura reluctantly agrees to visit her mother again. By now, she brings her husband and two young children. Because Laura has sworn by everything holy never to say a word to her father again, Eugen locks himself in one of the rooms for as long as his daughter is there and won't come out until after she and hers have gone. Adrian, who was set free after dutifully doing time in Graz, is allowed to come to stay on Kundmanngasse. He is even given a room of his own, a fact his father boasts about to everyone he does business with. Eugen also fixes up new jobs for Adrian and because his contacts are mostly in the restaurant or cooking trade, his son ends up as a bartender or a waiter. For instance, Adrian works for a while as an assistant bartender in the Hietzing casino frequented by British officers. That particular joy lasts for six weeks and then he is called in to see the manager, who is furious with him for not admitting at once that he has done time in prison. What would *he* think of a casino staffed by ex-cons and burglars? His father has to come to his aid again and find him a new job. A man he met once, one of the many casual acquaintances Adrian has made among saucepans and across cutting boards, once expressed his deeply serious belief that you can see if someone has a soul or not. It shows in a person's eyes, he insisted. The way they look at you. People without a soul won't look you in the eye and that's because their gaze has nothing behind it to keep it in place. That is why Adrian Ziegler wants to look at himself in the mirror as little as he cares to see himself in others. Seen from the outside, he makes a pleasing and perfectly respectable impression. He is slim-hipped and broad-shouldered, but perhaps a little on the short side, as if his legs had given up on growing while the rest of his body took on the size and proportions of a man. He has inherited his father's dark hair and strongly marked eyebrows. He observes his hands where they emerge from under the cuffs and thinks they look pale and somehow numb, as if they don't know what they should be doing next. His 'Semitic' ears still stick closely to the side of his head and it is hard to detect the gaze in his deep-set eyes, while his mouth, which knows that his eyes always seem evasive, tries to improve his appearance by putting on a smile that is meant to be open and trusting but comes across as ingratiating and unreliable. His father's smile, and perhaps his own most characteristic feature. So he becomes one of the soulless, a man who can't rest, who never gains the trust of others and stays at his different places of work only because they do not yet know everything about him. For a while, he works for a haulage company in Ottakring. He sits in the driver's cabin, ready to help with loading and unloading. His boss considers him a hard-working, decent chap and suggests one day that Adrian should drive the truck himself. If only he can get himself a driving licence, he will get a better-paid job. Adrian goes to the police station on Juchgasse and asks if they might not make an exception in his case so that he can get a driving licence. The policemen stare as if they think that he is out of his mind. The haulage company remains understaffed and the boss wonders why he hasn't got himself that driving licence yet. In the end, Adrian has to tell him straight: soulless people are not ever trusted with driving licences. This makes his boss furious, not because of the lack of a licence but because of the betrayal, the falsehood: why didn't he say straightaway that he had been inside? Daddy Ziegler says: don't worry, we'll fix it. But by then Adrian has had enough. When the war ended in 1945, he was fifteen years old. In 1955, when Austria was once more declared an independent country, he was twenty-five and had already been sentenced and imprisoned three times. During these ten post-war years, his sister Laura had gone from being a pale, withdrawn teenager to a self-assured and resolute mother of two. The day came when Laura decided that her mother had suffered enough, went to the police and charged her father with domestic abuse. Eugen stayed on in the Kundmanngasse apartment. It simply wasn't possible to shift him. However, Leonie was given a small flat of her own in Meidling that was out of bounds for her husband. Laura also thought it best that Adrian shouldn't go near it, although Adrian couldn't make sense of this. At first he had thought that Laura had been mixing up father and son without thinking since he officially still stayed in what had been the large family flat, although it had come to house only his father. It turned out, though, that Laura's reason for finding Adrian as hateful as his father was that she linked them both to a past which she felt was degrading and would have nothing more to do with. This was why she had forbidden Adrian to talk about his time with the Haidingers or about Spiegelgrund and what went on there: she wanted to lead a normal, respectable life, she said, and not have the past riding her all the time. She doesn't care one way or the other if Adrian *cannot* put his past behind him. Actually, she sees it as him trying to make a virtue out of his inability to forget and carry on. It is 1955, after all. Earlier that year, the occupying powers signed the new Austrian State Treaty, and perhaps it because the wartime past is now *definitely* behind them that Laura finally weakens and gives in to her mother's nagging: the whole family, including Helmut, is allowed to celebrate Christmas together. On that Christmas Day, Laura (who runs her own dressmaking studio) presents her mother with a lovely crepe dress. Adrian stands in front of the mirror and tries to pull up the zip at the back of the dress with his clumsy fingers and his mother stands in front of him, passively, her neck bent and her fragile shoulder blades drawn up, and suddenly he can't bottle the question up any longer: do you remember when you visited me in the pavilion, Mum? And of course she doesn't because it is the case with soulless persons that they don't become included in other people's memories and, just then, his father arrives, so drunk he can barely stay upright. I see the lad has bribed somebody to let him get at the festive spread this year as well, he says, first thing. And so Adrian hits him, perhaps enraged because his father had once more taken the trouble to turn up only to humiliate his son again. Or perhaps it is more that he wants to beat him up to make it clear that they are not of the same ilk, he and his father, and that Laura is prejudiced. But if that is what he hoped, he could not have been more mistaken. The effect is exactly the opposite. *Out! Get out now!* Laura screams and, that evening, his last glimpse of his sister is of her lips, so thin and bloodless you can hardly tell them apart. She slams the door after them. Father and son, peas in a pod. So much so, they are bounced from the same venue at the same time. What Adrian could not have known is that liver cirrhosis had been eating his father for years, causing his muscles to shrivel and his normally flabby face to slowly hollow out until only skin and bones remained. He could not have known that the only reason why his father hadn't sought medical help long ago was his fear that the doctor would take his booze away, even though had reached the stage when he could hardly drink a glassful before vomiting it up again. Though they no longer lived together as man and wife, Leonie visited him twice a week, on Tuesdays and Fridays, when she would shop for him and clean, and cook what little he was still able to eat. She kept this up until he was finally admitted to Allgemeines Krankenhaus, the city's general hospital. A few months later, by which time Eugen was obviously past all hope of recovery, Adrian was given leave from prison to visit him and stood in front of his father's bed with his cap in his hand and his neck bent, as if to apologise for something. He never worked out for *what* he wanted to apologise but it didn't matter because by then, his father no longer recognised him.

Interlude in Josefstadt One day in the 1960s, Adrian ran into Pototschnik in an ironmonger's shop on Josefstädterstrasse. *Can I help you?* Pototschnik's cauliflower hair was the same as he remembered it or, if it had thinned and greyed a little, Pototschnik's face was just as bulging and his eyes as small and sunken and pig-like as ever. Now, these eyes were fixed on Adrian without a glimmer of recognition. How can I help? the hair and face and eyes asked. Did

Pototschnik really not know who was standing in front of him? Or was he pretending because he wouldn't give anything away? Admission would be to lower his guard. He was wearing the same worn, grey cotton coat as the other shop assistants but Adrian found it hard to believe that he was just a simple employee. Surely he owned the whole shop? What started with a cartridge had ended up as an entire ironmonger's shop. Pototschnik did have the dignified stance of the owner as he leant forward with both palms resting on the hinged part of the counter that separated the shop from the space behind, where the assistants had to hurry up and down on the sliding ladders along the shelving that covered the full height of the walls in order to locate and bring down samples of all the stuff stored there: hammers, chisels, kettles, brass or iron braces. Pototschnik opened his mouth to ask his question for a third time but in that same instant, a tram passed just outside and a metallic clamour mingled with the quivering of the shop windows and their displays of ironmongery. Adrian thought the whole place would collapse. But the collapse was taking place only inside Adrian. When he looked at Pototschnik again, the man hadn't moved a single millimetre, presumably *couldn't* move because his hands were pinned to the counter with massive nails. Adrian stared at the nail heads protruding from the backs of Pototschnik's hands and the blood that had dribbled between his fingers. It clotted and stained the counter red. Pototschnik apparently hadn't noticed and was still looking at Adrian as if expecting an answer. No one else seemed to have seen anything unusual either. Behind the counter, the grey-coated shop assistants clambered up and down the ladders, or wrapped up buckets and broom handles, or poured nuts and screws into small cones of newspaper for the customers who were coming and going while the doorbell was ringing incessantly and the noise of the passing trams also continued, apparently unseen and unheard by all (at that moment) except Adrian. The doors leading to the past are never fully closed, Adrian would say later. But their positions change all the time and you can never predict where they will be and so it is impossible to prepare yourself before you arrive at this gateway or that, unsure if there is any other way of getting in.

The Long Arm of the Law When, in the end, he gave up on Austria and went to Italy, he had held down a steady job for quite a long time and even got married. He and his wife Elfriede had a daughter christened Maria but never called anything other than Missi. Little Missi's fifth birthday was due the year he went away. There is a photo of the two of them taken the previous summer: he stands holding Missi's hand on one of the tree-lined paths at Schönbrunn. Both stare attentively at the person behind the camera (is it Elfi?) as if they belived there would be no picture unless they looked hard into the lens. Above them rise the canopies of the trees to form a mighty arch of greenery, like in the Steinhof park, and it makes them look small and vulnerable. At that time, the family was still staying in a room in the Rudolfsheim appartment belonging to Adrian's parents-in-law. At first, this had been a practical arrangement because he and Elfi were working and needed someone to look after their little girl during the day. However, over time, Elfi had grown dependent on her parents. Even though she never said as much, it seemed as if she felt unable to trust her and Adrian's ability to manage a home of their own. Her lack of trust was inflated by her mother, who made it part of the household routine to slander Adrian. She was quite capable of doing this even when he was within earshot. She would tell her daughter that he was a wastrel who couldn't be relied on when it came to handling money. And, she would say, he has no practical sense, either. How could someone like Adrian, who had never had proper training in anything and couldn't provide properly for his family, ever be a master in his own house? He who had always leaned on the goodwill of others? Had he even tried once to find a family home? This last accusation was especially out of order because, when he had found a modern flat (two rooms and kitchen) for them on Laxenburger Strasse in Favoriten, his mother-in-law had objected, saying that it was far too large for their needs and, besides, much too expensive. And she immediately added another thing to her long list of things to criticise him for: he was ungrateful and had never appreciated everything his in-laws had done for him. Adrian had appealed to Elfi's common sense and pointed out that it was after all up to the two of *them* to decide how to lead their lives. The exchange became heated and the outcome was that Elfi locked herself and Missi into their one room. His mother-in-law promptly threatened to call the police if he ever so much as showed his face in her home again. For three weeks, he dossed down in the flat of an old acquaintance called Rolf Dellinger and spent all his spare time brooding on the unfairness of the accusations launched at him. In the first place, it was untrue that he had no training and no permanent job. He had done an apprenticeship as a welder and been fixing damage to chassis and finishes for several months in a car repair shop in Hütteldorf. His current boss trusted him and, before the miserable row with Elfi, he had often brought a car back for weekend trips with his family. It had made him pleased with himself to be able to do this, and Elfi had enjoyed it – at least in the beginning. He still didn't have a driving licence but no one was bothered or asked awkward questions. On the contrary, because he had access to a car, friends and even casual acquaintances would ask him for lifts or if he could pick them up after a night out. He was too proud or perhaps too uncertain about his skill with motorcars to say no. Or, typically, impatient. Soulless. One day, a much younger man came to see Rolf Dellinger. The visitor, a Yugoslav called Goran, asked Adrian if he would drive him and a few of his friends one evening sometime soon. If he agreed to do the job and kept quiet about it, there would be a 20,000-schilling fee. Of course Adrian twigged immediately that Goran was planning something illegal and that, if anything went wrong, the car could be traced to him, which would mean the instant loss of all he cared for, not only his job but also Elfi and Missi – and, as likely as not, for good. But even though he grasped this from the start, it didn't occur to him that he could simply say no. One evening in late September, he turned up behind the wheel of a Chevrolet Impala that was in good shape apart from a buckled mudguard. He looked forward to showing off the splendid car to his passengers. He had parked, as instructed, near the corner of Zieglergasse and Mariahilfer Strasse to make it easy to slip into the Gürtel, the out-of-town ringroad. Goran and his companions turned up fifteen minutes late and, even so, didn't seem to be in that much of a hurry. They slung their cases into the Impala's huge boot and Adrian turned right towards Westbahnhof and carried on driving the purring engine in the direction of Linzerstrasse. What he learnt later was that the police had been on their tail ever since he pulled out of Zieglergasse. They had identified the registration number and contacted the owner, who informed them that the car should be in a Hütteldorf repair shop. One more call to the owner of the workshop and they had the name of the perpetrator. Exactly what the police had asked, Elfi couldn't say because it was her mother, and not herself, who had opened the door. Elfi was too upset to say anything, wept incessantly and would not hear of him talking to Missi, which was the reason he had called. Adrian stood in a phone box in Graz with the receiver gone dead in his hand, knowing that he had to choose. He could go back to work, try to explain to his boss that he had acted in good faith to help friends of a friend. But then, his boss would surely say what they all said: why hadn't he come clean about his prison record? Or he could go for his only other option, take the consequences of all doors now being closed to him, keeping in mind that they had actually been closed all the time, and try to make a fresh start somewhere else altogether. He went to Italy and worked as a welder at a shipbuilder's in Genoa, then moved on to Bari in Apulia. Later still, he stayed in Marseille where he met a woman who, like him, had been married before and had had children but been forced to break with her family. He ended up being away for five years, but not a month passed without him meeting his responsibilities and sending money home to Elfi and Missi. Which was probably how they managed to track him down because he had hardly crossed the Austrian border before the police arrested him. He had received 20,000 schillings to provide a getaway car for four men who, on that day all those years ago, had robbed a supermarket on Schottenfeldgasse. His pay-off was a silly sum, a tiny proportion of what the takings had been that day, but the law was in no mood to show mercy. An extensive inquiry was set in motion. It did not only examine his involvement in the burglary and but also his life in general and especially his 'criminal' past. Until the investigation got underway, he was kept on remand in a small cell in the Landesgericht building in Josefstadt. From the start, everything seemed horribly familiar. One morning, the guard came to escort him. You're to see a psychiatrist, he said. This was in November 1975. Adrian Ziegler's forty-sixth birthday had just passed. They took him to an interrogation room. It was furnished with one table and two chairs, one of them already occupied by the well-known forensic psychiatrist, who didn't look up from the client documentation that he was leafing through until Adrian was already in the room and the guard had locked the door.

I am Doctor Gross, he said and took his glasses off.

XV

The Sentence

Hearing Witnesses Spiegelgrund is no more. The walls, meticulously built around the institution, are now demolished and what the staff had undertaken under oath to keep secret is now public knowledge. The papers frequently uncover new information about the 'murderous medics' at Steinhof. So far, no one has got hold of Doctor Gross but doctors Illing and Türk, later also Hübsch, are locked up in their respective police cells and, while there is much speculation about when they will appear in front of the People's Court in Wien, images are published of pavilions with bars over the windows, of smiling 'innocent' children and parents who claim that they had previously been 'forced to stay silent' but will now stand up and tell of how they entrusted their children to these kind, confidence-inspiring medical men and women, and then found that they couldn't get the children back or, when they insisted, were told that their little ones had died, as it happened, killed by the very professionals who had promised to save, even cure them: *abgespritzt* – the terrible word, which means 'killed by lethal injection' but should not be used to signify everything that had been going on in the clinic. Every morning when she wakes up, she is terrified that her name will be announced in one of these fat headlines. What worries her most is that her parents will find out – which is crazy because they have known all along where she was working and, in the end, everyone in their block of flats also knew. But it is one thing to know the kind of things no one really needs to talk about, knowing that gets you nowhere. It is much worse to be aware of something that you realise is common knowledge, spoken about by all sorts of people and, for instance, run in the papers day after day. Still, her father doesn't read newspapers and there are times when she thinks he wants to escape the stories. Perhaps his inexorable physical and mental decline is no more than a strategy intended to keep harmful knowledge at bay. Now that she no longer works, she takes her father out for walks every day. They descend the main staircase together. Once it was just that – a staircase – but now, to her increasingly frail father it is a dreaded chasm. It is as if the building they have lived in for so long is not constructed with floors and landings now, but with gaping shafts and hollows. Her father grips the railing with his trembling hand and, because his legs are as shaky, he is no longer sure where the next step is. One day, before she has time to grab hold of his shoulders, he falls helplessly down the stairs. As he falls, he gazes up at her with an astonished look in his eyes as if he could not have imagined that her hands, of all hands, could fail him. Afterwards, she sits with his heavy head in her lap and shouts up into the empty stairwell that someone must come and help her, and above her the flat doors open and people come to lean over the railings. But Mrs Katschenka is a nurse, of course, she hears somebody whisper, she'll manage on her own, surely. It takes time and effort to get her father to stand up again and, with a handkerchief held against the bleeding wound on her father's forehead, they continue the descent past the voices and smiling faces of people who quickly disappear behind their partly closed doors. Of course people had talked about the Katschenka family before, but it had been in a respectful tone. They were decent people who kept themselves to themselves. Of her, it has always been said approvingly that she had been such a support for her parents. They had said that to her face as well, in the street or the dairy round the corner. What mother wouldn't have wished for a daughter like her! But now they agree that she is hiding behind her poor, innocent parents. The shame of it! But they will come for her soon, mark my words. Soon, soon – no doubt about it. And Otto, who is the one telling her all this, instructs her that she must not speak to anybody about these matters. If you have done anything that can be held against you, keep it to yourself. Never confess. All they are after is someone to take the burden of guilt off themselves. Don't let them get away with making a scapegoat of you, Anna, he says. But when the summons to appear in front of the judge leading the investigation finally arrives, she feels almost relieved. She can't quite explain why. Perhaps because, at last, there is something concrete to discuss – claims and accusations but, be that as it may, these can be rejected or confirmed instead of the endless whispered hints and half-truths. She is a respectable person who has nothing to be ashamed of, and because she believes this she wants to confront the law head on. For the interrogation, she dresses in a skirt and a freshly ironed white blouse with a lace collar. She buttons the blouse all the way to the base of her neck. She puts on gloves and a hat. Throughout, the judge behaves very properly towards her. He is keen to emphasise that she is not herself accused of anything. She has been called by the defence of one of the persons charged, namely Doctor Marianne Türk, who feels that Mrs Katschenka could make a statement in her favour. Afterwards, she is presented with a transcript of the interrogation, and is asked to read it carefully before she signs it.

She does sign it.

Diagnosis

The first interview with the witness Anna Katschenka, November 1945:

THE JUDGE LEADING THE INVESTIGATION: Mrs Katschenka, you were employed at Spiegelgrund from January 1941 and until the liberation. That makes almost four and a half years. From this, one might reasonably conclude that you were well informed about the working conditions on the clinical side of the institution and also about the prevailing mentality of the staff. Is that so?

ANNA KATSCHENKA: I suppose so.

JUDGE: I have also been given to understand that you are an honest and fair-minded person. Hence, you presumably have nothing to lose by speaking out.

ANNA KATSCHENKA: I have already told the police everything I know.

JUDGE: Indeed, you have given an account of what you heard and saw. However, at this stage, I am looking for something else. Accusations have been made to the effect that children were subjected to euthanasia. And so on.

ANNA KATSCHENKA: Mostly rumours, I believe.

JUDGE: How would you personally describe such rumours?

ANNA KATSCHENKA: As false. Without any foundation.

JUDGE: I meant: what would you say that the rumours were alleging?

ANNA KATSCHENKA: I don't know. Rumours are rumours.

JUDGE: So, if I put it to you that certain persons have deliberately and with foreknowledge allowed severely ill patients to die. That is, in the expectation that death would occur in these patients although at a later stage. The aim would have been to shorten the suffering of the ill. Would you agree that this is a reasonable definition of the concept of euthanasia?

ANNA KATSCHENKA: I don't quite understand what you mean.

JUDGE: Please, just answer my question.

ANNA KATSCHENKA: Yes, I believe so. It depends.

JUDGE: Depends – on what?

ANNA KATSCHENKA: It is essential to understand all the circumstances in the case.

JUDGE: [*leafs through documents*] Mrs Katschenka, I think I'm right in quoting a preliminary interview with you in which you stated that the majority, not to say just about all the patients under your care in the clinic, required continuous medication with sedatives or painkillers of some kind.

ANNA KATSCHENKA: That is probably correct.

JUDGE: And it is also correct to say that the substances used in the clinic to provide sedation or pain relief were administered in doses sufficient not only to ease the patient but, conceivably, high enough to be fatal?

ANNA KATSCHENKA: All medication has damaging effects if taken at too high a dose level. The quantity must be adjusted from case to case. As I said earlier, one must have an idea of the history of the illness in its entirety and not just rely on single symptoms.

JUDGE: You stated earlier that there were sedative agents which were also given to control severe fits and spasms in some patients?

ANNA KATSCHENKA: That is what I meant when I said that one must have the whole picture. These matters are judged from case to case.

JUDGE: But surely what you say implies that it must be difficult, not to say practically impossible, to decide whether very ill patients have been given the sedating or pain-relieving drugs in a sufficient or in too high a dose? As it is understood that the same substance that can control the symptoms in certain instances also can contribute to accelerating the progress of the disease.

ANNA KATSCHENKA: You're trying to make me say something, but I'm not sure what it is.

JUDGE: Is it the morphine or Luminal that kills the patient? Or is it complicating conditions such as pneumonia or circulatory disturbances, for instance?

ANNA KATSCHENKA: I don't understand why you ask me all this. I'm not a doctor.

JUDGE: What I am asking you is whether you can exclude the possibility that in some cases, sedatives or painkillers were administered in such quantities that the drugs contributed to a worsening of the patient's illness and premature death?

ANNA KATSCHENKA: No. I'm not aware of any such case.

JUDGE: But you can't exclude that it might have happened?

ANNA KATSCHENKA: I am not a doctor. I can't comment.

JUDGE: But surely you have an opinion? You worked in this clinic for almost five years.

ANNA KATSCHENKA: All I know is that most of the patients that we treated were, medically speaking, completely hopeless cases. Death was a more than likely outcome. I can confirm that, and also the fact that we dealt with children who suffered so greatly from their torments that the painkillers or sedatives given to them, regardless of what their effects may be in the long run, the sufferer must have felt them to be blessings. However, to suggest that sedating or pain-relieving agents were given with intention to kill is quite a different matter.

JUDGE: So, I understand you to say that, in your view, it is utterly unthinkable that any medication with sedating or pain-relieving properties might have been prescribed with the intention of bringing about a fatal outcome?

ANNA KATSCHENKA: Yes.

JUDGE: As for an alleged circular, issued by a relevant authority, that encouraged the practice of regularly administering such medication with a fatal outcome in mind – and this has been said to exist – is it something you're aware of?

ANNA KATSCHENKA: No. I had absolutely no idea.

JUDGE: May I ask: if this circular had been in force, would you have been aware of it? Its existence, I mean?

ANNA KATSCHENKA: Yes, I assume I would have been.

'It wasn't part of my work to feed the children'

Transcript of a new interview with Dr Marianne Türk, January 1946:

I have to make it clear that I no longer stand by what I stated in response to questioning during the interrogations held on 16 October 1945. Then, I claimed that I had no knowledge of any mercy killings carried out in the institution and also that Dr Illing, at the time my immediate superior, had not in any way indicated to me that such acts took place. Now, on the contrary, I am prepared to state that I did know of this. Some time after I had taken up my post at the clinic, Dr Jekelius informed me of the existence of a law that permitted euthanasia in certain defined circumstances. Any relevant cases were to be referred to a state committee for scrutiny. The committee, on the basis of its findings and evaluations of the case histories presented to them, would decide whether euthanasia was to be carried out or not. The legislation conferring these powers on the committee would not be completed until after the war, since the authorities had not quite decided how the bill of law was to be drafted or how it would deal with the relatives. In other words, I knew of these regulations prior to Dr Illing's arrival at the clinic. Euthanasia cases also took place in Dr Jekelius's time. When the committee decision became known, it was enacted using Luminal or Veronal tablets. I did not personally administer these drugs since it wasn't part of my work to feed the children. However, I did pass the task on – or, to be precise, I ordered the nurse on duty to carry out the recommendations received by Dr Jekelius and, later, Dr Illing. [. . .] Injections of morphine-based preparations were used only very rarely: that is, in such cases where the tablets had not had the intended effect, because the parts of the brain normally targeted by Veronal or Luminal were dysfunctional due to the child's condition. [. . .] I would estimate that between seven and ten children were euthanised in this way every month. [. . .] The reason that I made different statements when interrogated about these matters on 16 October 1945 is that I was required by both Dr Jekelius and later Dr Illing to swear a binding oath not to disclose any of this to anyone. I saw it as my duty to keep my oath also on the occasion of this investigation. As I have already stated, I hardly ever gave the children these drugs myself. I occasionally administered injections. How many children were involved, I don't know. It was not very many. On the occasions when the nurses did the injections, it is my belief that they [the nurses] were completely aware of the significance of what they did. Exactly how well informed or briefed these nurses were with regard to particulars, I cannot say.

[Sign.]
Dr Marianne Türk

Symptoms

The second interview with the witness Anna Katschenka, 30 March 1946:

JUDGE LEADING THE INVESTIGATION: Are you familiar with this book, Mrs Katschenka? [*He holds up, with both hands, a heavy textbook in nursing practice; the cover says HAND- UND LEHRBUCH DER KRANKENPFLEGE.*]

ANNA KATSCHENKA: No, I'm not. It was not used during my training years.

JUDGE: No, of course not [*leafs through a few more pages*]. It was printed in 1940. If I may, I'll read a short extract to you. It is taken from the third chapter's second section, second paragraph. It is entitled 'Other regulations affecting professional healthcare practice'. This is what it says: *The National Socialist transformation [of society] has brought about extensive changes in the practice of healthcare. The thinking that now guides German care of the ill as well as general healthcare is based on new approaches to the welfare of the people as a whole. To replace the 'curative liberality' that previously dominated the medical profession and which entailed regarding the care of the ill as charity, often exercised by churches and other religious institutions, today's form of care is directed by the goals already established in our new legislation concerning matters of race and heritability of traits. Hence, new laws and regulations supporting those purposes have been introduced, such as the law defining a Uniform System of Health Care. Also, new organisations have been instituted with the aim of developing and practising NSDAP's political will and leadership.* Are these ideas at all familiar to you?

ANNA KATSCHENKA: I have never been a member of NSDAP. I

have already made that clear. Party politics do not appeal to me at all.

JUDGE: That's understood. But what we're talking about now is not membership of a political organisation. The passage I read to you sets out the law as it affected everyone working in healthcare. It was written in 1940, one year before you, of your own free will, applied for a post at the children's institution. I take it you can't seriously claim that you were unaware of the new statutes described in this textbook. Especially as you sought out this workplace yourself and Doctor Jekelius had informed you of the type of children admitted to the clinic. And, presumably, also of what kind of services were expected of you.

ANNA KATSCHENKA: I carried out my work in the same spirit as in the past. And with the same intentions.

JUDGE: I have asked you before if you noted any changes that followed immediately after Doctor Illing's arrival as medical director. You said no. Is that correct?

ANNA KATSCHENKA: Yes.

JUDGE: However, when Doctor Illing was heard in the People's Court, he emphasised himself that his powers in the institutional context, and the justification of his right to do what he did, were based on a circular that he safeguarded in one of the desk drawers in his personal office, number 15. I assume that you know of this room, Mrs Katschenka?

ANNA KATSCHENKA: Yes.

JUDGE: Would it be fair to say that you actually went there quite often?

ANNA KATSCHENKA: I don't understand your line of questioning.

JUDGE: This investigation was initiated to prepare for the court case against two defendants who were both your superiors, doctors Illing and Türk. Since the investigation began, a great deal has been unearthed which also changes the circumstances affecting my interviews with you. I believe that you by now have heard of the investigation that is underway in the case of Doctor Margarethe Hübsch, now that she has been found and taken into custody. Apparently Margarethe Hübsch also expects you to be a witness in her favour. But, before you do, I should inform you of the fact that some of your former superiors have changed their statements in view of what has come to light recently. To give you an example, Doctor Türk has admitted that so-called mercy killings were carried out during Doctor Illing's time as medical director of the clinic. She admits also that these practices were already taking place, although to a lesser extent, during the previous medical director's time in office. That is, during Doctor Jekelius's time. Doctor Türk states that she was called in to see Doctor Jekelius soon after she had taken up her post, and that he instructed her about a document issued by the Ministry of Internal Affairs in Berlin which set out the recommended procedures and, furthermore, he made it clear that this document was the equivalent of enacted legislation. Now, Mrs Katschenka, I'm sure you will recall that during our earlier conversation, you denied all knowledge of any such circular or document. You confirmed that *if* there had been such a thing you would definitely have known about it. This would be reasonable in view of your rank in the institution and the nature of your work, and possibly also because of your personal relationship with Doctor Jekelius. When you sought out this institution, it was, you have said, because you *wanted* to work under Doctor Jekelius. That is already on record and would seem to point to the very likely possibility that you, too, were called to the director's personal office, number 15, and informed about this document in just the same manner as Doctor Türk. Also, it would indicate that the suggestions that you earlier dismissed as false and groundless rumours were what actually happened.

ANNA KATSCHENKA: [...]

JUDGE: Mrs Katschenka?

ANNA KATSCHENKA: [*in tears*] You don't understand. You don't understand what it was like. There were so many of them and they suffered so dreadfully.

JUDGE: Mrs Katschenka. I must reiterate. You are called as a witness. You are not accused of anything. It is also recognised by all of us that we are bound by the oaths of service and that we all have committed ourselves to be loyal to our superiors and have a duty to obey their instructions. I do understand that you feel constrained by such binding declarations but surely you also recognise the absurdity of insisting that you had no idea of what was going on in the institution when those who were your superiors have already admitted that much. Now, you took up your post in 1941, at about the same time as Doctor Türk, isn't that so?

ANNA KATSCHENKA: [*faintly*] Doctor Türk was already there when I started.

JUDGE: Well, it's not important here. You began your work in 1941 and you have already said that you did so willingly because you felt such a great confidence in Doctor Jekelius. Now, it is a fact that even then it was relatively well known what kind of medical man Doctor Jekelius was – if I may put it like that. The condition for Am Spiegelgrund existing at all as a specialist clinic dealing with children with disciplinary problems and, also, very severely ill children, was of course that the majority of the previous in-patients were . . . let's call it 'evacuated'. Transported to another place. Eliminated. This, you must have known. With regard to the daily duties and procedures in your new place of work, you must either have been already aware of them or been told of the aims of the institution after a meeting with Doctor Jekelius, who presumably also felt great confidence in you . . . [*leafs through her personal documents*] I can't see here that you ever looked for another position somewhere else during all those years.

ANNA KATSCHENKA: But you don't understand. There were . . . look, I couldn't get a job anywhere else. All doors were closed to me by then. That was when I realised that there were posts at Steinhof, and that Doctor Jekelius . . . [*weeps*] I had been at Lainz but would so much have preferred to work with children. Before, at Wilhelminenspital, I had worked with children, many of them were so very ill but it wasn't . . .

JUDGE: So, it shocked you to see what kind of clinic you had signed up for?

ANNA KATSCHENKA: I was completely horrified. It was not at all what I had expected. Besides, I had never had any training to prepare me for nursing children who suffered from such extensive malformations or neurological diseases. This was actually true of most of the staff in the children's clinic – they weren't trained for this work either. There were some who had qualifications in paediatric nursing but most of them were leftovers from Steinhof. Asylum nurses. And nursing assistants. Soon after I had taken up the post, I asked to see Doctor Jekelius to tell him that I was not suitable, simply not the right person. That was when he explained it to me.

JUDGE: Explained what?

ANNA KATSCHENKA: Well, that letter . . . the document you were speaking about earlier.

JUDGE: When was this?

ANNA KATSCHENKA: I can't remember. Soon after I had begun my new job. Perhaps just a few days later.

JUDGE: And what did he tell you?

ANNA KATSCHENKA: He said that I had by then seen with my own eyes that the condition of the children who were admitted to the clinic was truly miserable, that some of them were incurable and, in such cases, certain procedures had to be followed.

JUDGE: And what were the procedures in such cases?

ANNA KATSCHENKA: He said that the final decisions were made in Berlin and that the local doctors never decided on their own. In that sense, the children on the wards were there for observation. Our main task was to observe them very carefully so that we could submit accurate and thorough case reports as bases for final conclusions.

JUDGE: When that conclusion from Berlin arrived, what did you do?

ANNA KATSCHENKA: The judgement was up to the doctors.

JUDGE: How did you react when you learnt all this?

ANNA KATSCHENKA: I simply didn't understand at first. I only realised when Doctor Jekelius let me see the Berlin document. He showed me that it was sent out from the Führer's own ministry and was signed by the Führer personally. Jekelius said that since it came from the person of the Führer, it had the same status as any law, only in this instance the situation demanded secrecy. I assumed that he referred to the war.

JUDGE: And then?

ANNA KATSCHENKA: Then he reminded me that I had taken an

oath and sworn to be silent about the work I do. And he said that I must not, in any circumstance, tell anyone about any aspect of the institution or about the principles which were applied and, well obviously, anything about individual cases.

JUDGE: Was that all?

ANNA KATSCHENKA: What do you mean?

JUDGE: Do you remember anything else? For instance, do you remember what the Berlin circular – that's what we're speaking about, surely – looked like?

ANNA KATSCHENKA: I was far too upset to notice any details. I remember that it was written on quite ordinary letter-pad paper, nothing special at all. Except the symbol, the eagle and the swastika in the top left-hand corner. And the signature at the bottom.

JUDGE: The Führer's signature?

ANNA KATSCHENKA: I believe so.

JUDGE: Then it would be fair to say that, from this time, from this talk, you *knew* – knew not only what was going on but also what the aim of it was. Is that right?

ANNA KATSCHENKA: [. . .]

JUDGE: I suggest that at this point, we should take a break. The court will rise and you can use the time to consider what you will include in your statement. You may want to discuss it with your lawyer. Then we shall have a look at the case of Doctor Hübsch.

Treatment

The second interview with the witness Anna Katschenka continued:

JUDGE: Now, Mrs Katschenka, have you made up your mind about what you want to include in the final statement? We had better start at the beginning, from the first day you took up your post at the institution.

ANNA KATSCHENKA: I started work at Am Spiegelgrund in January 1941. At the time, Doctor Jekelius was the medical director. My post was Ward Sister and I was allocated to pavilion 15. The institution, as it was then organised, also catered for children with difficult disciplinary problems. But some of the children were profoundly unwell, with differing types and degrees of malformation and debility. On admission, each child underwent a very thorough examination. Our task was defined as observing the children during a limited period of time in order to provide the required details that were to be the basis not only for a final diagnosis but also for any future evaluation of each child's condition. Each child was also photographed to illustrate the case notes. All sick children admitted to the clinic were then reported to the state committee in Berlin for scientific evaluation of heritable and family background-related severe disease. Then, at a later point, the committee would issue a recommendation about how we should proceed – that is, which children were to receive treatment or continue to be kept under observation.

JUDGE: If the decision was that a child was to 'receive treatment', what did that mean?

ANNA KATSCHENKA: It meant that the child should be killed. In the meantime, many children died anyway. It also happened several times that a child whom Berlin had ordered us to treat remained under observation because we still had some hope that their condition might improve. This was what we hoped for all the time. You must understand. These children were very ill and often had very severe inherited organic defects. For instance, some of them lacked certain parts of the brain. We cared for children with water on the brain – hydrocephalus – children with paresis or paraplegia, with spina bifida or spinal cord herniation. At the less serious end of the spectrum were children with cramps, atrophic conditions and paralysis. Most of them were quite heavily medicated. Many had to be tied down at all times, or kept in straitjackets to prevent them from sticking fingers up the rectum and then eating their faeces.

JUDGE: How was the treatment carried out?

ANNA KATSCHENKA: For those who were able to eat more or less normally, we mixed the medication into the food. For very ill infants who couldn't swallow, we administered drops of morphine in very small doses. The larger children were mainly given Luminal.

JUDGE: And everyone knew that a treatment of this kind would end in death?

ANNA KATSCHENKA: Yes, everyone knew.

JUDGE: How often was this done? Was it a daily occurrence, or weekly? How often would you say?

ANNA KATSCHENKA: I don't quite understand.

JUDGE: Was it part of, as it were, the day-to-day routine to carry out such treatments or to discuss further treatments?

ANNA KATSCHENKA: Yes, that's right.

JUDGE: On whose orders were these treatments carried out?

ANNA KATSCHENKA: The doctor in charge or, if not there at the time, the doctor on duty.

JUDGE: What you are telling me is that it would be impossible for drugs of this kind to be administered, and the intended effect achieved, without the knowledge of the doctor in charge?

ANNA KATSCHENKA: Yes, that is so.

JUDGE: Now, which doctors are we talking about?

ANNA KATSCHENKA: Doctor Jekelius during his time at the institution. If he wasn't available in person, doctors Gross or Türk would take over. And, later on, Doctor Illing.

JUDGE: And Doctor Hübsch? She was after all employed as second in command to Doctor Jekelius when he was absent at various times. In your view, was Doctor Hübsch also fully informed and aware of what was required?

ANNA KATSCHENKA: Doctor Hübsch was a senior consultant and didn't always join in the daily rounds, but because these recommendations were issued by the board and the director of the institution, it is hard to believe that she didn't know about them. After all, she was the director's deputy and attended board meetings when Doctor Jekelius was away. Besides, she was a committed National Socialist. She was always dressed according to regulations, displayed NSDAP party insignia and always used the *Heil Hitler* greeting. I think it's impossibile that she wasn't fully informed.

JUDGE: I think this is enough for today, Mrs Katschenka.

Anatomy

Extract from the hearing of the witness Dr Barbara Uiberrak, senior registrar and pathologist at Steinhof, January 1946:

I have been employed at the Steinhof asylum since 1933. Since that year, I have been in charge of post-mortem examinations for the entire hospital complex, i.e. not only for the mental hospital but also for all institutions linked to the Steinhof asylum. Over the years, the hospital has of course undergone several changes. The children's clinic was opened and then a reform school. In addition, a labour camp for women was established and then a military hospital.

Throughout these changes, I carried out autopsies as required by all these institutions, including the military hospital. Practically all dead bodies were autopsied. It was only when the workload became so large that we were no longer able to sustain the burden that we stopped carrying out post-mortem examinations on subjects who had died from old-age-related decay.

Doctors Illing and Türk I only know of as colleagues at work. We did not meet privately. Doctor Türk was known as someone who was not a National Socialist, while Doctor Illing was widely known to be a National Socialist. He wore his party badges prominently at all time.

I was not aware that there were state instructions about carrying out euthanasia in certain parts of the institution. My staff would talk about these matters, for instance the rumour that procedures in the children's clinic were not what they should be. Personally, I gave no credence to all that. There was a lot of loose talk going around at the time which turned out to be quite unfounded. As for the children's corpses, I never picked up anything untoward at autopsy.

All I can say about Dr Illing is that he gave me the impression of being an exceptionally meticulous physician who took a most unusual interest in individual cases. It often happened that he came to see me in order to examine more closely some particular autopsy observation or generally to survey the material. In brief, to my mind, he left a very good impression indeed, as a doctor and a human being – a morally highly commendable person and very devoted to his duties as a doctor.

As required, I shall here make short statements concerning some of the cases of morbidity I saw at the time:

I. Boys:

1) Sturdik, Anton: The child was unfit for life. It is hard to judge how long he would have survived. This boy was paralysed and, as shown in two of the photos, he is, as it were, lying on his head. This is normal in children with severe muscular spasms in the legs. The photograph of his brain indicates clearly the expanded ventricular system (internal). Otherwise, no marked changes. If one went by the brain development alone, such debility would be unexpected. As in so much research into brain function, the effects of lesions are obscure.

2) Wenzel, Johan: An advanced case of hydrocephalus (water on the brain) with diminished brain development.

3) Lasch, Wolfgang: A child of spiritually highly developed parents, Wolfgang sustained brain damage due to X-ray irradiation during the second month of the mother's pregnancy. The child was a complete idiot. He survived until his seventeenth birthday. I believe that the child's mother died before her son. Her nerves were completely damaged.

4) Rothmayer, Gerhard: Very severe brain damage, however, relatively difficult to find any lesions from external inspection alone.

5) Rimser, Günther: Severe brain damage.

This pattern continues throughout all the case histories of the children.

II. Girls:

1) Schmidt, Brigitte: Severe brain injuries shown on X-rays. Injuries of this type can be inherited defects or also have been caused during labour, e.g. at forceps delivery. Destroyed brain cells do not regenerate.

2) Kramerstätter, Maria Theresie: In this case, the cerebellum is almost entirely missing.

Almost all these cases are exceedingly interesting from a scientific point of view. We have preserved 700 or so brain specimens, which are kept here, 'Am Steinhof'. In most cases, fixed speciments of all endocrine glands have also been kept. The intention was that all these anatomical items should become available for scientific study, especially to illuminate neurological pathology. I think one or several cases could usefully be investigated annually. This would be a way to achieve a wide overview.

'Save yourself, Mrs Katschenka' You're out of your mind, Otto says when he realises the kind of admissions that his sister had felt that she must make. *You're out of your fucking mind.* His eyes have gone blank, his lips are quivering like an upset child. She tries to convince him that she had no choice. If her own ex-superiors, like doctors Illing and Türk, are retracting their previous statements and admit that the clinic's children were subjected to euthanasia – what can she do? Doctor Illing even insisted that he is proud of his achievements. He says that he has at all times been on the right side of the law. They will always have the law on their side or find a senior person to hide behind, Otto says, but who will protect and defend you? The war ended a year ago but Otto is still employed on clearing-up crews and is at this point out at Lobau, where the Nazis had been busy constructing a new facility for landing oil. The excavations were done by tens of thousands of Soviet POWs who had been transported there. Otto inspected the barracks where the workers were housed. They lived in quite a style, he says, and his voice is full of contempt. Much better than we did. Can you explain that? Why should they, who were prisoners after all, have been provided with all these goodies like housing and free food? Back then, they were much better off than us ordinary honest workers, and that's still true enough. She realises that his bitterness festers like a wound. She still remembers the day when he came home on leave and placed his hands on the table as far from the plate as he reasonably could, as if he didn't want to recognise them as belonging to him, and that was when she knew that his hands had been used to kill. For whom, for *what* had he killed? He is asking himself that and now she is aware that she, too, could ask herself that question. A few weeks after putting her signature to the last witness statement, she gets a phone call from a man who says that he is Doctor Illing's legal representative. She doesn't catch his name, maybe he never said, but he is punctiliously polite and enquires about her family and how she is managing *during these difficult times* before he launches into his real reasons for calling her. He asks her if she has completely grasped that Doctor Illing will stand accused in court of crimes which were lawful acts in the legal context that applied during the war. Surely, the man insists, the fact was that if Doctor Illing had acted in contravention of the regulations in force at the time, he would have been guilty of a punishable offence. He might have been dismissed from his post, and possibly brought in front of a military court. Perhaps, Mrs Katschenka, you have not given sufficient weight to the same considerations in your own case. You should do so without delay. You, too, followed the institution's rules and regulations at the time. No human being can set him – or herself – above history or commit themselves to obeying another, supposedly 'higher' form of law and justice than that which governs other citizens. You would be punished for such heresy. This is why I beg you: save yourself, Mrs Katschenka. Don't agree to say in court what you have been told to say. Everyone knows that you were the person responsible for seeing to it that the prescribed lethal doses of certain drugs were given to the children. Therefore, don't admit to anything that might compromise you further or, indeed, any of your previous superiors. By inducing you to make these admissions, the People's Court doesn't aim at arriving at a clear understanding of what happened in the interest of what they would call justice. Instead, they will try to turn your statements against you. Which is why I advise you to make no admissions whatsoever. Repeat to the court that you don't know and can't remember. I beg you, Mrs Katschenka. Lives depend on you. Not only those of your former superiors, but your own. *Who was that on the phone?* Otto asks when she has put the receiver down, but she doesn't know what to tell him so she says that she's in a hurry because of an arrangement to see one of her woman friends. Otto's gaze goes blank again. He knows that his sister isn't going to meet a friend. She has no friends, male or female. But he does not try to prevent her from going out. When she is in the street she can't think what to do and, because she is at a loss, she boards the number 6 tram at Matzleinsdorferplatz as she used to do every morning when she went to work. It is a mistake. She understands that at once. *There she is!* she hears a voice call out from the back of the carriage. When she turns to look, there *they* all are, of course. All the crazed mothers who used to hang around the hospital gates, waiting, are now seated around her and behind her. Mrs Barth and Mrs Schelling, the mother of the girl they had to tie down all the time; Felix Keuschnig's mother, and Mrs Althofer, whose daughter was the girl with the pigeon chest. They seem to re-enact their children's behaviours: Mrs Schelling strokes her wrists constantly, as if still feeling pain where the leather straps would have marked them; Mrs Keuschnig drags her feet and pulls her legs along one at a time, just like her son; Mrs Barth's hands are constantly visiting her broad behind and she licks her lips as if they were smeared with excrement, too. And, indeed, Mrs Althofer has a pigeon chest. She sits, as if up to her ears in concerns, her pointy chin jammed into the base of her neck while her stumpy arms wave in the air. All these women are fumbling to get hold of her, touching her with their small, repulsive hands, flapping about and squeaking and shrieking. *Kill her, kill her!* they yell. She throws herself forward, begs the driver to stop, while around her the mothers are barking with wide-open maws and wildly staring eyes. A tram-stop sign slips past, the doors open and she is free of them at last. The next morning, she walks to the *Landesgericht* and says that she wants to retract everything she said in her last interview session. But the investigating judge isn't there or, perhaps, doesn't want to see her.

Stone Faces The trial of the three main defendants in the so-called Steinhof case – doctors Illing, Türk and Hübsch – began on 15 July 1946. That day was a Monday and the trial continued for the rest of that week. Anna Katschenka, nominated by the press as the leading witness for the prosecution, was called to take the stand on the second day, the Tuesday. Earlier that morning, Marie D testified. She was the mother of sixteen-year-old Martha, who had been born with a cranium as thin as a bird's egg. Martha was unable to walk or to speak, and the slightest touch caused her pain. Mrs D directs her words alternately to the judge and to the members of the public who had struggled to get in and now packed the courtroom. Everyone is following the proceedings in and around the witness stand with tense attention. Mrs D speaks of how she, from the very first, had done everything in her power to make her little daughter better. She fed her special nutritional supplements and bathed the twisted infant body in rock-salt solution to strengthen her skeleton. However, none of the many doctors she consulted dared to give her any hope. No medicine in the world can save a child like yours, one of the doctors told her. In September 1944, she had used up the last of her strength and the angelic patience that everyone who knew her agreed that she had shown, and brought her daughter to Spiegelgrund in a taxi. She was received in the clinic by Doctor Illing, who initially impressed her as 'graciousness personified'. He asked her why she hadn't sought help earlier and assured her that, to him, there were no 'hopeless cases'. When Mrs D had explained her circumstances in more detail (the child was apparently born out of wedlock and the father was simply never mentioned) and her fear that her fragile daughter would be hurt at the hands of strangers, Doctor Illing became quite upset: *Do you really believe so ill of us, Mrs D? We are here to help people like you. I am a father myself and I treat every child in this clinic as if he or she were one of my own*. But despite his vehemence, Mrs D had not felt wholly convinced. In the days that followed after she had left Martha, she made several visits to the clinic, but every time she asked to see her daughter, the staff told her that it was impossible. Doctor Illing had banned all visits in view of the child's 'weak nerves'. After another few failed attempts to see Martha, Mrs D was finally ushered into the ward where Martha's bed was. Her daughter had changed for the worse:

> Her hair had been combed straight back, her lips were blistered, her head lay weakly on the pillow and her tormented body expressed itself in incessant whimpering and weeping. That upset me more than anything else, these tears that kept flowing from her eyes, my girl who had never as much as whimpered a complaint in her entire life. I immediately asked to see the doctor and demanded to know what she had done to my daughter. Then, Doctor Türk answered that, in the first place, your daughter is very ill, her temperature is very high, and that is only to be expected with a child like yours, you must prepare for the worst.

> And then, on 23 October 1944 when, after endless waiting, I was finally allowed to see my child, death had already left its mark. Under the thin coverlet, her thin body looked famished, like a skeleton, her eyes were unnaturally large and she no longer had the strength to even lift her head from the pillow. I was close to insanity, out of control. I wanted to speak to the doctor at once but the doctor was unavailable and wouldn't be back on the ward until the following morning. I had to wait.

Next, Mrs D received a notification of bad news – a *Schlechtmeldung*. By this stage, Mrs D's identification with her ill daughter had become so intense that she describes how it felt as if she had *herself* been given a 'dose of powder' by the staff. She was struck down by fever, her temperature rose to forty-two degrees centigrade and, when a doctor was called, he diagnosed 'nerve fever'. Two days later, the final letter arrived:

> *It is our tragic duty to convey to you that your daughter Martha passed away this morning at 07.30 a.m.*

Dead, after just three and a half weeks in a hospital, Mrs D says, turning to face the dumbstruck public, *and at home, with us, she lived for fifteen and a half years!*

There are other witnesses to follow Mrs D that day, including the nursing assistant Anny Wödl. Anny Wödl was not at Steinhof but was an employee of the Allgemeines Krankenhaus. She had looked after her little boy Alfred at home for six years and was a single parent throughout. Alfred, according to Wödl, 'understood everything you said to him but couldn't speak'. His legs were apparently also not entirely functional because his walking was very poor:

> Truth to tell, none of the doctors seemed able to give us a straight account of what was wrong with Alfred. Instead, they recommended that I should place him in care of some sort. And because I'm a single woman who couldn't work and look after Alfred at the same time, I arranged for him to be taken in at Gugging, which had a good reputation.

But then 1938 arrived, the republic was dissolved and the Nazis took over. Terrible rumours were doing the rounds among people who worked in healthcare, stories about how the new authorities dealt with the old and the mentally ill. One of Wödl's closest colleagues at the AKH had a son who was mentally retarded and had been at Steinhof since several years back. Now, she visited him as often as she could because she was so worried that something would be done to him. The day came when she arrived at Steinhof only to be told that her son was no longer a patient there. He had been transferred, as part of war-related measures, as they said – *kriegsbedingte Massnahme*. By then, all official decisions and all newly introduced systems of social order were explained in terms of the war effort and its demands. The boy's mother was told that he was now in a spa resort on the German Baltic coast. A couple of weeks later, she received a letter telling her that her son had 'died suddenly'. Around this time, thousands of other women in Wien also received letters speaking of 'sudden death' having struck down their children, parents or close relatives. Those who approached the hospital board at Steinhof and demanded to be told more about these deaths, and in particular what caused them, were referred to the city's main office for public health, the Hauptgesundheitsamt, on Schottenring, but once there, the enquirers were referred on again, this time to various committees within the Ministry for Internal Affairs in Berlin. By then, all important decisions were made in Berlin. One group of distraught women decided to club together and send a representative to Berlin, charged with making enquiries and demanding answers. The women chose Anny Wödl to represent them (even though Wödl herself had not yet shared their experiences; her son Alfred was still in the Gugging home and well cared for). 'People from Wien plead for their relatives' – *Wiener bitten für Angehörige* – is the entry in the visitor's book at the ministry on Tiergartenstrasse 4 in Berlin on 23 July 1940, the day Nurse Assistant Anny Wödl arrived in the capital of the Reich. She was received by Doctor Herbert Linden, Secretary of State with responsibility for Section IV, which dealt with healthcare and public health – *Gesundheitswesen und Volkspflege*. This section (abbreviated T4) had final say in decisions about which individuals in the Reich should be weeded out for reasons, as related to racial purity or social medicine, that turned them into so many millstones around the neck of the healthcare system, already under severe strain from the war effort. What must be prioritised, after all, was to make the system ready to serve the essentially healthy and fit for work, whose contributions of course include producing future generations of children in sound mental and physical health and, thus, enhancing the racial stock. Doctor Linden explained all this in precise detail to Anny Wödl and his calm, matter-of-fact kindness included an element of firmness. He also commented on the need for the transport of patients to take place at night since it prevented unnecessary and potentially damaging rumours from spreading among the general public. Furthermore, it must be obvious to all that Wien and Ostmark could not be exempt from a healthcare policy that by definition applied to the entire Reich. There was a war on, after all. Germany must be prepared to strengthen its preparedness on all fronts. That means the internal front as well, he said. How are we to keep up our preparedness to go into battle if, for reasons of sentiment or similar feelings, we end up soiling our race, undermining our morals and weakening our will and our strength of character? And that was that. Wödl had to accept that this message was all she would ever get to bring back from Berlin. She set out for Wien and, in January 1941, half a year later, she learnt in various underhand ways that her son Alfred had been forced to undergo a new medical examination which showed that the boy suffered from what the doctor described as 'athetotis'. The symptoms are spasmodic, involuntary movements that are often slow and oddly writhing; in addition to the motor effects, co-ordination was also disturbed. The doctor suggested that the condition might have followed an attack of encephalitis, the same inflammation of the membranes around the brain that had also caused Alfred to develop 'a medium degree of debility' and meant that he became almost permanently bedridden. On 6 February, Anny Wödl received a card, sent to the AKH ward where she was working at the time. The card stated:

Your son, Alfred Wödl, on the date as shown above, was admitted to the clinic for children under the control of Wiener Städtische Jugendfürsorgeanstalt known as 'Am Spiegelgrund', 109/14 Sanatoriumstrasse 2, Wien.

On 15 February, Doctor Heinrich Gross examined Alfred and also took a photograph of him. In the photo, the miracle-boy Alfred Wödl stares with serious, eerily enquiring eyes at the doctor and his camera. Perhaps the child had not quite grasped what an enlightening observation Gross felt that he had just made. The doctor added a triumphant note to Alfred's record: *The child is half Jewish! (15.02.41).* Clearly, the pieces had clicked into place: Alfred was born out of wedlock, the Wödl woman had never disclosed who the father was and the boy's condition had never been ascribed to a credible medical cause. Meanwhile, Anny Wödl succeeded in getting in touch with the Spiegelgrund clinic's medical director, Doctor Erwin Jekelius. Many years later, she tells the court that she had completely given up on hoping to save her child and says this about the meeting with Jekelius:

> All I wanted was to stop them from transferring Alfred to somewhere else. If it was necessary for him to die then I at least wanted to make sure that he wouldn't suffer. So I asked Doctor Jekelius in case he felt that he could not save my son's life, he could surely see to it that Alfred's death was as quick and painless as possible. If he did, or if he passed the task on to someone else and, if so, what that person did – I don't know.

Anny Wödl sits looking down and crying quietly. The courtroom is still and silent. The chairman of the bench calls the witness Anna Katschenka. The chief witness for the prosecution. Now, the atmosphere among the public changes to outrage. Someone screams *murderess!* when Katschenka is escorted into the court. She walks at her usual slow pace but to the public it looks as if she tries to resist the two court attendants who hold on to her arms. To those who know her, she seems wearier than before. She will now be asked to testify about the actions of the defendants, who are seated together, Hübsch and Illing on either side of Türk. They all stare at her with inexpressive faces. Faces set in stone. It is impossible to tell whether they feel ill at ease or are supremely indifferent. The prosecutor starts speaking at once about the so-called mercy killing of children. He reads aloud from a text which sets out the events following a child's admission: the physical examination followed by a report to the committee in Berlin, and the subsequent response by Spiegelgrund staff to the ministry's decision about the child, including any recommended 'treatment'.

Have I described all this correctly, Mrs Katschenka?

Anna Katschenka doesn't know what to say. She looks at the stone faces opposite her, then down at her hands – worn, rough-skinned but clean hands, used to doing what they intend, effectively, be it to tuck in a corner of a sheet or compress a vein before inserting the syringe needle; they are supportive, helpful and sometimes punitive hands and not the kind that are mere tools. You cannot ignore what they have been up to. Sometimes, she has thought that her hands are her: all she is. And sometimes, at night, she has put them on her face and thought that they should stay there, stay for so long that they fuse to her skin. She doesn't know if this would be a gesture towards expressing shame or grief or abandonment or all of these things at the same time. But she knows that she will sit with her face resting on those hands until the sentence is announced and the stone faces will observe her with their high-minded or indifferent eyes and everyone will think that she is to be punished as it is only what she deserves, given the acts these hands have carried out.

PROSECUTOR: Can you tell me when and by what means you were first informed that the euthanasia – mercy killing – was practised on the clinic's children?

ANNA KATSCHENKA: I had never in my entire professional life seen patients who were as ill as these children and, in no other hospital, experienced anything like this clinic.

PROSECUTOR: That is not what we're talking about at present. When did you find out that children were euthanised at the clinic where you were working?

ANNA KATSCHENKA: I had heard rumours suggesting that adult, mentally ill patients at Steinhof had been killed.

PROSECUTOR: As for the children . . .

ANNA KATSCHENKA: I knew nothing about that.

CHAIRMAN OF THE BENCH: [interrupts] Mrs Katschenka, you have stated in interviews prior to this trial that even Doctor Jekelius systematically terminated the lives of children who had been deemed unfit to live by the committee in Berlin and that your allotted task was precisely this: to judge who was due for termination and who should continue to be under observation. It was the point of the whole enterprise, if you excuse the levity. Children were subjected to euthanasia in the clinic. Is that not so?

ANNA KATSCHENKA: There might have been certain suspicions.

PROSECUTOR: Suspicions about what?

ANNA KATSCHENKA: About the procedures not being quite right but more . . .

PROSECUTOR: *But more*?

ANNA KATSCHENKA: More than that I can't say.

CHAIRMAN: [interrupts] Excuse me, Mrs Katschenka, but you initially were the Ward Sister and later also Deputy Matron. It was part of your conditions of work – indeed, of your duties – to see to it that the sick children were treated according to doctor's orders. It is simply not possible that you remained unaware of what the medical staff prescribed for the children.

ANNA KATSCHENKA: Yes . . . that's true.

CHAIRMAN: Or are you suggesting the children themselves got hold of these powerful drugs?

[*Ripples of nervous laughter in the audience.*]

ANNA KATSCHENKA: [. . .]

CHAIRMAN: In the preparatory hearings, you stated the following about how the 'special treatments' were carried out: [*reads*] *For those who were able to eat more or less normally, we mixed the medication into the food. For very ill infants who couldn't swallow, we administered drops of morphine in very small doses. The larger children were mainly given Luminal.* Furthermore, in your answer to the question 'And everyone knew that treatment of this kind would end in a death?' you replied unconditionally that yes, it would would end in death, and yes, everyone did know. On whose orders did you do these things?

ANNA KATSCHENKA: [*weeps*]

PROSECUTOR: Were the orders in fact not given by the three defendants, seated here in the courtroom today?

the stone faces

ANNA KATSCHENKA: Doctor Illing . . . and Doctor Türk both paid great attention to the well-being of the children and there were no objections to the manner in which they treated the children.

CHAIRMAN: [*speaking sharply*] Mrs Katschenka! Who or what has caused you to say these things today which are completely the opposite of what you said in the investigation interviews? During the time that has passed since then, what kinds of pressure you been under? And who has exerted this pressure?

ANNA KATSCHENKA: [*weeps*]

the stone faces

CHAIRMAN: I would like the two court attendants to step forward.

[*The court attendants approach hesitatingly.*]

Please, Mrs Katschenka, will you stand up now?

[*Katschenka attempts to stand.*]

I hereby order that this witness is arrested and imprisoned with immediate effect on the grounds that she is suspected of being an accomplice to murder. From now on, this woman is under arrest.

Much celebration in the courtroom. Anna Katschenka does try to stand up but on hearing the words of the most senior judge present, she sinks back onto her seat and almost falls forward, burying her face in her hands. When the attendants put their hands under her arms to support her, her weeping makes her shoulders shake so much it is almost impossible to raise her. For a brief moment, the woman, her face streaming with tears, looks up at the three stone faced doctors on the defendants' seats: superiors whom she for this last time could not bring herself to betray. When she is led away, the audience is in uproar. This is more than anyone dared to hope for: a murderess who is arrested right in front of witnesses and victims. The three stone faces stay where they are. Illing turns his head slightly away, as if he found the entire performance repulsive.

Atonement The sentence in the separate trial of Anna Katschenka was announced in April 1948. She was condemned to eight years in prison with the additional punishment of three months' hard labour every year. She was to do her time in Maria Lankowitz, a women's prison near Graz. The prison housed more than three hundred inmates who had to sleep in cells shared between up to twenty prisoners at a time. The cells lacked toilets and running water. The only source of warmth was a big stove in the middle of the room which was only sparingly supplied with fuel, even in the winter. Of course, tightly packed human bodies give off their own warmth. During the first few months, before her cell was changed, she had nowhere to keep her personal belongings and nowhere to sit except on her bunk. The prison board did not encourage differentiation between inmates on grounds of their offences. Women who had been served more than year-long terms for theft, fraud or falsification of official documents sometimes shared cells with murderers on life sentences. For a while, Anna Katschenka was courted by a younger woman who had poisoned and killed her own daughter. To look at, this woman seemed ordinary enough. She kept clean and neat, was always polite and respectful, if perhaps a little distracted at times. If spoken to, she inclined her head and smiled enigmatically with her eyes fixed on the floor or a nearby wall. Her interest in Katschenka was quite rational: she had read about the Steinhof trials and was simply keen to know how Katschenka and her colleagues had 'gone about doing it'. They never shared a cell, which was just as well, because Anna Katschenka soon came to dread her like the plague. The woman was a curse that had taken on human shape. Katschenka tried her best to avoid having to pass her in the corridors and always left the prisoners' canteen as soon the poisoner turned up. She even went to the length of formally asking to be moved to the so-called Labour Building where prostitutes and drug addicts were held. Later on, she withdrew inside herself and deliberately avoided all contact with people, warders and fellow prisoners alike, and stayed silent unless ordered to speak up. She was haunted by a recurring image of herself *alone* on the defendant's seat. Again and again, other details from the trial proceedings also came back to her mind. Officially, the prosecution's case was not just against her but also her colleagues in pavilion 15: Maria Bohlenrath, Erna Storch, Emilie Kragulj and Cläre Kleinschmittger. But she had been given to understand that the police had failed to find and arrest any of them, despite extensive searches. What would have happened if she hadn't returned to the hospital that day? What would have happened if she had stuck to her original witness statement regardless of Illing and Türk's confessions and washed her hands of the accusations, insisting, as had Marianne Türk, that what she had done only amounted to carrying out orders given by others. After all, decisions about treating or not treating were made in Berlin and not in the clinic at Spiegelgrund. *I only did my duty*. Now and then, she forced herself to go even further back in time: what if she hadn't applied for that post at Spiegelgrund with Jekelius? But at that point, her speculations had to stop. There had been a war on. If she couldn't earn, what would her family have lived on? She was her father's supporting arm, her mother's map of the world. She felt now that, by being locked up, she had let her patients down and betrayed her responsibility towards them. The days went by, and the years, each day being added onto the previous one like a small cog in a wheel that moved a tiny little bit closer to the end of her prison term. All the while, another bigger wheel, whose cogs made it move in the opposite direction towards her own ageing and death, seemed to drive her deeper and deeper into darkness. The burden of punishment never became lighter but instead ever more impossible to endure. Altogether, she was to spend four years, five months and eight days of her life in prison, including the time in police cells. Throughout, she who had spent her professional life watching and judging others had to put up with being watched herself, having every aspect of her body and personality measured and weighed, scrutinised and analysed. Her lawyer's application for parole led to her being subjected to a wide range of medical examinations in April 1950. The records show that her already sparse hair had thinned further and gone grey. Her body, always a little on the sturdy side, had swelled and hardened. Katschenka cannot stand being touched by strangers and bursts into tears easily. She is said to suffer from cyclical attacks of depression and these pronounced mood swings, together with her enhanced sensitivity and marked secretory activity, were considered by the examining doctor to be symptoms of excess thyroid hormone production, which would also fit with her irritability. From the application for parole, it is also clear that Katschenka has gained exceptionally high approval ratings for good behaviour. She works as an assistant in the prison hospital and is praised by the doctors for her 'diligence and sober attention to detail, her willingness to help at all times and her gentle and sensible manner'. She is allowed to leave the prison in December 1950, but her release is conditional and the remainder of her sentence has been changed into a five-year-long trial period. She is now allowed to look for real work and manages to land a job after about six months of applying: the post is in a children's hospital, the St Anna Kinderspital on Kinderspitalgasse in Wien's 9th Bezirk. Now she can work with children, the kind of nursing she loves better than any other, as she has claimed in her witness statement and parole application. But the St Anna Kinderspital is a private hospital. Her position in the city health-care system was lost the moment she was sacked from Spiegelgrund. A permanent post, with the possibility of a payout on retirement of what she had saved for her pension, is out of her reach unless she becomes fully rehabilitated. So far, all her applications have been refused. In September 1956, when a last application has again been turned down, she appeals in a letter to the Minister of Justice, Otto Tschadek, pleading that he should intervene on her behalf:

> Most highly esteemed Minister,
>
> I believe that I need not try to express how hard this refusal has been for me other than to say that, after all these years of worry and grief, I hoped once more to have the right to feel a worthy human being. The documentation I have enclosed demonstrates

that, since my release from prison, I have strenuously devoted myself to return to my previous profession of nursing, and also what difficulties my efforts encountered. I have to support my elderly parents and also build a new existence for myself. My sentence entailed the loss of my post in the Gemeinde Wien after 21 years of service and also my old-age pension since I can work only in privately run institutions. In January 1951, I applied to Gemeinde Wien for reinstatement in the healthcare services but have to this day not had any reply even though influential civil servants have intervened on my behalf.

I grew up in a Socialist family. My father, Otto Katschenka, was a printer and has been a member of the Social Democratic Party since 1895. On his 80th birthday (14 November 1954), the party honoured him in many ways and he was also given a photo of President Doctor Körner, dedicated and signed, as my father and the President worked shoulder to shoulder on the construction of the ski-jump slope in Kobenzl. I was a member of the Social Democratic Party from 1923 to 1934 and re-joined in 1945.

My father had a stroke in July this year and I live alone with him and my mother, who I have to both care for and support with money.

Most revered Minister, I beg you with all my heart to help me so that I no longer have to carry the burden of the legal consequences of the verdict against me. I have received the most laudatory recommendations throughout my years of service and have never been a bad human being, but was dragged into court proceedings due to unfortunate circumstances. I was only the executive arm of the Spiegelgrund board and have surely atoned for the acts that the conditions of my post forced me to carry out.

Please, Herr Minister, help a decent human being and a Socialist who will always be deeply grateful and work hard to be worthy of your support.

With greatest regards,
Anna Katschenka

Also this last application is refused. Anna Katschenka is never rehabilitated. Sixty-one years old, she dies in Wien in February 1966.

XVI

The Survivors

What's the point of digging up the past, we must learn to look ahead There's a kind of forgetfulness, Adrian Ziegler says, that isn't the same as failing to remember but makes you feel that your brain has gone numb. Believe you me, he says, I'm very familiar with that kind of forgetfulness. I've suffered from it all my life. You do things as if life is just a meaningless backdrop, and nothing of what other people say or do to you matters. Not even the very worst or most horrible events really get through to you. You might call it 'not remembering' or you begin to think that you don't understand the meaning of your own acts. Can an entire country be in the grip of that kind of forgetfulness? Heinrich Gross was on the run from the collapsed Eastern Front, made a failed attempt to cross the river Elbe and was captured by Soviet soldiers. That was in May 1945. He then spent more than two years in a Soviet prison camp at Kohtla-Järve in northern Estonia. The camp held almost fifteen thousand POWs but had only twenty doctors. Gross realised that he could be seen to be useful and the camp bosses soon came to appreciate him as a keen and trustworthy doctor. He was allowed to study Russian in his spare time. When he returned to Austria in December 1947, a recently released POW, the court proceedings against the three principal defendants in the Steinhof trial were already completed. Doctor Illing had been condemned to pay the maximum penalty and was executed by hanging on 30 November 1946. Doctor Hübsch was freed and Doctor Türk sentenced to ten years in prison. Heinrich

Gross knew that he would have to face the court and made some half-hearted stabs at lying low, but was found and arrested after only a few months. However, despite Anna Katschenka's witness statement naming Doctor Gross as one of the superiors who had ordered her to kill the children, deaths that she had herself been condemned for, the *Volksgericht* of Wien sentenced Gross to spend just two years in prison. The guilty verdict was promptly challenged in a higher court, which declared the entire *Volksgericht* trial invalid due to technical errors. Unlike Doctor Türk, who could not appeal against her verdict because she had admitted in interviews that she had acted knowingly and with intent to kill – as Türk had stated: *On the rare occasions when the child in question failed to respond normally to the sleeping drug, I would administer an injection of Modiscop* [a combination drug of two morphine-based compounds and scopolamine], *usually, say, three to four ampoules, a dose that led to death within twelve hours* – Doctor Gross admitted to nothing, neither acts nor intentions. Gross knew all about death by natural causes as well as the other kind and, as far as he was concerned, the children cared for at Spiegelgrund had died from natural causes, that is to say illness, inherited or acquired. Anyone could read that in the case notes. Pneumonia, for instance, was the most common cause of death. Certainly, if certain sedatives or hypnotics like Luminal, for argument's sake, were given in excessive doses it could lead to symptoms similar to gastrointestinal disorder, as had been described in some of the children. However, many diseases are also associated with such symptoms. Doctor Gross, unlike Anna Katschenka, never contradicted himself and maintained an aura of composed, somewhat arrogant vagueness throughout the proceedings. He admitted only to things that could definitely be pinned on him, ignored everything else, and made a show of regarding whatever was presented as 'evidence' of his alleged wrongdoing as no more than a ragbag of isolated items, all capable of different interpretations depending on your perspective. He also consistently talked down his own contributions as a doctor at the institution:

Yes, in 1941 I took over the responsibility for the infant care in pavilion 15.
Doctor Jekelius tasked me with medical photography of sick children under his supervision. I worked there until the summer of 1942, kept case notes and took photographs of children.
[. . .]
Certainly, a photographic record was kept of all the children. Including the children in the reform school.
[. . .]
Was there any psychiatric value to be had from the photographs? That I can't say at present. With regard to the children I photographed, some of the marked malformations were certainly of medical interest. Dreadful cases, sometimes: children with hydrocephalic skulls a metre in diameter. That kind of thing!
[. . .]
No, this had nothing to do with racial biology. It is essential that you grasp the distinction between the photographs I produced for the clinic to use with the case notes, and those of the youths . . .
[. . .]
Jekelius might have used the photographs for some purpose to do with racial biology, that's possible but I can't comment . . .
[. . .]
Indeed, the work was very demanding. There were only two or three doctors attached to the clinic and each one had to be on call just about every second or third night. The doctor on duty also had

to establish death and sign the death certificate. But signing the certificate didn't imply that you were certain of the cause of death or were even familiar with the case.

[...]

No, I have no idea of any circular [from Berlin]. *And you say it stated that members of the clinical staff were to administer medication in higher doses than recommended? Are you trying to make a fool of me? No doctor of sound mind would ever dream of doing anything of the sort.*

In May 1951, all further proceedings against Doctor Gross are cancelled, the accusations against him withdrawn and he is free to carry on in his old career. Which he does, with immediate effect. During the next two decades, he publishes very frequently in medical journals. His publication list runs into hundreds of articles concerning neurological defects and appropriate diagnostic methods. In 1959, Gross and colleagues publish an article in the *Vienna Journal of Neurology and Related Specialisms* (*Wiener Zeitschrift für Nervenheilkunde und deren Grenzgebiete*) that is entitled 'Concerning Major Malformations of the Cerebral Ventricular System'. It is a study of common pathological changes of the fluid-containing spaces of the brain, with an attempt at explaining how these defects could come about. In his introduction, Doctor Gross informs his readers that he bases his research on having been offered *access to the remarkable collection of good-quality anatomical specimens kept by the autopsy unit at the healthcare institution Heil- und Pflegeanstalt 'Am Steinhof'.* This archive of hundreds of preserved brains *is probably the greatest and most wide-ranging collection of its kind available anywhere in this country.* That the institutional source of the fixed brains was Gross's earlier place of work is clear from the anonymised case histories that the authors describe in this article and in a later series of scientific articles. In other words, the specimens are the brains and assorted endocrine glands that the senior registrar in charge of autopsies, Barbara Uiberrak, spoke of during the Steinhof trial as 'exceedingly interesting from a scientific point of view'. She then went on to suggest that, every year, a few of them should be studied, and Doctor Gross obviously followed up on her suggestion. While Doctor Heinrich Gross carries on analysing the cases of the children he had helped to kill, his reputation as a scientist and psychiatrist spreads ever more widely. In 1957, he is appointed as medical director at the Rosenhügel hospital in Lainz. By 1962, he is back in his former doctor's villa on the Steinhof site and is applying for the directorship of the entire hospital. In 1968, he is offered the post as head of the Ludwig Boltzmann Institute's unit for research into malformations of the nervous system and, at about this time, he also starts out on a long and successful career as a forensic psychiatrist. During the 1960s and early 1970s, the courts consult him almost routinely for his written assessments of many criminals whose mental health is in question. Decisions on sentence tariffs and eventual treatments are based on his judgements. He states himself that, by 1978, he has found time to write no less than 12,000 of these reports. Doctor Gross is widely regarded as knowledgeable, thorough and efficient, and this efficiency of his is particularly appreciated by the courts. Requests never stay for long in his in-tray. And it is in his capacity as forensic psychiatrist that Doctor Gross, one morning in November 1975, encounters one of his former Spiegelgrund patients. It takes some time, though, before he realises just whom he is dealing with.

A Talk with My Psychiatrist

DOCTOR GROSS: [*reads*] Ziegler, Adrian . . . Where were you born, Mr Ziegler?

ADRIAN Z: In Wien.

DOCTOR GROSS: So you're an Austrian citizen?

ADRIAN Z: Yes.

DOCTOR GROSS: And your mother's name is?

ADRIAN Z: Dobrosch.

DOCTOR GROSS: [*takes notes, no noticeable reaction*] And your father?

ADRIAN Z: What do you mean?

DOCTOR GROSS: Do you know who your father is? Have you met him?

ADRIAN Z: Ziegler is my father's name. He and my mother married in 1939.
They divorced later on.

DOCTOR GROSS: Is your father still alive?

ADRIAN Z: No, he died in 1970. He was an alcoholic.

DOCTOR GROSS: And before that? Did your mother and father live together?

ADRIAN Z: Periodically.

DOCTOR GROSS: And what about you, Mr Ziegler? [*His lips pout and twist into something that is meant to be a smile.*] I can assure you that you can be completely open with me.

ADRIAN Z: My younger brother and I were given away to be adopted. I was taken in by a family called the Haidingers. However, they didn't want me. Instead I was sent off to Spiegelgrund. It was in 1941. Early that year, in January. Which must have been about the same time as when you arrived there, Doctor Gross.

DOCTOR GROSS: [*Says nothing, lets his gaze float up towards the ceiling, then slowly back down.*]

ADRIAN Z: [...]

DOCTOR GROSS: [*in a surprisingly sharp voice*] It means that you were there . . . now, between which years, Mr Ziegler?

ADRIAN Z: That ought to be on record in your papers, but perhaps you'll remember anyway. There was a largish examination room that was used as a lecture hall on the ground floor in pavilion 15. Because Doctor Illing regarded me as a sample of a mixed-race person – a *Mischling* – I was made to stand naked in front of a lot of nursing students until he dispatched me with a slap on the bum like some tame animal. When the treatment was done with, I was to be sent off to labour camp but the truck that was to transport us never turned up and because a young woman cleaner had left an upstairs window in the pavilion open I had a chance to get out. Which led to my first punishment. Doctor Illing ordered a report on me by a forensic psychiatrist. That was in 1944.

DOCTOR GROSS: These documents are not available anymore, I believe.

ADRIAN Z: Yes, they are. In his report, Doctor Illing writes about my grave inherited defects, about my sociopathic mentality and says that from psychiatric and psychological perspectives I must be regarded as a chronic recidivist criminal.

DOCTOR GROSS: Have you ever spoken to anyone about this?

ADRIAN Z: No, there has been no call to do that.

DOCTOR GROSS: Are there any other people from that time whom you know or are still in contact with?

ADRIAN Z: Yes, Some of them are still around. But I won't name any of them. I don't think that would be appropriate just now.

DOCTOR GROSS: [*baffled*] Well, yes. Indeed, no need to talk all that at this point. Other times, other times. I for one am glad all that is in the past. And I feel sure that you too, Mr Ziegler, are glad that the times are long gone. Indeed, we won't rake over these old stories. If you agree to keep this between you and me I promise in my turn to put in a good word to the court on your behalf and arrange for you to be let off as lightly as possible.

Crime and Punishment But Doctor Gross doesn't keep his promise. He does exactly the opposite and uses Doctor Illing's report from 1944 as the basis for what he himself writes about Adrian on the same day as their talk. Already as a child, opines Doctor Gross, Adrian Z proved that his seriously disturbed ability to sustain relationships by betraying and cheating and engaging in various forms of incestuous and homosexual acts. Several placements in foster homes followed until he was admitted to a clinic for paediatric nervous disorders.

He goes on to quote in detail from Illing's 1944 report, the very same document that he had tried to deny existed during his talk with Adrian:

> *It follows that from psychiatric and psychological perspectives the accused must be regarded as past rehabilitation. The accused is not only an active sociopath but must from psychiatric and psychological perspectives be regarded as a chronic recidivist criminal.*

Adrian Z's crime consists of receiving 20,000 schilling as a fee for being an accomplice to criminals who had done a major robbery. The court, after consideration of the psychiatric report by Doctor Heinrich Gross, sentences Adrian to six years in prison followed by ten years in a special detention centre for gravely disturbed, recidivist criminals.

Safe Haven Adrian Ziegler's cell in the prison in Stein an der Donau was not much larger than the solitary-confinement cell in pavilion 9. There was just room for a toilet, a wash-hand basin and, high up on the wall, a barred window which he covered with a blue curtain. He had sewn the curtain himself on an old treadle-powered sewing machine that he kept in a worn, brown suitcase right at the back of the wardrobe. This was how he gradually transformed his appalling, bitterly cold exile into a thriftily and effectively furnished home, full of useful things, though there was no room for anything superfluous. Above and underneath the neatly made bed (if there was one single thing I learnt at Spiegelgrund, he said, it was how to make beds) books were stacked, either in double rows on the shelves or in tottering piles to save space once the shelves were too packed to hold any more. His books were of every kind. He had Thucydides's *History of the Peloponnesian War*, translated novels by Steinbeck and Conrad, and political biographies, as well as textbooks in social medicine and pedagogics and accounts of the development of modern psychiatry. One treatise that he had become particularly intrigued by was a 1916 essay by Julius Tandler, the well-known Social Democratic spokesman for the rights of the working classes to sanitary homes and working conditions. The essay is called 'Krieg und Bevölkerung' ('War and the Population') and was one long plea that society must stop supporting the people Tandler called society's 'negative variants' (*Minusvarianten*; Ziegler had underlined the word) or else, if one carried on propping them up, there was a risk that racially inferior traits would be propagated into future generations instead of grafting characteristics such as strength, skill and capacity to survive onto the human breed. I realise now how little I knew as a child at Steinhof, Adrian said later. I never understood how deeply views of this sort had penetrated into every pore of society and how devilishly calculated and regulated, to the very last detail, the whole system was. How just about all parents were visited by agents from the social services, just as my mother was. And how people who worked in the social service offices, as well as the staff in all children's homes and hospitals, had to fill in a form for every child that they figured might be flawed in some way or who seemed not to measure up – to whatever standard. And then, these children were simply taken away from their parents. While I was in Spiegelgrund, I had to sit for two weeks alone in a cell like this one. *Einzeln gegeben*, that's what they called it. It was just routine; the slightest thing that annoyed the nurses could mean that you were punished like that. It's a fact that I can't quite remember what I was punished for, only that I, just once, after having spent something like a week, maybe ten days in the cell, I asked if I couldn't have a book to read or a sheet of paper to write on or anything at all to keep me occupied, but instead of a book or a sheet of paper I got Doctor Illing. And he brought the clapper and was in a furious mood and said that I had no right to ask for anything at all and all I needed to learn was to bend down and obey. He made me stand on all fours like an animal while he flogged me with the clapper. If the punishments really were senseless, if they didn't keep us locked up in order to do what they said the school was for, which was to educate us, teach us to read and write and behave decently, then what *was* the intention behind it all? Why hit and hit and hit until the child can neither sit nor stand afterwards? What was the point? At least I'm allowed books to read now, he said. Ziegler was regarded as an oddball by his fellow prisoners at Stein, and by the wardens and social workers and other people he came into contact with as well. Nobody else had a cell like his, kitted out like a cross between a haberdasher's and a library. He was known as a talker who held forth without anybody understanding much of what he was on about or even picking up what was the meaning of all that talk. The words formed a screen that he held up in front of himself to prevent anyone from seeing and finding out what was buried deep inside. Ziegler was a loner who had learnt to socialise with his loneliness as if it were a kind of company. His face had grown sharp-edged and square, with its strong chin and prominent frontal and cheekbones which made it look almost like a mask, an impression that was emphasised by the broad-rimmed glasses he habitually wore at the time. His skin was coarse and grey as if all the concrete and stone that surrounded him had settled in his pores. But the look in his eyes was frank and curious although, now and then, it could start shifting about and make him seem utterly absent. At these moments, his mouth would keep moving and he became involved in long arguments with many tangled details only to say, suddenly, *I don't remember, I've no memory of that.* He often showed photographs and documents he had collected and stuck carefully into different albums. He showed pictures of his mother (Leonie Dobrosch-Ziegler) wearing her bridal veil. And one of Uncle Ferenc, relaxed on the bare riverbank down by Hubertusdamm, lying on his side with his head supported by his hand. The naked skin on his chest shows under his jacket and is as dark as the skin on his face. The pictures of Adrian's brothers and sisters show Laura, who looked determined even as a child, with her broad arms crossed and resting on the table the children have gathered around: Helmut clinging onto the back of a chair and the two younger sisters, Helga and Hannelore, sitting on their mother's lap. Leonie's red lips almost part in that anxious, cherry-lipped smile that Adrian would so often describe. He also had pictures of the woman he married and later ran away from, Elfriede, and of his daughter Missi. He had laboriously copied each and every one of the letters he wrote to her from prison into a large, black notebook and then stuck her letter in response on the opposing page. He used to write to her at least once a week. They didn't meet that often, of course. When they did speak together, they only rarely talked about his childhood and never about his time in Spiegelgrund. He was not unwilling to tell others about Spiegelgrund, but as time went by it became harder for him to find concrete details to catch and hold people's attention. He said that he increasingly didn't remember things or that the monotony and uneventfulness he had experienced later in life set everything adrift in his mind. He would revisit certain sensations and events, though. One was seeing Nurse Mutsch's mane of black hair, that one and only time when she let it down. It had made an overwhelming impression on him. Then, there was the night when Julius Becker had stabbed himself in the belly with a pair of scissors, and the battle of the bullet casings or the period of 'Pototschnik's rule', as he called it. But he remained vague about what happened after his escape, when he spent time with 'the idiots' and then with the dying in the gallery of pavilion 17. He did say that he was subjected to one of Doctor Illing's air-into-the-skull X-rays and described the pain and other side effects extremely convincingly. But the notes in his diary are very unclear and it is impossible to be certain that any such investigation was actually carried out. When his sentence was reduced and he was released from prison, he went out to Steinhof a few times, though it seems that these trips didn't do much to help him remember more of the past. He walked along the long lateral driveways that extend from the rising track that forms the central axis. In early afternoon, the only sounds are the persistent cawing of the crows and the hollow whispering of the wind as it blows through the canopies of the trees; always the same unchanging wind, wide and calm. Because many of the pavilions are still in use, it is difficult for an ordinary visitor to get access. On one visit, a pavilion stands empty for refurbishment and Adrian takes the chance to have a look inside. Near the entrance, the corridor has been piled high with old enamelled items, toilet seats and the like, giving off an acidic smell of dust and damp. All the wash-hand basins have been ripped off the washroom walls and only the rust-eaten tap sockets are sticking out from the bare plaster walls. But the long row of shower cabins is still there, and even one of the big tubs where the bed-wetters were dealt with by being rolled into wet sheets and then alternately dunked into the water and lifted up again. *Schlempern lassen*, Adrian recalls that the procedure was called officially. (Nurses Mutsch and Demeter standing on either side of the tub with the leaden weight of the wet body dangling inside the sheet they have stretched between them.) As Adrian remembers it, the doors to the dormitories were equipped with hatches to let the nurses on night duty check that the children were in bed, but in this pavilion at least, the doors are smooth and in one piece. The waist-high band of evil-smelling brown oil paint that he remembers so clearly as running along the lower part of the corridor walls is not there anymore. But the rhomboid pattern of the floor tiles is the same and, at the doors and along the skirting boards, the tiles are so worn that the pattern is fading. And the windows, with their grilles and lockable braces, let in this very special, empty light that has all colour and substance filtered out and leached away. It is a light without shadows or space: a light without memory. In the area around the hospital, the tracks run along their old, accustomed paths, the same tracks where the children marched off to their excursions, with Mrs Rohrbach or Mrs Krämer leading them. Gallitzinberg is also there to be climbed and the air-defence culverts and passages can be examined on old blueprints. On one of the south-facing slopes, hidden behind rough boulders and half-overgrown with mosses and roots, you can locate the entrance to the entire system, the same entrance through which Baldur von Schirach must have made his way to safety when Wien capitulated in the last days of April 1945. The angels on the top of the mountain are missing, though. They were the children's guardian angels who, or so Hannes Neubauer insisted, looked exactly like the stone angels that were part of the ornamental façade of the church overlooking the pavilions. When the air-raid sirens screamed at night he'd always thought the sound came from the angels. But only young women, not much older than the boys, worked inside the bare, cement-lined rooms carved out of the rock. They had earphones clamped to their heads and spoke into microphones. Once, when Hannes Neubauer was listening to the radio in Nurse Mutsch's room, he had heard one of these women speak. She was *Mrs Cuckoo* who, in her cool ethereal voice, told of air raids to come and reported on the damage afterwards. There is a picture of her sitting at her post, a very young girl, perhaps fourteen or fifteen years old, with shoulder-length hair cut with a straight fringe, and a face that radiated scared self-confidence. The wall behind her was hung with abstract-looking maps showing the movements of the enemy planes. If the Allies had bombed just this installation, if only they had known that the Austrian Nazi regime had concentrated their entire air-defence control system inside the mountain, all of it could have been wiped out with one precise hit. One huge blast could have eliminated them all, not only those who were keeping watch around the clock inside the Mountain, but all the sick and retarded, the degenerate and the useless, all these *inhuman* creatures who inhabited the pavilions at the foot of the mountain. No angelic alarm call in the universe could have saved them.

The Archive of the Dead In March 1997, a previously locked cellar under the old autopsy rooms at Steinhof was opened up and, inside it, the body parts of almost eight hundred children, all one-time 'patients' at the Spiegelgrund clinic, were discovered. The items removed from their corpses were stored in thirty-centimetre-tall glass jars, carefully labelled, numbered and lined up on the dusty shelving. No personal details are given on the labels. The specimens were sorted by age and gender (e.g. *4 J* – it stood for: boy [*Junge*], aged 4) or body weight (e.g. *10 kg*) but the labels usually also state the main diagnoses, written with blue ink that has faded over the years – *Results: Normal; Diagnosis: Idiocy*. All belong to what Doctor Gross has referred to in innumerable scientific articles as his personal set of anatomical specimens: *a remarkable range of good-quality anatomical specimens . . . probably the greatest and most wide-ranging collection of its kind available anywhere in this country.* Behind the grimy glass, whole brains or dissected bits of the central nervous system float in viscous formaldehyde solution; a child's jaw with a preserved growth clinging to it like swollen seaweed; an entire face floating as if in a dream, with its eyes closed while its slightly parted lips curl in an expression of perennial wonder. Between the rows of tightly packed glass jars, the jars on the next rack of shelving can be glimpsed. An ever-unfolding perspective, as one line of shelves opens out into a view of another in a space that seems without end. The search for the identity of individuals will surely also go on forever, with the numbered jars being checked against case-note entries to find the diagnosis of the brain damage so that each anonymous specimen is seen to have been part of someone once alive. *Whole body paralysis. Hermine A.* Hermine is admitted to Spiegelgrund on 8 February 1943 and Doctor Illing's diagnosis is *profound idiocy* (*tiefstehende Idiotie*). On the same day, the state committee in Berlin is notified of her case. The girl's general health is 'deteriorating markedly' (a case note records 'fever, 39 degrees') but despite this, a full pneumoencephalographic investigation is carried out five days later. Doctor Illing has already scheduled the autopsy of Hermine's body but wants a set of the images of the live brain tissue. After the skull X-rays, Hermine dies without regaining consciousness. *Fifteen-year-old Ingeborg S.* Ingeborg S suffers from paraplegia but also occasional muscle spasms and cramps. The case notes show that her fits are treated with Luminal. The girl has to be 'tied' so as not to 'tear herself free' during the night. Doctor Illing notifies the Berlin committee of Ingeborg's case – his stated reason is that the Luminal has failed to bring about any 'progress' – and then she, too, is subjected to a pneumoencephalography, even though she fell ill with measles the week before and, as the day nurse notes, 'runs a high temperature'. Two days later, Ingeborg succumbs to 'bilateral pneumonia'. As in all other cases, it is Doctor Uiberrak who carries out the post-mortem examinations, usually with either Gross or Illing present as curious observers – as Doctor Uiberrak made a special point of stating in the pre-trial interviews. The brain is lifted out and placed in the correct strength of formaldehyde solution. A selection of glands are also removed and preserved. The girl has been transformed into a nameless object to be taken out and examined, again and again. The dead don't die just once. They keep dying.

The Last Interview with Doctor Gross In April 1997, a court case is once again brought against Heinrich Gross. This time, the charges are based on new evidence that includes a document recovered from an old Stasi archive in Berlin. In it, Doctor Illing asks the committee to approve a retrospective grant to the clinic in order to finance the work done by Doctor Gross during the summer of 1944, in view of his record of 'support for the great task of the Reich committee'. Gross had previously claimed that, during the summer of 1944, he was resting and, in any case, he had not set foot in the clinic since he was called up to join the Wehrmacht in 1943. This time round, the prosecutor can prove that Doctor Gross was fully engaged in the work of the clinic throughout the summer, and that he, during that time, examined, notified the authorities and subsequently 'treated' twelve children or more, of whom the youngest was ten days old when examined, and the oldest fourteen. Hannes Pichler was one of these children. He was seen by Gross on 19 July 1944. Hannes was three months old and had been born with a severe malformation of the face. Evaluations of the child's psychological or neurological status were 'impossible in the circumstances', according to Doctor Gross's notes. Following routines that were by then established since years back, the boy is taken to the infant ward in pavilion 15, pneumoencephalograms are produced, and Berlin is notified of the case. Presumably in view of the child's malformed face, the committee recommends 'treatment' and the baby dies on 26 August that year. But even though both the record of the examination and the report to Berlin carry his signature, Doctor Gross continues to deny everything.

ANONYMOUS INTERVIEWER: Does the name *Hannes Pichler* mean anything to you?

DOCTOR GROSS: No.

INTERVIEWER: It doesn't remind you of anything at all?

DOCTOR GROSS: No, nothing whatsoever.

INTERVIEWER: But you have, after all, referred to his case in scientific articles published in 1956, 1957 and 1973. Also, in the articles you discuss histological specimens of his brain tissue that you prepared yourself.

DOCTOR GROSS: So what if I did? It still doesn't mean that I know who he was.

INTERVIEWER: This is a case of a child admitted to Spiegelgrund, who died or was murdered there. You examined him and he died during the time you had taken on the post as Doctor Illing's deputy.

DOCTOR GROSS: It is possible, but I don't remember anything about it. Not by now.

INTERVIEWER: But Illing wasn't there! Who was ultimately responsible when Doctor Illing wasn't in his post?

DOCTOR GROSS: I have no idea. Decisions may well have been made earlier. I don't remember.

And so, Doctor Gross, through the medium of his team of lawyers, continues to contradict and deny everything, despite the prosecution's presentation of solid evidence for his participation in twelve murders. In parallel with these denials, the defence also attempts to persuade the court that Doctor Gross is incapable of following the proceedings. The court is shown medical certificates stating that the defendant is suffering from a whole array of illnesses: diabetes; chronic infection of the bladder; angina; impaired mobility; and partial deafness. 21 March 2000 turns out to be the last day of the trial. Doctor Gross is eighty-four years old, his back is bent and he moves with small steps, dragging his feet across the floor. He wears a cap pulled down over his eyes and leans on his stick while gripping the arm of his lawyer's son, who slowly escorts him to the defendants' seats. He sinks rather than sits down, then slumps so that all you see under the brim of his cap are his large, broad-rimmed glasses and a part of his bulbous nose. As the hearing gets underway, Doctor Gross sags so much that he almost falls off his chair, a disaster prevented only when a court attendant reaches out to support him at the last moment. By now, the judge is worried enough to incline towards the defendant: *Mr Gross, do you understand what I'm saying?* he asks. The reply is indistinct but something like: *not so well. A bit.* At this juncture, the lead advocate in the Gross team opens his document case and produces a trump card: a recently done CT scan of his eminent client's brain. It demonstrates advanced dementia, a process which, according to the psychiatrist who had requested and then analysed the scans, would bring about memory loss and recurring states of confusion. It takes only another five minutes for the court to decide that, in view of the defendant's failing health, the proceedings should be postponed for another eighteen months. However, Doctor Gross is spared more court attendances. He dies on 15 December 2005, aged ninety, in his home town of Hollabrunn. He seems not to have recovered from his selective memory loss. And he is never convicted of the murders of the Spiegelgrund children, or even of being an accomplice to the murders.

DOCTOR GROSS: No – no! With the utmost respect to the court.
I have never, be it directly or indirectly, participated in acts that could have led to deaths, of children or of adults.
Never. Exactly that: never. I don't remember.
I remember nothing whatsoever.

One night, as I lay in bed listening to the flow of the river, I felt it was true; I was like a river with the earth below and the air above. The true river had stopped, and I was the one who flowed farther and farther away, all alone in the center, trees on both sides.

From *Death in Spring* (*La mort i la primavera*) by Mercè Rodoreda. Translation from the Catalan by Martha Tennant (Open Letter Books, University of Rochester, 2009)

XVII

The Nameless Dead

From one day to the next, without any noticeable resistance, a hospital in Wien turned into a camp for children with alleged mental handicaps. At Spiegelgrund, these children were subjected to tests of their fitness for life; they were measured, reported on, maltreated, tortured and murdered. The authorities slandered their parents and operated behind their backs. 'Once the child has died, its relatives tend to stop caring', one murderous doctor wrote in someone's case notes. He does not mention that he had prevented the parents from being in contact with their child before as well as after the murder. He would later deny what had happened and stay silent until all was forgotten. Some of the children escaped from this lethal institution, others survived inside it. All those who survived have for decades borne witness to what went on at Spiegelgrund. They have described, carefully and circumstantially, the individuals who tormented and murdered the children there but who still have, unhindered, carried on living and working in this city as if their pasts were clean. After the sentence passed in the court of Oberlandsgericht Wien on 30 March 1981, it became possible to declare everywhere in this nation that Doctor Gross, a senior consultant, had collaborated in 'the killing of an unknown number of children diagnosed with mental illness, mental retardation or severe malformations (who may or may not have been ill for genetic or other reasons) and that the unknown number of victims, while likely to have been very large, at least can be stated with certainty as amounting to several hundred'. Here, in the city graveyard of Zentralfriedhof, more than six hundred urns have been buried. As of today, we are aware of seven hundred and eighty-nine murdered children. The number grows with every passing year. Today, we also know that no less than fifteen per cent of the total population of Wien were destined to be eliminated. This was the estimate of the 'required negative selection' recommended by eugenics specialists as an essential measure of 'racial hygiene'. Even so, the doctor who had made euthanasia part of his work could continue in the post he held in 1981: medical director at Steinhof. At the time, the Secretary of State for Healthcare was Alois Stacher. Gross became a recognised forensic psychiatrist. The Minister of Justice at the time was Christian Broda. Gross kept his post at the Boltzmann Institute. The research community did not find it problematic in the slightest when we presented evidence proving that the specimens used by Doctor Gross were taken from murder victims. Herta Firnberg was the Minister for Science and Bruno Kreisky the Chancellor of Austria. At the time, only the survivors, who are represented here today, protested against this terrifying indifference. Since 1981, they have been striving towards a single aim: that the children who were reduced to medical specimens should be mourned and buried. What Antigone demanded for her brother, slain by Creon, is what we, too, have demanded for two decades on behalf of the innocent children who died at Spiegelgrund: a grave. Why deny them a grave for so long? Why has society refused to believe in the witness statements made by the survivors? Why has everyone seemingly chosen to trust the forensic medical men and women, and not the historians of medicine? The answer is there for all to see but no one cares to take it on board. We therefore want to make it clear, in front of everyone here, that the injustice has not been wiped from the slate of history, that all the perpetrators have not been punished but that they have been forgotten through a deliberate loss of memory, a forgetfulness legitimised by the authorities. Justice has not been done. There is not even a verdict of 'guilty'. To question the usefulness and value of human life brings nothing but misery and it must never again be done, never and by no one . . .

I incline my head and contemplate the painful deaths of these children. May the earth be light in which we let them rest.

A Father, Hannes Says As he grew older, Hannes Neubauer began to collect maps. One of them was a poster from the Nazi era which illustrates the river systems of German-controlled Europe's (*Germanische Europa* – that's what it says): it is beautifully done, with the rivers drawn to look like long blood vessels, coloured black, red, blue and turquoise. They wind their way across a continent so bloated with annexed and occupied territories that the landscape characteristics cannot be made out. Look, here, Hannes says and points to the region of Mähren, which has been crossed by a strong turquoise line, here's where the Nazis wanted to dig a canal to link the Oder and the Donau. They were going to use Russian POWs to dig it. If they had succeeded in linking the two rivers, all the waterways of Europe would have been interconnected in one great vascular system and they would've ruled over everything, not only the roads and railtracks and harbours but also the internal flow in our circulatory systems. Why do you think getting rid of us mattered so much to them? We didn't occupy any space; we weren't visible on their maps. But we prevented their blood from attaining purity, from running freely. Simply by existing, we cast a shadow of doubt over the obedient and pliable type of people they had hoped to foster. The ruling race wanted to invent a slave race. But they failed. We were the stain, the shameful last resistance that they had to conquer inside themselves and never managed to break down. We were the flaw in their system, the stumps at the ends that would never join up, the ghostly voice that whispered in the night to remind them that you will all remain other than you ought to have become, other than you were meant to be. Hannes said all this, and then explained that he had been one of the last inmates left at Spiegelgrund. When the clinical side of the institution finally closed down, he was moved to another hospital. It was on Kollburggasse, in Ottakring. He was allocated a bed in a ward full of other children who nobody had come to claim. He can no longer remember what the specialty of his ward was or for how long he was kept there, but he realises that they must have thought him very ill. A doctor came to see him several times a day and he was given medicines. A psychologist came along as well to talk to him. The psychologist was a kind young woman, quite different to Mrs Baar, who had tormented him for so long; however, even this sweetly patient creature gave up when she received no answers to any of her questions. He was given injections to make him talk but that only made him drowsy and even less willing to speak. The nurse who injected him also brought him food. You must eat now, Hannes, she said. You must grow big and strong. Her voice was warm and kind, and he deeply distrusted everything about her. The war is over now, she said in her treacherously gentle voice. Someone from the 'administration' visited at regular intervals, escorting an embarrassed-looking adult or a couple of them. It always went the same way. The 'administrative person' produced sheaves of paper and found some name or other to read aloud. The charge nurse pointed at a bed and the adult, or adults (mostly women, rarely men; sometimes a man and a woman together) sobbed loudly or howled, and rushed along to the bed where the child was lying, or else the child was forced to get up and walk obediently with lowered head towards his or her waiting relatives. Finally, the ward had emptied. Only Hannes was left. He had recovered a little by then and spent most of his days by the window, looking out. Windows had no bars in this place but were windows all the same. Then, he suddenly hears somebody come walking along the corridor and, when he turns, the nurse stands in the doorway and tells him, sounding happy and also a little relieved:

Hannes, your mother has come for you.

She steps aside and a strange being reaches out for him and advances as if she expects him to run straight into her arms. He lets out a dreadful scream and then something close to complete pandemonium breaks out. The nurse has to call for help and two male nurses come along at a run and in the end extract him from his hiding place under the bed. Later, an administrative person turns up and there is quite an argument. The strange woman is required to state again and again that her documents are correct. The last thing he remembers from that scene is how he was clinging to the door frame with both hands and how they had to loosen the grip of his fingers one by one to manoeuvre him out of there. Of course, everything is sorted out in the end. The strange woman, who is kind and patient and not at all like the repulsive monster he believed her to be during the first few days, takes him for a walk in the park one day and tells him things. Hannes's real mother is dead, she explains. She died soon after Hannes's father divorced her. The woman says that soon after the divorce, she married Hannes's father. And that was the worst mistake of my entire life, she adds. His father told her that he was a widower and really seemed to be someone who needed the help and support of a woman. Though what he actually needed was someone to vent his anger on, daily. My father is a soldier, Hannes says. The woman understands. Yes, in a way, he was a soldier, she agrees. He worked for the armaments industry and spent day after day at a metal press, a huge machine where you had to put your whole head inside before you depressed the pedal that operated the pressurised air inlet, which in turn powered the entire machine. And, well, one day he forgot, put his foot on the pedal before he had time to move his body out of the way. He had the end he deserved, if you ask me.

You're lying, Hannes says.

But then, people have been lying to him all his life. How is he to work out what is true and what isn't? This woman is, as we know, understanding. She says that she did everything to convince the authorities that she must be allowed to give Hannes a real home. Where else would he be? By now, the woman had found a new husband called Heinz Rehmer who teaches in technical college, and Hannes Neubauer grows up with these two. But he can't get over the lie. All the time, he sits poring over his maps and books, and thinks about *what if*. What if this or that happened or didn't, *then what*? If they really had had time to complete that canal? If their shame had not existed? If his father really had been a soldier and come to take him away after the war as he had said he would? Or if he at least had had the sense to die properly, like all the others?

The Nameless Dead On Sunday 28 April 2002, the remains of the nearly six hundred children were buried, all retrieved from the 'memory room' in the cellars under the autopsy unit at Steinhof. The memorial service in the chapel in Wien's Zentralfriedhof is attended not only by Hannes Neubauer but also several others from the 'old' reform school intake. Hannes is still in touch with some of them, for instance Walter Schiebeler (Miseryguts). Schiebeler tells Hannes that he recently went to see Pawel Zavlacky, who has got himself a place in sheltered housing in Simmering. I never thought the old fucker would hang on for this long, Miseryguts said. Adrian Ziegler is not present. When people he knows bring up the subject of Spiegelgrund, he usually says things like, *I've put all that behind me long ago*, though hardly anyone believes a word of it, because he still speaks about the place all the time and also carefully cuts out and saves everything he can find about the Nazi euthanasia project. On the day of the funeral, he and his son-in-law are off to pick up flower bulbs and manure from a wholesaler out in Schwechat. Adrian's son-in-law is called Ewald. He and Missi run a small flower shop together in the 16th Bezirk and Adrian enjoys helping them by collecting goods or stacking sacks with compost and topsoil. During the few years when he worked, it was the simple, practical jobs he always liked best. In 1983, he finally acquires a driving licence, thirty-five years after the law forbade him to drive any vehicle. But his son-in-law does the driving; Ewald and Missi own a red SEAT Combi. The spring day is almost like summer; over the fields, the span of the sky is open and boundless, and a faint, light line of haze at the horizon erases the already ill-defined boundary between earth and sky. The wind blows down from the open sky and sweeps up dust and loose soil from the fields. The wind also makes the tall poplars shudder and creates swooping waves in the dense growths of willow along the verges. They have just come out of the underpass at the Ostautobahn and are on their way towards Albern when Adrian turns round and remarks to Ewald that they were driven just this way from the youth prison in Kaiserebersdorf that time when they were sent out to clear the rubble left behind by the air raids. It must have been in March, in March 1945. Never, says Ewald, they always used POWs for that kind of work. Who did? Adrian asks. Why, the Nazis, obviously, Ewald says. They have discussions like this quite often: Adrian tells Ewald about something and the younger man says that it couldn't possibly have happened that way. Ewald is a stubborn and argumentative type who believes he always knows best, even about events he hasn't been part of. But he listens to Adrian good-humouredly and, on the whole, quite enjoys the company of his father-in-law. Adrian of course knows perfectly well that this was the road. He remembers clearly the strange sensation of being in the sharp light of an early spring morning, and how the mud and half-melted ridges of snow along the verge fused into a depressingly grey mist. He also remembers that Jockerl had been sitting next to him in the back of truck. Jockerl was dead but there all the same, pale and shivering with his knees pulled up close to his body. How can you remember seeing someone who was dead at the time? But it makes no difference to your memory if whomever you remember is alive or dead. By then, the tall grain silos at Albernen Hafen are towering up above the line of the forest. Please, turn off here for a while, he says to Ewald.

After the ceremony in the chapel, the congregation walks to the burial ground. By now there is quite a crowd: politicians in dark suits and journalists wielding microphones and TV crews with their heavy cameras slung over their shoulders. Of course, the camera-eyes are directed almost exclusively at the politicians and their wives, and the Mayor of Wien and his entourage. In the gaps between the dark-suited backs, Hannes glimpses a row of about fifty schoolchildren. Each child carries an enlarged photo of one of the murdered Spiegelgrund children and has raised it to head or chest height. The photographs were presumably taken by Doctor Gross because there are hardly any other ones. The urns are carried along an avenue lined with these faces. The names of the dead are read out aloud. Slowly and methodically, name follows name, but the reading voice is a little rasping or perhaps it is the wind rustling in the low trees and shrubs around the gravestones. Hannes cups his hand behind an ear to hear better:

Baumgartner, Herbert   Bayerl, Wilma   Becker, Anna

He tries to catch names he recognises. But those who get a mention are children from pavilion 15. *Becker, Julius*, he thinks, the boy with the scissors; but, of course, Becker's name is not there. And the voice reads on:

Braun, Anton   Brückner, Gertrude   Brunner, Hilde
Czech, Anton . . .

Please, turn off here, Adrian had said to Ewald and, without asking any questions, Ewald had swung the car to the right and driven down the long slope to the quayside. Down here, between the silos, it feels much warmer. The air flows and quivers in the roar of the engines as if the entire harbour basin were enclosed in barely transparent, curving glass. Tankers are reversing out towards the loading jetties, the drivers hanging halfway outside the opened cabin doors. They shout and gesticulate to each other but the noise is so tremendous that it is practically impossible to pick up any sounds other than the rumbling of the engines and the rattling of the crane chains as the heavy loads are swung on land. Two harbour workers in hi-viz vests stand with their legs wide apart, ready to grab hold of the long feeder tube from the one of the tankers, then they slowly guide the end of the tube to a gridded opening and, soon afterwards, the grain starts rushing down into the cistern while both men step back and light their cigarettes. Adrian looks around. He doesn't recognise the place but it must have been here. And it must have been here in Albernen Hafen where dead bodies ended up after being carried downstream, all the dead who Uncle Ferenc had been talking about, the nameless ones who exist nowhere except possibly in the memories of some of those who missed them but never knew where they went after leaving their homes. He and Ewald drive past the long row of harbour store-buildings until the road ends at a turning circle. Two trucks with concrete mixers mounted on the back are parked here. The massive engines are idling while the mixers are being cleaned by two workers. One of them strides around, directing the jet from a high-pressure hose so powerful that it sounds like a gunshot every time the stream of water hits the metal shell of the mixer. The other one follows, using a broom with an extra-long handle to try to scrape off clumps of concrete that still stick to the metal. Both men are wearing brilliant orange overalls but their bare, tanned skin shows underneath. They're just like Ferenc. Now, Adrian knows that he is in the right place and, for a moment, he feels almost happy. He gestures to Ewald to stop and climbs out of the car. Ewald wants to say something but knows he won't be heard over idling engines and the concrete mixers, which are rumbling emptily. By now, it's incredibly hot, as if the daylight itself has been heated and begun to melt in the diesel fumes and is pouring down into the narrow cleft between loading jetties and store buildings. On top of it, insects fill the air. Insistently buzzing flies and horseflies seem crazed by the greasy exhaust smell. Adrian tries to smack them with the back of his hand but it doesn't help much. On the far side of the tarmacked area, two gateposts mark where a couple of roughly made steps lead down to a small burial chapel half-overgrown with shrubs and climbers. You see the graves first when you come down the cracked, mossy steps. Unlike a proper cemetery, the paths between the gravestones do not run straight and have no distinct outlines, but instead wind and probe, as if seeking the right direction on their own. Actually, these are not pre-prepared paths but tracks worn by the footsteps of visitors. On one of the long summer afternoons when Adrian and his uncle had been keeping an eye on the cattle down by the Hubertusdamm,

Ferenc had told him of the forgotten, partly buried cemetery down by Albernen Hafen. They had been lying side by side on the rough, gravelly grass and looking up into the warm, empty evening sky, and the insects had been swarming over the riverbanks in big, black clouds, just as they do now. The river took many of them back, Ferenc had said. Especially when the plan was to control the flow by constructing a cut to make the river go where it does now, and then dam and drain the old river branches. Several of Ferenc's relatives had joined the labour crews. Most of those who didn't die from typhus during the digging years were taken by the water and either disappeared for ever or else surfaced with all the other drowned corpses just here, down at Albern. For some reason, one of the river currents created an eddy right there, Ferenc had said. The flowing water forms whirlpools as it always does when surface water clashes with stronger and very much deeper currents. Where many currents meet you'll get a pool of still water, and in it a lot of rubbish from miles away upstream will tend to collect, like grass, pieces of wood, old boxes and even whole sets of furniture. And human corpses, of course. Lots of corpses. Some of them had been in the water all winter and were so inflated with gas that they seemed barely human. So, this is what happened: they were all buried where they were found, at the tip of the promontory. The graveyard grew quite large in the end. Not that the diversion digging was of any use, Ferenc had added. Even though the river was supposed to be regulated, it flooded its plains again and again and, after each flood, they had to strengthen the high-water dam even more and add a new cemetery on the land side of the old one, just to make room for all the new dead bodies that came floating along.

The banked-up ridge running along the shore to Adrian's right is the latest attempt to stop the river from flooding this burial ground. There, the dead lie close to each other in disorderly rows, side by side because there are so many of them. Some graves are marked by a wooden board stuck in the ground that says *Unknown, nameless.* Or else, nothing, or only a date: *14/04/1931*. Is that the day when the dead, one or many, were buried? But not all the graves are untended. Here and there, tree seedlings and weeds have been cleared away and fresh flowers put into an old paint-pot, or else the image of a saint has been left on guard, or perhaps a lantern with a burnt-down candle placed inside a glass container stained on the outside by muck and dead insects. The boards or stones on some of the graves even carry inscribed names: *Martin*, it says on a wooden stick, and on a stone a bit further away, *Hildegard*. Adrian wants *Jockerl* to be written on a memorial and, at one point, almost thinks he sees a *J*, just a faint mark on a stone. When he tears the moss away it is another name and there are so many critters crawling around his mouth and nose that he hardly dares to breathe. And there are insects creeping and swirling on and around the back of his neck and head, and swarming around his forehead and eyes. Strangely enough he can hear the angry whining of their wings even though he can no longer hear the clamour of the harbour with its loading cranes and stores from only a stone's throw away. The marshy, sodden ground of the graveyard is on another level, as if it belongs to a different world. Using what strength he still has, he clambers up the embankment, holds on to shrubs and roots until he stands in the sunlight at the top. Up there, the wind blows and the insects vanish as if by magic. In the glow of the setting sun, the branch of river spreads out in front of him, all the way down to the power stations at Freudenau. Turning to look in the opposite direction, there is Albern and its narrow harbour entrance, and there is Ewald, smoking a cigarette next to his bright red SEAT. In the middle of the river, a barge is chugging upstream as if moving across a floor of light. Someone shouts. It is Ewald. *Adrian!* he calls.

Adrian sees his mouth opening and closing and his hand pointing to his watch. He turns back to the river for a last look. The barge has disappeared and only the shapeless expanse of water is left, in constant motion but apparently immobile, only reflecting the light from above as if from the unseen inner surface of the sky,

and the voice reads on

Weihs, Ingrid *Weinzierl, Johann* *Weiss, Hildegard*
Wick, Alfred *Wödl, Alfred* *Woina, Franz* *Zehetner, Gerhard*
Zipfl, Aloisia *Zipko, Hedwig*

and then starts again from the beginning and so on forever

Afterword

There is by now a very extensive literature about and around the project of euthanasia of children that was initiated at Spiegelgrund by the Nazi regime, and it would create too long a digression to refer here to the material that I have relied on. However, I must take this opportunity to thank especially Friedrich Zawrel, whose childhood and youth and late, unexpected encounter with his former tormentor Heinrich Gross have inspired corresponding passages in this novel. In many interviews for books, films and lectures, as well as in conversations with me, Zawrel has given insightful and detailed accounts of what an upbringing at Spiegelgrund could be like and this has been invaluable for my writing. I also want to thank Andrea Fredriksson-Zederbauer for all her help with research for and editing of the book, as well as for her many critical and constructive comments. Thanks also to René Chahrour and Herwig Czech, and to Werner Vogt, whose talk on 28 April 2002 at the burial in Wien's Zentralfriedhof of the remains of the several hundreds of Spiegelgrund victims of child murder is quoted here in an abbreviated form (pp.546–7).

Translator's Note

The translator is responsible for translations of German words, phrases, text extracts (e.g. from case notes) and concepts, and also, now and then, the brief explanations.

Also by Steve Sem-Sandberg

ff

The Emperor of Lies

In February 1940, the Nazis established what would become the second largest Jewish ghetto in Poland, in the city of Łódź. At its heart was the ghetto's leader Mordechai Chaim Rumkowksi, a sixty-three-year-old Jewish businessman. Mysterious, ambiguous and monarchical, 'King Chaim' forced adults and children alike to work punishing hours in workshops to provide supplies for the German military, as thousands of others were transported and never seen again. Was Rumkowski an accessory to the Nazi regime driven by a lust for power, or was he a pragmatic strategist, actively saving Jewish lives through collaboration? Steve Sem-Sandberg draws on genuine chronicles of life in the Łódź ghetto to create a compelling meditation on power, corruption and compromise.

'Irresistible . . . absorbing from first page to last . . . Dickens would have been very pleased with this novel.' *Guardian*

'Fiction of true moral force, brilliantly sustained and achieved . . . stunning.' Hilary Mantel

'[The] cinematic richness of detail . . . invites immersion in the way few contemporary novels of serious ambition do.' *New York Times*